WRITERS
HARVEST
2

SOS

WRITERS
HARVEST
2

•

Edited by

ETHAN CANIN

A Harvest Original

Harcourt Brace & Company

San Diego   New York   London

Library of Congress Cataloging-in-Publication Data
Writers harvest 2/edited by Ethan Canin.
p.   cm.
"A Harvest original."
ISBN 0-15-600246-9
1. Short stories, American. 2. American fiction—20th century.
3. United States—Social life and customs—Fiction. I. Canin, Ethan.
PS648.S5W75   1996
813'.0108—dc20   96-18702

Printed in the United States of America

First edition

A C E F D B

CONTENTS

ACKNOWLEDGMENTS

Share Our Strength has expanded steadily for more than ten years now so that our antihunger efforts reach literally millions of Americans. The engine driving our growth has been the unique creative skills and talents exemplified by the eighteen wonderful writers who donated their work to make this book. On behalf of SOS and all of those we serve, I thank them for giving the best of themselves.

The efforts required to recruit and coordinate the contributions of so many fine writers could take another book just to describe. Katherine Wanning and before her Meghan Russell of the SOS staff managed this process single-handedly. This book would not have been published without their persistence, skill, and dedication. And lucky us for Diane Sterling at Harcourt Brace! Diane's judgment, talent, and patience helped turn our love for writers into writing that readers will love.

I owe special thanks to Ethan Canin, our first guest editor, who undertook this responsibility despite his very busy schedule. His contributions to SOS began nearly a decade ago. That kind of steadfast support is rare, but essential, if our work is to succeed.

Finally, there is no one in the world of books who has given more than our agent, Flip Brophy at Sterling Lord Literistic. Again Flip, and again, thanks.

William H. Shore
Executive Director, Share Our Strength

PREFACE

●

Ethan Canin

People love stories. What a delight this fact is—that despite their utter uselessness to timing the market or keeping out Bermuda grass or beating the traffic, people still crave them and go out of their way to hear them. And not just stories written down: people will stop everything to hear what is known in crude form as gossip and in refined form as literature: the drama of other people's lives—alliances made, chances lost, losses born, fortunes seized. To me this is a continual and I must say surprising delight. Surprising because if a person glanced out the window into the five o'clock crowd in, say, New York City, he might very well conclude that human beings don't care at all either about each other or, in a disheartening way, even about their own selves—in the sense of their real, private selves, their *souls*—the mystified, curious, striving, frightened, awe-able mendicants all of us on this strange planet must feel ourselves to be. People are running to get home from work. People are fighting for cabs. People are making after-hours trades on cell phones and stepping over bums and cursing the uptown traffic and never slowing the pace.

Yet the thing is, so many will pause for the hint of a story—for the lover singing at the window or the child rescued from the well or the athlete caught in adultery. To a writer this is a delightful fact and to anyone with sympathy for the down-and-out this is nothing short of a saving grace. By this I mean that the urge to hear a story—to gain access to turning points of another person's life—is the same urge, I think, that might bring us as a culture to keep caring for our members in trouble. It's the urge to empathy, the *instinct* really, and it is one of the true necessities of civilization. Reading stories deepens and strengthens it.

The writers in this collection donated their work to help Share Our Strength, an organization that supplies millions of dollars to literacy and antihunger programs across the United States and throughout the world. If you buy this book, you are donating part of the price to help these causes. Our thanks to all of you.

THE SNOW THIEF

•

Melanie Rae Thon

M Y FATHER FLED without waking. Snow fell. The ghost of an elk drifted between trees. Mother called that November morning. *Gone,* she said, as if he might be missing. He was sixty-nine, still quick and wiry, a tow-truck driver who cruised county roads rescuing women like me.

A single vessel ruptures; blood billows in the brain. That fast. Impossible to believe. Eleven years since he'd caught me with his friend Jack Fetters in the backseat. No one could blame his bursting artery on me. No one except my father himself. He filled my one-room flat on Water Street. I smelled smoke in damp wool, saw the shadow of his hand pass close to my face.

Simply dead. How could this be? He'd wounded the elk at dawn, tracked it for miles down the ravine. Near dark, the bull became an owl and flew away.

Lungs freeze. Hearts fail. It's easy. I know it happens everywhere, hundreds of times a day, to daughters much younger than I was then. Still, each one leaves a mystery.

As my father slipped into bed that night, he said, *My shoulder hurts. Could you rub me?*

And Mother whispered, *I'm too sleepy.*

It drove her mad. Over and over she said the same thing: *I was going to rub his shoulder in the morning.*

I thought we'd lose her. She kept asking, *How could I sleep with your father dead beside me?* I remember how suddenly she shrank, how nothing she ate stayed with her. My brother wanted to put her away. *A home,* Wayne said, *for her own safety.*

One night we found all her windows open, the back door flapping. We caught her three miles up the highway. She stood in the middle of the road, as if she'd felt us coming and had paused to wait. Our headlights blasted through worn cloth, revealed small drooping breasts and tense legs, bare feet too cold to bleed. She wore only her tattered nightgown. No underpants beneath it. Nothing.

She wouldn't ride in the truck. I gave her my coat and boots. I wore Wayne's. He had to drive in stocking feet. Mother and I walked together, silent the whole way. I held her arm to keep her steady. But this is the truth: she was the one to steady me. It made sense, this cold—a kind of prayer, this ceaseless walking.

When we got home, she let me wash her feet. I told her she was lucky, no frostbite, and she said, *Lucky?*

Then she slept, fifty-six hours straight.

The doctor said, *She needs this. She's healing.*

I washed her whole body. She hadn't bathed for twelve days. My mother, that smell! Air too thick to breathe, tight as skin around me.

She woke wanting sausages and steak. Eggs fried in bacon grease. A can of hash with corned beef. She ate like this for days and days, stayed skinny all the same. *It's your father,* she said. *He's hungry.*

He took her piece by piece. For thirteen years my mother stumbled in tracks she couldn't see. Every year another stroke left another tiny hole in her brain. I thought of it this way, saw our father standing at the edge of the pines, his gun raised. He was firing at Mother; but it was dusk, and since he was dead, his aim was unsteady. Each time he hit, she staggered toward him. He was a proud man, even now. It was his way of calling.

In the end, he defeated himself. All those scars left spaces empty. She forgot why she'd gone to the woods and who she wanted to find there. She loved only her nurse, and almost forgot my father, and almost forgot my brother and me.

I caught the pretty boy smoothing her sheet. Thin as an angel, this Rafael, so graceful he seemed to be dancing. He held her wrist to feel the pulse. He checked her IV. He said, *What a beautiful way to eat.*

He loved her too. How can anyone explain? He wasn't afraid of burned thighs or skin peeling. He touched her feathery hair, sparse and fine as the wet down on one of the not-born chicks my brother kept in jars of formaldehyde the year he was fourteen. *Specimens,* he called them, his eighth-grade science project. Every two days he cracked another egg to examine the fetus. I hated myself, remembering this, seeing my own mother curl up like one of these. But there they were, those jars of yellow fluid, those creatures floating.

I stroked her arm to make her wake.

What do you want now? she said.

To say good night.

Not good-bye?

Not yet.

It's not up to you, she said. She was seventy-seven years old, seventy-three pounds the last time anyone checked.

What did I want?

I wanted her big again. Tall as my father. Wide in the hips.

Think of me as a child. Once, when I was sick, my mother sat three days beside me, afraid to sleep because I might stop breathing. Sometimes when I woke, I smelled deerskin and tobacco, felt my father's cool hand on my forehead.

I have this proof they loved me.

What went wrong?

I turned fifteen. Jack Fetters said, *Someday, Marie.* Jack Fetters whispered, *We're not so different as you think.*

He was a guard at the state penitentiary. He said, *Man goes crazy watching other men all day.* His wife, Edie, had some terrible disease with a jungle name. Made her arms and legs puff up huge, three times their normal size. Jack Fetters said, *Sometimes the body is a cage.* They had a little girl just five, another seventeen, four boys in the middle. The one I knew had found his profession already: Nate Fetters was a sixteen-year-old car thief.

I thought, sooner or later his own daddy and a pack of dogs will chase him up a tree. Would Jack Fetters haul his son back to town, or would he chain the animals and let the thief escape?

A trap, either way.

I liked that boy, Nate Fetters. But he never noticed me. It was the father who touched my neck under my hair. It was the father I slapped away. The father who kept finding me. After school, at the edge of town, throwing rocks down the ravine. The patient father. *Someday, Marie.*

Was he handsome?

How can I explain?

He was the wolfman in a dream, a shape shifter, caught halfway between what he was and what he was going to be. Even before I unbuttoned his shirt, I imagined silvery fur along his spine. Before I pulled his pants to his ankles, I saw his skinny wolf legs. I knew he'd grunt and moan on top of me. Bite too hard. Come too quickly.

This part I didn't see: a car pulled off the road, a backseat—my father with a flashlight, breaking glass above me. I never guessed my own belly would swell up huge like Edie's legs.

Wayne sat on the window ledge. Our mother's room. Another day.

She's worse, he said.

At last, I thought, *it's ending.*

But he didn't mean this.

He said, *She promised that little fairy her damn TV.*

I knew Wayne. He wanted the color television. He figured he'd earned it, living with Mother. Thirteen years. *I've done my time.* That's what he'd say.

Her eyelids fluttered. She was asking God, *What did I do to deserve children like these?*

Listen, I felt sorry for my brother. He was soon to be an orphan. Just like me.

Once we hid in the ravine, that dangerous place, forbidden, where fugitives dug caves, where terrified girls changed themselves to pine trees. We buried ourselves under dirt and damp leaves. We couldn't speak or see. We couldn't *be* seen. God only glanced our way. If he saw the pile of leaves, he thought it was his wind rustling. He turned his gaze. He let us do it. He let us slip our little hands under each other's clothes. Warm hands. So small! Child hands. So much the same. God didn't thunder in our ears. God didn't hurl his lightning.

But later, he must have guessed. He came as brittle light between black branches. He was each one blaming the other. He showed himself as blindness, the path through trees suddenly overgrown with thorns and briers. He came as fear. He turned to root and stone to trip us.

The man on my mother's window ledge had split knuckles, a stubbled beard, bloated face. He said, *It's late. I work tonight.* He said, *Call me if there's any change.*

First love gone to this. If I said, *Remember?* Wayne would say I'd had a dream. He'd say I was a scrawny brat. He'd say the closest thing he ever gave me to a kiss was a rope burn around my wrist.

This is how God gets revenge: he leaves one to remember and one to forget.

The boy I loved had been struck dead.

At twenty, Wayne said, *This whole town is a penitentiary.* He meant to climb the wall and leap. No barbed wire. No snags. He moved up and down the coast, Anchorage to Los Angeles. He wrote once a year. Every time he was just about to make some real money. But after our father died, Wayne came home to Mother, safe, took a job from Esther McQuade at the 4-Doors Bar on Main Street. *It's a good business,* he said. *Everybody has to drink.*

Six months later, he married Esther's pregnant daughter. Some kind of trade. He said, *I know this first one's not gonna look much like me.* Now he was Esther's partner instead of her employee.

But he was still jealous, thought I must be smart and lucky. Because I went to college, two years. Because I got as far as Missoula and stayed. Eighty miles. I wanted to tell him, *No matter where I go I'm just the same.*

Did he blame himself for Mother's last accident?

I never asked. I knew what he'd say. *Just because she lives in my house doesn't mean I trot to the bathroom with her.*

She spent two days in bed before she told him. A tub of scalding water, thighs and buttocks burning. She was ashamed. *I just sat down,* she said. *I wasn't thinking.*

By the time she showed him, the skin was raw, the wounds infected. She couldn't ride a single mile. The doctor who came to the house gave her morphine. He said, *How did you stand it?*

And she said, *I forgot my body.*

This doctor was a boy, blinking behind thick glasses. He couldn't grasp her meaning. Mother said, *Go ask your father. Maybe he can tell you.*

The doctor shook his head. No way to help her here in Deer Lodge. He said, *We'll have to fly you to Missoula.*

Yes, she said, *I'd like that.* She meant the ride, the helicopter.

Now this, three weeks of antibiotics and painkillers pumped into veins that kept collapsing. She had a doctor for each part of her: one for skin and one for brain, one to save her from pneumonia. But all of them together couldn't heal her whole body. The neurologist rubbed his clean hands as if they hurt him. He stood near the window—gray light, white jacket, all I remember. He tried to explain it. *Common with stroke victims, immune system impaired, the body can't fight infection.* He said, *It's one thing after another, like stomping out brush fires.*

We were alone at last. I smoothed her hair. She curled into herself, tiny bird of a woman, still shrinking, becoming my child, my unborn mother. I leaned close to whisper. *It's me,* I said, *Marie, your daughter.*

Rain hit the glass. Then Rafael appeared, off duty,

wearing his black coat draped around his shoulders. He washed her face. He said, *She likes this. See? She's smiling.* He said, *Go home if you're tired. I can stay awhile.*

His coat was frayed, not warm, not good in rain. Maybe he had nowhere else to go. No house, no room, no bed, no lover. Maybe this was the reason for his kindness. Who can know our secrets?

I saw my father in the parking lot, gun propped against a Dumpster. He searched his pockets. Found no bullets. He knew Rafael was with my mother. So close at last, and he'd lost her all the same.

I meant to go home and bolt the door. But rain turned to sleet, sent me spinning. One wrong turn and I found myself at the Bearpaw Bar on Evaro.

Animals hung. Buffalo, moose, grizzly. This last one had its hide attached. I thought their bodies must be trapped behind these walls. I told the man beside me I'd break them free if I had a pick and axe. He had pointy teeth, a glad-dog grin. He said, *Where were you when they locked me down in Deer Lodge?* His skin was cracked, a Badlands face. When he smiled that way, I was afraid the scars might split open. This Tully bought my third beer, my first bourbon. He gripped my knee. He said, *I like you.*

By the jukebox, two sisters swayed, eyes closed, mouths moving. Sleepdancers. My father leaned against the wall, watching their smooth faces and the dreamy tilt of their hips rolling. I passed him on my way to the bathroom. His coat was wet. I smelled metal and oil, a gun just cleaned, grease on his fingers.

Too many beers already. I knew how it would be, how I'd follow Tully to the Easy Sleep Motel, take off my clothes too fast to think.

But when I saw my father, I had hope I could be saved. I thought, *I won't do this if you'll talk to me.* I said his name. I whispered, *Daddy?*

He didn't hear. Deaf old man. He looked away.

Listen.

They never brought my son to me. They let me sob, sore and swollen. They let my breasts bleed milk for days.

In every room, another girl, just the same. In every room, the calm Catholic women said, *Gone, a good family.*

Listen. There were complications. Narrow pelvis, fetus turned the wrong way. They had to cut my child out of me. Days later, they cut again.

Infection, the doctor said. *It has to drain.*

One slip of the knife. And a girl becomes a childless mother forever. It's easy. The good women promised, *No more accidents.* Between themselves they murmured, *It's a blessing.*

Listen.

No father lets you tell him this.

In the bathroom, I tried to see myself, but I wasn't there. I was black eyebrows and lipstick smeared. The rest of me was hidden, inside the wavy glass. I imagined opening a door, falling on a bed. I saw the marks my mouth would leave, bright blooms on scarred flesh. I saw a spiderweb tattooed on Tully's hairless chest.

What did I care if some old man judged me?

Listen. I'm snow in wind. No one leaves his imprint.

I went back to the bar, another beer, a third bourbon. Tully's hand moved up my leg. I'd hit black ice, locked my tires in a skid.

And then, a miracle, an angel sweet as Rafael sent to rescue stranded women. God spit him from the mouth of the buffalo head. Skinny boy in black jeans and leather. He pulled me off my stool. He said, *Maybe we should dance.*

The old man shot coins into the jukebox. My friend, after all. They were in this together, partners, a father and son with a tow truck, saviors with a hook and winch sent to pull me from the ditch.

Those thick-thighed sisters took care of Tully. One lit his cigarette, one stuck her tongue in his ear. They'd fallen with the snow, melted in my hair. They were my strange twins, myself grown fat. Their nails were long and hard, their lips a blazing red. Angels, both of them. You never know how they'll appear.

That boy's big hands were on my back. He whirled me in a dip and spin. His leg slipped between my legs.

What are we doing? I asked.

Only dancing, he said.

Yes, dancing. There's no harm in it. But later it was more a droop and drag, a slow waltz, one of us too drunk to stand.

The old man sat at a table in the back, holding his head in his hands. I saw how wrong I'd been. No angels here. The scarred man and the twins left. I was alone, reeling with the boy called Dez.

He ran his hands along my hips, pressed me into him. I said, *You're young enough to be my kid.*

But I'm not, he said.

He wrapped his fingers around my neck. He said, *Listen, baby, I'm low on cash.*

One last chance. I bought my freedom, gave him fifty-two dollars, all I had. He stuck it down his boot. I thought he'd vanish then, blow out the door, a swirl of smoke. But he said, *Let's go outside. This cowboy's got to get some air.*

In my car, he kissed me in that stupid way, all tongue and no breath. I lost my head. Then we were driving somewhere, snow-blind, no seat belts, nothing to strap us in. I saw broken glass, our bright bodies flying into tiny bits.

I took him home. Who can explain this? His long hair smelled of mud. I found damp leaves hidden in his pockets. His palms were cool on my forehead. He opened me. With his tongue, he traced the scar across my belly. It was wet and new. In a room years away I heard a child crying.

I expected him to steal everything. He touched the bones

of my pelvis as if remembering the parts of me, veins of my hands, sockets of my eyes. *Like a sister,* he said. I thought he whispered *Darling* just before we slept.

In the morning he disappeared. Took my sleeping bag and cigarettes.

Then the phone rang and a voice said: *Your mother, gone.* Imagine.

Everyone you love is missing. The voice on the phone never tells me this. The voice says, *Body, arrangements.* The voice says, *Your brother's on his way. You can meet him here.* I don't argue. I say, *Yes.* But I don't go to the hospital. I know I'll never catch them there.

Hours gone. *While you danced. While you lay naked in your bed.* That's what the voice in my own skull says.

I go to the ravine where the wounded elk staggers between pines. It's always November here, always snowing. It's the night my father died. It's the morning my mother is dying.

Sky is gray, snow fills it. Trees bend with ice, limbs heavy. I climb down, no tracks to follow. Snow higher than my boots already, a cold I hardly notice. I forget my body. How will I find them if they don't want me?

Flakes cluster, the size of children's palms now. They break against my head and back, so light I cannot feel them. I glimpse shapes, trees in wind shifting, clumps of snow blown from them, big as men's fists, big as stones falling. They burst. Silent bombs, scattering fragments.

Nothing nothing happens. Nothing hurts me.

And then I see them. He's wearing his plaid coat and wool pants, a red cap with earflaps. She wears only her pink nightgown. He carries her. She's thin as a child, but still a burden, and the snow is deep, and I see how he struggles. I could call out, but they'll never hear me. I can't speak in these woods. A shout would make the sky crumble. All the snow that ever was would bury me.

Deeper and deeper, the snow, the ravine. He never slows his pace. He never turns to look for me. Old man, slumped shoulders. All I ever wanted was to touch him, his body, so he could heal me, with his hair and bones, the way a saint heals. I hear my own breath. I stumble. How does he keep going?

Now I climb the steep slope. With every step I'm slipping. The distance between them and me keeps growing. I know I'll lose them. I know the place it happens. I know the hour. Dusk, the edge of the woods. The white elk takes flight as an owl in absolute silence. Wings open a hole in the sky, and a man and a woman walk through it.

No one says, *Go back.* No one says, *You'll die here.* But the cold, I feel it. My own body, I'm back in it.

I can stay. I can lie down. Let the snow fall on my face. Let its hands be tender.

Or I can walk, try to find my way in darkness.

I'm a grown woman, an orphan, I have these choices.

THE IMPOSSIBLE TO
KILL ME GAME

●

Po Bronson

THIS IS HOW WE LIVED: the year my mother
met Michael, she and a friend owned a used bookstore near
the Pike Place Market in Seattle, and after school I rode the
32 James downtown to help her shelve boxes of donated books
and pester the panhandlers until they moved from the en-
tranceway. It wasn't much of a store—I had to go to the
Vietnamese restaurant next door to use the bathroom—but
Mom made enough money to cover mortgage payments and
buy us new shoes every eight months. Mom encouraged me
to read, but I faked it by memorizing the descriptions on
the jackets and copying any drawings that were inside. We
closed at six and took the 11 Madison home, getting off to
buy dinner at Dick's Fast Food, where we ate in time to catch
the next bus. We split up and stood in both lines to get to
the window faster, winking at each other when the servers
told the man in front of me that they didn't make fish

sandwiches and couldn't take the catsup off his cheeseburger. Mom loved hot fudge sundaes and ate only those, while I hauled home a bag of six burgers and french fries for my older brother and me.

Ron was a sophomore at the high school and that winter had basketball after school until five-thirty. He played football in the fall, basketball in winter, and track in the spring, in which he threw the javelin, but he was no big-shot teenager—he never went out on dates and didn't even own any albums. Girls didn't call at night, and he didn't hang out with friends. Instead he listened to the radio a lot and couldn't fall asleep without it on. He listened to the late-night talk shows where people called in to talk about their sexual problems. At six foot four he was so skinny that Mom still bought his belts and underwear in the boys' department. He wore leg weights strapped to his ankles and every day practiced jumping behind our house—he would jump as high as he could and as soon as he landed take off again. He did this in the dark after he got home. He had read about the training in *Sports Illustrated,* and to my knowledge it worked; fifty times in a row, then a two-minute rest. Ten sets a night. He could reverse-dunk a basketball.

Ron bragged to me that he would be sixteen soon and would drive to Montana by himself that summer, despite the fact that we had no car. Our grandparents lived in Missoula, and he wanted to drive the hay truck and herd cows on their range. In three months, he would gain fifty pounds and five years of experience, come back with hair on his face and muscles on his bones. Or maybe not return at all—get a job with the state game warden and spend his days in the mountains chasing poachers and counting grizzlies.

We had a game that we played, the Impossible to Kill Me game. Ron would invent a situation in which I was sure to die, and I would invent ways to save myself. He would slowly increase the impossibility of saving myself, and I would become more and more inventive. "I've pushed you off a cliff," he would say. "You're falling toward jagged rocks below."

"Before I fall, I flip around and grab your shoelaces," I would say.

"You can't hang by my shoelaces," he would argue. "Your fingers couldn't grip that hard."

"I could if I had to save my life. Unless you've been there, you can't say I wouldn't be especially strong."

"Then I would hit your hands with rocks until you fell."

"The cliff is slightly sloped. I would crash through bushes growing on its side until I was going slow enough to stop myself."

"No, the cliff is a cliff of cement. There's no bushes growing." He would begin to get angry, as if I was cheating. I would begin to laugh, which would only make him angrier.

"I'm carrying a huge umbrella," I would say. "I open it and float to the rocks."

"They're jagged rocks. You weren't listening."

"So maybe I break both legs. Maybe I break both legs and wrench both knees, but I'm still alive."

Mom let us know that life in the city was not easy, and the rain and the cold did not make it any easier. She often said her lungs were better suited to California.

To make it a little easier for her, Mom had a few rules. We had to take the garbage out every night, so the kitchen wouldn't smell like french fries in the morning. She wouldn't let us turn up the thermostat, but because she didn't get up in the morning until just after we had left for school, we abused this rule with a fifteen-minute tropical blast. Most of all, Mom screamed if she had to take a cold shower. Our water heater was small, could only keep two showers' worth of warm water, so when I turned twelve she made Ron shower at night. He'd been taking morning showers for three years, and it was my turn. As a result, he went to bed with his hair wet and woke up with it molded into awkward sculptures. A wet comb never seemed to bring it back to normal, and I envisioned my brother being known at the high school as the skinny boy with the uneven hair.

Michael was Mom's boyfriend. Ten years before, he had written a memoir about growing up in Tacoma a second-generation Greek immigrant. But he couldn't write anything more after that, and instead he sold men's suits at a down-town department store on commission. He didn't have any kids but had been married once. He told us that he had lost all his body hair after his divorce, and this seemed strange because he was a hairy man, with bushy black curls on his head, eyebrows, and forearms. When he ate dinner with us, I sat across from him and squinted my eyes and tried to make the hair go away. Mom had met him in line at Dick's Fast Food. He had a studio apartment near there. I was with her. She recognized him, she had seen his picture on his book in her store. When we had our food, we sat down together on the orange plastic benches outside Dick's, and twice Michael gave me money for scoops of double-mint ice cream. At school that day I had learned about centrifugal motion—it's how we get the water off the lettuce—and I demonstrated the principle for him by swinging around a pole. We missed three buses. When we got home, Ron was already out back jumping into the darkness, and his hamburgers were cold. I watched him from the window, silently counting sets with him, listening to the scuff of his shoes as he fought the five-pound lead sacks belted to his ankles. Thirty-two. Thirty-three. I could hear his high-school coach in the background, Frank McCuskey, who taught history war by war and was old enough to have fought in several, warning Ron

that hands on the hips between sets was a sign of weakness.
Forty-eight. Forty-nine. Forty-nine and a half. Fifty.

A few weeks after the night at Dick's, Mom and I went to
West Seattle for one of Michael's soccer games, where he
played on a team with fellow Greeks. We went straight from
the store, transferring from the 5 Central to the 42 Alki
down by the Rainier brewery; she had invited Ron, too, but
he had lied and said he had a history paper due.

The game was in a small outdoor stadium under the
lights. I knew nothing about this strange European sport,
but Michael's team had silky royal blue uniforms with skull-
and-crossbones patches on the shoulder. It couldn't have been
more than a few degrees above freezing, but these men braved
it with only baggy shorts and tall socks. Michael played
somewhere on defense, and when he stole the ball he gave it
a great kick down the field, toward the other end. That his
kicks went right to the other team's defenders didn't matter;
everyone else was knocking the ball in tight little passes,
while Michael's kicks soared fifty yards, and I assumed he
was the strongest on the field. I imagined bringing him to
the school yard for a kickball game and watching him send
the red rubber ball into orbit.

Mom sat beside me, her face white despite the winter
cold, completely silent until halftime, when she let out a
huge breath that she seemed to have held for the entire
period. I was used to this, though, it was the same way she
watched Ron at his basketball games. Her silence was a
constant prayer. Sometimes I would catch her whispering
to herself. She feared for her men in these situations, they
could make a mistake and cost their team the game, or they
could tangle up legs and ankles and get them broken. She
never objected to sports and always went to our games,

because she knew we needed support. But they scared her. All those men in one place.

During the tiny breaths that followed, where she brought oxygen back to her lungs and blood back to her face, I took advantage of this weakness and hit her up for popcorn and hot-dog money. We didn't have much money, but the entrance of Michael into our lives distracted us. I ate the dog and the popcorn before I could make it back to my seat, so I turned around and went back for more. I was always hungry when it was cold. Mom took a single bite with her front teeth from the back end of my hot dog. She was dieting, she said.

The second half began. Mom started to talk then.

"You have to get used to them not scoring much," she said. "There's a fine appreciation to this sport. They don't have cheerleaders and halftime shows."

"I like it," I answered. It was a men's game, clearly, and I'm not sure Mom could appreciate it fully herself.

"Someday you'll travel, Lou. Someday you'll go places and learn about what they do in other countries."

"In Greece they drink lots of wine, I know that. And eat olives."

"Michael told you that?"

"Sure." But he hadn't, and he didn't need to. It was intuitive. Salty cheese, sexy women, old men in overalls and little caps working the fields. It was better than Montana. It beat Montana hands down.

"I'm glad Michael can share with you," she said then. "It's important to me."

There was a corner kick. Michael came up from the back to stand at the rear of the crowd and then rushed in just as his teammate booted the ball hard and straight into the mob of players. Michael ran straight at the ball and got his head on it, flicking it backward, over the top of the goalie and into the far side of the net. With his head! I thought they might call it back because he didn't kick it in, but he kept on running right past the goal and then in a big circle back onto the field at full sprint with his arms high over his head. I knew then that Michael was in our future, and it seemed impossible that he hadn't been my real father all along. His teammates lifted him off the ground and tried to carry him several yards, but their legs gave way and they all spilled to the ground. I was in my seat with my arms over my head.

Mom let out another breath, and this one led into silent crying, which she disguised by reknotting her scarf around her neck at the same time. She asked if I was hungry again. She took my hot-dog napkin and blew her nose. She straightened her wool hat.

This is what Michael and my mother would do at night: they would get out a bottle of wine, sit around the table, and talk. For years I had asked to be excused as soon as I could finish the last of my peas or french fries. Mom never minded, because Ron and I would only argue at the table anyway, or play Impossible to Kill Me, or shave off our calluses with a steak knife. Ron would brag about how long he could keep his finger in a candle flame, and I would challenge him, and then we would argue over whether he had counted too fast. But then, when Michael appeared, I suddenly wanted to stay at the table and listen to their talk. Michael convinced my mother that a shot glass of wine every few days wouldn't hurt a twelve-year-old. Michael always brought copies of magazines with him, for my mother to read a fascinating article he'd found, and they would discuss it together. While they talked, I copied the little drawings that were tucked in at the bottoms of the pages.

I liked to hear my mother's voice with a man's, talking, two voices in a dining room, and sometimes I got so relaxed I fell asleep in my chair. When I woke, it would be close to midnight, the lights would be dimmed, the portable radio would be tapping out a light jazz tune, and Michael would be waltzing my mother across the kitchen floor. For a while I would pretend to still be asleep, but when they started kissing I would go upstairs quietly, and I would hear Ron's radio, more talk shows. I would open the door to his room and very slowly turn down the sound to nothing. I would stand over Ron's bed and watch him sleep. Sometimes I reached out and touched his hair, which was still just slightly damp, hours after showering.

A couple of Saturdays later, Mom sent us down to Michael's department store for new suits. The store had a sale, and it was time, as Mom told us when we walked out the door, to dress the part of the young men we were quickly becoming. It was early February. It had snowed more the night before, and in the streets this had melted and refrozen into invisible ice patches. Our crowded bus kept getting stuck on the hill, and we had to get out to lighten the load and walk to the bus stop ahead, then get back on. By this time we had lost our seats, and since I couldn't reach the overhead railings, I hung on to Ron's parka. He kept jerking it away from my grip and I tried to stand for a while, but as the bus lurched I stumbled and reached out for his parka on the way down. From the floor I noticed he had his leg weights on. When Ron picked me up, he said, "Okay, stop that," like a parent, and it made me laugh. When I wouldn't stop laughing, he started in on a scenario.

"You're taped into a seat on a bus. Big wide strips of that gray tape they use for pipes. You're the only one on the bus, and the bus is headed down an icy hill without any brakes. At the bottom of the hill is a brick wall."

"That wouldn't kill me. I would be protected by the frame of the bus."

"Yes, it would. The bus would crunch up like an accordion, with you in it."

"Then my faithful dog Sparks chews me free of the tape, and I rush to the wheel of the bus and steer it down a side road."

"You don't have a dog. You haven't had a dog since Teddy died when you were six."

I lied. "Michael's going to get me one for my birthday. He told me."

"This is before your birthday. This is right now."

"Then I've been eating these special seeds that make my saliva able to dissolve any glue, and I spit on the tape to free myself."

"That would take too long."

"I work very fast under pressure."

"Then I've chloroformed you before taping you in. You're unconscious."

"I only look unconscious. I'm faking it. These special seeds also make me immune to chloroform. In fact, not only do I avert disaster, but I drive the bus all the way to Montana."

"No way, you'd be dead."

"I'd be a game warden. I'd be arresting poachers." I think he would have hit me if the bus hadn't been full of witnesses. But soon it was our stop, and once off the bus we gave up arguing. Ron walked ahead of me, as if he didn't want anyone to think we were brothers. Once he turned around and warned me not to touch anything when we got in the store. None of this mattered to me. A doorman swung the great gold doors open for us, and then I smelled the warm air and the perfume that all the dressed-up ladies were spraying onto themselves. I considered stealing a small bottle for Mom, but she would know I had stolen it, so I kept my hands in my pockets until I got to men's suits.

The walls were covered in dark shiny wood, and the

carpeting was so thick that I didn't make any sound when I walked. Glass cases of ties circled the room. Michael had told me about the ties—no two the same. I looked carefully, checking his assertion, tried to find two that were identical. Then Michael found us. He helped us off with our coats as if we were regular clients, then went to measuring us, down our inseams, around our waists and chests. He whistled when he measured Ron's shirt sleeve. Ron's arms were extra long, they could almost reach his knees, like a gorilla.

"I'll have a hard time fitting you two," he said. He got on the phone, called downstairs, and asked for someone to bring up a blue suit in my dimensions. Michael told me they usually kept stuff in special sizes in the basement. I knew he was just calling the boys' department, but I didn't say anything. It would be a suit.

While we were waiting for that to come up, Michael took a long look at Ron. He went off and came back with a herringbone wool jacket, which fit the chest and shoulders but barely covered his elbows. Then Michael came with a huge one that almost covered the wrists but was big enough in the body for two Rons. They tried some more, and then Michael had to sit down. He was sweating lightly on his forehead.

"Look," he said. "I can get something specially made."

"They have stores for people my size," Ron said.

"Maybe you'd like a tie for now. Why don't you pick one out?"

"Yeah, Ron," I said, trying to help. "No two ties the same."

So I got a suit and Ron got a tie. Michael showed him several ties, but Ron just shrugged his shoulders and took the nearest one, blue with gold squares. Michael offered a quick lesson in tie knotting, and Ron answered that he was too old for Boy Scouts. I wanted to wear my suit out of the store, like new shoes, so we waited for Michael to have it pressed. I gave him my old clothes, and he said he would bring them that night to dinner. I had a new suit. It was light blue, with wide lapels and white buttons that were probably carved from elephant tusks. We took the elevator downstairs. Everywhere I walked, I caught glimpses of myself in the mirrors and window reflections. I told Ron that the tie looked nice, but as soon as we were outside he yanked it from his neck and balled it into his pocket.

"What do you remember about our father?" Ron asked, when we were waiting for the bus.

I said I remembered what he looked like and that he sold insurance in a big building downtown. I said I remembered going to his office and looking down at all the little cars on the freeway. His secretary's name was Mary. But I didn't really remember any of these things. They were just things that Ron and Mom had told me over time.

"You know what I remember?" Ron said. "I remember his suits. They weren't cheap polyester like the one you're wearing. I used to camp out in his closet in the dark, wrapped up in his old army-issue sleeping bag, eating roasted peanuts. His suits used to hang down and tickle my ears. They were wool, and scratchy. They smelled like smoke. Then next morning Dad would find peanut shells in his shoes, and he would come into my room, where I was sleeping, and wake me up by slapping the shoe against the wall, right over my head. In a couple days I would go back to his closet. I *liked* it in there."

"You did?"

"Sure," he said. "I made drawings on the walls that I never got in trouble for because nobody bothered to bend down and look. When Dad moved out and took his clothes, my drawings were revealed. I got away with it because so much else was going on."

"Wow." I tried to sound impressed.

"What do you mean, *wow.* Is that all you can say about a father leaving a family?" Ron didn't look at me as he talked.

"Why do you lead Mom on with Michael? Do you want her to get hurt again, is that what you want?"

"No."

"You make her think it's going to be all okay with him."

"Isn't it?"

"*Man,* sometimes you can be so stupid. What do you think we're getting these suits for?"

"Because they're on sale?"

"It's so we'll be men, and so we'll be able to take care of ourselves."

I didn't know what to do. I started to get cold, and I wished I hadn't given my parka and mittens to Michael. I was hoping that if I gave my face just the right look, one of the taxicabs would stop and give me a ride home for free. Several buses went by, but they weren't ours. I turned my lapels up to cover my neck, even though I knew it looked stupid. It was a thin suit, a spring suit, fabric made from plastic, and I could feel the slight wind as if I weren't wearing anything. I wanted to stand close to Ron so he'd block the wind, but for every step I took toward him he took one away from me. Finally our bus came, and I got a seat next to a huge black lady. I tried to smile and make her like me, but my teeth were chattering and my breathing made me sound like I was growling at her.

Michael came that night just as Mom was setting dinner on the table, so they didn't get a chance to talk between themselves. Michael didn't say anything to Ron about the suit. Normally Michael liked to have a feast at the end of a hard week, and he liked to talk a lot. But now he was quieter. He kept his elbows off the table and set his glass down carefully and looked around at us only when he had his glass to his mouth, like it was his first date with Mom all over again. Then Mom asked me to do the dishes, and she and Michael took the bottle of wine into her bedroom, which was on the same floor as the kitchen. They left the door open, and they were talking in hushed voices. I decided to have some ice cream, and I ended up eating the whole two quarts, right from the box, with a soup ladle. The ice cream made me really cold again, and I tried to wish warm air out of the heater vents. I expected Michael to spend the night—it was Saturday—but before too long he came out and closed the door behind him, walking straight through the living room and out the front door. After about fifteen minutes Mom came out with all her clothes on, the bottle empty at least a few days ahead of schedule. I was in the corner of the kitchen with only the stove lamp illuminating the room, and when Mom cracked the refrigerator the light caught me in the corner.

"What are you doing there, Louis? You're not spying on your mother, I hope."

"I was eating ice cream. I did the dishes."

"Why don't you have the lights on?" She closed the refrigerator, turned on a light, and then struck a match and lit a cigarette. It'd been a while since I'd seen her smoke a cigarette—because she hadn't wanted us to start, she'd smoked only in her room when we weren't around, or in the store in the mornings—and I knew something was going on if she'd smoke one in front of me.

"I was saving electricity. I thought maybe we could turn on the heat if I turned out the lights for a while."

"Is that what you'd like, Louis, to turn the heat on? You can do it if you want. Go ahead. Fire it up. I wouldn't mind a sauna. I wouldn't mind a little warmth around here."

I wasn't going to do anything then, but she spun the dial on the thermostat, and I heard the old furnace boom in the basement and the blast of the pump igniting.

"There you go, Louis. That'll make everything all right for you now. You can be happy now."

"I didn't say it would do that, Mom."

"No, of course you didn't. Where are your friends, Louis? It's Saturday night. Don't you have friends you should be out with?"

I didn't say anything then. I didn't bring friends home, mostly because Ron would give me a hard time in front of them, and when you don't bring people to your house you don't get invited to theirs. I wanted to leave, but I also didn't, because I felt she needed me then, not in her usual way but in Ron's way—she needed me to be angry at.

Then Mom said, "Come over here, Louis." And I did that, I went and stood next to her, where she leaned up against the fridge. "Would it bother you if I opened another bottle? There's one in the cupboard over the sink, if you'd get it." So I did that, and I opened it, and I poured her some, but not much. It was red wine, and Ron had told me that was the strongest kind, and I didn't want her to have much more.

"What does Ron teach you, Louis? Does he teach you how to be nice to girls?"

"No."

"Your father used to say that he couldn't wait until you two got old enough and he could teach you about that." Then she reached out to me with her arms and pulled me to her body. I was almost as tall as she was, only a few inches shorter, and it was easy to hug her lightly. But when I started to pull away, the hug over, she said, "No, you'll never get a girlfriend that way. You have to hold them for a long time."

So we stood there in the kitchen, holding each other, for several minutes. I was afraid to move, afraid to hug her any tighter or any softer. "When some man does come along to teach you about women, Louis, you remember this: you remember we like to be hugged. Don't let them skip over that part when they start talking about the other things."

"I wouldn't do that," I said. I could smell the smoke in her hair and on her clothes.

"You just stand here and hold. You don't try anything, you just make her feel good." Finally she let me go. "Why don't you see what your brother's doing upstairs?"

The next morning, Ron came in my room around nine-thirty and woke me up with a slap on the shoulder, saying I had to rake the lawn so he could burn the leaves. He threw a pair of jeans at my chest and said I'd slept through breakfast and had missed my chance to eat. I got a glass of milk and then went outside. Ron had already started a fire in one of the garbage cans, which he had set down in the middle of the yard. He was burning the regular garbage, and it bled a deep black smoke that refused to rise to the sky.

The rake wasn't any help against leaves stiff with frost, so I had to use a pitchfork. I didn't know why we had to rake the leaves on that day, or in the winter at all, but it was either Mom's idea or Ron's, and I would surely lose an argument against either. Ron stood guard by the fire and shoveled my growing pile of leaves onto it. For a moment the fire would appear to go out—all that frost dripping onto the flames—and then the smoke would seep through again. In about twenty minutes I had done half the yard, and the neighborhood air was dark gray. The garbage can couldn't hold all the leaves, and burning them didn't seem to reduce their size, so he'd let the fire leap from the can into my pile. He shoveled some snow around it as a protective ring and told me not to get too close, he was in charge. Then the neighbors started to call. First Judy Lightfoot from the house behind ours, and then Mr. Cable and Mr. Hawkes. What the hell were we burning? Who the hell was supervising it? Did we have a permit or should they call the cops? Mom took the calls, and it only made her mad at them. She stood by the door in her faded jeans and gray turtleneck and told us to keep going and make lots of smoke. Light the whole world on fire, she said. It started to snow lightly, but she didn't let it stop us. She waited until we were finished, and

then she disappeared into her bedroom before I had a chance
to talk to her.

For dinner that night Mom picked up little boxes of
chicken and mashed potatoes. We ate and did not argue.
Mom stared out the window at the falling sleet that kept the
world hidden. Even our black ashes were hidden from sight
under a sheet of ice. Ron finished quickly and did not ask
to be excused when he left to watch television upstairs.

"It's Ron's birthday soon, isn't it?" Mom said.

I nodded. "A few weeks."

"What do you think he really wants?"

"He wants to go to Montana. He wants to drive there."

"Is that it, huh? It's that simple?" She let out a sigh.

I didn't know what she meant by that. I pulled one of
Michael's magazines closer and started to flip through the
pages.

"Well, maybe I should let him. He'd do a lot better hitchhiking across the country than I would."

"It's cold there this time of year. People turn to ice statues
just walking out to the car."

"Is that what he said?"

"And if you go out to feed the horses in the yard, sometimes it's snowing so hard that when you turn around you
can't find your house."

She laughed a little. She started crumpling up our
chicken boxes and napkins and threw them in the garbage.
After she rinsed our glasses and put them away, she went
back to the window.

Then she said, "We were close, you know. It was almost
working."

"What, Mom?"

But she didn't answer. She went to the hallway closet,
where she put on her yellow suit coat and scarf, which made
her look like a schoolgirl at college. She came back into the
kitchen only briefly.

"I can't stand this," she said.

"What, Mom?"

"I'm going to Michael's," she said. She opened the front door, and I could feel the draft. "I'll be back." Then she left.

So this is what I did: I sat at the kitchen table, reading the backs of cereal boxes and milk cartons, waiting for them to return. I waved my chicken bones over the candle flame until they were striped black zebra bones. I poured a glass of wine for myself, a real one, not just a shot glass, and I pulled out a stack of magazines to thumb through. I read old jokes over and over, but it was better than the milk cartons. I forced myself to laugh. Then I practiced laughing, because Michael had a laugh that boomed, and I wanted to have a laugh like that. It came from somewhere way in the back of his head, at the base of his skull, and it vibrated his nose as it came out.

Of course Ron came downstairs and wanted to know what was so funny. He had just taken a shower and his hair was combed in place. I said nothing was funny and that his hair looked nice. He asked where Mom was, as if I had kidnapped her, and I told him what had happened.

"She said she'd be back soon," I added.

Ron nodded. "What are you reading?"

"One of Michael's magazines. There's a fascinating article on the future of atomic energy."

"There is not."

"Sure there is." I had read the introduction in the table of contents, just the way I read the flaps on Mom's books. "Now they not only explode the atoms, they collapse them. The atoms *implode*."

"So?"

"They disappear. Poof! You've heard of black holes, this is how they start. They eat laboratories and buildings and earth. It's happening all over the East Coast." I hid my lies by offering him the magazine. "Here, read it yourself if you don't believe me."

"Nah." He opened the refrigerator, then closed it. He did the same with a couple of cabinets. "I made a basketball court in the television room," he said. "You want to see it?"

I followed him upstairs. He had pushed all the chairs and the couch up against the walls. A coffee can was nailed above the doorway, and a strip of masking tape marked the free-throw line a few feet away. A small Nerf ball sat in the middle.

Ron spotted me fifty points, and we agreed to a game to a hundred, which took about fifteen minutes. I failed to score a single point. It was impossible to get the ball in the can unless you stuffed it, which I could not quite manage. My balance was off from drinking the wine. Each time Ron drove past me and stuffed it, he also called a foul, which put him at the free-throw line. He couldn't make the shot either, but he could leap past me for the rebound. He had no need to dribble—he could cover the court in two steps—and sometimes he passed the ball to himself off the walls. Once, wrapped up in his defense, I tried his trick and accidentally threw the ball out the open window, where it soaked up a puddle like a sponge. Ron wrung it out and then dove past me for the last few buckets. Several times I expected him to get angry or dispute my calls, but he was all business, with a killer instinct that could not be stopped once begun. He gave no pointers, and throughout the game his only words were the increasing tally. At one hundred it was as if he woke from a trance, sweaty and open-eyed, wondering what I was doing there.

Still Mom hadn't come home.

I sat down on the couch, and he turned on the television.

"Are you hungry?" I said.

"You already had dinner."

"But not a feast. I always feel like having a feast at the end of a hard week."

Ron kept flipping channels. "You haven't had a hard week," he said. "You're in sixth grade."

"Maybe we should call her," I said.

"Yeah, we probably should." Ron went for the phone book. "What's his last name?" he asked.

I didn't know. He had always just been Michael to me. Not mister anybody. Not like the old boyfriends.

"*Stupid*," Ron said. He threw the book on the floor.

The book! I ran down to Mom's bedroom and looked at the book Michael had written, which she kept under her pillow. There was his last name, Asimakapoulos.

Ron got a busy signal.

"Michael probably got a call from his sister in Tacoma," I said.

We sat on the couch and didn't say anything for a while. Ron went into his room. I could hear the radio going. They were talking about cars. The wine had made me sleepy, and I curled up. I thought I would go to sleep like that, just like when Mom and Michael were around, but I couldn't get comfortable that way, so I went to bed. I stole some pillows from the sofa chair in the living room and put them on the foot of my bed, so from under the sheets it would feel like a dog was sleeping there.

When I woke, the snow had turned to rain, and the world was turning to mud. I ran downstairs to Mom's bedroom, but she wasn't there. I ran back upstairs and pushed Ron. He told me to go away and threw a pillow at me, but I wouldn't stop.

"They're not here," I said.

"Who?"

"Mom. Mom and Michael."

He got out of bed and turned off his radio. I could see his ribs under an oystery blue skin that hadn't seen sun in years. We sat on his bed. The gutters on our roof had flooded and the rain ran right down the window.

"Do you think we have to go to school today?" I asked.

"You can do what you want."

"It doesn't start for a couple more hours anyway. It'll probably start snowing again by then."

We sat there for some more time and just watched the rain. I wanted to know what time it was, but Ron didn't use an alarm clock. He believed he could condition himself to wake up at an exact time every day just by picturing the time in his mind before he went to sleep.

"They're probably stopping off at the pound," I said.

Then, a little while later, I added, "And at the grocery. They're probably planning a big brunch for us. Smoked ham."

Ron pulled a blanket off my bed and threw it over his shoulders. His hair was all bent up on one side. I took the other blanket and put it around my shoulders.

"And at the bakery," I said. "You know how Mom likes cinnamon rolls."

"Look, don't you get it? *They're not coming back.*"

"What?"

"You see how happy they are with each other. They want to start a new life together. They want to have new kids of their own. They don't want to have anything to do with *us.*"

"They don't?"

"They're probably halfway to California by now, cruising through the Siskiyou mountains in Michael's Impala."

"But Mom left all her stuff..."

"That's her old stuff. It's her old life. She's not taking that with her. Do you think Dad took anything with him when he left?" Ron spoke with scorn, not for my mother but for me, for not seeing this earlier.

"She said she'd be back."

"But she didn't say when."

"But, Ron, we're alone here."

"Shut up. You've got your suit, you can handle it."

I was numb. I was scared. Ron took me into the bathroom. We stood next to each other facing the mirror, the top of my head came even with his shoulder.

"What do you see?" he asked.

I saw myself. I saw his bent hair. I looked into our eyes for something else. I thought he was going to talk about how much older he was than me, how my face would thicken and an Adam's apple would grow in my throat and how my wavy hair would begin to curl. I expected a sermon about how I was going to have to grow up fast. How I'd have to become more like him.

"Now step on the toilet," he said. The toilet was right beside me, its rim had been pushing up to my shin. When I stood, my shoulder came even with Ron's, our eyes on equal level. "What do you see now?" he asked.

I turned to the mirror. But now my head was above the mirror, I could only see my mouth and neck and trunk extending down to my feet on the lid of the toilet.

"This is how I live," he said. "I have to bend down to see myself."

I could only see his mouth as he talked. I couldn't see his eyes, I didn't know where they were looking, but I imagined they stared off to the upper right, as if he were talking to someone else.

"I have one for you," he said. "This one's going to kill you for sure."

"No," I said. "It's impossible to kill me." He was finally getting to me, all his meanness.

"I break both your ankles with a spiked mace, and you've lost three quarts of blood. Then I tie you in ropes and throw you into a pool of starving great white sharks."

"Great whites hate the taste of rope," I said.

"Not when they haven't eaten in two weeks. Not when they're starving."

"I quickly swim to the bottom and pull the plug on the pool. The water runs out and the sharks are left yapping like harmless poodles."

"You're still bleeding."

"But I'm still alive," I said.

"Yes," he said. *"You're still alive."*

Ron ran out of the room and went into his, where he started packing a duffel bag with his clothes. He picked out his jeans and his rugby and flannel shirts and rolled them into tight balls.

"What are you doing?" I said.

"I'll be sixteen in two weeks anyway," he said. "I might as well get a head start."

The bag quickly filled. He unplugged his radio and put that in there, along with a toothbrush and a towel. He went down to the kitchen and got a small knife and a can opener and three cans of beans. He didn't even have to think, he was just checking off a mental list that he must have gone over many times.

"I was going to wait 'til summer," he said. He zipped up the bag and set it outside his door. "Look," he said. "I could give it a week. We've got some food downstairs to live on, and that would give you a couple of days to get your own bag and make some plans. I was going to take the umbrella, but you can have it."

I didn't know what to do. I thought I could handle this but I just couldn't, not with Ron around. I decided to go back to bed, to crawl under the covers and kick the pillows onto the floor. I didn't want to believe him, but I found myself making plans. I still had the house, and I could just live here on my own, go to school during the day. I could get a job in the afternoons bagging groceries and steal some food from the storeroom. I wouldn't even have to tell anyone that my mom was gone. The milkman brought a half gallon of low-fat and some cottage cheese on Tuesdays. I could eat cottage cheese if I had some jam. Then I remembered we had most of last summer's raspberry jam in the freezer. It would be okay. It would be tough on my birthday and on holidays, but people lived alone all the time.

We'd come so close—Michael'd been there, in our lives. It was almost working. I drew my legs up to my chest and closed my eyes and counted to ten, then I went over my plan again. People lived alone all the time.

I heard a car outside, its doors opening and closing. I threw off the covers and ran to the window as I heard voices, two voices. Michael's Impala sat at the curb. In one arm Michael held an umbrella over Mom's head. Draped over the other arm, protected by a thin layer of plastic, was a brown herringbone suit.

With my arms high over my head, I ran, first in tight circles, then out my door and into Ron's room, victory on my lips. But he was not in his room. I could see him through his window—he was out back again, jumping, lead sacks on bony ankles. He jumped from a puddle and landed in his own footsteps, taking off again before the water could cover his shoes. His pants, shirt, and hair clung to his body. Near the tops of his jumps his face clenched.

With the sleeve of my pajama top I wiped away the mist on the window. From his bed I stole a green wool surplus blanket and draped it over my shoulders, and I watched my brother and said nothing, even as I heard the front door open and the voices come closer, calling our names: *"Lou? Ron? Louis?"* In ten minutes I'd be downstairs, trying not to crack the yolks on the eggs Mom had bought as Michael checked the length of Ron's new trousers. But at that moment I had lost my thoughts—I counted up toward fifty, waiting for his set to end.

S P I K E S

•

Michael Chabon

O N E   A F T E R N O O N   toward the middle of April, Kohn's lawyer, her patience exhausted, called and said she was giving him one last chance. He was to come into Chagrin Harbor that afternoon and sign the petition in which he and his wife informed the state of Washington that their marriage was irretrievably broken. If he once again failed to show, his lawyer regretted she would have to toss his file into a bottom drawer, send him a bill, and forget about him. His wife, and *her* lawyer, would then be free to reap uncontested the rewards of his recalcitrance. So Kohn pulled on his big rubber boots and slogged up the path to the slough of gravel where he and his neighbors on Valhalla Beach parked their mud-encrusted Jeeps and pickups. There was a chill in the air, and Kohn's large, unshaven head with its spectacles and stunned features was zipped deep into the hood of a parka the vague color of boiled organ meat. He peered out at the world through a tiny porthole trimmed with synthetic fur and heard only the sound of his own respiration.

His marriage had been short-lived, a brief tale of blind hopefulness, calamity, and then the dismantling ministrations of psychotherapists and lawyers. Jill was ten years older than Kohn, a Mudge Island native, a Lacan scholar who taught at Reed College. She yearned to have a child. Kohn was an easterner, socially awkward, obsessive. He was an instrument maker who built custom electric guitars, mostly for the Japanese market, and he preferred to keep his own yearnings pressed between the clear panes of a marijuana habit, where he could safely observe them. He spoke with a slight stammer. His only good friend was one he had made in his freshman year of high school. Jill had mistaken his carpenterial silences, and a shyness that was purely physiological, for the marks of a sensitive soul. She was thirty-five and perhaps not interested in looking too closely or too far.

She had gotten pregnant right after the wedding. They left Portland and moved back up to Puget Sound, to her parents' old brown-shingled house on Probity Beach. The baby arrived in March, a son, and for the length of a baseball season the three of them were contented, in a blurred way that at certain moments resolved itself into sharp foci of happiness no wider than a dime, no more substantial than a smell of salt in the hollow of the baby's neck as Kohn carried him up the beach to his grandparents' whitewashed porch. In October, the baby spiked a fever of 106 degrees. He lost consciousness on the ferryboat, in his mother's arms, on the way in to Swedish Hospital. He was buried, along with his parents' marriage, in a corner of Mudge Island Cemetery, with some of his ancestors and cousins. They got therapy, but it was a waste of money and time because Kohn didn't like to talk in front of the therapist. He grieved at odd moments, privately, minutely, invisibly almost, even to himself. He did not, it was certainly true, grieve enough. He withdrew. Jill left him. She left the island and moved to an ashram in the California desert. But Kohn had stayed, or had been left behind. He'd rented a tiny cabin on Valhalla Beach, set up his workbench, and resumed the slow production of his signature model, the Kohn Six, a flying wedge of flamed maple with locking tremolo and tuners and deluxe hum-bucking pickups with coil taps. He waited for the next intervention of fate, hoping this time to miss it when it came.

When Kohn reached the muddy parking area, out of breath from the climb, he saw Bengt Thorkelson standing in the rain beside his mother's Honda Civic, with a length of PVC pipe, swinging for the fences.

Bengt was eleven years old and lived with his widowed mother in the Wayland house, three doors down the beach from Kohn. He was short for his age, and pudgy, with wiry dark hair and big eyeglasses. He ran with a slight wobble in his hips. On the beach at dusk, when he thought no one was looking, he practiced seagull impersonation, with some success. His best friend, Malcolm Dorsey, was currently the only black child on Mudge Island. That was all Kohn knew about Bengt, except that, walking on the beach one stoned morning the winter before, Kohn had come upon the boy sitting on a driftwood log, in the rain, with his orange Lab mongrel, Nerf, holding a polka-dot Minnie Mouse umbrella over both their heads, and sobbing. Kohn had hurried past him, head down, zipped tight into his parka. The boy's father, Kohn knew vaguely, had drowned or somehow been killed at sea. His mother was a buxom, energetic, foulmouthed, kind of sexy woman, who had once brought Kohn a strange casserole involving tofu, buckwheat noodles, and currants. Kohn avoided her, too. He kept his distance from all his neighbors, whose lives extended across Mudge Island from Valhalla Beach to Rhododendron Beach, from Chagrin Harbor to Point Probity, from the tops of the transmitter towers

along Radio Beach down to the deep Cretaceous bones of
the island. Kohn's life fit into the back of an Econoline van.

"Hi, Bengt," Kohn said, moving slowly toward his van,
the mud sucking in and spitting out the soles of his boots as
he went. He was never comfortable saying the boy's name,
which must be the curse of his entire existence. Generally
he veered between leaving off the *t* and trying to slip in as
much of the *g* as he felt Swedish custom would allow.

"Hi, Mr. Kohn," Bengt said glumly. He crouched and
picked up a penny from the ground by his feet. He was
dressed in a bright red-and-white hooded sweatshirt that
said "Rangers" in blue script across the chest, a pair of stiff
new dungarees, rolled, and a pair of ancient, pointy men's
cleats, tied with dress laces, much too large for his feet and
apparently a hand-me-down from some remote ball-playing
ancestor. A brand-new fielder's glove lay on the ground at
his feet. His fingers, on the length of plastic pipe, were pink
with cold. He rocked back on his heels, raised the pipe like
a hatchet behind his head, and tossed the penny into the air.
Then he swung, as Kohn had seen him swing before, putting
everything he had into a huge, wild hack that spun him
around so far he almost fell over. The penny hit the mud
with a splatter of rude commentary on his form.

"Shit. I mean, shoot." He picked the penny up, tossed it,
and took another swing. He missed again. "Shoot." He tossed
the penny and swung wild again. "Shoot!" He glanced toward
Kohn, then away, his cheeks reddening. "I can hit it," he
assured Kohn. He pointed, and Kohn saw that the ground
before him was sprinkled lightly with pennies.

"You have a game today?" said Kohn. He had spoken to
no one but his lawyer in days, and the bassoon twang of his
voice struck his ears oddly. He unzipped his hood a little.

"No, I have practice. Today's the first day."

"In the rain?"

"It's not raining." Kohn guessed that he was right; it had

rained all winter, every day but January 11 and February 24, from early December to mid-March, a magical-realist deluge that made fence posts sprout green leaves and restored Mudge Lake, lost thirty years earlier to a failed Army Corps of Engineers drainage project. This spring weather was something different, hardly weather at all—a thin, drifting blanket of sparkling grayness that would not prevent islanders from mowing their lawns, washing their cars, or working on their home-run swings. Again Bengt tossed the elusive cent into the air. This time he connected, and the coin chimed an E-flat against the tube. It hooked foul, toward the Civic, ricocheted, and landed in the mud ten feet from Bengt's shoes, leaving a white scar in the blue flank of the car. "Yes!" he cried grimly. He reached into his pocket, fished around, and brought out another penny. "I suck."

"Pennies are small."

"Baseballs are small, too," Bengt observed. He probed at the mud with the end of his pipe. "I'd like to shoot a crossbow one time," he went on irrelevantly. He operated an invisible crank, took aim along the stock of his PVC pipe, and then let a bolt fly with a *thwok!* of his tongue. He looked down at his feet. "These shoes were my uncle Lars's. I know they're stupid looking."

"No," said Kohn. "Not really." Kohn looked at his wristwatch. A few seconds later he looked at it again. Lately he was always checking his watch, but the next moment he never seemed to remember what it had told him.

"Huh," said Bengt finally. "Well, okay. I'm late now. I guess I must be pretty late. I guess I might as well not go. I hate baseball." He glanced up at Kohn, then away, looking to see if he had shocked Kohn. Kohn tried to look shocked. "I'm much more interested in archery."

"Is your mom driving you?"

"She's with my gran in the hospital. She fell off a step stool in the kitchen, my gran I mean, and broke her hip. My uncle Lars is staying with me supposally, but I don't know where he is. I called Tommy Latrobe, and his mom is supposed to come over to pick me up. But I guess she forgot."

Bengt tossed a penny and connected again, pulling it to the left but keeping it more or less fair this time. Then he dug down into his pocket again.

"You sure have a lot of pennies in there," Kohn said.

Bengt brought out a handful of fifty-cent penny rolls in crisp, tight red-and-white wrappers. He held them out for Kohn to inspect, then slipped all but one back into his pocket. From this one he peeled down a quarter inch of wrapper and loosened another handful of coins.

"They were my dad's," he said. "My mom said he used to have a lot of time on his hands. On the boats." The Mudge Island Thorkelsons ran an outfit that went up to Alaska, rounded up ice floes, and drove them to Japan, where they were sold, suitably shaved and crushed, in elegant bars. Wondrous the things a Japanese person would buy. "There's a whole box of penny rolls under my mom's bed." He tossed a penny, swung, and drove it toward the ivy- or vinyl-covered wall of his imagination.

"Don't hit them into the mud!" Kohn was appalled. "Your father's pennies!"

"I don't need them."

Bengt pressed another penny between his thumb and forefinger and prepared to toss it into the air. He brandished the length of pipe behind him. Just as he tossed his hand, Kohn reached out and grabbed hold of his wrist. The boy looked at him, astonished. He wrenched his hand away and gave it a shake. His arm bore briefly the pale impression of Kohn's fingers.

"Oh, my God, I'm sorry," said Kohn, surprised by himself. They were only pennies. They rolled under the refrigerators of the world, wedged themselves into the joints of desk drawers, disappeared into the bowels of auto seats, slipped behind breakfronts, bureaus, and toilets. No one bothered to fish them out. They fell from the hands of careless pedestrians and lay for hours on the sidewalk without anyone stopping to pick them up. Kohn himself had tossed ringing handfuls into the garbage. "Did I hurt you? God, I'm sorry. Let me give you a ride to practice. I'm on my way in to town."

Bengt studied Kohn, his forehead wrinkling. He checked Kohn's adequate build. He appraised Kohn's knotted, strong-looking hands. "Do you like baseball?" he said.

Kohn considered the question. He had first come to the game at the age of eight, in Washington, D.C., and had fallen in love with Frank Howard, but at the end of the season Howard and the Senators departed for Texas. That November his parents had ended their own marriage. The candy manufacturer for whom Mr. Kohn worked as an accountant transferred him to Pittsburgh. After a nasty legal battle, the young Kohn went with him. The following spring his father took him many times down to the big, ugly ballpark at the Confluence. The Pirates had a handsome Puerto Rican outfielder who hit in the clutch and cut down runners at the plate with strikes from deep right. He collected his three thousandth career hit on the last day of the season and died the following winter in a plane crash. After that Kohn gave up on the organized versions of the sport.

He shook his head. "To be honest, I kind of hate it, too."

"I know," said Bengt, banging the ground with the end of his pipe. "God!"

"But I play a little softball sometimes." Kohn had played on an intramural team in college. He had been the second-worst player on a team that finished in ninth place out of twelve.

Bengt looked a little surprised. "What position?"

"Outfield." Kohn had a sudden craving for the broad skewed vista from far right, the distant buzz of chatter from the bench, the outfielder's blank bovine consciousness of grass and sky. If you backed up far enough out there on a hot summer day, you could sometimes see the curvature of the earth.

"Do you have a glove?" Bengt was getting a little excited now.

"Somewhere in my van, I think."

"Cool," said Bengt. He dropped the piece of pipe, picked up his own mitt, and started toward Kohn's van, cleats spraying clodlets of mud as he went. Kohn trudged after him. When he climbed in behind the wheel, he saw to his dismay that the boy was smiling.

"I have to go see my lawyer," Kohn said. "Did I mention that?"

Ordinarily Kohn drove the island roads with unstudied recklessness. His work demanded that hours of intense care be paid to very small things, and when he got behind the wheel of a car he always came a little unwound. But he drove his twitchy, voluble young passenger toward town carefully and slowly. He worked at it. He was doing a good deed, and a part of him was afraid of doing good deeds. They often seemed to result, he had noticed, in tragedy and newspaper articles. A kindly, heartbroken neighbor drives a troubled young fatherless boy to his baseball practice. Their van flips over and bursts into flames.

"My uncle Lars is like eighty years old," Bengt was saying, warily watching his shoes. "He played for the St. Louis Browns. He was the pitcher who killed somebody, you know? With a baseball, I mean, in a game. Johnny something, I don't remember. It was in a book. *Strange but True Baseball Stories.*"

"Lars *Larssen?*" said Kohn. Kohn had read this same book, or one like it, as a child. "That's your uncle Lars? Wow. Johnny Timberlake, wasn't it?"

"Timberlake."

"What happened to him after that?"

"He died!"

"I mean, your uncle. Did he have to go to jail or anything?"

Bengt shook his head. "He had to retire, I guess was all," he said. "It was an accident. It was just bad luck."

At the intersection of Cemetery Road and Mudge Island Highway, they pulled up to the traffic signal, one of only two on the island. The light turned from green to yellow, and Kohn slowed the car to a stop. He looked over at Lars Larssen's old spikes, with their reptile skin, their rats' snouts, their laces like quivering feelers. Kohn would not have wanted to put his own feet inside them.

"I have to wear six pairs of socks," said Bengt.

"Can't you just buy new ones?"

Bengt didn't immediately reply. He looked at the cursed shoes that were swallowing his feet, at the curling, scarred black toes of bad luck itself.

"I wish," he said.

In spite of Kohn's fears, they arrived safely at practice. Kohn cut the engine, and they sat. They stared through the windshield at the men and boys gathered on the grass. The team practiced on the dirt-infield diamond behind Chagrin Harbor Elementary School, on the edge of a cow pasture frequented, autumn midnights, by the local island coven of shroomheads. The fathers were standing around in their baseball caps, in a knot, smoking and talking. They looked over at Kohn's van, trying to identify it. Many of them would have known each other all their lives. On this field they would have tormented the chubby, bespectacled goat of their generation. Their sons sat clumped along the bench like pigeons on the arm of a statue. One boy stood off to the side taking practice swings with a red aluminum bat, and two others were playing some private martial art that involved kicking each other repeatedly in the behind. At last a tall, heavyset man separated himself from the group of fathers and approached the boys, clapping his hands. The men spread out behind him, arms folded across their chests, suddenly all business. The boys scrambled to their feet and went to string themselves out along the third-base line.

"You'd better get going," Kohn said, looking at his watch.

"I can't," said Bengt.

"Go on. You'll be fine."

"Aren't you coming?"

"Some other time," Kohn said. "I'm serious, I really do have to see my lawyer."

Bengt didn't say anything. He affected to study the engineering of his fielder's mitt, picking at its knots and laces. Kohn checked his watch again. He was already ten minutes late for his appointment.

"Who's your lawyer?" Bengt said at last. "Crofoot? Toole? Overholser?"

"Banghart," said Kohn.

Bengt nodded. "Are you making out your will?"

"Yes," said Kohn. "And I'm leaving everything to you. Now, go on."

Bengt looked down at his lap. His glasses started to slide off, but he caught them and pushed them back up his nose. His eyelids fluttered and he took a deep breath. Kohn was afraid he might start to cry. Then he opened the door. Before he got out of the car, he reached into the muff of his sweatshirt and took out a neat, tight roll of pennies. He handed it to Kohn.

"I can get someone to bring me home," he said. "Thank you for the ride."

Kohn hesitated, but he felt that because of Bengt's father, because of the fruitless nights he had spent rolling stacks of coins as he drove the broken ice across the sea, he could not refuse payment. He took the pennies, then watched as Bengt, slow, hunched forward as if he were dragging some huge, cumbersome object, trudged over to join the other boys. Kohn put the pennies in his pocket and got out of the car.

The boys stood in a broken line along the base path between third and home in bits and pieces of outgrown and hand-me-down uniforms, ripped jeans, dusty caps bearing the insignia of a dozen different major league teams, but all of them wearing complicated polychrome athletic shoes tricked out with lights, air pumps, windows, fins, ailerons, spoilers. They were skinny, mean-looking boys, scratch hitters and spikers of second basemen, dirt players, brushback artists. One of them was almost as tall as a man, with a faint pencil sketch of a mustache on his upper lip. They all stared at Bengt as he sidled up to the line. He was shorter than any of them and ten pounds heavier, and as he looked up at the coach he blushed and gave an apologetic little laugh that, amid the gang of tiny hard cases, came off inevitably as shrill and unbecoming. Standing with the other boys, Bengt reminded Kohn of the leather button used in his family for many years to replace the shoe in Monopoly, ranged at "Go" alongside the race car, the top hat, and the scrappy little dog, plump and homely and still trailing a snippet of brown thread. When Bengt saw Kohn, he colored again and looked down at his feet. This time his glasses fell off. They landed in the mud. A few of the boys laughed. Bengt picked them up and wiped the lenses on his sweatshirt.

"I guess now we know what happened to Joe Jackson's shoes," said a father, and all the men and boys laughed.

"Hello," said the coach, walking over to Kohn, looking a little suspicious. "Glad you could make it. You must be..."

He held out his hand, waiting for Kohn to supply the explanation, the narrative that would plausibly connect him to Bengt Thorkelson.

"I'm just a neighbor," Kohn said. "I was just giving him a ride."

He went over to Bengt, took the roll of pennies from his pocket, and handed it back.

"No charge," he said. Then he zipped up his parka, turned, and walked off the field.

He was steering the van back into the swamped half acre of mud and gravel above Valhalla Beach when he realized he had forgotten about his lawyer. When he called to apologize, her secretary said she wasn't in and would not be able to take his calls anymore. A few days later, when Kohn went into Seattle to buy lumber and saw blades and screens for his bong, he spotted a pair of flashy baseball sneakers in the window of an athletic-shoe store on Forty-fifth. The knowledge of his missed opportunity came over him like a spasm; he was breathless with regret, doubled over, dizzy. He went in and dropped a hundred and forty-five bucks on the shoes in a boy's size twelve. They were absurdly beautiful things, a cross between architecture and graffiti, but the salesclerk, lumbering, slow, had too many customers on his hands, and by the time Kohn got back out onto the street his van had been ticketed, it was getting dark, and he had twenty minutes to get out to the specialty hardware place in Ballard where he bought his wood. Kohn tore the ticket from his windshield and tossed it, with the shoes, into the back of his van, where they were soon lost.

LIFE PRERECORDED

●

Jill McCorkle

W HEN I QUIT SMOKING, I dreamed of ciga-
rettes. They were everywhere: dangling from lips, burning
in ashtrays. I felt the thin cylinder between my fingers, my
words shrouded in fog, heard the zip of a lighter, the scritch-
scratch of a match. I could smell cigarettes from blocks away.
When hordes of people poured into the subway, I knew instantly who smoked and who didn't. I leaned in close to those
who did, envying the habit, the rustle of cellophane in their
purses or shirt pockets. I wanted to suck the stale tobacco
from the fabric of their clothes.

I begged a cigarette from a complete stranger, a man
with dreadlocks who carried a brightly colored duffel (I
didn't *look* pregnant, after all), and dipped into a dirty
public rest room, stood in a nasty stall that had no door, and
read still nastier graffiti while inhaling and exhaling, common breathing elevated to enormous heights. As I got down

close to the brown filter (a much harsher brand than the one
I'd abandoned), I kept hearing my doctor say how he could
tell which women smoked by the appearance of the placenta,
and I envisioned all that I had just taken in settling like silt
onto that little cluster of cells safely hidden from the world
by skin, underwear, jeans, sweater, heavy down coat. He said
that he had seen quite a few tar-filled, blackened placentas
in his young career.

The nurse who took my little cup of urine and poured it into
a vial, sample after sample lined up to go to the lab, didn't
know how to look when giving the results. A wedding ring
was no guarantee. Age was no guarantee. It was easier for
her to telephone, easier to deliver the news without a face,
only in monotone syllables: "Your test is positive," confirm-
ing the little home stick test that I had anxiously tried twice
already. I found myself reassuring *her*. "That's wonderful,"
I said, and I could hear her lengthy sigh at the other end
of the line, like a balloon let loose into the air. She faced a
waiting room full of the others: the young girl with mascara-
stained cheeks, Clearasil and homework assignments in her
synthetic leather purse, the one with some boy's ring and
promise strung around her neck, the one who had no earthly
idea how it could have happened.

The dreams started early, odd little snippets. I was at a table
with friends, in a lively, colorful café with hot-pepper lights,
and I felt so jolly, robust and jolly, that when the cute young
waiter, his hair slicked back like a flamenco dancer's, came
whirling by, I asked for another fruit-juice concoction like
the one I'd just finished. Delicious stuff. I ate the cherries
and sucked the pineapple. I discreetly picked my teeth with
the frilly little parasol. "Fruit juice?" he asks. "Fruit juice?"

The music stops, all heads turn to my table, to me, my abdomen clearly visible under a tight tank top like I have never owned in reality. "Lady, you just sucked down your fourth double tequila sunrise." What? "Lady, you seem discombobulated," he says with an incredulous look, and that word, *discombobulated,* with every loud harsh syllable, ricochets around the room. I get stuck on the word, my head bobbling, reeling, about to fall off.

The images came to me, woke me, the blackened placenta slipping onto a clean hospital floor, the wide-spaced stare of fetal alcohol syndrome. It was a recurring dream; it was right up there with the one where the bathtub is steaming and bubbly and this beautifully shining naked baby shoots from your hands like a bar of soap into the well of an empty tub or out an open window. There was the one where you leave it on the hood of the car and speed off down the highway, and the one where you accidentally pierce the fontanel, that soft spot, with something as innocent as the wrong end of a rat-tail comb.

There were times in those early weeks when I couldn't help but smoke. How bad could one cigarette really be? How bad could one little paper tube be, as compared to nervous energy and honest-to-God cravings? I walked blocks to a different neighborhood, a drugstore where no one would recognize me, to buy a carton of cigarettes, and then I carefully hid them in the apartment, here a pack, there a pack, so it seemed as if they weren't really there at all. Early mornings I stood in my nightgown and watched from our fifth-floor window. When my husband disappeared around the corner, I climbed out on the fire escape with matches and an ashtray. The knowledge that I *was* going to smoke allowed me to slow down, take my time, angle myself so that I had a good view, red-brick buildings and sidewalks rising up Beacon Hill.

Then I puffed furiously, the late November wind making me shiver as people down below scurried past in their down coats and scarves and hats. I watched our neighbor walking toward Charles Street, his steps slow, as methodical as the metallic click of his prosthetic heart valve.

Our neighbor. While moving in, we had been told by another person in the building—the single woman below us, who wore faux zebra spandex minis and catered to at least five Persians I'd seen lounging in her bay—to avoid "the old man" at all costs, to look the other way. "He'll talk your head off," she whispered, and then rushed off to her job at a small gallery on Newbury Street. She never once asked what I did, somehow having gotten stuck in the groove of my husband's being an actuary; like many people who weren't sure what an actuary was, she simply stopped talking and left.

I met our neighbor that same day, while the mover was bringing in our things. It was late August but already felt and looked like what I knew in the South as the beginning of autumn; there was a breeze off the Charles, and with it the sharp river smell that I grew to appreciate, even to welcome as home. The light seemed sharper, whiter, the shadows longer. It was a surprise to find that I *loved* this city, the street, the building. I thought about all of this while sitting on those old concrete steps—smoking one cigarette right after another—and watching our belongings come off the truck.

It was while I was carefully watching over my great-aunt Patricia's piecrust table, which was being angled and turned through the door, that Joseph Sever stopped to introduce himself and then (as the other neighbor had predicted) proceeded to talk. He told me how he used to smoke, how he smoked Lucky Strikes, started during the war, liked them so much he continued. He said that if he hadn't had such a good reason—his life—to quit, he'd still be smoking three packs a day and enjoying every puff. But of course that was before his wife of forty years, Gwendolyn, died, before the heart valve, before his temples atrophied. He had been an accountant right there in the downtown area, and he described those April evenings when he worked so late, lighting cigarettes without even thinking, sometimes finding two lit and burning in the ashtray, as if he had an invisible partner.

He asked (with great consideration given to any possible answer) how I spent my time. When he stopped speaking and there was a lull in the hoisting and heaving of the movers, I could hear his valve, a metallic click as it swung closed to prevent his blood from rushing back to its source. I told him that I worked as a copy editor for one of the publishers in town and that my work load fluctuated in a similar fashion. With that entrée, he talked about books, his favorites from as long ago as he could remember: *Look Homeward, Angel* as a young man new to the city, then *Anna Karenina* and *For Whom the Bell Tolls,* all of Hardy and Conrad, a little Jack London. "I'm a bit of a literary dabbler," he said. "I have written some perfectly horrible poetry myself." He liked T. S. Eliot and he liked Yeats. He liked to pause and quote a line or two with great drama, always stopping, it seemed, when his breath gave out, at which point he tipped his latest L. L. Bean hat and bowed.

I came to learn that he purchased a new hat each season: the panama in the summer, the wool huntsman cap in the winter. I imagined a closet filled with hats, stacks and stacks, as in *Caps for Sale*—a favorite book in my memory as read in the voice of Captain Kangaroo. It turned out that at the end of each season he continued to do what his wife had called "purging." He gathered up everything he could live without and took it to the Salvation Army bin down on Cambridge Street. "Except books," he said. "And of course the cats." He and Gwendolyn had always had cats, sometimes one, usually two. During his fifty years in the building he had had fifteen different cats and could name them all in one fluid motion, their names rhyming and rolling as each received an appositive: the friskiest of them all, the one with a terrible urinary problem, the one Gwendolyn never got over, the one who ate a rubber ball. He said that I should come visit his apartment and see what fifty years of books looked like. "This will be your future," he said as he slowly mounted the stairs. "There are rows behind rows of books, in closets and in one very special kitchen cabinet. Gwenny always used *Heart of Darkness* to balance the lamp that wobbles by our bed." He paused on the landing before taking his flight to the second floor, the big brass-plated door propped open by the movers. "I keep it there. The lamp is a hellish thing, old and shorted out, but I keep it there."

Over and over I dreamed I was having a kitten. I looked at the faceless doctor and said, "Oh, thank God, she didn't have her claws out!" I told him that, yes, she was really cute but I was kind of disappointed, I really wanted a baby. At which point he laughed, just slapped his knee and laughed in a way that marked the absurdity of it all: imagine wanting a child. Then I dreamed that I *couldn't* have a child, there was no child, and I went to a special clinic seeking help. I rode the T, changing trains twice; I took a boat and a bus and a taxi. The building was no bigger than the small drugstore around the corner, and women of all ages and sizes and shapes were pressing up to the counter, behind which stood a woman in white guarding the shelves of test tubes. "Ah, yes, Mrs. Porter," she said, and nodded when it was my turn. "We have your child." Suddenly the other women were gone, and I was carefully handed a small glass tube. I held it up to the light, and there I saw a beautiful little girl no bigger than the pictures of Thumbelina I remembered from my childhood fairy-tale book. She had dark brown hair that waved onto her shoulders and big blue eyes that I was certain I saw wink and blink in affection.

"Freeze-dried," the woman said. "Same process as coffee. Just go home and add a little water, you'll see." The woman looked like someone I knew: a former teacher, the mother of a classmate—I couldn't quite get there. "Be very careful with her now," she added, and handed me a special cardboard tube much like what you'd use to mail a stool specimen or a radon test. Carefully I kissed the precious glass tube and slipped her into the sturdy container and then into the special zippered section of my purse. I put that into a brightly colored duffel and looped the strap over my head for extra security. In the dream I had dreadlocks and a joint hidden in my bra.

"Oh, by the way." I was almost out the door when I remembered the important questions I had planned to ask, all the things that my husband and I had discussed before my long journey to this place. "Her medical history." The room was buzzing with grappling, grabbing women again, and I was being shoved out of the way. "Please. I really have to know all that you know about her." The woman seized my arm and pulled me around the counter and back behind the heavy rows of shelves. She leaned close and whispered. Now I knew that I had never seen her before in my life. I would have remembered—the shiny broad forehead, the missing teeth. "You must never reveal what I'm about to say. If you do, people will want your baby. They will never let her alone." She leaned closer, her mouth covering and warming my ear as I strained to hear. "Her mama was Marilyn Monroe," she said. "And her daddy—" She paused, looking around nervously. "JFK." I felt stunned, disheartened. Why couldn't my baby just be the product of Flo Taylor and Ed Smith from Podunk, Wisconsin? I didn't even think to ask why they were giving *me* such a burden. Was it all random or had I been singled out, especially chosen? My worries turned to mental health issues, substance abuse genes, square jawlines, and prominent teeth. But then, all because I was wondering about the rich and famous, I found myself thinking about good looks and talent and southern roots. I said, "Do you have one from Elvis?"

At three months, that magical time when you supposedly cross the threshold from morning sickness to a sudden burst of energy, the uterus slightly larger than an orange, my husband and I decided to take a vacation. The reason was clear. It was freezing in Boston, not to mention the fact that everywhere we turned people were saying, "Your life is about to change. It will never ever be the same." Like birthdays, weddings, funerals, it seemed important to mark this transition, to remind ourselves constantly that something was in fact happening. We chose the Virgin Islands, as a way of feeling we had gone very far and yet not left the country. I just didn't feel I could be pregnant *and* in another country.

The trip was like a perfect dream that first day as I lazed in the sun, calypso music playing down the beach, the warm clear water as blue as the sky. I listened to the birds and the steel drum while running through lists of names in my mind—names of relatives long deceased. In and out of my thoughts, I heard the man who was trying to interest my husband in a time-share. This man sat there in his shorts and Hawaiian shirt, canvas shoes with the laces untied, smelling like Hawaiian Tropic and some kind of musky aftershave. He asked my husband if teenage girls were better looking than ever before these days, or was it just him? I heard him tell my husband that he preferred younger women, always had. "Like that one, *mmmm, mmmmm,*" he said, his words oozing in such a way I half expected to see them crawling off his tongue like black oily leeches. Instead

I opened one eye to his gleaming white teeth just in time to follow his look to a string bikini, oiled brown thighs too young for cellulite. I wanted to sit up and tell him that of course he "liked 'em young," that any grown-up woman with any sense whatsoever wouldn't want to touch him or a thing he had. But the warmth of the sun and the distant drums, the secret knowledge that the young woman who had just passed would not give this two-bit Peter Pan salesman the time of day, seemed satisfaction enough. That and the fact that I had already lifted his almost empty pack of Marlboros and hidden it deep in my beach bag. I listened to him pat his pockets and look all around. Let him have a little nicotine fit, get a grip on the libido. I devised a plan that I would get up in the middle of the night and tiptoe out onto our balcony. I would huddle off to one side and blow my smoke with the wind, just as I had done through the screened window of a locked bathroom as a teenager. A little mouthwash, deodorant, hair spray, cologne. If no one saw me, if I didn't confess, it was as though it never happened.

The next morning I woke to the sensation of wetness, the gray numb of sleep suddenly startled by recognition as I hurried to switch on the fluorescent light in the bathroom. It was real; I was bleeding. Slowly, carefully, I called out to my husband and lay down on the cool tile floor. I felt detached, as if I was in someone else's room, on someone else's vacation. I imagined a honeymoon couple whirling and dancing, drunk and giddy, collapsing on the bed while the stark sunlight and still blue sea lay beyond the sliding glass doors. Same place, same room, same toilet, different life. I lay there and questioned everything. Why did I buy the crib so early? Why did I smoke that Marlboro Man cigarette? I lay there wishing that we were home. I wanted the broken black tiles of our own bathroom; I wanted Joseph Sever seated on the front stoop, the smell of the Charles River, our pots without handles and the rickety three-legged couch I complained about every time I sat; I wanted absolute normalcy. I said, "Let's make a deal. Let me win this round and I will never ever again smoke. I will go on great missions and try not to gossip. But more than anything, I solemnly swear to never again smoke."

It seemed to take forever: phone calls, a slow walk, the idle chatter and words of sympathy and well-wishes from the time-share man, his gaze taking in the freshly raked beach. There was a boat ride and then an ambulance that really was a station wagon with a light on top. There was an emergency room and then a closed door, a hall where pregnant women perched like hood ornaments on cheap aluminum stretchers, some crying out in labor, their wings spread in pain. They had no ultrasound; they had no answers. I caught myself thinking about the used-car lot that was across the street from my grandmother's house when I was growing up. I thought of the little plastic flags strung across that lot and the way they whipped in the wind. IT'S A GOOD DEAL, the sign said, and whenever anyone commented on it, my grandmother simply leveled her eyes at the person with a solemn stare, as if to say, "You better work hard to *make* it a good deal." Woman by woman, I rolled past. They looked lifeless—used and worn and tired.

I spent a week sitting in my hotel bed or on a chaise on the balcony, the room littered with room-service trays; the choices were limited—conch chowder, conch fritters, conch omelet, conch conch. I could hear my husband down below, forced in my absence to hear more time-share news, to have supple young bodies pointed out for his perusal, while I clicked a channel changer round and round hoping that all of a sudden I would find more than one station. Over and over it advertised a parade that had taken place the week before, people in large bird suits, feathers and bells,

marching. I lay in the bed and watched little yellow sugar
birds fly up to suck on the jelly packets I placed outside, the
breakfast tray discarded on the dresser. The Kings Day parade. The Kings Day parade. It was a bad *Twilight Zone*.
It was as if the world had stopped suddenly and thrown
everything askew.

Everyone has a story. Perfect strangers will come up and
tell you the most horrible story they've ever heard about
pregnancy and childbirth. They will say, "I shouldn't be
telling this to *you*, but..." Then they will proceed without
ever pausing to draw a breath. You hear about the woman
who miscarried after the three-month mark and about the
woman who knew at seven months that her baby was dead
but was asked to carry it into labor all the same. "Oh, sure,"
people will say. "It's common to bleed like that. Happens all
the time. No real explanation. *Que sera, sera.* A miscarriage
is just one that was never meant to be, you know, a genetic
mistake. If you lose this one, you can always have another.
But look at it this way—you haven't lost it yet! It ain't over
'til it's over. The fat lady ain't done singing."

"The river is within us, the sea is all about us." Joseph Sever's
voice quivered with the line as he leaned closer to me, all
the while looking at my abdomen now two months beyond
the nightmarish scare. He insisted that I read aloud, anything I was reading, anything my husband was reading.
We should be reading aloud all the time now. He had read
an article about it, the words traveling through the layers
of clothes, skin, and thick hard muscle to those miniature
ears, lanugo-coated limbs gently swishing and bathing. "Who
knows what's for real," Joseph said as he tipped his hat and
once again reached for my grocery bag piled high with cig-

arette substitutes like licorice whips and Chunky Monkey ice cream, greasy Slim Jim sausage sticks that I hadn't eaten since childhood. "We know nothing of this world, this great universe." He paused, hazel eyes squinting in thought as he waited for me to nod. "Take God, for example," he said and laughed softly, "and which came first, knowledge or man's *need* for knowledge?" I motioned him on with his errand, his own marketing trip. It was our daily struggle trying to help one another on the icy brick sidewalks. We argued over who was more in need, an old man with a bad heart or a pregnant woman who would not believe that everything was really okay until she gave birth to, saw, held, heard a healthy infant.

I dreamed of my grandmother. She was naked and alone in a rubble of upturned graves. I squatted and cradled her in my arms, so happy to find her alive after all these years. Forget the damp orange clay and what seemed like ancient ruins. Forget the pale, shrouded family members wandering aimlessly in search of loved ones. (Was this Judgment Day?) Then I dreamed myself sleeping, my husband on his side, his face a comfort. My own head was inclined toward him. I wore the very gown I wore in reality, and within the dream I woke to a chill, a cool draft that filled the room. I sat, startled, and turned on the lamp by the bed. Stuck to its base was a little yellow Post-it note with the words "I came to see if you believe" written in a small deliberate hand. "Yes, yes, I believe. I believe." I woke myself with this affirmation. I woke to discover that my husband was already up and in the shower and that I wasn't entirely sure to what or to whom I had given this great affirmation of faith. I woke to the tiny buzz saw, vibrating uterus, a pressed bladder, the dim gray light of day.

Early that summer—week twenty-eight, the time designated
for a baby to be "legally viable"—Joseph and I went to see
the swans being brought back to the Public Garden. It was
warm and we walked slowly, taking our time to point out
lovely panes of amethyst glass, the little catty-corner building that looks just like the drawing in *Make Way for Ducklings,* the bar that was used as the model for *Cheers,* crowds
of people waiting in line to get inside and buy T-shirts.

Joseph remembered when there *used* to be swans in the
Public Garden; Gwendolyn was alive then. We sat on a bench
in the shadiest spot we could find, the ground in front of us
littered with soggy bread that the overfed ducks had ignored.
I told him about the Peabody Hotel in Memphis and how as
a child I had gone there to see the ducks marching from
their penthouse to the elevator and down to the lobby pool.
I told how I had looked around that lobby and marveled at
the people staying there, in this fine hotel with its rugs and
chandeliers and fountains. I was with a church group, a
busload of kids stopping here and there to sing for other
congregations. It was supposed to be an honor (not to mention an educational experience) to get to go on the trip, but
I spent the whole time reading Archie comic books and wishing myself home. This was the summer before Martin Luther
King Jr. was shot. It was when Elvis still walked the rooms
of Graceland in the wee hours of the morning. It was when
my sister was practicing to be a junior-high cheerleader and
my grandmother was walking the rows of her garden.

With the arrival of the swans (they had been staying
across the street at the Ritz), Joseph cleared his throat
and began reciting. "Upon the brimming water among the
stones / Are nine-and-fifty swans." He paused and laughed,
adding, "Or what about two swans?" With Yeats's wild swans
he had once again opened his favorite topic, which led eventually, as the crowd began to thin—strollers pushed away,
children led to visit the bronzed ducklings in a row, couples

spreading picnic blankets—to Eliot and one of Joseph's all-time favorites, "Journey of the Magi," which turned to "The Gift of the Magi" and then to his own Christmas story, one I'd heard on several other occasions: Christmas with Gwendolyn. The picture of Gwendolyn I always conjured in my mind was that of a Gibson girl, even though I knew that she wore her straight gray hair cut close, with bangs, and that the waist of her dark wool coat hit high around her short, thick middle. Joseph kept a photograph on top of his dresser—Joseph and Gwendolyn in 1945, standing on a busy sidewalk, each cradling a shopping bag, his face filled out in a way I'd never see.

"It was just the two of us," he began, as he often did, pausing over the unspoken question—one I never asked—about whether or not they had ever wanted a child. His close attention to my own growth, his comments on my coloring and my hair, seemed answer enough. He described their Christmas Eve, the rushing home from work in midafternoon to find the other waiting on the stoop—her with a black wool scarf wrapped around her head and tied beneath her chin, him with a gray fedora he felt certain she was about to replace that very night. He said that when he looked back it seemed as if it always snowed right on cue: Let there be snow. Inside, their windows fogged with cold dampness, the lights they strung glowed as they pulled old boxes from the closets and tied red velvet around kitty-cat necks. They waited until dark and then walked down to the waterfront, the freezing wind forcing them to huddle up like Siamese twins. They listened, ready to stop with the sound of any carolers, any church bells, and they paused and looked up into windows to see the lights and children and greenery. The city was never more beautiful.

They ate in a small dark restaurant at a table by the window. First they ordered bourbons (hers with a lot of water), and then they spent the first hour just talking over the year behind them. Oh, there were those years when the plans went awry, when one or the other was upset about this or that, work or a sick family member. And there was that year when, for reasons he didn't feel it necessary to discuss, they were further apart than they had ever been, complete strangers coming and going for a period of three months. They feared that they would lose each other, that there would be no forgiveness. He said this part quietly, nodded a slight nod, as if to say, You must understand what I'm saying. "That was the worst Christmas," he said quietly. "Really the only bad Christmas." He laughed then and looked at my abdomen, gestured to it as if speaking to the child. "Trust me. We were better people once it was all over. We made it." We watched the swans circling in all their splendor, necks raised proudly as they didn't even acknowledge the various bread and cracker crumbs tossed out onto the water. "In my mind, the Christmas—*the* Christmas—is the way I've described it: our dinner talking over us, our life, and our future."

On all those Christmas Eves it seemed as if they were the only people out. Others had rushed home to family gatherings, but neither of them had relatives close by. They were alone with each other. The best part of it all was that they always got the very best tree left at the Faneuil Hall lot for just three dollars. (It had gotten up to ten by the time Gwendolyn died.) Then they dragged the tree home and decorated it with common little items, things they already had—paper chains cut from glossy magazine pages, tinfoil stars, spools of thread, her jewelry, his neckties, fishing gear, chess pieces tied off in twine. "We had a glorious time," he said. "Brandy and poetry and her crazy ornaments until the sun, that cold winter light, came through the window."

That day, the temperature at least eighty as we left the Public Garden and made our way back down Charles Street, we once again argued over who was in worse shape, a thin old man with a prosthetic heart valve or a pregnant woman so far beyond her normal weight that she thought she'd never wear shoes other than the rubber clogs purchased at Woolworth's. "A hard time we had of it," he said in short gasps as we began our climb up the dark apartment stairs.

I dreamed my husband and I went to a party. We were greeted at the door by the mother of an old friend of mine, a friend from childhood whom I had not seen in years. In real life I knew that the mother had recently died of leukemia, and in the dream I knew this truth. I knew that it was not my friend's mother who greeted us but a three-dimensional image of her. Somewhere in this room there was a silent projector. My husband said how wonderful she was. He said, "No wonder you love to be over at their house all the time." (I had not seen the house in twenty years.) I could not bring myself to tell him the truth, that we could pass our hands straight through her body, that there was absolutely nothing there.

The dream jumped, as dreams often do, and the party was over. We were almost at the car when I remembered that I had left my coat behind. I raced back only to find an empty room (had the other guests been projections as well?), and there on the wall was her image, stilled. They were projecting an image I'd forgotten. It wasn't the way she had looked racing up the gold-carpeted stairs of her house, demanding that we explain the cigarette burn in my friend's brand-new windbreaker, or the one she wore a year later when she handed me my first sanitary napkin and elastic belt, or the one she wore the day the moving van arrived to take them to California. Rather, the expression I saw, frozen there on the wall of the dream, was one more subtle and fleeting: it was the way she looked most of the time.

My friend and I are in the backseat of her Country

Squire. We are taking turns inking the initials of the boys we love (high-school boys we've never met) in cryptic fashion on each other's Blue Horse notebooks. In the way-back, her brother and his friend are bouncing up and down until her mother casts a quick glance in the rearview mirror. "Settle down, boys," she screams, a forced furrow in her brow. They obey, at least while the light is red, and she goes back to her humming. This is the moment—the second glance in the rearview mirror, the look after she yells, when her face re-laxes into a pleasant half smile. On the radio is "We'll Sing in the Sunshine" and she sings along, her voice a little nasal, twangy with confidence. That's what I see on the wall, over and over, that look, and in that look I see Indian summer, the fashionable ponchos my friend and I have shed balled up at our feet, the flat terrain of our hometown passing us by.

I had back labor. We took a taxi across town to the hospital, me stretched and riding as upright as I could manage, my face pressing into the soiled gray ceiling of the cab, traces of smoke lingering in the upholstery. Now the cab was smoke free, or so the driver said when my husband hailed him; at the time I was squatting in front of our building with my face against the concrete steps. Just the day before, Joseph had been in that very spot waiting for the cab that took him to the very same hospital for a brief stay, a series of routine tests. In the hospital, we were still neighbors, though wings and floors apart, and I wanted to get a message to him, but at the moment I felt discombobulated and all tied up. Would I like narcotics? Why, yes, thank you very much. I said that I'd also appreciate a needle in my spine just as soon as they could round up an anesthesiologist. "Epidural, please." The words rolled right off my tongue; I had forgotten everything I knew about breathing.

My friend and I were eleven years old and in love with Tommy James and the Shondells, "Crystal Blue Persuasion" playing on her little hi-fi on the floor, when we heard her mother coming up the stairs.

"Where did you girls get cigarettes?" She flung open the door to my friend's room and stood there, hands on her hips, frosted hair shagged short on top and long at the neck.

"Junior's Texaco," my friend whispered meekly. There was no need to paint the picture, the two of us riding double on her banana-seat bike, me pedaling furiously while she held onto my waist, her legs held stiffly out from the spokes. We were on the service road of the interstate, glittering black asphalt still steaming from a recent rain.

Labor went on forever, a monitor strapped to my belly for contractions, another to the baby's head for its pulse. I was telling jokes and calling my sister long-distance by then. I was watching a contraction rise like an earthquake reading, the needle going wild to register my unfelt pain. I was ready to push when I realized that I'd been talking for hours and that the doctor had never left my side. I suddenly realized that all was not well, my husband was too quiet. I had come this far—no cigarette had come close to my mouth—and yet there was a problem. Things happened suddenly. The baby's heart rate dropped, a heart so small I couldn't even imagine. It was a simple procedure, this C-section, but it had to be done quickly, now, this instant. They knew what to do; they had all the right equipment to slice through the layers of skin and muscle, to suction from my body a fully formed baby.

My friend's mother reached into her bathroom cabinet and handed me a sanitary napkin and a little elastic belt. I had seen them before. I had practiced wearing one at home; I had envied those girls who had already turned the monumental corner. She said that she would understand if I felt I needed to go home, but she really hoped that I'd stay the night as we had planned. I stood barefooted on the cool tile floor of her bathroom, my eyes still red from chlorine, my hair bleached like straw, from an afternoon at the local pool. I watched the toilet paper and the fancy little embroidered guest towels sway with the blast of central air conditioning. She sat on the end of her bed, the first queen-size I ever saw, and talked while I nodded embarrassedly. Here was the moment I had been waiting for, the threshold, and I felt gawky and foolish and uncomfortable. I stayed, and we went to teen night at the community pool, where we played Ping-Pong and sat on the hard wooden benches that lined the chain-link fence. I felt as if I was sitting on a garden hose but maintained my position for fear that the outline would be seen through my shorts. I kept thinking about my friend's mother sitting at the foot of that bed, ankles crossed, a flash of pale pink polish on her toenails. Years later, when I heard a tale about a girl several years older who faked sick to stay home from school and then slept with her boyfriend in her parents' house, this was the bedroom I pictured, even though they had long since moved to California. I saw the bed, the chenille spread pulled up tight, pillows rolled and pressed against the scratched solid headboard. I saw the brown tiles of her bathroom floor, smelled that blast of central air and the lingering chlorine. My friend's sixth-grade school picture was on the dresser in a heavy gold frame. Years later, at the height of first love, Saturday nights in parked cars or on the busted couch of somebody's forsaken game room, the friction of adolescent passion driving me forward, I thought of that same picture—the bed, the coolness, the distant

glance, all insecurities and reservations temporarily brushed
aside.

The day after my daughter was born, I woke to great relief,
which was quickly followed by a fit of anger, a cold seizing
of what might have been or might not have been. Fifty years
ago, and maybe my child and I would have been the slight
numbers on tombstones, the young mothers and children I
had always wondered about. Many times I had gone with
my mother and grandmother to tend my grandfather's
grave; they weeded and planted, brushed the pine needles
from his marble foot marker. My grandmother guided a
whirring push mower up and down the hill of his plot. I
never knew him, her husband, my mother's father, my grandfather, but I imagined him stretched there beneath the dirt;
I saw a young man in a World War I uniform, even though
I knew he lived to be a very different man, a much older,
frail man with wiry gray hair. There was a tiny stone lamb
on a nearby grave and a date that equaled nothing: the baby
was born and died on the same day; the mother died just
one day later. The more I looked over the mossy slabs, the
more I found. "Oh, honey," my grandmother said and squeezed
my hand. "It *is* sad." So many of them died for such simple
reasons, and that was what I kept thinking that first morning, a healthy infant asleep in her hospital bassinet. I asked
that the stitches in my abdomen be eternally blessed; I
praised modern medicine, saluted and sang. I called everyone I knew or had heard about who had squatted out in the
woods like an animal, gnawing tree bark and umbilical cord,
stoically delivering in absolute isolation. "You idiot. You god-
damned selfish idiot," I raged, and hung up before they knew
who I was. In some places I am thought to have an accent.

Hurricane Andrew took the hotel in the Virgin Islands and all of the nearby time-shares, but I find myself thinking of the place as if it still exists. I do the same with Joseph Sever. We moved a year after my daughter was born, and when we left, an August day much like the one of our arrival, he was out on the stoop wearing his panama straw and reading the *Boston Globe*.

Right before the move, we had done all those things that visitors do: the bus tour, the battleship, the Old North Church. I spent a whole afternoon at the top of the Prudential building, my daughter tucked away in the little sack I wore strapped to my chest, and fed quarter after quarter into the viewfinders. In a random glance toward Beacon Hill, I spotted the steeple of the church on our street, and from there it was easy to swing back and find our building, to travel up the red brick to the roofline. I found our bay window, the plant on the sill; I half expected to see myself enter the room, my abdomen round and hard and waiting. I had that same odd feeling I get from time to time. The feeling that maybe I can pick up the phone and call my childhood friend or my grandmother at that number long disconnected but eternally memorized; that I can find a clean path into my childhood where I could race my bike down the street and into the yard, the wheels spinning and clicking, a triangle cut from an aluminum pie pan clothespinned to a spoke; that I can run inside and find my parents thirty years younger, younger than I am now, as they talk over some event that will soon be lost to that hour. I moved the lens just one-hundredth of an inch and there was Joseph's living room, the outline of what might have been a cat.

We exchanged greetings over the next couple of years— Christmas cards, postcards. The last card to arrive was addressed to my daughter, an Easter card, one of those you open and confetti comes out. I hate those drop-what-you're-doing-and-go-get-the-Dustbuster cards, and yet there I was, my daughter delighted by the sparkling shapes while I imagined Joseph there on Charles Street in one of the fancy stores thumbing through racks in search of the right card. From past reports I knew it was a short matter of time, that very soon a card I sent would be unanswered or returned unopened. Actually the news that he had died came from another neighbor in the building, and even then, seeing it in writing, it didn't seem quite real. I couldn't imagine the orphaned cats being given away or the years' worth of warped musty books pulled from the cramped shelves, the dilapidated bedside lamp left on the curb in a heap of garbage bags along with all the makings for a thrown-together Christmas. Instead I see him out on the stoop, or down at the corner grocery picking his fruit from a table out front, his breath visible and keeping time with the click of his heart.

My friend and I went to the cemetery to smoke cigarettes. She pedaled the bike that time, her legs not as strong as mine, so we wobbled and nearly fell on the small dirt paths. It was a new cemetery, the kind where there were no raised stones, only a flat slate of marble at the foot of each grave. The flowers, whether artificial or real, looked as if they had sprung up from the graves. People in our town liked the new look: the sleek even lines of the plots, the serene white statue of Jesus in the center. But as I inhaled and exhaled, narrowed my eyes the way I'd seen smokers do, I told my friend that I preferred where my grandfather was buried. I liked those huge trees, trees perfect for tire swings or clubhouses had they not been in a cemetery. I liked the damp mossy undergrowth and the dates from before I was born. Here the people started dying in the sixties, and it all seemed too recent. I told my friend how my dad could palm a Camel

nonfilter and hide it in his pants, how he had once done that
in high school when the principal walked by. I had heard
the story many times, and I had seen enough old photos to
picture him there, his hair combed back high off his
forehead—a pompadour—as he leaned, tall and thin, against
the brick wall of the gymnasium. I turned my cigarette
inward, heat near my hand, to demonstrate. My friend did
the same, the fabric of her jacket singeing when she tried to
slip her hand into her pocket. We smoked and smoked, until
our heads felt light, and then we each chewed three pieces
of Teaberry gum and rubbed our hands in the yellow clay
of a grave recently dug. Everywhere else there was perfect
green grass, rolled out like a carpet, flowers sprouting up
from the dead.

I think of that place every autumn when I kneel to plant
bulbs, when I sprinkle a teaspoon of bonemeal into each hole,
as my grandmother advised. And at Christmas I picture
Joseph's scene, the walk to buy the tree, the brandy and
makeshift adornments. I give Gwendolyn Gibson-girl hair
and a rhinestone cigarette holder. I give her the face of my
friend's mother, what she looked like thirty years past when
I knew her. "How old will you be when I'm one hundred?"
my daughter asks, enunciating in a way I will never master,
and I say, "One hundred and thirty-six." I catch myself
looking at her in absolute amazement that she is here and
the time is now. A faster sperm and she wouldn't be here;
there would be another child or no child at all. No day
beyond that moment would be exactly as I know it now. It
might not be a bad life, just a different one. What we don't
know is enormous. "I want you to live forever," she tells me.
"I want a guinea pig and a Fantastic Flower kit. I want long
wavy hair and I want to be like Jesus and have people pray

to the god of me forever." I tell her that I would like nothing better, that it's every young mother's dream.

Sometimes I think of the woman cheered by the long-awaited phone call that she is pregnant. The nurse on the other end is relieved. Everyone is overjoyed. The woman goes upstairs to take a nap and never wakes, an ectopic hemorrhage. Would the fanatics in the street argue that the life within, this bundle of cells unintelligible to the human eye, killed *her*—these people who rummage the back-alley dumpsters of emergency rooms to find some hideous example of sin in a jar, these people who take someone else's worldly loss and turn it into a freak show? I can barely keep my car on the road when I see them gathered in protest, their hideous pictures waving in the air. "Why don't you *get* a life?" I want to yell. "Go after handguns. Go after R. J. Reynolds."

I dreamed of my grandmother. I lifted her as she had once lifted me, my feet potty black from her garden, through the damp dirt-floored shed where she had stored her jars of tomatoes and peaches, floating jewels pickled and preserved. In the dream I watched people wandering, stones over-turned, granite lambs tilted on the heaving mounds of cracked earth. Was this Judgment Day? "I don't know what all the fuss is about," she said, and I was there holding her, pulling her closer, corn and tobacco fields beyond the up-turned graves, holding her and whispering the song she had made up years before, a lullaby sung to the tune of an unknown hymn: "You're my baby. You're my baby. You're my baby. Yes, you are."

When I was fifteen, I spent many afternoons cruising the streets of my hometown with a friend who drove a baby-blue Mustang. It was a car to be envied, and we were like queens, the radio blasting the Top 40, our suntanned arms hanging out the window to flick our cigarettes. I was a bona fide smoker then, a pack of Salems in the zippered part of my vinyl purse, fifty cents in my pocket in case I ran out. Sometimes we drove way out past the city limits, out where we were surrounded by flat fields and small wood-framed houses, churchyards overgrown, the rush of the brisk country air drowning out the music of the radio. Those rides gave me a rush, tingling scalp and racing heart; I felt powerful, as though I could look out over those fields to the end of the world.

Now I find my daughter all dressed up in front of a mirror. She is almost five and is wearing a faux leopard poncho and a little pillbox hat with netting over her face. Her high heels are silver sequined and wobbling to one side. She has a pencil held between two fingers and, with her other hand on her hip, takes a deep drag from the imaginary cigarette. She tilts her head back, purses her lips, and blows at her image, eyes closed, while she says, "I must be running now, my dear." She turns quickly and stops when she sees me there, her shoes leaving marks as if she had suddenly put on brakes. "Oh, hello," she says in that same affected way. "I'm pretending it's long, long ago. Back when cigarettes were good for you." With that, she takes another puff and blows her smoke my way, and I lean close to breathe it all in. I breathe in as much as I can take for now.

SLEEP

•

Gary Krist

DONALD'S EYES WERE CLOSING just as
the London markets opened.

Paul Brockman, standing over his infant son's crib in
Piedmont, New York—three thousand miles from the opening bell in London—glanced at his watch. It was 3:32 A.M.,
and Donald, thank God, was finally showing the signs of
imminent sleep: the licking of thick lips, the enormous, oddly
petulant sigh, the lolling of veiny head from side to side.
He'd be gone in thirty seconds, Paul guessed. A minute tops.
Paul leaned over in the faint blue radiance of the Popeye
night-light and put his hand on his son's hot, damp hair.
Sleep well, he said silently, enviously.

That was when the telephone rang in the living room.

"Christ," Paul hissed aloud. He looked down anxiously at
his son's face, but Donald was already sleeping ferociously—
mouth gaping, forehead wrinkled with determination, at the

stage when nothing short of artillery or the sound of his mother's voice could rouse him.

Paul made a last adjustment of the blanket and then stepped out to the living room to answer the phone. He knew that the call had to be London. The Tokyo market had already closed, and everyone in the New York office was still asleep—as Paul himself should have been, with Harriet, his wife, snoring away in the luxurious depths of their chestnut sleigh bed down the hall. Last night had been Harriet's turn to sit up with Donald. The two of them alternated odd and even dates; it was an agreement they had worked out together, a system. The only flaw in the system, Paul thought, was that Harriet, on leave from her job at Price Waterhouse, couldn't sit up with Tokyo and London on the nights when Paul was supposed to be sleeping.

"Disasterville, Paul. We've got trouble." It was Derek Peabody, the deputy rep of Paul's firm in London. Paul had never met Derek Peabody, but he knew his voice well enough. It was high-pitched, overly jocular, and—at least at 3:35 A.M.—deeply annoying.

"Okay, give it to me," Paul said, collapsing into the couch and pressing his hot eyelids.

"Renzer is down three and an eighth at the opening and sinking fast. So's the rest of the market, but not as badly."

"So our deal . . ."

"Obsolete would be my guess. Hey, I just work here."

"Does Tokyo know yet?" Paul asked.

"I leave it in your capable hands, guy. I've got phones beeping off the hook here. Bye now."

Paul hung up the phone. He stood a moment, watching the tendons move beneath the smooth skin of his telephone hand. A three-plus-point drop was bad, he knew—so bad that everyone involved would have to know as soon as possible. That was Paul's responsibility. He was the coordinator on this deal, the "harmonizer," as his boss, Pete, liked to say.

In his more cynical moments, Paul would define "harmonizer" as the person who wasn't allowed to sing but who took the rap for any sour notes. And it had certainly been easier to harmonize deals in the days before 2 A.M. feedings and the various other gurps and gurgles that would rouse him from bed every other night.

Paul stopped himself. He thought of that helpless, all-powerful presence in the crib down the hall. "Priorities," he told himself firmly.

The first number he punched into the phone was Ben Farley's in Tokyo. As it rang, Paul looked again at his watch: late afternoon, early evening in Tokyo. Ben was probably in transit. "Hello, Kimiko," he said when Ben's wife picked up the phone. "It's Paul from the New York office. How are you?"

"Very good, Paul, thank you." He had never met Kimiko Farley, just as he had never met Derek Peabody, or Roger Billings's daughter in Hong Kong. They were all just voices to him, currents on a telephone wire with personalities attached.

"Well, we're not so good on this side, businesswise. Ben around?"

"Sorry, Paul. Not home from work yet."

"I figured as much."

"His cell phone is still out. But I have him call you the second he comes in."

"Ask him to keep trying if it's busy. It probably will be."

Pete Demiehl in New York, the next person on Paul's list, was somewhat less gracious. "This better be a calamity, at four in the morning, Brockman," he said, only half kidding. Paul explained to him quietly that it *was* a calamity. Renzer was their biggest pending deal. "Set up an early meeting," Pete growled, his voice still heavy with sleep. "E-mail the details so everybody's up to speed by then."

"How early is early?"

Pete paused a moment before saying, "Eight should do it."

Paul checked his watch again: 3:47 A.M.

"You'll have to contact the others—Clay, Boulding," Pete went on. "And let Billings in Hong Kong know. He may still be at the office. And I guess you spoke to Ben."

"He's on his way home. I've left him a message."

"Good. See you at eight. Now, damn it, let me get some sleep."

Paul heard the line click dead. "Kill the messenger, why don't you," he muttered to himself. Sighing, he pressed the disconnect button for a dial tone.

First Clay, then Boulding, then Billings. It was a familiar litany by now. Just like that other litany—London, Frankfurt, Hong Kong, Tokyo, Chicago, Toronto, New York. The financial markets, an empire on which the sun never set. Paul yawned. He shifted his weight on the couch and began pressing the memorized numbers on the telephone's keypad.

One night, standing alone in the philosophical orange glow of the light above his kitchen sink, Paul had amused himself by trying to imagine the twistings and turnings of the great communications network he stood at the center of, waiting like an attentive spider for a tremor from some far corner of its global web. He imagined the thin copper wire—or fiber optic or whatever the hell they were using nowadays—leading from the end of his kitchen extension, spilling over the counter to the wall jack, where it connected up with a line that ran to the front of the house, to the outside wire slung over the front lawn, to the other wires that coursed along Grand Avenue, branching off east, west, north, south, feeding into the main lines, the switching stations, the transoceanic cables gnawed (if the *New York Times* was to be believed) by sharks. And then, at the other side of the ocean—in Brighton, Yokohama, Kowloon—the wire would emerge from the waves and reverse the process, telescoping down to main line, street line, house line, to the blunt, hairy hand of Derek Peabody, the graceful fingers of Kimiko Farley, the sweaty palm of Roger Billings or his daughter. It was an enormous electronic octopus, a world-wide nervous system (the metaphors kept coming to him), and he was at the heart of it all, information central, the control tower, ground zero. The thought had given him—as he stood there in the sweet specificity of his maroon-and-beige kitchen in the Hudson valley—a heady, ambiguous feeling, like the combination of confidence and insecurity one feels when climbing half drunk into the driver's seat of a car.

But now, as he made the required calls to Clay, Boulding, Billings—and then dropped the necessary E-mails and voice mails methodically into the boxes of everyone in the New York office—the only thing Paul felt was fatigue. It was already past four, and dawn was approaching invisibly from the east. Exhausted, he shuffled into the bedroom and quietly slipped under the covers next to Harriet. It felt good to be off his feet, off the telephone. The bed smelled wholesome and familiar, like warm grain. Harriet, rising a level or two from the depths of sleep, inhaled sharply and then rolled over toward him. Her hair seemed to be radiating heat. Paul angled his arm around her waist and closed his eyes. A fluid darkness seemed to swim beneath his eyelids. He told himself that he had two and a half hours ahead of him. Two and a half hours of oblivion.

He was almost asleep when he heard the little muffled cry from Donald's room next door.

"At least," Harriet said, changing Donald's diaper, "it's not as if your job is at stake." It was the next evening, after the meeting about the Renzer deal. Paul sat at the kitchen table watching his wife wrap the white Pamper around Donald's dimpled thigh, wondering idly if this—changing a diaper on the same surface that dinner had just been served on— was something that childless couples would find distressing. Donald, meanwhile, was staring up into the lights of the imitation-crystal chandelier, mesmerized. "Is it?"

Paul looked up suddenly. "What?"

"This deal," Harriet repeated, raising her thin, expressive eyebrows. "It's not as if your job is at stake, right?"

"Oh," Paul said. Then: "No, no, of course not." Paul had not slept in two days. After the 4 A.M. feeding that morning, Donald, ailing from what their insufferable pediatrician called "a frolic with colic," had been unable to get back to sleep. Paul had spent the rest of the night giving his son an in-depth tour of the living room, hoping to make him so bored that he'd drift off. But Donald had apparently found the living room interesting enough. So, when Harriet woke up at 6:30, Paul had simply handed the baby to her, show-ered, dressed, and driven over the bridge and down the highway to his office. By the time he arrived, Renzer had already fallen five and a quarter points in London. Pete Demiehl was furious. At the meeting, he shouted and sneered and seemed to hold Paul personally responsible for London's plummeting market. It was finally decided, after much dis-cussion, that the deal with Renzer should be put on hold until the economic climate had stabilized.

"You would let me know, wouldn't you?" Harriet asked now. "It's just that I'd need a new outfit for bankruptcy court."

Paul smiled. "The markets are just a little shaky at this point," he said. "It'll be fine."

When the phone rang, Paul jumped up so fast that his head grazed the hanging crystals of the chandelier, causing Donald to gasp in approval. "Must be Tokyo," Paul said, but when he picked up the phone it was Ridgewood, New

Jersey—Harriet's father. "So everybody's telling me it's time to bail out of the market," he began, without bothering to say hello.

"Hi, Pop," Paul said. He should have been expecting this, a communication from that other network of financial information in his life—Harriet's family. Harriet had an uncle who was a retired bond trader, two brothers in merchant banking, and a father who had his grandchildren's trust money (hard-earned during a blessed forty-three-year career as a housing contractor) invested in growth-oriented mutual funds. Every big rise and fall in the Dow Jones industrial average typically brought a flurry of phone calls from in-laws considering changes in their investment strategies. Somehow, despite the credentials of his wife's siblings, Paul was considered the family expert. Harriet said it was because he was so solid and upright, unlike her brothers, who reportedly played with money the way they used to play with stray cats—carelessly, ruthlessly, without regard for the sanctity of life.

"I keep thinking October '87," Pop went on. "So what do you think?"

"Hard to say. This is probably just a technical correction. The market has been due for a breather."

Harriet glanced over at Paul and made a face. She recognized his comment as an exact quote from the analyst they had just seen on the *Nightly Business Report*.

"Well, I'm nervous," Pop said then. "Don't you hotshots have software or something to let you know for sure? Special Internet tip-offs or whatever?"

"Yeah, Pop. There's this little farm up in Connecticut, and when the hens stop laying eggs, we know it's time to sell. But here's your no-good unemployed daughter, who's been waiting to talk to you all day." Paul quickly handed the phone to Harriet, who handed the baby to him. Donald looked up into his father's face with the same calm, all-accepting attention he had earlier given the chandelier. "Hi, Pop," Harriet said into the phone as Donald moved his lips.

Wearily, warily, Paul carried his son into the living room. He turned on the cable news and started pacing around the room. No, he assured himself, this couldn't affect his job. Paul took a deep, slow breath. He was feeling strange—bone-tired but restless. Too much caffeine, he guessed. His mind was speeding. He tried to concentrate on the television, where an unfamiliar anchorwoman was reporting about mounting tensions in some godforsaken place or other. A fat man came on after her and reported that a low-pressure system was approaching from the northwest. "And let's have another look at that wild day on Wall Street."

Paul sank into the armchair in front of the TV. Then he got up again. A low-pressure system. The Dow. He was a hopelessly entwined person, he told himself. He lived surrounded by complex, interrelated systems, magnifying every little disturbance, collecting the emitted impulses of an entire globe and focusing them on that little space halfway between his eyebrows and scalp line, where they pulsed and ached and wouldn't go away. Of course, it was that same sense of interconnection that had attracted him to finance in the first place—the continuousness of those systems, which made the market sensitive to everything from a corporate rumor to a tiny dip in interest rates. Plugging into that network was like playing a game with enormously convoluted rules that changed almost as quickly as they could be learned. He had loved playing that game. He still did love it, in fact. Only now he wished there was an off button somewhere. Now that he had a wife and child. Now that Renzer had fallen five and a quarter points in London.

All it would take, he told himself, would be a big drop in Hong Kong—call options would plummet, margin calls would be triggered, portfolios would collapse. A chain reaction, like the one that would follow the deceptive cloud on the radar screen, the button pressed, the silo in North Dakota opening, the needle-nosed missile maneuvering into position . . .

Oh, sure, sure, sure. Stop it, Paul told himself. He was tired. He wanted to rest. He wanted to look up into the spinning lights of a cheap chandelier and just be amused.

Paul found himself in the kitchen again just as Harriet was hanging up the phone. "Where's Donald?" she asked him.

Paul looked down. He wasn't carrying the baby anymore. He must have put him down somewhere. "Playpen," Paul guessed.

Harriet frowned. "When I go back to work," she said, sweeping past him, "we're going to redistribute the duties in this house."

Paul followed her into the flickering light of the living room. "I was up with him all last night, remember," he said.

Harriet lifted Donald from the couch and hooked his chin over her shoulder. "And I'm afraid you'll be up with him again tonight," she said, beginning to pat his back. Paul only then noticed the wet gleam around her eyes. "My father didn't want to say anything to you before talking to me. He wants my brothers and me to go over there tonight. My great-aunt May is dying."

Paul got some sleep that night. Ben Farley called once, at 7:15 P.M., to tell him that Tokyo had stabilized nicely at the opening; Derek Peabody in London didn't call at all. Donald, meanwhile, woke only twice, at 12:45 and 4:10, and each time went right back to sleep after a warm bottle and a short, bouncy walk around the house. Paul slept—in the empty bed, alas—from 10:25 to 12:45, from 1:05 to 4:10, and from 4:30 until the alarm went off at 6:00.

He and Donald were already sitting in the kitchen, eating

bananas for breakfast, when Harriet called to tell them that
Aunt May had died. Paul winced, but of course they had all
expected this news for some time; Aunt May's health had
been deteriorating for months. But Paul could sense the
upset in Harriet's voice. When she showed up about a half
hour later, she looked foggy-eyed and pale, her dirtyish black
hair pulled back in a sloppy braid. "May went quietly," she
said, handing Paul the car keys. He was already late for
work.

"Donald fell asleep playing in the laundry basket, so I
left him there. And I've asked Judith to come over to watch
him later so you can crash."

Harriet nodded and then tipped forward into his arms,
pressing her cheek against his tie.

"She was old," Paul whispered to the top of her head.

"Oh, I know that," she answered. "I know it, I know it,
I know it. It was just sitting there, though, in her bedroom,
waiting. She was wearing all of her jewelry, everything—
bracelets, rings, this old cameo my great-grandmother had
given her. I didn't feel sad, exactly. I don't know. I felt alone.
I missed my husband anbaby."

Paul rubbed the back of her shoulders. "Get some sleep,"
he told her gently, his eye on the clock behind her.

Harriet's father had a heart attack at Aunt May's funeral.
Paul and Harriet found out about it after the ceremony.
Harriet's cousin Ruby told them, just as they were heading
out toward the parking lot. During the eulogy, apparently,
Pop had pulled Ruby's mother aside and told her that he
was having chest pains. They were sitting in the back, where
Pop always sat in any gathering, waiting to be of use: to
turn up a thermostat or help the funeral director get the
limos into place. He didn't want to disturb the ceremony, so

the two of them had departed quietly for the hospital, leaving word with Ruby. Pop, it seemed, had forgotten his nitroglycerine tablets at home.

He had already been admitted by the time the family reached Englewood Hospital. The little blond martinet at the desk would allow only two visitors at a time, so Harriet's brothers offered to stay behind and let Harriet and Paul go up first. She agreed without another word, and the two of them pushed through the swinging glass doors into the ICU.

They found Pop lying in an elevated white bed, at the center of an intimidating tangle of hoses, wires, and tubes. He had an IV stuck into his hairy left arm, an oxygen tube taped under his nose, and various wires and electrodes running from his chest to three beeping and humming monitors that stood officiously around the room. Ruby's mother sat in a vinyl armchair next to the bed, holding Pop's hand. Both of them were grinning.

"You got nothing to worry about," Pop said to Harriet as they stepped into the room. "It was all over by the time we pulled into the emergency room." He took Harriet's head in one of his enormous hands and kissed her on the temple. "Now they got me all pumped up with nitro and I'm just fine, really. They're not even sure it was a real attack, per se. Bad angina, maybe. They just want to monitor me for a few days."

Harriet took his hand. "Damn you, Pop," she said. "This time I'm going to sew a packet of those damned pills into every shirt you own."

Pop chuckled, making the line on one of the monitor screens jump alarmingly. "Whatever you say, kid. Just don't worry."

Ruby's mother was watching him dreamily from her chair. "He was very brave," she said.

Harriet smiled uncertainly. "Anyway," she went on, "now

that we know you're safe, we should tell Ron and Bill. They're downstairs waiting to hear."

"I'll go down," Paul offered, stepping up to the bed. "Glad you're okay, Pop."

"You!" Pop said, just now noticing Paul. "You, on the other hand, got something to worry about. Have you heard a news report lately? The market's crashing. I heard it on the car radio on the way in." He pulled his hand out of Harriet's and waved a gesture of disgust in Paul's direction. "The market's crashing, and taking my grandkids' trust funds with it!"

Ruby's mother clucked her tongue. Paul closed his eyes.

"This is not something a man in the process of a heart attack needs to hear," Pop said then, to his daughter.

Paul got home from the office at ten that night, while the Tokyo market was in midsession. Yes, the New York markets had been crashing as Pop spoke—the Dow down 424, the NASDAQ even worse—but stocks had recovered quickly from the breathtaking plunge. By the close, the Dow was down only 73 and change, while Tokyo had actually opened slightly higher. But Paul was still in a state of semishock. He had been swamped all day. Communications were down for minutes at a stretch. Pete Demiehl, looking ill, had called a meeting at 4:30 to try to pick up the pieces. The meeting had lasted until almost nine.

Harriet was in her flannel nightgown when Paul walked in. "Here," she said, handing Paul a big, comfortable mug of cocoa. "It'll relax us. We both need it."

Paul took off his tie and jacket and threw them unceremoniously behind the couch. "How's your father?"

"Depends on who you ask," Harriet said. She was standing in the kitchen doorway, leaning against the jamb in an

unnatural way. "Pop says he's fine. Dr. Bernaducci is carefully noncommittal. He says Pop will be in intensive care
for at least four days."

Paul nodded. "And Donald?"

"Sleeping like a baby."

Paul took a sip of his cocoa. He could feel the hot liquid
spreading through his body. "Listen, I know it's your turn
with him tonight," Paul said. "But I'll be up all night with
this market thing anyway. There's no way I'll get any sleep."

Harriet came over behind the couch and started kneading
the muscles in his neck. He put his head back against the
warmth of her belly and closed his eyes. Little blue dots were
flashing under his eyelids. He felt he could hear the fax
machine in the laundry room bleating already.

"Scary," Harriet said, quietly, over his head. "You feel
so vulnerable." Paul heard her breathe, and then, after a
moment, she said, "I appreciate the offer. I'm worn out." She
leaned over and pressed her lips against Paul's scalp. "The
hospital says they'll call if there's any problem," she said,
heading toward the bedroom. Then she stopped and turned
around. "If you do get a chance to sleep at all, I'll be keeping
it warm in there."

Paul watched her through the rising steam of his cocoa.
"Do that. I'll disconnect the living room extension so you
and Don won't be disturbed."

She nodded and shut the bedroom door gently behind
her.

Paul was dozing, hours later, when the first call came.
In his dream (searching for a path through rush-hour traffic,
trying desperately to deliver something to a place he couldn't
remember), he had identified the sound as the telephone.
But as he came awake, he recognized it as Donald's telltale
hungry squeal. Paul got up slowly from the couch. His watch
read 4:13. He was amazed, and then worried, that he hadn't

received any calls yet. Could there be something wrong with
the telephone? He would check the fax and his E-mail after
the bottle, check if anyone anywhere had left him a message.

He padded into Donald's room and lifted his son from
the crib. Donald's cheeks sagged comically in the dim blue
light. His oversized head seemed to sink down into the white
softness of his shoulders. "Suppertime," Paul whispered to
him. He put the baby over his shoulder and carried him out
to the kitchen.

London called while he was warming up Donald's bottle.
"It's looking bad," said Derek Peabody's voice. "Magnifi-
cently bad." Paul groaned while Derek told him exactly what
he had been fearing and expecting—that the London and
Frankfurt markets were crashing, that they were sinking
even further and faster than in 1987.

"Oh God," Paul said, staring out the kitchen window at
a haloed streetlight. Everything seemed perfectly normal
out there. This was the way it happened now, Paul told
himself. Disaster struck abstractly, announced by voices on
a telephone, numbers on a screen—never seeming quite real.
"Sounds pretty grim."

"Hey," Derek replied, "it's only the end of Western civilization as we know it. Anyway, my father always wanted
me to join the family dry-cleaning business. 'Derek,' he'd say,
'whatever happens, the ladies of the world will always need
clean blouses.'"

"Listen," Paul interrupted, "call me back when you hear
something more. Whatever time, doesn't matter."

"You bet. Hang in there."

Paul hung up the phone. "Crashing," he said aloud to
himself. It was such a strange word, he thought. So ambiguous. Crashing was what you did at a friend's house when
your car wouldn't start. Crashing was what you did on the
highway when your car did start. Paul thought suddenly of
his dream about traffic, of rubber burning, and then realized

that something smelled, something was burning. He ran over to the stove. The water he was using to warm the bottle had boiled away and now the plastic was melting in the pot. "Shit!" Paul flipped off the stove, grabbed the pot with one hand, and threw it into the sink. It hissed vigorously as he filled it with cold water from the tap. When the pot was full, he turned off the water. Little bits of charred plastic floated up in a roiling mixture of formula and water. Paul and Donald looked down at the mess in silence.

"So much for supper," Paul said into his son's ear. Then he swept Donald's tiny body over his head and held him toward the ceiling. His arms felt weak and unsteady. "London market's falling down, falling down, falling down." Donald slobbered delightedly as his father sang to him. "London market's falling down . . ."

The telephone rang. Paul stood there, staring at his son high above his head, as it rang five times, then eight, then ten. The phone finally stopped ringing. He lowered Donald to his shoulder. "My fair baby."

The telephone started ringing again. This was something important, Paul told himself as he walked over to the instrument. It was Hong Kong this time, or Frankfurt or Paris. Or maybe it was the Englewood Hospital, telling him that Pop was dead. Or his own sister, telling him of a brain tumor, a fire at his parents' house, a plane wreck. Paul could almost picture the next wave of calamity—the biggest and last, perhaps—building somewhere out in the distance, just out of sight. It was a matter of minutes until it hit. Or even seconds.

The telephone was still ringing. Paul knelt next to it. Calmly, deliberately, he pulled the telephone wire out of the modular jack in the wall.

He stood up again, the baby still clinging to his shoulder. He took a slow, agonizing breath. "No," he said aloud.

Then, imagining the storm of electronic impulses flashing

around the thick shell of his house, he carried Donald into the master bedroom. He stood at the foot of his bed and took off his suit pants with one hand. Kicking them aside, he climbed into the gorgeous warmth of the bed. And there, with his son and his wife in his arms, he lay, patiently waiting for sleep.

A BATHROBE,

A STEAK

•

Jay Gummerman

W HEN CORRINNE GOT BACK to the dug-
out, Jeff told her she didn't have to swing at every pitch. If
she'd only be a little more selective, she'd be on first base
right now. The October sun was behind them, casting a flame-
colored light on the field and the players and the church
across the street, and she felt grateful for once that the city
was too cheap to put up lights in this park. She had told
him in the morning, when he was waxing his car, that she
was pregnant, that she'd stopped taking the pill two months
ago, that the rabbit had died a slow and intolerable death.
But she was lying, like the time she said she'd put LSD in
his sangria and didn't back down until he had dialed the
paramedics. She wasn't going to have a child.

He sat on the little wooden bench in the corner of the
dugout away from the rest of the team, sipping a beer behind
his glove and looking out on the field. She had begun to

notice that whenever he gave her advice during softball, he would look out on the field as if someone there were giving him signals on what to say next. She sat down by him, though not very close, and began rummaging in her purse for some gum. When she found the empty pack, she remembered that she'd given him the last stick on the way over. He had spit it out quickly, his mouth puckered like a little baby's, saying he couldn't stand the taste of saccharin.

She looked at him now in his silly uniform, then at the field, then back at him again. She decided she liked the way his nose was after all. It was tacky what she was doing to him, she knew that, but sometimes it seemed that tacks were all there were to their lives, these little tacks that irritated you but never punctured your skin. This was the sort of behavior he expected from women anyway, she thought, and it was a trip sometimes just to go along with it, the same way it was a trip to do this whole bygone softball thing.

"Got any more beers?" she said loudly, with her voice directed toward the field. Your team forfeited the game if the umpire caught anyone drinking in the dugout.

"About so high," he said, gesturing with his naked arm. "That's your wheelhouse. For chrissakes, you can't hit a ball that's over your head."

For chrissakes, she thought. She had struck out her last three times up. She didn't like the high, arcing pitches with all that spin that they threw in this league. She had only gotten on base once in five games, and even that was because the gangly blond playing second that day had bobbled the ball. Ron, the first-base coach, had also given her advice then: "You can't leave the bag until the ball crosses the plate." He had said it over and over again, but she left too soon anyway and the umpire called her out, telling her that rules were rules. She thought if she could just get to second base she'd be away from all these assholes.

"For chrissakes," she said aloud this time, though not so

he could hear. She didn't know why she had let him talk her into playing this game. Supposedly this league was only for married couples, but he had lied on the application. It was a boring game, she thought, and the players were boring, and the places they played this boring game were boring.

He picked at something on his fingernail, using the edge of his thumb. "Why don't you sit over here?" he said in a kinder voice.

She waited for him to say it again. When he didn't, she began scraping the clay out of her cleats with a little stick that he brought to the games for just such a purpose; he had showed her how to use the stick last week after she had tracked mud on the carpet in his MG.

"Please don't make fun of me," he said. "I'm not in a very good mood right now."

"Who is?" she said.

He turned his head in her direction but without moving the rest of his long, angular body, like a heron regarding a distant splash. "Why don't you sit over here?" he said again and smiled.

"Why don't *you* sit over *here?*" she said, and he looked sorry. But she didn't want him to apologize—she knew she could make him do that. And she didn't want to make him cry either. Men his age weren't capable of crying anyway. "Tell me what you told me in the car this morning," she said.

"What did I tell you?"

"You remember," she said. "You just choose not to remember."

"It was that traumatic?"

"Say it."

"You mean the thing in the car?"

"It's getting dark," she said.

"Is that like getting warm?"

"Oh, please."

He took a large swallow of beer and wiped his mustache

with his glove. Down the bench, a man who looked like an aspiring Hell's Angel was laughing loudly with a tiny woman who had "Cheesecake" written across her flamingo pink tank top. She didn't think the woman was the man's wife, but she couldn't exactly remember.

"I don't know what to make of you," he said.

"That's not how you said it this morning."

"How did I say it then?"

"You were looking in the rearview, or you were trying to look in the rearview, but I had it turned so I could take off my makeup."

"Why would you want to do something like that?"

"Like what?"

"Take off your makeup."

"Just say it right."

"I can't."

"Why not?"

"I meant it when I said it the first time."

"And?"

"And I don't mean it now."

"You mean you know what to make of me?"

"No, I didn't mean that," he said.

She liked this answer, but she made a conscious effort not to smile. "I took the paint off my fingernails," she said. "And you thought you had problems with no mascara." She laughed half a laugh. "I took it off while I was playing right field. While I was supposed to be standing there, knees slightly bent, glove held out from my chest, like you told me." She held out her nails for him to see, but it was too dark and he was too far away.

"Why would anyone want to do that?"

"I want to be plain," she said. "Wasn't your first wife plain?"

"She's not my wife anymore."

"Boffo."

"Boffo?"

"Like hooray, only European."

"I thought you wanted to be plain."

At the plate now, the future Hell's Angel had just hit a pop fly. He stood there watching the ball as though it were a living thing. "Run, you bastard," she wanted to scream.

"You write a check every month, don't you?" she said.

"I'm up next," he said.

"And in the little space where it says memo, you write 'Child support,' don't you?"

He leaned over and set his beer under the bench. The aluminum scraped the concrete and made a noise that was satisfying to her in an odd way, like the smell of gasoline.

"Don't you?" she said.

"The check goes to wife number two."

"Details," she said, and they both looked out on the field as if it was the ocean, as if it ended a great distance beyond their horizon. She had lost track of the score, and she hoped that he had too, and she hoped that he had lost track of everything else, everything except what she wanted him to keep track of.

The bases were empty and there were two outs and Bob of Bob's Tropical Fish, their team's sponsor, was the batter. He hit a slow grounder to the pitcher, who examined the ball before underhanding it to first for the third out. The umpire held up his hand as though asking permission to speak and told the catcher he was calling the game on account of darkness. The players all shook hands by the mound and trailed off to their respective vehicles, a few of them saying good-bye.

"We could have played another inning," he said, after Ron had given him the drinking sign and walked away with his chunky wife.

She tried to laugh wickedly, but she wound up coughing instead. "Why do they call it softball anyway?" she asked. "The ball seems pretty hard to me. It should be soft. Like a baby."

"You couldn't hit it very far then." He looked at her and smiled, but she was glaring at him. "You just won't drop this, will you?" he said and moved next to her on the bench. He put his arm around her, but she made herself stiff and he released her.

"Ron's wife is plain too," she said. "Do you think she calls me a slut behind my back?" She grabbed him by the sleeve of his jersey. "Well, she can't anymore." She brought his sleeve to her mouth and wiped off her lipstick in one swift motion. "The rain in Spain falls mainly on the plain," she said.

He looked at her blankly as she stood up with her purse.

"You can tell everyone at the bar that you soiled yourself sliding."

"Where are you going?" he asked.

"Madrid," she said. "Or probably my plain old condo. I can slip on my plain old bathrobe and do plain old things for the rest of the evening."

She turned and walked briskly toward the street, hoping he would follow, hoping she could lure him away from this awful place where they played that awful game. Maybe she could crack him on her home turf, she thought. But instead of coming after her, he began to laugh, not a mean or cruel laugh, but a laugh of helplessness, a laugh she had never heard from him before.

She turned around again, a good distance from him, with one foot anchored on the mound. She couldn't really see him in the blackened dugout, but she was pretty sure of his whereabouts. "What's so funny?" she asked innocently.

"What you said. I guess it reminded me of someone else."

"Who?" she said and moved a little closer.

"This guy in a bar."

She didn't think he was telling the truth. "You're not being very helpful," she said.

"It just doesn't seem very important."

"It must be important or you wouldn't have mentioned it."

"I didn't mention it," he said and laughed, but he stopped abruptly. "It was right after my second divorce. I was a free man again and all the crap that goes with it, and I'd been sitting at the bar all night in this singles joint with this young guy, you know, probably your age. He wasn't bad looking or anything. He just seemed a little depressed, that's all." He paused as though remembering some detail that didn't quite fit in the story. "So anyway, we hadn't said a word to each other the entire night, and we were just sitting there finishing up our last calls. Then he sets his empty glass down on the counter and gets up to leave. He turns to me and he says, 'All the good women are at home right now in their bathrobes frying steak.' I guess he thought that was a virtuous thing, frying steak in your bathrobe at two in the morning."

"I still don't see why it's funny."

"I told you there wasn't very much to it."

"But there's more to it than you're telling me."

"Neither one of us got what we wanted, and we wanted opposite things." She didn't say anything to this, so he continued. "He wanted something meaning*ful* and I wanted something meaning*less*."

"You met me in a bar," she said, as if she were repeating some incredible fact.

"But I was better off by then. I wasn't looking for anything when I met you. You were pretty much an accident."

"A head-on collision."

"You don't think I take you very seriously, do you?" he

said. "Well, just because I don't say I love you all the time doesn't mean anything. If you say it all the time it loses its impact, like trying to get laughs out of a joke you've told a million times. Believe me, I know."

"It's not a joke," she said.

"I love you. I do. But not the way you wish I did."

"Once more, with feeling."

"You're young," he said, "and you're pretty, but you think it's time to be more than that. You think it's time to settle down. You want to be married. You want to have a family. I thought everyone your age was too cynical for that."

It wasn't what she wanted, though. She had never even thought of it that way before, being married to Jeff—or not seriously—living out her life with him in some middle-class setting. But the way he made it sound, the way it was clear he was withholding something merely by not making her the proposition, made her angrier than before. Maybe it would be a good thing to be married to him, just as it would be a good thing to divorce him. At least then you could say you had fallen from grace. You could act worldly and sulk in shabby little cubbyholes like this one and think about how put-upon you were all the time.

A car passed in the street, and as its headlights shone on the field, for one brief moment she could see him huddled in the dugout, his face buried in his hands. "Free love was big for a while," he said. "Then everyone got VD."

"I want to help you," she told him. But she wondered if he would ever fall out of his time warp, or if he would merely wind up being pathetic. He believed and acted out all this corny stuff. Nobody used that term *VD* anymore, for instance. And hadn't everybody stopped eating steak? It was bad for you. She had told him that herself a hundred times before.

A light went on in the church across the street, and she

could see the shadow of someone in the window. She wondered if it was some religious guy, some guy who had it in his head he could save the souls of other people. She was sure he couldn't see them, the cover of darkness and all that, but she was nervous enough about this whole scene already—it was beginning to wobble. It was headed in a direction that wasn't on the map.

She walked briskly back to the entrance of the dugout and called in to him, "Let's just get out of this place, okay?" Her voice had risen for the first time that evening. "Let's just leave before the ghost of baseball past turns this into more of a bad movie than it already is."

He didn't say anything for a while, as if he sensed he might have gained a little momentum. "You get older," he said finally, as though she hadn't made him an offer at all. "You look at pictures of yourself, and you wonder what you were like, because you can't remember. You try to be whatever you were."

"Nobody changes," she said. "Even I know that much."

"Everybody changes. Your mind, your body, your situa—"

She pulled him up by his jersey, but she lost her balance and fell backward against the chain-link fence of the dugout, with him right on top of her. She couldn't remember his ever being so malleable, but she realized now that she didn't want him this way either, some quivering invertebrate feeling sorry for itself.

"Give me your keys," she said. "Just give me your fucking keys."

He complied silently, much to her further disgust. He had never let her drive the MG—in fact, he always insisted on driving her car too—and she thought at least he would have put up some flimsy argument. But he was fully morose now. He was pushing forty and she was twenty-three, and

he was so worried he would have to do something responsible
that he might not say anything the rest of the night.

She drove the car fast, just as he did when he was angry, as
though a change of scenery might actually change how they
felt inside, and she thought he had probably assumed her
usual role too, the way he just sat there, inwardly frightened,
trying hard to look bored as he stared out into the row of
houses whizzing by. She deliberately avoided the freeway so
she could extend their wild ride, but still he didn't say anything, even when she nearly grazed a pedestrian and sailed
through an intersection on a full red light.

By the time they got to her building, the moon was coming up over the breakwater and she could see a lot of people
milling around on the pier, which seemed strange to her for
a weeknight. Then she remembered the sign she had seen on
the little chapel out there among the rows of shops and
restaurants—TUESDAYS: TWO FOR ONE. She could just imagine the two tacky couples and all their tacky friends doing
this thing they knew was tacky and thinking that the tack-
iness somehow made the whole thing cool, but really it was
just tacky, out there with your hooting friends, side by side
with the tanks of death-row lobsters and the bins of saltwater
taffy.

Instead of pulling into the resident lot, she parked at the
yellow curb in front of her building and got out, taking the
keys with her. At the elevator she pressed twenty and waited.
When the doors finally opened, he was there beside her, and
they stepped inside together as though nothing was wrong.

Why would he ever think she wanted any part of that,
to drive around in a fucking armada of limos, throwing her
garter belt out the sunroof on their way to their Vegas honeymoon? She had a hard time understanding now what she

had ever seen in him—just that he had seemed like a gentle-
man was all, that he wasn't such a sex fiend, like the guys
she knew her own age. He was shiftier about everything is
what it came down to, though. At first this whole chivalrous
thing he was into—paying part of her rent until she finished
school so she could have a decent place to live—had seemed
like respect, but now it felt like the opposite, a way to pa-
tronize and control her and in the end get exactly what he
wanted.

And what was this condo he rented for her anyway, this
place that people paid a lot of money for so they could all
share the same view? So they could all look out at the same
man-made harbor filled with man-made paraphernalia, complete with steeples and churches and people who had faith
in all the tackiest ideas in the world? He could have his tacky
condo and he could have a different woman to keep in it,
the genuine tacky article. To think that at some point she
had felt sorry for him because she'd lied. She understood
now why older women used all these tacky vamp tactics. It
was the only way to get to the bottom of things with tacky
guys like Jeff.

Sullenly they moved into her apartment. He sat down
on the love seat he had bought for her and then stared plead-
ingly in her direction, but she would have none of it; she
left him sitting there and went into her bedroom. She wanted
to get out of her softball clothes forever. She wanted to lose
this bad dream, to forget about the world of tacks that guys
like Jeff had created, but they were everywhere: at the bank
where she worked, at the mall where she shopped, even in
the neighborhood where she had grown up, these little re-
minders that things weren't quite right, these pricking sen-
sations that were never painful enough to ever cause you to
change the course of your life.

"You always wanted to hear about my first wife," she

heard him saying as she opened her closet door. "She was an innocent girl, a *plain* girl, as you already know, which I guess was what made her appealing."

She looked frantically through the hangers, but all she could see were clothes she had bought to impress him.

"This was just as the whole sixties scene was taking off," he continued. "And as I look back on it, we were just trying to hold on to the last part of the fifties, when people got married and had kids and lived happily ever after."

She took off her pants and jersey, thinking how you couldn't tell his life from a million other guys' his age. He really thought he had come so far, but he always looked to someone else for ballast. If his buddies had never gotten divorced, he'd still be out there in the suburbs with his wife and three kids reseeding his lawn.

"But of course," he said, "it didn't last. The country was flying in a million different directions by then, and what Marla and I had simply dissolved. At least we didn't have any children."

Couldn't he hear how clichéd his life sounded? Didn't he have it in him to remember one original experience? It was as though he'd watched his own life on a television documentary. She wanted to shout at him to once and for all just turn the set off.

"Suzanne was much more the earth mother. We lived together for a lot of years before we ever got married, which only happened because she got pregnant and we were afraid the kid would suffer from some kind of stigma if we didn't. As it turned out, that was the end of us. We just couldn't hold up in the face of commitment."

God, she wanted to tear her hair out. She wanted to pour nail polish all over her body and light herself on fire. Why had she ever thought it was romantic to play this little mistress game? She would never ever dress up for him again or put on makeup or take his hush money or try to act the way she thought he wanted her to act.

"Corey," he said. "Corey, are you listening to me?" And when she didn't answer, he started to cry, just a sniffle or two, but she heard it anyway. There was no mistaking it. "This baby," he said, his voice all strangled now. "This baby will only wreck things. Things are going really good. They just are. Why would you want to ruin that?" He stopped for a moment, and when he started again he was making a great effort to keep his composure. "I don't know if I love you— is that what you want to hear? I don't know if I love you, and I don't care if I do or not."

She threw on her bathrobe and sat down on her bed, listening to hear if he would say anything more. She couldn't believe this situation, how it was built out of nothing, how what she did for the entire day amounted to nothing and she got paid for it anyway, and the higher up you went the more nothing you did and the more money you got paid for it. That's why they were really giving you a salary, she thought, to keep this whole conspiracy of importance alive. The older you got, the further you moved away from the idea that your life meant nothing. If you couldn't distract yourself in some convoluted way, if you couldn't get married or have kids or get divorced or have an affair or buy yourself a speedboat, you would have to look at yourself and realize how unimportant you really were. Sooner or later something real would happen, she thought, the world would collapse on itself under the weight of human ignorance. But even then the pathetic thing was everybody would just get off on their own self-destruction. There would be this huge crying jag, but nothing would ever get fixed.

It made her want to cry herself, but that was the saddest part of all—you couldn't cry about something so petty, the pettiness of their lives and everybody else's she knew about and probably ever would know. All she could do was shake her head and listen for his voice from the other room. He really believed he was sad, she realized that now, and she realized, too, that this capability of his to believe something truly important was happening in his life was what she envied in him most.

But he didn't say anything else, and after a time an ambulance blaring outside snapped her from her reverie, and she got up and went to the bathroom to wash her face.

When she saw herself in the mirror, she had to smile: she was wearing a bathrobe after all, just like all the fabled good women in the idealist's story. Could she honestly say when she was Jeff's age that some twenty-year-old wouldn't look at her and think how misguided she was, how set she was in her own foolish ways? Maybe these older people really were more sophisticated after all. Maybe *she* was the one who was being vain and egotistical. It was just a matter of hypnotizing yourself, she thought. It was just a matter of convincing yourself that whatever you received in life was what you wanted all along. To do anything else was to selfishly call attention to your own suffering, as though everyone else wasn't living their lives through the same dull ache.

She was suddenly overcome with a tremendous shame, imagining all the pain she had caused him this night, and all the nights before. She had taken things too far as always, she thought; she had expected too much, and she vowed to herself that she would never take them that far again. She would go to him and tell him the truth, and afterward, when things had smoothed over, she could send him down to the all-night grocery for steaks, and she would fry them up and eat hers too, pretending that she liked the taste of it, and maybe someday she actually would.

She opened her bedroom door, but he wasn't there, and when she saw the open window she let out a genuine gasp and ran to it, staring down through the layers of thick dark air. But there wasn't any crowd assembled on the pavement, nor an ambulance or a policeman. A loud noise like a fire-cracker going off was followed by a round of cheering, and she looked out over the water where a lot of people were still gathered on the pier. It was no doubt a champagne cork, she thought, from a bottle of cheap champagne, where they mar-ried couples at the rate of two for one. And then her eye caught on something in the miniature world directly beneath her: it was a tiny version of Jeff, parking his MG in the resident lot so it wouldn't get towed, and she watched with only a small amount of horror as he withdrew from the trunk a tarpaulin and carefully covered his car in vinyl.

THE GLORIOUS
MYSTERIES

●

Alice Fulton

for Mary Callahan Fulton and Maureen Murphy

As the second-eldest daughter, it was my job to call Papa and tell him his sister Edna was having trouble breathing.

"Oh, she'll get over that," he said.

This morning I had to tell him Ed was gone. "You know, I've been thinking about her," he said. I could hear him drawing on his pipe through the telephone lines. "She was always an oddball."

Those words kept repeating on me as I stood in the parlor of the house on Seventh Avenue, trying to decide whether I could sneak outside for a smoke. If I'd opened my pocketbook once, I'd opened it a dozen times, checking for matches. The house belonged to my maiden aunts, Min, Bess, and— I nearly said Ed. We always spoke of the Flanagan aunts in just that order: Min, Bess, and Ed. There was a naturalness to the habit by now.

You have to understand. My aunts were not modern people. They had lived together in perfect contentment since they were little children. Their house made you feel the previous century was still at large. It was brown as a horehound drop, inside and out, with mossy green shades on every windowpane. The parlor had some tintypey, arthritic-looking furniture, under hand-tatted linen doilies, and a wide-open Bible on a library table. There was a picture of the Sacred Heart of Jesus on the wall, with a sick-call set and the crucifix from somebody's coffin laid out underneath. The mahogany radio was the most with-it thing in sight. As I reached for my pocketbook again, I disturbed Ed's sewing basket. Something white and sharp jumped out at me. I LIKE IKE! it said. I gave a yelp. Only a campaign button from the last election. But in this room it seemed offbeat as something come from outer space. I was struck by it. It gave me butterflies. A can of Fluffo, a box of Tide—anything up to date looked strange in the house on Seventh Avenue.

"Dora, get in here and rest," Aunt Min called. I joined them in the dining room, which was nearly cheerful. The table was pine with a sunny sheen, stenciled with green and yellow Dutch tulips. A corner cabinet showed off some Fiestaware and a set of china with a hand-painted underglaze. "Sit down before I knock you down," Min said, setting a cup of Postum on the table in front of me and wiping her hands on her pinafore. She was bossy as a floorwalker. "Sit, Scotty," she told the dog. She and Bess were discussing the details of the wake. I was there to help, and I couldn't leave till everything was set. Right now they were deciding the easy stuff, like what to put on the holy card.

"First come the five Joyful Mysteries. Then the five Sorrowful Mysteries. And last are the five Glorious Mysteries," Aunt Bess said. Bess always seemed to be wearing gloves, whether she was or not. Her hands were folded on a stack of altar linens with lace that deep, waiting to be laundered.

"No, the right order is Joyful, Glorious, and Sorrowful. Isn't it, Dor?" Min said, to draw me out. She usually looked a little puzzled, like somebody trying to do arithmetic in dim light.

I knew they were talking about the rosary, though I am not a religious person. I was still working as a waitress, even if my husband, Itch, wanted me to quit, and when I heard "the five Glorious Mysteries," I thought of a Chinese blue plate special. I wouldn't let on, though. I wouldn't give them any lip. Maybe it's that I'm their second-eldest niece, or that I do their taxes, or that I'm named Dorothy after their sister who was a Sister of Mercy. For some reason the Flanagans seemed to think a lot of me. I wanted to stay in their good graces. I reached down to straighten the seam in my stocking and realized I was still wearing my Puritan uniform and white seamless mesh from yesterday. I hadn't had time to change after being up all night with Aunt Edna at Saint Mary's Hospital.

"The paper will want to know she worked for Cluett's, the Model Shirt Company, and the George P. Ide Collar Shop," Bess said. Min, Bess, and Ed had a nice little arrangement in their day. Bess and Ed went out to earn a living as seamstresses. Min stayed home to cook and clean. The whole setup worked like a charm. You had to admire it.

"And they'll want her full name. Edna Theresa Flanagan. After Saint Theresa, the Little Flower," Min said. She was watering her patient lucy on the sill. "Just like my middle name, Zita, is after the Saint of Pots and Pans." Min considered housekeeping her vocation. In the spring and fall she'd rip everything apart and wash the walls from the bottom up, which only made the dirt drip down. "Remember how Ed got her first name?" she asked. This story always tickled her.

"You wouldn't remember because you weren't born yet," Bess told her.

"Bess and them got our mother to name Edna after a cow," Min said to me. "Some old Holstein. On account of the cow was the first thing Mother saw after she saw Edna."

"She was our best milk cow. A Guernsey," Bess corrected.

Even in old age, Aunt Bess had stunning skin. The sort that never shines but always boasts a dusting of down like cornstarch. She also had a beauty mark. Min had nothing of the kind. Edna had been sweet tempered but homely as a hedge fence. Her complexion was sallow, almost jaundiced, and pools of wrinkles widened out over her face like somebody had thrown a pebble in it. The aunts all had middle parts and hair yanked back into buns. Only Ed's hair was rusty pink, and her nose was a shame, being like a beak, pushed to one side, and bumped. You noticed it. None of the Flanagans were the kind of ladies who'd wear their stockings rolled to the ankle. But Edna's fashion sense was truly lacking. It must have been because she felt the cold that she favored big, shabby, shapeless brown sweaters year round. She was the shyest of the sisters, to boot.

"Remember how Ed wanted to go on the stage?" Min's laugh was short and jolly. It took you by surprise. I wasn't surprised, though, to see the aunts were treating Ed's death like something they had gotten over even as they were going through it. That was the Flanagan way. Saint Thomas Aquinas said to purge all passion. Despair was a sin against the Holy Ghost. And that accounts for the milk in the coconut.

"Remember how Ed used to talk about opening her own dress shop called the Fashion Plate?" Min said. "Remember how she answered the phone 'Ahoy! Ahoy!' instead of 'hello?' "

"I think she should wear her dark blue suit, relieved by lace at the neck," Bess said. She reached down to straighten Scotty's collar.

"And when we went to visit Sister Dorothea, remember how Ed stayed home to go to the movies?" Min said. Every summer Min and Bess took the train all the way from Troy to Asbury Park, New Jersey, to vacation with the nuns who were their relatives. They thought that was living, vacationing with the nuns.

"She'd go twice a day if the picture changed," I offered.

"What should we do about her tooth?" asked Min. She sashayed around to pour me more grain beverage from a teapot shaped like a cottage.

"I think we should let Tom Fleming decide," said Bess. That was the undertaker. We all knew about Ed's tooth. Every morning before work, she used to mold a front tooth out of wax and wedge it into place. How couldn't anybody know? It stuck out like a sore thumb.

"Tom Fleming looks down his nose at us. And Fleming's is too far. We won't get a good turnout. MacChestney's needs our business." Min sat down in a definite way.

Bess adjusted her reading glasses and unfolded an issue of *The Evangelist.* "Send her good dark blue over to Fleming's," she said.

"I don't know, Bess." Min took a swipe at the table with her apron. Maybe it's because of my arthritis, but I admired the nimbleness of her hands. They were always up to something. "Before she went, Ed said something to me that's got me thinking." Min stopped and stared at a bannister of sun falling through the bay window. "It's got me thinking she should wear that dress she made herself."

"Not *that* dress!" Bess's famous good skin turned a fretful red. If she'd gotten the breaks—if her mother hadn't died after Min's birth, say—I think Bess might have gone to the Convent of the Sacred Heart and wound up the high muckety-muck of some women's club. I see her as the ringleader of her own salon. And I don't mean hairdressing. "We dasn't. What would the priest say? And the board of health!" She asked the saints to preserve us.

"I only want to honor my sister's wishes," Min threw in.

"Anyway, it won't fit," Bess added.

"Now you're fibbing. Ed never got stocky," Min said, shaking a finger.

Bess raised her nose ceilingwards and rolled her eyes. "I mean to say, it won't fit in the coffin."

"That's as may be," said Min. But you could tell she wasn't giving an inch. If they'd had a mother, any of these girls might have made something of themselves. Min was practical. She might have become a rock hound or taken up animal husbandry. I see her with pick in hand. I see her as a beekeeper, sticking her whole arm into the hive. Any of these girls might have had more drive than their brothers. Look at Papa. He hadn't been right since his prostate operation. They might as well have taken his brain out, Mother used to say. As for me, I was sitting there dead on my feet all this time, sipping little pretend sips from my cup of dust and wishing like the dickens for the real stuff.

"Dora, you look all in. Why don't you go lie down while I fix us a bite to eat?" Min said with a kindly smile. I'd been eating Min's cooking since I was a kid, so I knew what was coming. She was a believer in all-day boiling.

"We're having the specialty of the house," she said. Her specialties included mutton with flour gravy gray as a rat and chicken stewed in its pinfeathers. She kept the heavy syrup from canned fruit and fed it to her guests as juice. "And for dessert, my pieplant pie," Min said. This was cake crumbs she'd saved in a jar, scraped together with suet, condensed milk, and rhubarb conserve, slow baked.

"Once, when you were little," Bess said, "Min made you a cup of cocoa and left out the sugar."

"It must have been terrible bitter. But you drank it politely, like a good child," Min added.

"Another time, Dor said she couldn't eat your creamed corn because of the hairs in it," Bess said, touching the net that kept her bun in place.

" 'Hairs! That's silk,' I told her." Min shook her head.

And I'd eaten her creamed corn, too, though I was particular about hair in my food. As a girl I'd fasted on tea and crackers, which ruined my looks and health and digestion forever. That is why every time I ate Min's cooking I got sick as a dog.

"Nothing too heavy," Min continued. She poured the kettle dregs of cereal coffee onto a gardenia in a galvanized tub. "In honor of your dyspepsia. It must be hard to be a waitress, with your nervous stomach."

"I'd rather serve people than be catered to myself," I said, getting up to bring my cup out to the sink. I wasn't one to lounge around like the Queen of Sheba letting people wait on me. But I knew better than to interfere with Min's kitchen. She had a real bad cook's temper. I've worked with a flock of chefs, and she could hold her own with any of them in the giving-some-poor-soul-what-for department. She'd get mad as heck if anybody questioned her seasonings. Thinking of Min's cooking made me remember how Edna claimed to have tastebuds not just on her tongue but all over the inside of her mouth—on the sides and roof and lips and halfway down her throat. She was funny that way. You had to wonder whether Min's cooking wasn't another cross for her to bear.

I decided to lay low for a while on the chaise lounge in the parlor. I must have been suffering from tired blood. Somehow I couldn't get comfortable. Everything looked cockeyed. I had the loop-de-loop feeling you get when terra firma says so long. A little table that was also a bookshelf held poetry called *Heart Throbs* and other doodads. *The Silver Chalice, The Life of Christ.* I tried to focus on that with no luck. I tested myself by trying to remember what month it was. May came to mind.

It seemed like yesterday I was a kid, sitting here with Min, Bess, and Ed, watching the style—including the choir prima donnas and lead tenors—going to high mass at Saint Patrick's. Edna could do fine stitching. If one of her nieces appeared in a new blouse, she'd eye it and pinch it and report on the weave and quality. She'd say, "I think that outfit should be a little shorter," and kneel down and hem it where you stood. We'd exchange opinions on the Freihofer breadman who tried to slip treats in with their regular order. We'd talk about the all-girl band they'd seen at Proctor's Theater or how people became saints. I'd ask what they thought of eating pitted cherries at the movies or describe a pair of spectator shoes I was saving to buy. When we mentioned items we wanted, we could see their faces taking notes. Before we left, Min, Bess, and Ed would vanish into their bedrooms. We'd hear the pocketbook clasps snapping. They'd each call us into their rooms so none of them knew what the others gave. Min gave thirty cents, Bess fifty, Edna sixty. "Here you are, old-timer," Edna would say.

Thinking all that made me think how *oddball* was a tough thing for Papa to call his sister. And this morning was not the first time I'd heard him say it. In the car on the way home from Mother's funeral, Edna had told us she'd have to go right back to the shop. They needed her to do something special with the machines, some smocking or dart-and-gusset work just she could do. They'd only given her the morning off. That was the first time I heard Papa call her an oddball.

It was but a week ago she'd come down with a cold. When she got so she couldn't breathe right, Min rubbed camphorated oil on her chest and made a mustard plaster for her. Their medical man gave her something, but her temperature was a hundred and four, her pulse was racing, and she was delirious when my sister Annie, the family nurse, appeared. Annie called the ambulance right away. When I got to Saint Mary's last night, I didn't like the sound of Edna at all. She kept breathing fast and then stopping. This was around dawn, when the night shift changes, and they bring in the trays. I hailed a nurse who was coming on duty. "She's having trouble breathing," I said, pointing to Edna. Oh honey, the nurse says. That's the death rattle. She won't last long now, the nurse says. She must have thought I was a cafeteria worker and not a relative because of my uniform. She might have been an LPN. I don't think so, though. When she saw me smoothing Ed's mussed blankets, she went on to say, that's Cheyne-Stokes respiration. Her lungs have consolidated. I guess there's a name for everything these days, I thought. After that I waited, listening to Edna struggle, puffing and puffing and then quitting cold. Every time she stopped, I held my own breath, wondering if she'd breathe again.

You have to understand. The Flanagans were saintlier than any nuns I'd known. Ed's life had been nothing but innocence and kindliness. And there she was, tucked in that ward with hospital corners where no one knew her, like some castoff or castaway, with nothing to make her feel at home, no rings or handkerchiefs of Irish linen, without a friend in the world. When she opened her eyes, I saw despair and abandonment and terror in them, and I had to think where was the happy death they said true Catholics died? That God could turn his back on this poor good little thing in her last moments was what I couldn't get over.

"Time to keep body and soul together," Min called from the dining room.

"Doesn't that smell grand!" I said. I thought it smelled like she'd cooked Scotty. At least she served measly portions. I offered up a slice of toast she'd sulfurated on the coal-burning part of the stove.

"... and he was a man whose second helpings were as ample as his first," Min was saying. "It did your heart good to see him. Dora, don't be stinting yourself on the gravy."

"Have you made up your mind about everything?" I asked. They'd put me at the head of the table.

"All but the dress," Bess said. "Edna said something to *me* before she went. What she said meant she mustn't wear any such dress." She swiped daintily at her mouth.

"What did she say, Bess?" Min asked. Min was nosy as a terrier.

Bess shook her head.

"What did Ed say to *you*, Min?" I said.

"I wish I could tell you, Dora." And I could see she wanted to in the worst way. "Then you'd know she has to wear that dress she made herself."

"Say." I took a stab at my boiled cutlet. "If neither of you will tell what she said, how will we decide?"

Min passed me the gravy. "I don't mind telling *you*, Dor. It's Bess I worry about. It's Bess who would be shocked."

Aunt Bess made wit's-end, tongue-ticking sounds.

"I know!" Min said. And her ears seemed to perk with eagerness. "Let's you and me go into my room, Dora, and I'll whisper it."

I could see Bess thinking the jig would be up if this happened. "All right," she said with a sigh. "And I'll tell Dorothy in private, too."

With that, Min and I adjourned to her room, which hadn't changed in forty years. It was as mingy as Aunt Bess's. There was a three-quarter-size bed, a throw rug on the oilcloth floor, and some pinch-pleated drapes. It didn't take long for me to hear their little secrets. I returned to the table feeling almost victorious.

"Well, old-timers. I have a surprise for you," I said, taking a swig of peach syrup like it was a Tom Collins. "Edna said the same thing to both of you. She said, 'Bury me in my Rose of Sharon Mermaid Dress.'"

Bess twisted her Catholic Daughters of America ring. "God help us," she said.

Min sneaked a scrap of mystery meat to Scotty under the table. "What could be plainer?" she said.

"I won't have it," said Bess, tapping her black oxford like a gavel on the floor. "People would say we were putting on airs. The Rose of Sharon, my foot. And Mermaid! A dress like that is impious. We could all be excommunicated."

"It's what Ed wanted. The Rose of Sharon," Min reflected. "Wasn't she the one whose teeth were like a flock of sheep that are even shorn?"

"Edna wasn't herself when she asked for this. She was raving. It's our duty to save her from sin, not lead her into it. Any fool can see that, Mary Zita. She's our sister. We have to take care of her!" Bess always spoke sparingly. I'd never seen her get this way before. Though I did remember Mother calling her Bibleback Bess, God love her.

"It's not that I approve of that—that taxi-dance dress." Min's face looked discombobulated. "But I'm not worried about Edna's soul either. Remember she made the Nine First Fridays. And she was wearing the Scapular of the Sacred Heart when she died."

"Edna loved God. I won't have her wearing that—thing—for all eternity—for all to see," Bess said. Her milk-white nose was trembling.

"Edna loved God the way chorus girls love furs," Min said, snatching Bess's plate away while Bess's fork was in the air.

"Dear hearts," I said. Min and Bess had been best chums, ticking together like the hands on a clock till this minute. I was worried about them. I honestly was. "Don't be arguing over a dress. Edna wouldn't want that." I could hardly believe they were squabbling over something so picayune. "I have an idea. The solution has just come to me." I must have been getting punch-drunk or I'd have kept mum. Talking to the aunts right then was like playing pickup sticks. You had to be delicate and move one part without rattling the other. "Let's let Scotty decide," I said.

There was a queasy silence. The aunts looked baffled.

"There's that trick Scotty does." The dog only has one trick, and believe me, it isn't much.

"You don't mean the one where we wag a bone over his head and he spins around and around till he gets all balled up and falls over playing dead?" Min said.

"That's it. The solution is, you stand on one side of the room, Min, and Bess gets on the other. I wave the bone over Scotty's head, and whichever one of you he falls toward decides about the dress."

Either they were weary or their supernatural respect for me made them go along. Edna always did like Scotty, Min said finally, and we were in business. I feel like a jackass now for not getting them to toss a coin. But that is the wisdom of hindsight. Min handed me a greasy gray bone fresh from the pot, and we took up our positions. Those Scotty dogs get awful excited. I twirled the bone above his head, and he spun himself faster and faster, yipping and yapping like there was no tomorrow. Then didn't he fall over with his head on my foot and commence to slobbering on my good white work shoe as though I was his only friend. There was no if, and, or but.

"Looks like it's up to you, Dor," Min said.

"Now hold your horses." I hemmed and hawed. It was not my place to act as judge and jury, taking sides.

"If Dora's going to decide, she has to see the dress," Min said.

"Dorothy doesn't want to see that dress," Bess said.

I had to admit to being a little curious by then about what manner of garment we had in our possession.

"We'll show you, Dor. And you can give us your opinion," said Min.

She led the way into Edna's bedroom. Like the other two, it was small and dim, with a window right on top of the neighbors, a little iron bed, and a dresser with some silvery lady things—a brush, mirror, and comb set—on it. Min opened the closet and rummaged around till she found a garment bag that looked handmade of maybe muslin. She ripped open the metal snaps, and I was nearly asphyxiated by a sudden gust of camphor with a mild undertow of vanilla. The Flanagans put camphor (it looked like gray ice cubes) into every blessed dresser drawer to protect their wardrobe from the moths. Once at Christmas, Bess gave me a box of candy she'd stored all year in camphor. It smelled to high heaven. Camphor was also a cure-all used to ward off germs and maintain health. The well-known remedy Save the Baby had a camphor base. Mother used to warm the tonic up and feed it to us on a spoon. Min, Bess, and Ed wore little crocheted bags filled with camphor around their necks. So I guess I should have been ready for it. But I wasn't, no more than I was ready for the dress itself.

I jumped back onto Bess's toe when I saw it. I put my hand over my heart like someone at a parade when the flag passes. Even in the gloom, the material was stunning, with a finish unlike any I'd known. It changed colors depending on which way you turned. It was as if the manufacturer had taken embers, spun them into thread, and woven that molten stuff into dry goods. The fabric was burnished coral in the folds yet bright rouge in the higher places where it grabbed the light. There was nothing indecent about the cut, I could see that. I could see it would cover every mortal inch of her. Buttons began at the right neckline, zagged to the left, and plunged on the bias to the thigh. Around the hips a swanky swathing of rose sateen gathered in a vee that gradually blurted out into a fishtail someplace near the ground. But what knocked the wind out of me was the tailoring. Every single solitary seam was showing. The seams were even and pinked at the edges with delicate sawteeth.

You heard stories of exotic furs in the family. You heard of marmot maybe in the aunts' far distant past. You heard of caracal coats cut to look like Persian lamb. But I'd never seen the aunts wear anything beyond crispy clean house-dresses in dimity prints or solid suits. This was something different. I had to admit it.

"Mercy," I said. "My word!" Ed must have sweat blood over this was my thought exactly.

"Regular people will see it and start to weep—," Bess added.

"It's," I stopped. "Inside out."

"—to think she had such sisters as would let her be laid out in this," Bess finished.

"That's the way Ed planned it," Min said, brushing some imaginary dust from the bodice. "She thought her best stitch-ing went to waste on the inside. This shows all her fancywork to the hilt. Wait! I almost forgot. It has a tail." And from the bottom of the bag she hauled out a seething massiveness of mauve charmeuse.

"A train," I said. I reached out, almost against my will, and petted the dress's tiny gray velveteen collar. It felt warm and numb as frostbite. "Marmot?" I whispered, full of won-der.

"That's mouse, child," said Min. "When we lived in the country, your uncle Mike trapped rodents in the pantry. And didn't he tan their hides and give them to Ed. He was a good egg."

"The board of health!" said Bess, clinging to the white metal bedpost like a mast.

"But can you tell me," Min said, twisting herself away from the dress to look me dead in the eye, "why anybody would want to be buried in a dress like this? I call it a mystery."

I was feeling kind of woozy, like I'd had one highball too many. You got the jitters, kid, I said to myself and sat down, thunk, on the bed. "Folks, I think I might take a little nap after all," I told them.

"Min, Dorothy here is all in," said Bess.

"And no wonder! Off you go—to the Land of Nod," said Min.

"Have a good rest now. Sleep tight. Bye-bye." And they backed out of the room taking great care to be quiet, like I was already under, leaving the dress on display in the open closet.

Having been awake for over twenty-four hours, you'd have thought I'd fall into a deep snooze posthaste. But I lay there awhile with the aunts' voices dozing through my head like the Latin at Mass. Gradually I drifted off, and it might have been an hour or two later, though I couldn't say for sure, that I woke to find myself petrified from head to toe. I couldn't shut my eyes or lift so much as my pinkie. As I lay there paralyzed, I noticed a flickering Something taking shape at the foot of the bed. This shimmering What-Not appeared to be loosening a watery garment. Then, making it look easy, this What-Have-You opened its chest like the skin was a jacket to show me everything within. I saw the satin lining and I saw the heart, which was on fire. Flames careened from it with every beat. Before I had time to be completely surprised, the Whatever reached inside, pulled the heart right out of its body, and held it in midair— suspended, red, and wrapped in twine. It gave off a perishing light! My own heart was going to town, and a liniment warmth was creeping through my side and spreading out. This feeling was new to my knowledge, not like aches and pains. It was then I mustered all the oomph I had left and sat up in the iced air of after-trance, out of breath, on Edna's bed.

"Well, Miss Rip Van Winkle, did you get your forty winks?" Min asked as I toddled into the parlor.

I sat down on the prickly edge of the horsehair love seat. What I wouldn't have given for an old-fashioned just then. Under ordinary circumstances, wild horses could not have dragged what happened from me. But I was so befuddled that the experience began to tell itself without a by-your-leave.

"That's a humdinger," Min said when I finished. "I never hope to have a dream like that."

"At least I got my second wind," I said. It was true. My get-up-and-go had returned. And I couldn't believe I'd gone the whole day without a smoke. Maybe I'd quit after all.

"A dream like that will put hair on your chest. Something you ate must have disagreed with you," Min said with satisfaction.

"No," said Bess. "Have you forgotten? This is a household consecrated to the Sacred Heart. Father Carey performed The Enthronement of the Sacred Heart in the Home ceremony in this room last year." She went over to their little bookshelf and grabbed a thin gray pamphlet. "I can't see without my glasses. But here's the record of payment in somebody's hand. Look, Dora."

"Ten dollars to Father Carey for performing the Enthronement of the Scared Heart in the Home," I read. "Pardon me. *Sacred* Heart. But somebody wrote 'scared.' "

"It's a sign," said Bess.

"We've been given a sign," Min said. "I can't get over it."

"Did the heart appear in a clutch of flames, banded by a crown of thorns and surmounted by a cross at the top?" Bess asked.

"I don't know about the cross," I said.

"I believe you've had an apparition of the Sacred Heart," Bess said. Her eyes were big as banjos.

"For heaven's sake," I said. I was beginning to lose patience with the religious jiggery-pokery. I honestly was. "I don't think it was anything of the kind. I honestly don't."

"What does it mean, Bess?" Min asked. "Read more, Dora."

" 'Enthronement implies that hereafter this image will have its place in the home and be honored by its inmates,' " I read. " 'By such means, Christ asks us to make reparation for the indignities inflicted upon him by others and for the ingratitude directed against his heart. Our reparation would soften in some sort the bitter sorrow he felt in being abandoned by his Apostles.' "

"But the dress," Min said. "What's it telling us to do about the dress?"

A hush came over the room. It was so thick you could hear the dust burp, as my husband, Itch, would say.

Finally Bess spoke. "Didn't Edna knit a sweater with heart-shaped buttons once?"

Min said she wasn't sure, but she'd go check. We all trooped after her into Ed's room. She pushed the Rose of Sharon Mermaid Dress aside and began rooting through the other few items in the closet. "Here!" she said, and flung on the bed what looked like some old rag Scotty had dug up. It was plate-scraping-leftover brown, and so dilapidated. But the buttons were hearts. I'll give them that.

"We'll put this over the dress. And no one will be the wiser," Bess said.

Min looked at her with real admiration. You'd have thought she'd solved a problem hard as King Solomon's about the baby with the two mothers. "And we'll tear off that darn tail," Min added.

Why didn't some one of them switch on a lamp? It was getting dismaler by the minute. When I'd arrived at the house on Seventh Avenue, it had been a beautiful spring morning, with sun all over the place. Now night was moving in. I'd have to hurry if I was to catch the last bus. "Is there anything else I can do?" I asked. I'd been hoping since morning to get home before dark. And now I might have to steer by the stars. Now there was no telling.

Min had the sweater on a hanger and was trying to work the heart buttons through the holes. They were giving her grief. "You try, Dor," she said.

For once I was happy to say my arthritis was acting up.

"I can't imagine Edna making something that wasn't just so. I can't imagine her picking buttons too big for the holes," Min said.

"I can't get over it," Bess said.

I told them again I was going, but they were wrangling in a genteel manner, and I don't think they heard. Bess wanted to redo the buttonholes. Min wanted to put the thing on Edna backwards so the gap wouldn't show. As I walked by the bay window, I waved in at them, but I couldn't catch their eyes. All I could see was their center parts bowed over the sweater, and their hands crossing as they tried to force the wayward hearts through the holes and button it, close it up nice and snug.

DALLAS

●

Frederick Barthelme

W E W E R E I N D A L L A S because Jen's father
was an assassination buff. It was his hobby, something to do
when there was nothing else to do. He wasn't new to it, but
he wasn't a freak about it, either. Some people go overboard
on everything, but that wasn't Mike. He was just interested
in the assassination, the research, the testing, the theories—
he perked up whenever anything about the assassination
came across his line of sight. Mike was fifty-three and already
retired from an Aetna Casualty job, so he had plenty of time
on his hands to study the books, the videos, the gray-market
paperwork he'd ordered from tombstone ads in magazines,
the geek view he downloaded from assassination bulletin
boards and the Internet, and the dozen or so assassination
CD-ROMs he owned, including one he'd shown me called "A
Practical Guide to the Autopsy" and others on the Warren

report, conspiracies in general, and great assassinations in history.

Mike had never been to Dallas. Jen and I hadn't been there, either, and we weren't particularly interested, but even though Jen and I had been living together for better than two years, Mike and I hadn't been introduced except by telephone, so one Sunday during the weekly call we decided to go see Dealey Plaza, just the three of us. The next day Jen added an old college friend of hers, Penny Mars, to the mix, because she thought Penny would be good company for Mike, who was long divorced and a confirmed bachelor and twice Penny's age. We were sensitive to age because I was twenty years older than Jen, nearer Mike's age than hers, and we thought there might be some talk about that. So Penny had various uses.

The four of us were going up in the carpet-and-glass elevator of the Dallas Ramada with a young guy who had "Rhumbo" stenciled on his name tag. He was handling the bags. He was disease thin, gangly, burr cut, tattooed, and properly earringed. A man of his time. For the job he wore a too-big maroon uniform with bad gold piping.

"Where'd you get the name tag?" Jen asked the bag guy.

"The name or the tag?" He seemed just naturally unpleasant, impatient and full of disdain. "Which?"

"Name," Jen said.

I couldn't figure out why she was bothering—maybe she was suffering highway stroke or something. She was wearing cutoffs and a washed-out T-shirt and looked younger than the twenty-seven she was. Penny looked younger than that. Mike and I looked rumpled and tired and like we were on the wrong side of middle age.

"I was in prison in Minnesota," the kid said. "B and E. They called me Rhumbo."

"Oh," Jen said.

The guy was too tall, and he stooped to look at her as he explained things, pointing with one finger at the palm of the other hand, like he needed that for emphasis. "See, some dead man there had this kid's book about an elephant named Rhumbo, it was the only thing he could read, and he figured I favored this elephant, so that's what he called me all the time. I was, like, his pet."

"Cool name," Jen said, giving a little nod and digging into her purse searching for something.

He gave her a look. His skin was blotchy and sore red, patches the size of fists ran around his neck, and his eyebrows were furry and queer looking on his shaved head. He had some kind of vinegary smell coming off the costume. "You want the tag?" he asked. "I can tell these Ramada dorks I lost it, I can tell them anything. That's something you get inside—how to take what you need, just rip it out of some-body's hands if you have to. These dips, what're they going to do? They're not going to fire me. They need a guy like me around here at night." He unhooked the name tag from his jacket and held it out to Jen. She hung back a minute, then took the tag.

"What about the Rhumbo-Dumbo thing?" Penny said, dodging her head back and forth to suggest she meant the question in a friendly way. "That a problem or anything?"

The guy rolled his eyes big, leaning his head off to one side. I watched his reflection careen around the elevator glass.

"Look," he said, like he was explaining something to a ten-year-old. "The Rhumbo book is *fact*. Elephants sleep on their stomachs. An elephant's height is calculated by mea-suring twice around the largest part of its foot. Real stuff. Dumbo was just some Disney slop."

Jen snapped the tag over the pocket of her T-shirt. "Hi, my name's Rhumbo," she said, shaking hands with an im-aginary elevator rider, practicing her introduction. Then she poked some high floor numbers on the elevator panel. "Rhumbo, up!" she said.

The bag boy led us to our rooms on the ninth floor. He went in and did a lot of curtain swishing and bed patting in each room, then stood there waiting for his reward. Mike gave him a twenty, and the guy went away grinning. We were still in the hall talking when he got to the corner by the elevators, did an elephant-trunk wave, and then disappeared.

In our room, Jen stripped to the waist, went straight into the bathroom, and came out wiping herself down with a damp washcloth. "I'm calling Penny and taking her for drinks," she said. "You want to come with?"

I was on my back on one of the beds. "I think I'm staying in," I said.

"You're getting along all right, aren't you? With Dad?"

"Sure. Everything's fine. He's not so bad—I don't know why we were worried. He doesn't seem to care how old I am."

"Well, he was prepared," Jen said. "He was talked to. You think he likes Penny?"

"I think he thinks Penny is a great big apple on a stick."

We'd been driving for so long that I was still swaying like we were out on the highway. It was nine, and the city was lit up, and all I wanted to do was stay still and let things stop moving. The downtown buildings were all outlined with lights. One place had twin spires and these circular towers and looked like it came from Buildings R Us. Downtown wasn't that big. One building had green wiggly lights all over it, reflected in its glass. I couldn't tell whether the lights were strange or it was fabulous architecture.

The room was cheesy in that motel way—silly-looking dressers, veneered night tables, a nondescript table-and-chairs set by the window. If somebody you knew owned the stuff it would be horrifying, but at the Ramada it was comforting. You knew where you were. No mistakes.

Jen called Penny and arranged to go out for drinks, then knocked on the connecting door to her father's room. Mike opened up wearing a royal blue satin smoking jacket.

"Check it out," he said.

"Where'd you get that?" she said.

"Found it," he said. "On a hanger in here." He thumbed back toward his room.

"Looks mighty suave," I said, getting out of the bed. It didn't feel right being in bed with Mike in the room, like I shouldn't be that relaxed. When I sat on the edge of the bed, I saw some kind of crumbs of food on the floor right by the night table. "There're crumbs here," I said to Jen, pointing to the floor where the crumbs were.

She came over for a look, then swept her shoe back and forth a couple of times over the spot. "There. All gone," she said. She invited Mike to go out and have a drink with her and Penny, but he asked what I was going to do, and when I told him, he said he thought he'd just hang out with me, if that was okay.

She said, "Sure. Fine. You guys can give each other lectures or something."

"No lectures," Mike said, raising his eyebrows at me as if he hadn't a clue what she meant. I didn't either, so I shrugged.

"This traveling together isn't so bad, is it?" Jen said, sliding past him, headed for the door.

"No, it's great," Mike said. "I mean, it's okay for me. I'm doing fine." He sat down in one of the chairs by the window.

"You guys stay out of trouble," Jen said.

We both waved at her, the same kind of wave. It was odd happening the way it did. Mike had a can of Coke he'd gotten somewhere, and he was flipping the tab making thumb piano sounds.

"So, Mike," I said, climbing into the second chair by the window. "You okay?"

"Pretty much," he said. "I guess I feel a little awkward. It's hard to be the father, us being the same age. I guess I never was a father to Jen all that much. With the first two I wasn't so tolerant, I didn't give them a lot of leeway, but by the time Jen came along I'd just given up. I mean, I knew whatever happened would be okay."

He was alternating between thumping the tab on the can and rubbing his thumb on the wood-grained Formica table between us, making a squeak sound, like he was trying to rub some spot off the tabletop, some sticky spot that wasn't giving up without a fight.

"Uh-huh," I said.

"I'm sorry, Del," he said, putting the can down and rubbing his forehead instead of the table. "I didn't mean to bother you with that. It's just I've been thinking about things all day. You know—Jen, the other kids, the family. I haven't seen her in a long time."

"Yeah, I know. And it didn't bother me, I just didn't know what to say. I don't have any opinions about parenting, families, all that. Well, I mean I have ideas about *my* family, but not about the parent side of it, or not any general sort of ideas about parents, just about my parents, you know, like from the point of view of the kid. Me, I mean."

"Sure," he said. "You live one way and I live another. All my life I'm a little tucked-in fella, sitting in my neat house, paying those bills right on time. Looking into problems and acting like I knew what I was looking at. I guess I had more order than I really needed."

"Actually, that sounds great to me," I said. "No kidding. Mine's been a mess, first to last."

He laughed. "Yeah, I gathered that from Jen. What I don't get is how come you're not worried? Fifty, aren't you? Close to it? You've got a good job, but it's not paying you a fortune, is it? And I'll bet the retirement program's not going to turn out the way the brochure described it. It takes a lot of nerve to be in your shoes."

I glanced at him trying to see if this was criticism, an aggression, but it wasn't there in his face, so I said, "I guess I am kind of worried. I mean, I never was before. I was always too busy being this or that, looking down on this or that—you know how that goes. But by now I'm a little nervous."

"Maybe I could help out," Mike said. "I mean, setting things up, some plans so you're sure you're okay when you retire."

"You think you could do that? That'd be very nice. I could use help."

"Sure," he said. He got up and leaned against the window looking down to the freeway below us, first left, then right, scratching his cheek. He had a heavy beard so there was a loud sandpapery sound. "You think we ought to go over to Dealey Plaza tonight?" he said, tapping the glass.

"We can if you want to." I was watching a helicopter flying on the other side of downtown. It reminded me of some movie. I couldn't hear it, but it was moving lazily around the buildings over there doing that spotlight thing.

"I was playing golf," Mike said. "When he was shot. Somebody came by in a cart and yelled at us, and we headed back for the pro shop where there was a TV. I watched for a while, then went home and stayed there for days. Saw Ruby shooting Oswald—all of that. I liked the music at the funeral, the cortege, the boots backward in the stirrups—that's what got me, that riderless horse. Walter Cronkite talking about the riderless horse—he must've said those words hundreds of times. 'And now the riderless horse...' That got me. The drums, the music. The procession. All that walking. The backward boots—damn. That was something. That was new as hell."

I got up and skirted the table, then picked up my wallet and keys from the dresser where I'd put them earlier. "So why don't we go over there now? Take a look."

"Should we eat first?" he said. "We can eat. You want to eat?"

The light coming up from the freeway caught his face in an odd way, and suddenly I saw him as a much younger man. This had happened to me before—in some odd second you see what somebody was like when he was twenty years younger. Most of the time it wasn't particularly attractive, but with Mike it was nice, it made me like him more than I already did.

"Chicken-fried steak, mashed potatoes, brown gravy," Mike said. "Let's hit a One's-A-Meal. Open-face roast beef with mashed potatoes. Either one."

"Hey now," I said, doing the guy on the Gary Shandling show.

"I've got that mashed potatoes thing going." He grinned and caught my shoulder.

"I'm right there," I said, touched by our sudden camaraderie.

We started down the hall for the elevator, but Mike had to go back and get something in his room. I waited in the hall, remembering a scene with Eddie Constantine in some early Godard movie I couldn't even remember the name of—*Alphaville*, it suddenly came to me. That's what the Ramada hallway looked like—desolate, frighteningly utilitarian.

"The art of the chicken-fried is a lost art," Mike said, coming out of his room and raising both hands as if to forestall any argument. "Now, I know that mostly what happens in life is that stuff gets lost, all kinds of stuff, and that food's the least of it, but you'd think they'd be able to hang on to chicken-fried steak, wouldn't you? The rest I don't care so much about. These days it's all rude people and their rude hair, anyway. That elephant boy in the elevator. You and me, Del, we're the old cars out there in the way." He soft-popped my shoulder with his fist. "But sometimes don't you just want to bump the little creeps, you know? Just nudge them with the front end—bam! Sixty miles an hour, that kind of thing. I'll bet you know that feeling."

"Yes, sir," I said.

"See," Mike said. "Yet another reason."

Rhumbo was backward on a plastic chair at Jen and Penny's table in the Twin Sisters, the Ramada's house bar. We stopped there to see if they wanted to eat.

"You taking a break?" I asked him.

"I was just asking how come these girls were with you guys," he said. "What, you can't find women your own age?" He switched to a too-intense expression. "Just kidding. Jen told me she's . . ." He hesitated, ready to point at one of us, not sure which one until Jen nodded toward Mike. ". . . your daughter, right? And you," he said, wagging a finger at me, "are the boyfriend."

"Good work," I said, then turned to Jen. "We were thinking of eating something."

"I can tell you where I'd go," Rhumbo said, swinging his leg over the back of the chair, getting up. "I'd hit that IHOP. Right around the corner here. Get me a batch of German pancakes. Real good." Something wet shone on his teeth when he smiled. He smelled sour. His little maroon suit was wide open over a white T.

"I don't play that pancake game," Mike said. "We're looking for chicken-fried."

"California Café, off Eleventh," the kid said. "Go there all the time."

"I wouldn't hate pancakes," Penny said. She was fooling with her long and auburn hair, finger-combing it.

"We're going to see Dealey Plaza afterward," I said to Jen.

"He wasn't in prison," Penny said, patting the bag boy's head. "That's just something he made up. He's in grad school here. His name's Roy."

"Hey," the kid said, holding his hands out. "Caught me. But I can't believe you're going over to Dealey. I've been here eight years and I've never been there."

"Hello, Roy," Mike said, shaking the kid's hand.

"How about Roy shows us the café and then we all go to the plaza?" Penny said.

"What about work?" I said. "Don't you have to work, Roy?"

"Fuck 'em," he said. "I'm on my break."

The California Café was greasy and small, just right, and chicken-fried steak was present. No brown gravy, only white gravy. It was nearly midnight when we got to Dealey Plaza, which was just a couple of highway feeders, half a city block with nothing on it, and a concrete train overpass. All the streetlights were orange.

"What a joke," Roy said, looking around from the sidewalk across from the Texas School Book Depository. "Oswald's up here, and the limo goes there, and *blam!* Even I could have made that shot. Do it in my sleep."

"Oh, settle down," Penny said. "You couldn't make the shot."

"On TV it always seems bigger," Mike said.

"What is it—a hundred yards from there to there?" Roy said. "It's tiny. Why'd they make a big stew about this? Anybody could make it. Glenn Ford could make it. It's a groundhog deal."

"Six FBI marksmen," Mike said. "They tried it with pumpkins and missed. I mean, using pumpkins for Kennedy's head. Did it here, and did it in a field in Iowa or Wisconsin."

He looked a little shell-shocked. I grabbed his arm, and we walked across the street to see the Texas School Book Depository close up, then we came back and walked the route Kennedy's car had taken, then climbed up the grassy knoll and went around behind the fence into the vacant lot where the other shots were supposed to have come from. A train was going by on the overpass. "This is where the three tramps were," Mike said. "Maybe they were getting into a boxcar over there." He pointed toward the tracks. "But some reports say they were over behind the depository building there, that back corner there. This lot was full of cars."

Jen, Penny, and Roy were sticking close to the terraced part of the plaza, where there was a reflecting pool and a commemorative plaque explaining everything. There was a spotlighted American flag in the middle of it, looking like red-and-white vinyl flapping up there. "I'm going to go see what Jen's doing," I said. "You okay here?"

He nodded, and I went back around the fence and crossed the street, climbed the little rise to the terrace. Jen drifted away from Penny and Roy.

"How're you doing?" she said.

"Fine," I said. "But what's the deal with Penny?"

"She thinks he's interesting."

"Roy? She must be starved to death," I said.

"He's right about how small this joint is," Jen said. "Where's Dad?"

"Over there," I said, looking back toward where I'd left Mike. "He's behind the fence, above the grassy knoll. He's being the second gunman. He seems kind of forlorn."

Across the street I could see Mike's head poking out above the wood fence that separated the grassy knoll from the

parking lot. The train going by behind the parking lot was
squeaking and squealing, rocking on the tracks.

"Places are always letdowns," Jen said. "I wish it was
scary, at least. You know, an eerie feeling like going back in
time, or time could switch around and you'd be caught there
that day, running to the limo, but it'd be snaking off toward
the underpass. You know what I mean? *X-Files*. That'd be
cool."

The big flag was snapping overhead, the wind was driving it so hard. Mike came out and stood for a minute in the
colonnade on the other side of the grassy knoll. Then he
headed our way. When he got to us, he looked like somebody
who'd gotten real depressed.

"You feel all right?" I asked him.

"Fine," he said.

"The depository isn't open," Jen said. "It's open days but
not nights."

Penny and Roy came up behind us. "Everything okay?"
Penny asked.

"I don't want to go there anyway," Mike said.

"This is cheap shit," Roy said. "It's a toy, like a scale
model where a toy president was killed. Toy people scattering. Toy shots. What a shank."

Jen was trying to bring Mike around. "We can come back
tomorrow, and you can get right up there to the window
where Oswald did the shooting," she said.

"Unless he was hanging upside down from one foot with
a squirrel in his teeth, it ain't worth it," Roy said.

"I think I'll go back to the Ramada for now," Mike said.

Jen looped her arm through his. "Aw, c'mon, Dad. Let's
sit here and just soak it up. Maybe it gets better if you hang
out awhile."

"History's always so small when you see it in person,"
Mike said.

"Yeah, this is Buck-A-Day," Roy said. "Who cares,

anyway? It's like about as important as John Wilkes Booth or whatever."

A busload of tourists came in behind us, maybe twenty Hawaiians in Hawaiian shirts carrying cameras and wearing funny hats. The tour guide gathered them on the terrace alongside the reflecting pool in front of the Dealey Plaza plaque and started explaining stuff. Mike went for the street and hailed a cab that was going by.

"I'm going to the motel," Mike said. "Anybody want to go with?"

"We're ready," Penny said, yanking Roy with her.

"Are you okay, Dad?" Jen asked. She looked at me as if I was supposed to stop him. I started toward the cab, but he waved me off.

"Forget it. I'm fine. I'll get some rest."

Then the three of them climbed into the backseat of the Yellow and rode off. The car squatted as it accelerated.

Jen and I went back to the grassy knoll and sat down, watching the traffic dip left to right into the underpass. For so late at night, there were plenty of sightseers, not a crowd, but fifty or so, circling and pointing out the highlights, the School Book Depository, the spot below where we were sitting where the president was shot, the knoll, the fence. There was a big road sign in front of us, and I couldn't figure out if it was the one the president's car disappeared behind in the Zapruder film or if it was some new sign. It seemed as if it was the same sign, but it was in the wrong place, as if it had been secretly moved, as if they didn't want anybody to notice.

"This is a big deal, isn't it?" Jen said. "I'm supposed to get the weight of history here. Great events upon which our future turned."

"Jen?" I said.

"It's not really working," she said.

"Maybe you have to believe things would've been different if he wasn't shot. You know, like coherence and history and all that," I said. The train had been squealing nonstop for twenty minutes. "I like this train pretty much."

"You would," she said.

"I like the way it's shimmering, and that steely noise the wheels make, and the way the cars shift back and forth into each other, kind of lurching," I said. "It's like a car-crash audio slowed way down."

"I wasn't even born," she said. "I think that's why for me. It's textbooks. . . . You're supposed to think about it, feel stuff, maybe that's it. You're supposed to, so you don't, blah blah. Pretty quick you resent it."

"Yeah?"

"I really don't feel shit, except I'm kind of pissed because it disappointed my dad."

I put an arm around her, then leaned against her, dropping my fifty-year-old head on her shoulder. "Still, you don't want Kennedy killed, there's that. He got his skull exploded right down here in front of us. Think of that. We're ringside."

"People get that everywhere," Jen said. "Plus, who cares? Why's the president getting it worse than somebody else? He's just one more goofball going down."

"He had big ideas," I said.

"He was just another guy with a sore dick," Jen said.

She got up and I followed. We went behind the fence where Mike had been earlier and toured the parking lot, then leaned up against the fence. It was kind of broken down at the corner. I wondered if it was the real fence. Then I wondered if I cared if it was the real fence. We walked through the colonnade Mike had been through and back up alongside the Texas School Book Depository, went and looked at the entrance to the museum part, and came back to where we'd started.

"I think things were different back then," I said. "There was a whole different deal, I vaguely remember. The idea is things changed because he was shot—that wised us up, made us all callous."

"That's junior, Del," she said.

"Hey, it hadn't happened before. Nobody thought it *could* happen. It was like something in those fifties movies with Henry Fonda or somebody, you know, the black-and-white ones?"

"Oh, please. If there's a change, it was you and your buds cheating each other, stretching truth, pushing at the edges of things, getting that little extra. Everybody got used to it. You all held hands and evolved into us."

"My generation."

"That's it," she said. "Do the crime, do the time." She waved toward the depository, then the rest of the Dealey setup. "This whole show looks like it's lit with bug lamps. It's yellow. Isn't everything kind of yellowish, or is that my imagination?"

"It has a parchment-colored aspect," I said.

"Part of the plan, I guess," she said. "It's shitty to charge for the Oswald window. That's like kill a president so your town can make six bucks a pop on the yahoos. How many you figure they get a year? They even charge for kids."

"Do not," I said.

"Yes sir. It's on the sign."

"So," I said, brushing off my jeans. "Let me see—you want to go back to the Ramada and get in bed and see what's on TV?"

"Exactly right," she said, smacking my arm. "Maybe that *JFK* movie. That'd be cool. Or some real rainy movie like that Kurt Russell Florida thing where he's the blown-out reporter and that Hemingway woman is his girl—that's really great rain in there." She kissed my shoulder. "I tell you, you older guys are slow but you're okay. You get there."

"Thanks," I said. "Now all we've got to do is refocus Penny, get her back on track."

"I'm getting her some new heels," Jen said. "Saw them in a catalog—chrome toe, six-inch stilettos, the works. They moan when you walk."

"She'll use 'em on Roy," I said.

"Well, then I'll keep them just for us," she said. "How about lemon?"

We walked back to where we'd parked the car, which was next to some architect's idea of a Kennedy memorial—thick slabs of concrete making a sort of room that stood up off the ground in an open half-block space. You were supposed to stand inside it and feel the gravity of events. Somebody had posted a clown-show sign on its side. We got in the car and headed for the hotel.

The streets of downtown Dallas were almost empty, so it looked like one of those end-of-the-world pictures, one of those movies where all the people have been killed and we get long shots of the empty downtown streets. There's a wind blowing coffee cups across the pavement, and pieces of paper are flapping in the breeze, but nobody moves. It was nice, so we ran the windows down on Mike's car and floated through the streets for a while—going six or eight blocks in one direction and then turning, coming up the next street going the other direction, the wind whipping into the car, twisting our hair. It smelled that strange way empty cities smell at night, clean and metallic. Jen switched on the radio, and we turned that up and let it thump as we rode through the streets.

Roy met us in the corridor outside our rooms. He looked the worse for wear, like he was loaded or he'd had too many drinks since the plaza. "So?" he said. "How're you guys? The big man turned right on in. You want to come down to Penny's and get trashed? We've got some shit."

"I don't think so," I said.

"Why not? What're you doing? Don't go getting all historical, okay?" he said, his hairless little face twisted into a smirk.

"Don't know much about history," I said.

We tried to get past him but he followed us.

"Where's Penny?" Jen asked.

He grinned way too big. "She's freshening up. Just, you know, freshening up." Then he laughed a kind of snort laugh.

"Great," Jen said.

"See, what I figure," he said, "I mean Kennedy and all that, is there's no difference. Starkweather, Nam, this cute Oklahoma trick—it's all settled. It's going down. That's what's out here. You gotta have the hard stuff or you got nothing. The government does it best. Blowing hands and feet off Iraqis on that road out of Kuwait or whatever—you see that? Real-time morphing. Big trade in corpse and body-part snaps. Big profits."

"Slow it up, pal, will you?" Jen said.

"And great TV, too," he said. "Sometimes I like that militia thing, that time-to-clean thing that we're doing now—flush the bad, act with maximum efficiency, scrape out evil's eye. Know what I'm saying? That appeals."

"You're a moron," I said, giving him some strange half-real, half-phony thumbs-up that I didn't quite have control of.

"Maybe history is calling," he said, grinning.

"Yeah, and maybe it's not," Jen said.

In the room, Mike's connecting door to our room was closed. Ours was still open. I started to shut it as quietly as I could, fearing the latch. "I guess I'll just leave this alone," I said to Jen. "He's probably asleep."

"He's got a model of the plaza," Jen said. "It's wonderful. Made it himself, took years. Perfect scale, perfect grass, lampposts, signs, cars, and the different people who were there that day, all reconstructed from video and photos." She was hooking her notebook computer up to the telephone.

"I want to see that when we get back," I said.

"I'm sure he'll show it to you," she said.

I flipped on the television and went through a few stations until I got to the Weather Channel and stopped there and watched a new hurricane named Camellia messing around with Hawaii. A lot of the video of Hawaii was quite beautiful, so I watched that for a while. Buildings were falling down. A Holiday Inn fell down, or part of it did, the sign and the portico over the drive-in entrance. The trees were all bending vigorously, and the whole picture looked wet. It was lovely and relaxing.

In a minute I heard Jen's modem screech as she made her connection. She turned around and caught the tail end of the Hawaii video and asked me what it was.

"Hawaii," I said. "They're having a hurricane."

"Cool," she said.

There was a light knock on the door. I eyed Jen, then got up to answer. It was Penny. She was done up in a short black dress and lots of makeup. I let her in.

"Look out in the hall and see if jerk boy is still hanging around, will you?" Jen said.

"Oh, don't be that way," Penny said. "He's harmless, he's okay. Besides, he's down in my room."

"Here's what he is," Jen said, clicking some computer keys. Then she read something off the screen. "With skillful manipulation of the Japanese rope harnesses you first find the middle of the rope and make a sizable overhand knot so you have a loop big enough to fit your partner's head.

Employ a rope of appropriate dimension and surface. Consider the path of the rope from the breasts, just above the vagina, taking care to border the labia, with the length running then to her head and neck, and have her hold her hands behind her back—"

"Okay," Penny said. "I get it. But he's doing the best he can."

"Like us," I said.

"Exactly. He's trying to be somebody."

"Why couldn't he try to be Alf?" Jen said.

Penny smoothed her skirt, what there was of it. "He wants to impress us. He's just trying to make himself more interesting. Anyway, we're going out for beers."

"Everybody always wants to be so interesting," I said.

"Yeah," Jen said. "That's our generation."

"I thought I'd tell you so you wouldn't worry," Penny said. "I don't think we'll be out too long."

"Okay. We won't worry," I said. "You look mighty, uh, breezy."

"Let me be, will you?" Penny said, looking at Jen. "What's with him?"

"He is just a rat," Jen said, walking Penny to the door. "Go. Have fun. Be lucky."

When Penny was out of the room, Jen tossed herself onto my bed. "Oh, baby, you're so right it just gives me chills. I just want to watch some TV with you. Watch those news gooks, potatoes with olive eyes talking as if it mattered. I wish we had that Saturday night one with the guy from the *Wall Street Journal,* Novak, and the woman with the prissy little mouth and the mole. Everybody sits up so straight on those shows."

"You're a true postmodernist," I said.

"No alternative," Jen said.

They were doing local stuff on the Weather Channel—

chance of rain. Jen shut the computer down, unplugged the phone cord, and stuck it back into the phone.

"I thought Penny hated men," I said.

Jen shook her head and rolled her eyes and did a little doll jerk, as if she were being controlled on strings from above. I took this to mean I was being stupid.

I clicked through the channels, stopped again at CNN. There was something about Whitewater, new revelations, et cetera.

"Now *that* is pissing in the wind," Jen said, looking over my shoulder.

"You guys are supposed to be less cynical than us," I said.

"That's another generation," Jen said. "The one before us, I think. They were less cynical than you. We're more. Our cynicism takes paint off warships, knocks planes out of the sky—this is a problem for you old guys when you get three or four generations out of touch."

The O. J. backdrop came up on the screen along with the O. J. theme song. Jen lunged for the remote. "Change it, quick."

I was the last one down for breakfast. The motel restaurant was all light wood and light Formica and plastic flowers in fifty shades of light green. It was almost empty. Mike and Penny and Roy were sitting together at a small table near a window that looked out toward the freeway. I saw Jen in the lobby as I came out of the elevator. She waved me into the restaurant. She was getting a newspaper. Mike had scrambled eggs and toast. Roy was slicing his fork through a tall stack of pancakes covered with pretty syrup. Penny was eating a piece of bacon off his plate. I said good morning.

"Morning," Mike said. "Long time no see."

"I slept," I said. "What time is it?"

"Eleven," he said.

Penny was patting Roy's arm. She picked up her fork and got a one-inch square of pancake off his plate. She had coffee and a roll in front of her, but she was more interested in Roy's pancakes.

"Dealey wasn't too great, I guess," I said.

"It's putz country," Roy said, waving his fork off toward town. "That's the real deal."

"It's deadly," Penny said. "That's what we decided."

"Maybe if we go over today that would help," I said. "You know—it was night, we were tired, we'd been driving."

"I don't think so," Mike said. "I've seen enough."

"It's fucking pathetic over there," Roy said. "So what are you anyway, some kind of investigator? You trying to figure how many gunmen there were and all that?"

"Yeah," Mike said. He was smiling, reaching out to pat the kid's shoulder. "You got it. How many gunmen. It's just as simple as that."

THE STONE

●

Louis B. Jones

I N   O N E   O F   T H E   N E W   P L A C E S north of Terra
Linda, Roger Hoberman lived with his wife, Beverly, and
his children, Jessica and Justin, in a house on the corner of
Sunstone and Wheatstone that had almost all the available
options, like a beamed ceiling and a yard area and a hobby
nook. Roger was then the owner-manager of an unpopular
and seldom-noticed Shakey's pizza franchise, across the freeway from the place that used to be the Holiday Inn and then
got turned into offices, on the frontage road that is for some
reason always under construction, year in and year out, with
great floes of weather-bleached asphalt tipped up and striped
hazard barriers blinking in the sun and scaring off customer
traffic. Inside the windowless Shakey's, where the cold black-
ness swarms up to your eyes and dizzies you after the con-
cussion of parking-lot sunshine, Roger could be found most
days between noon and midnight. He was there, lying on his

back under the bar with a flashlight—a big man, too big for this cramped project—trying to fix the canister of soft-drink syrup whose plastic hose had become clogged, when he felt the first pain deep in his belly. It was a thud, a tympani note of pain. It made him stop work, bring his knees up a little, drop his head gently to the concrete floor, and think about his crowded schedule and how remiss he was in everything.

It wasn't any mortal disease. It turned out to be the first symptom of a kidney stone. Actually, the *first* symptom had occurred two days earlier, when Roger had run down to the Marin True Value to buy a mop handle to replace the one broken by the new apprentice pizza chef, and as he was walking across the parking lot toward the store, there was a faint sweet flush of pain in the basin of his guts, which he ignored altogether. Roger Hoberman was a man who achieved a state nearest to perfect mortal happiness when he was walking across parking lots. With the slam of his car door, the flash of keys disappearing into his pocket, the unpacked spring in his stride, the renewed consciousness of his wallet, Roger was his truest self when he was walking toward a purchase. Or just walking. Toward anything. In heaven, the goal of his walking would always be just out of reach, receding into an intimate infinity. It's arriving that kills you. What do you get when you arrive? A mop handle. And then you stand around on the linoleum of the True Value holding this humiliating wand, awarded you as evidence that you're handling a job beneath you because others are too irresponsible, waiting for the teenager in the green True Value vest to say, "May I help you?"

At forty-two, Roger was always impatient for everything to be over with. When he was at Shakey's, amid the clang of the jukebox and the silent bombs of light from the wide-screen video, while only two stingy customers dawdled over their crusts, he couldn't wait for closing time, to get back to

the peace of his home. But then, at home, it wasn't long before
he ached to get back to the million things that needed doing
at Shakey's, and he couldn't stay seated in the furniture
because his muscles longed for exertion. Everything Beverly
said invited contradiction irresistibly, and then he was sorry
when she gave up and merely pursed her lips. Even in bed,
he lay out with the acid slime of coffee rising in his throat
wishing he could fall asleep immediately by force of will.
But then when he did get to work he wished he could be at
home. He dreamed about the half acre of unimproved land
he had bought way up in the cold sunshine of Mount Shasta,
way outside the radius of commuter colonization of every
city, where he wanted to build a cabin and sink a well, but
where in fact he never visited. It was only on parking lots,
on the great black rink where his own muscles propelled
him, that Roger walked through whatever grace is, fleet-
ingly. The hardware store turned out not to have the right
kind of mop handle. All they had was tapered-end handles,
and Roger needed one that was threaded, to screw into the
mop.

"That's how they come," said the dull boy in the True
Value vest. "Wade" was written in Ipana blue script on it.

"What?" said Roger. "I just *jam* it onto the mop? And
after I mop the floor for five minutes, the mop *falls off?*"

The boy smiled. "I guess so." He was delighted.

Roger began to speak very slowly and distinctly. "And
then when it falls off, do I pick it up? And jam it back onto
the handle? And try to mop for another two minutes before
it falls off again?"

"I guess so," said the boy, but his smile was getting filmy
as he realized that this guy wasn't being humorous, and
might even be weird, so Wade—you could see it in his fu-
gitive eyes—didn't want to be responsible here anymore.

Roger said, "I'm going to have to drill this. And bolt it."

The boy averted his eyes and shifted his weight from one

foot to the other. Roger cut himself off and went to the cash register and got out his wallet, his big old leather wallet, thick as a bar of soap, fattened encyclopedically by receipts, Post-it notes, a matchbook cover, salesmen's business cards, jotted-on napkins, a five-dollar rebate coupon, his hole-punched Video Paradise card entitling him to a free video after twelve punches, his driver's license and credit cards and organ donor card—a mound of a wallet, old as high school, its leather burnished at the corners by the years' rub of denim, its hem warped in the pocket's humidity, curved to the shape of his gluteus maximus, all held together by a girdling, necessary rubber band. It sat on the True Value counter between them while the boy rang up the sale. Roger had gone to high school in this town. He was born here. Through clenched teeth, valvelike, he let out a sigh. And then at last he walked out of the store with this mop handle, one end of which the boy had stuck into a paper bag. He tore off the bag and threw it into a trash can. That boy had probably never mopped a floor in his life, maybe literally never. Nobody cares about anything anymore. There's no payoff in it. "That's how they come" is the excuse for everything. A hardware store doesn't even look like a hardware store anymore. It looks like a ladies' department store or a bookstore or a drugstore. Everything is hanging on revolving racks, packaged in heat-sealed plastic on cardboard backings, so you can't even examine what you're buying. You're not supposed to *care*. The one guy who cares comes off looking like an asshole. Comedians on TV crack sly jokes about marijuana and cocaine, which Roger's nine-year-old doesn't yet laugh at, but someday soon she will. People have to *care* about things. Things *mean* something. Everything isn't just a pile of shit. Everything isn't just a pile of stupid shit to stand around in grinning. He knew when he got back to work there would be the busboy's guileless torpor to face; he would be *relieved* the mop wasn't fixed yet. And Roger would lose an hour of his valuable time bolting the mop to the handle, because he couldn't trust the boy to do it. The boy would botch it up, as if intentionally. In fact, the right bolt wasn't on the premises at Shakey's, and Roger ought to turn around right now and go back and buy one. But he kept on walking, right past his car, clutching this mop handle, because just walking felt good. And when he got to the end of the parking lot, knowing there was nowhere to go but back, he just stood there at the edge holding this stick, looking like a jerk.

When the kidney stone made itself felt for a third time, he was immobilized. It happened at Shakey's again. As in that childhood game of statues, he felt "tagged." He couldn't afford to take time off for illness. Everything was so heavily mortgaged. The only thing he owned outright was the land on Mount Shasta. Slowly, slowly, imperceptibly, he set down the SuperSlurp! paper cup he was holding in the gaudy dark, and one of the employees folded him into the passenger seat of the car and drove him to the Kaiser Medical Center. It was a kidney stone, X rays immediately showed. The doctor (his eyes never once met Roger's) was so flippantly *bored* by Roger's problem that his professional touch—on Roger's elbow, spine, breast, throat—was divine, angelic. And the valley of Terra Linda flooded with God's intentions again, of course. Surgery wouldn't be necessary; renal calculi were irritating as all get-out but never fatal; the only thing to do was take it easy, be patient, relax, and eventually the stone would be passed in urination. It was a tiny grain that had crystallized over the years. As a fact, that was astonishing. A stone had grown inside him, and it would emerge from his very penis. He was instructed to urinate into a fine mesh sieve. The doctor handed him a prescription, which he carried in his hand like valuable new currency, like a ticket to somewhere, as he rode back to work in a taxi, slightly alienated now from the place he'd grown up in, scenery passing the cab window. Then, at Shakey's, he drove his own car home and—feeling perfectly fine now—clipped the prescription with a magnet to the refrigerator in the kitchen, calling out, "Hey, Beverly."

She wasn't home. He was angry with her for not being home. She was always home. After pacing around the empty house for some time, he settled down at the hobby nook in the garage, where paperwork piled up, a mountain of evidence that the Shakey's was failing, basement-clammy, frigid with air conditioning, too heavily mortgaged. In spite of his medical condition, he could make efficient use of his time. Indeed, he was well into the pleasant, coffee-enhanced trance of miscellany when Beverly's familiar Toyota sound interrupted him. She would have seen his car in the driveway. But then there was some pausing outside in the carport, some tenderness in opening the front door, some pausing again in the kitchen, before at last she called, "Roger! You're home!" and the totally fantastic certainty crossed his mind that she was having an affair. It was decreed by the tarot he'd spread before him, of unpaid bills. She called out, "What's this?" because she'd found the prescription on the refrigerator. It made him instantly angry, her asking. He didn't answer. He just stared down at the computerized HandiKup bill on the work bench, his pen poised in air.

She appeared in the doorway beside him, puzzling over the Sanskrit on the slip. "Roger, what is this?"

"Oh, that. Nothing. Something from the doctor." It was all so annoying he was almost blind.

"What's it for?"

"I have a kidney stone. Okay? It's no big deal. I went to the doctor, and he said I have a kidney stone."

She stayed in the doorway. The HandiKup bill swam beneath his vision.

"A kidney stone. Don't people remove those?"

"No, they just go away. Look, I'm right in the middle of

this. Could we talk later? It's no big deal. It will go away in a few weeks."

"A few weeks," said Beverly, standing there ruminating as this stone took shape in her mind. She drew breath to ask another question but then didn't. Vanished silently from the doorway. Giving up on him again. Good-bye, good-bye. Soon the radio came from the kitchen, that easy-rock station she loved so much. She had always loved music. The sound of a paper grocery bag. He remembered her in high school, how she loved music then, too, which seemed sad. Regret, at a certain point in life, involves a hard swallowing motion. He could picture her reaching up on tiptoe to put cans on the top shelf: her calf, her thigh.

Over the weeks, the crystal kept looking for the passage of exit, creeping down, but then it would be driven back by the ejaculatory spasm of pain. He tried to go on at the Shakey's for a while, but the pains kept creating awkward situations. That inner cord would yank tight, and he would double over. Once, the Styrofoam straw hat that he and all the employees were required by the Shakey's International by-laws to wear at all times fell off and knocked a Coke into a customer's lap. Driving was dangerous, because if the pain came back when he was on the freeway he might not be able to lift his foot to the brake pedal. "Honey," said Beverly, lying beside him in bed with the *TV Guide*, "couldn't you let one of the older kids there manage the place for you? Why do you have to be there all the time?" At this point, the stone had dwelt within him for six weeks. It wasn't going as easily as the doctor had hoped.

"Those kids," said Roger in answer.

She tossed onto her side toward him, nudged by an idea with all her fake happiness. "Couldn't Shakey's International send a manager out temporarily?"

"It has to be me. It's my franchise. Stop making the bed jiggle." But there was something else. He was in debt. He had borrowed heavily to make the down payment on the franchise, and he had taken out a second mortgage on the house. When customers came in, looked around the empty place, and decided to stay, he would put on his Styrofoam hat, light as popcorn, and appear like a puppet behind the bar, saying merrily, "Howdy, folks. Y'in the market for a pizza?" and start swabbing down the bar—as if he'd just opened up, as if these were only the first guests arriving at what would be a large party. But of course the party never materialized. If the customers didn't put a quarter in the jukebox, they would eat their pizza within the melancholy rumble of the kitchen equipment, the roar of refrigeration that held them all—him, them, the two employees leaning against the counters soaking up their minimum wage—the huge ovens drinking up electricity and making the aluminum disk with the calibrated rim, out back in the utility company's meter, whirl and whirl and whirl, measuring.

"Bev, it doesn't work that way," he told her, revolving himself gently away from her onto his side. "Just don't *try* to help, okay?"

That put an end to it, and she went back to the *TV Guide*. But a minute later he made the mistake of holding his breath, expecting a pang—which never came—so that Beverly noticed. She said, "You haven't had your cranberry juice tonight, have you."

"Fuck the cranberry juice. I hate that goddamn cranberry juice."

She didn't say anything. Then she got up and put on her robe.

Roger heard her in the kitchen opening the refrigerator, pouring a tall glass of the juice the doctor had prescribed a daily gallon of. He recognized the clink of the nice Crate & Barrel glassware. Then for a long while there was silence.

She seemed to be just standing alone in the kitchen. His heart went out to her. That his intuition was right—that she was having an affair with a twenty-five-year-old named Jacques—was something he found out only later. But even now there was a persistent sense of a missing piece, an uncrossed borderline in the vicinity, or of her taking colder breaths alone in other rooms. When she appeared in the doorway with the scarlet glass of juice, she was smiling, with only a faint rubbed redness about the eyes. "Now drink this," she said. "If we don't do what the doctor says, how can we make you better?"

According to the lab tests, the stone was probably composed of calcium oxalate minerals. He supposed it was like the sliding gravel that accumulates over the years in a teakettle. Its crystalline structure had sharp edges that kept getting caught as it bumbled blindly toward birth. The doctor prescribed a drug, penicillamine, that was supposed to dissolve it; but the side effects were nausea and dizziness as well as severe diarrhea. Roger couldn't go to the Shakey's at all. He dwelt within a dim den at home, where the children ventured only with a shyness and fearfulness, as if they were visiting a dying dragon. In their pajamas after their baths, glowing through the dusk of his nausea, they appeared in the posture of bashful acolytes for the ceremony of saying good night to Dad, and then he waved them away into the world. Beverly kept bringing him, like red candles, offerings of cranberry juice, and then—when the doctor changed his mind, deciding that Roger's system should be extremely alkaline—cloudy baking-soda potions. There would be lucid periods when the miasma would lift, during which he might put on a robe and prowl the house, tipped slightly forward, waiting for the pain to trip him. But the drug-induced dizziness would always rise around him again, and he would make his way back to the den, grasping swimmingly at passing furniture. He slept alone on the den couch now because Beverly jiggled the bed too much. Her motions in his vicinity were clumsy and apologetic. She was beautiful, from this remove, her clumsiness was beautiful, and behind a distancing teardrop lens he fell in love with her again. He actually stopped worrying about the Shakey's, which was rapidly failing under the management of a Shakey's International troubleshooter. According to the faint and refracted rays of news that penetrated into Roger's den, a new trainee had left the ovens on all night, set on high, so that there was a small fire during the night. But Roger was so seasick it was difficult to care much. When the Shakey's representative phoned one day to say that his franchise had been cursed with a bad location from the very beginning and that the San Rafael bank that carried his loans was going to attach the premises and liquidate everything, Roger told him he couldn't think about it, and he hung up the phone gently, with an odd sense of victory. He laid his head on the pillow and went under again.

It was two weeks later that Jacques was discussed. Beverly had left home in the morning, saying she would be spending the day at her mother's house in Santa Rosa. Then in the afternoon her mother happened to phone, and it came out during the conversation that Beverly wasn't there. A number of unaccountable absences and silences now arranged themselves logically in Roger's mind. When she came home that evening, he watched her—her adulterousness a kind of unmentioned sunburn on her face—and found himself filled with compassion, as if it were all his fault. After dinner, when the children were safely enfolded within the sound of gunfire and reckless driving on the TV sound track, Roger sat in his usual vinyl swivel chair while Beverly rinsed dishes. She made small talk. Her hands made healing motions as she laved each cup and plate in water. Finally, in a lull, Roger said, his heart pounding, "Your mother called today."

"She did?" Beverly said mildly, drying off her hands. "Just a sec." And she went into the bedroom. Roger heard the bathroom door close. For a long time he waited. He knew she was crying in there. He stood up to go to talk to her, and he realized the stone was making progress again, working its way down into the dangerous zone where, in a spasm, it might be bitten back up into his insides once more, losing what it had gained. So he walked carefully into the bedroom and leaned against the bathroom door, trying to relax himself as much as possible, trying to imagine himself a slack chute of exit.

With his forehead leaning against the closed bathroom door, he said, "Beverly?"

No sound within.

"Beverly?" he said. "It's okay."

There was no reply. Roger turned around and leaned his back against the bathroom door.

"Really, Bev. It's okay. I mean it's understandable."

After a minute Beverly said, "It's understandable!"

"I mean I understand. I mean it makes sense."

"It makes sense?" she said, her voice beginning to wobble. Why was this making things worse? He turned around again to project his voice through the door. "I'm trying to tell you, you shouldn't feel bad, honey. I mean, I'm aware that I'm not exactly..." Not exactly what? Not exactly Mister Wonderful these days?

"Exactly what?" said Beverly, her voice not at all weepy, suddenly dry. "You're not exactly what?"

But Roger couldn't answer; he was making a slow-motion lunge to sit down on the bed, anticipating a pain, which was announced by the familiar contraction—but which luckily never came.

Beverly opened the bathroom door, holding a box of Kleenex in her hand, and said softly, "You're not exactly what?"

He couldn't answer for a minute. She could see that. She sat down on the bed beside him, but at a slight distance, leaving a gap big enough for this invisible person to sit between them.

"Who is he? I mean, whoever he is, I'm sure he's a nice guy."

Beverly sighed. She was pleating an edge of a Kleenex against her thigh, hemming it.

"It's nobody. I'd rather not tell you."

"What do you think? I'll find him and beat him up? I just want to know his name."

She kept pleating the tissue all the harder. "Jacques," she said. "You don't know him."

"Jacques?" said Roger.

She didn't say anything.

After a moment, he said, "Mm."

"What do you mean, 'mm'?"

"Nothing."

But she was looking at him. He sighed. "Just the name, Jacques. You get a picture of him. What does he do?"

"He's a recording engineer."

"Yeah, and I bet he writes songs, too."

"Oh, Roger."

She looked at him, then stopped looking at him and started tearing little notches in her Kleenex. There was a long silence. She tucked her knees up under her chin and hugged her shins. She said, "But Roger, I love you. I want you. He's not . . . he's okay, he's nice, but he's not . . ."

Roger said, "I know."

She hugged her knees tighter.

After a while, she said, "This is happening at the wrong time."

"I know."

She sighed and rubbed her ear on her kneecap. "Actually it was stupid. Actually, as a matter of fact, you wouldn't like him."

"No, it wasn't stupid."

"Yes, it was," she said, and the tears started to come.

That night they lay fully clothed side by side on the bed, both waiting, as if to see where the bruise would rise or how exactly it would bloom. The expectancy was something they shared now, like when they were a young couple at the beginning of their marriage. The children were asleep.

Roger started. "I'm going to owe a lot of money on the Shakey's thing. I think we'll probably have to sell the house."

"Okay."

"I was borrowing on the house to cover the franchise payments."

"Okay."

"But, Bev?"

"What."

"Would it be okay if we separated? Just for a bit? Do you think that's a good thing to do?"

"Well, why?"

He didn't want to think about why; or even know why.

"We'll be fine," he said.

The pain had started to come with such frequency that, at night, he never really sank to the deeper levels of sleep because it kept yanking him back up to the surface on its embedded hook. So in the daytime his bones ached from tiredness, and the ring of his consciousness shrank and bulged so that he could only focus on immediate and present objects—a countertop, a bowl of cereal, a document from Shakey's International to be signed, a picture Jessica had drawn in school. It was as if he were limited to viewing life through the queasy viewfinder of that old childhood Viewmaster of his, whose plastic against his nose smelled like comfort while pictures of unattainable icy mountain peaks revolved under the squeeze of his finger. Cowering in the den, he was only peripherally conscious of the real-estate agent's voice, which said, "Excuse us just for a minute, Mr. Hoberman. Folks, this is the recreation room, but it could serve as a child's bedroom. This is Mr. Hoberman," addressing prospective buyers, who always filed past reverently, like gentiles in some weird mosque. It got so he didn't even lift his eyes. When Beverly had packed him into the Toyota and driven him to the Kaiser Medical Center for one of his consultations, the doctor sat down and clicked his tongue, reviewing a computer printout of test results, and then said, "Roger, I think it might be time for us to go in."

"Go in?"

"The prevailing philosophy is to stall off surgery as long as possible, but this has been going on for too long. It's taking a toll on your system."

Roger didn't say anything.

The doctor said, "Really, it's too bad. There's a technology in development involving high-frequency sound waves that will just *explode* renal calculi in vivo. But that's years off."

Roger still didn't say anything, guiltily, stubbornly congealing within.

"Let me just describe this operation."

"No," said Roger. "No surgery."

The doctor leaned back in his tilting chair. "Well, I'm recommending surgery."

"No. I want to go on with this."

Beverly hired an accountant, to whom Roger gave power of attorney over his affairs in his present exalted weariness. He only had to sign an occasional document that Beverly would slide into the shrinking circle of his field of consciousness. As more home buyers kept trooping through the house, he started to feel more and more like a discovered squatter on the premises, and it became clear he and his family would have to clear out.

"Well," Beverly said, "there's always my mother's place. The kids love it up there. She'd be glad to have us. Since Dad, she's just been rattling around."

"Fine," Roger said. They were sitting side by side on the living-room couch in the jerky light of the television. Beverly had cut the sound track with the remote-control unit. They both faced the screen. She said, "We could put all this stuff in storage. It won't be too expensive. And if we do it now, Jessica and Justin can start the school year fresh in Santa Rosa."

"Okay," said Roger.

After a silence, while the image on the screen zoomed and smashed, Roger said, "But, Bev? I'll move into a motel."

She stood up to go to the kitchen. Then she came back and stood in the doorway, silhouetted against the kitchen's fluorescent lights. She said, "It's this *thing,* isn't it?" shrugging her delicate shoulder toward her own ongoing penitence. She seemed to *want* penitence. There was no way of saying to her how irrelevant that was. People have to want what they want. And get what they get.

"No," he said.

She said, "What motel? For Christ's sake, Roger. You're too sick to be alone."

"The Bermuda Palms," said Roger. "I'll be fine. I can mix my own bicarbonate of soda. And I'll always be within six feet of a telephone. They have a monthly rate. I called them. I've thought about this."

"I see." She started to bite a cuticle, holding one elbow in the palm of her hand, and she leaned against the doorjamb. She set one foot atop the other, the way she always did.

"I love you," Roger said.

Nothing in the motel room was his except for the open suitcase on the floor in the corner under its heap of clothes. Even
his wallet was stored away in the boxes of stuff in his mother-
in-law's garage in Santa Rosa, so that when he took his short
limping walks around the seedy neighborhood of the motel,
his pockets were empty. The new circumstances of his life
—the telephone without a dial, the small wrapped soap, the
stiff sheets and rough granular towels, the sandpaper daisies
stuck to the tub's floor, the view outside onto the motel's
grimy marquee announcing water beds and cable TV—
everything provided the pleasant abrasion of anonymity. It
was his cure. He spent most of the time sitting on the floor.
The constant ache focused his mind. Sometimes he was interrupted, by the accountant phoning to say that the buyers
for his house had arranged financing, or that Shakey's International had paid the first installment of his franchise
return, or that the land on Mount Shasta had been sold at
a loss, or that State Farm's cashed-in policy had paid a small
refund. Or Beverly came by with the kids, who fidgeted and
brought him small rehearsed bulletins from kindergarten or
the playing field. But mostly his head was raised in visu-
alizing a very specific pain as he sat alone on the floor. His
fingers idly plucked and whorled the yarns of the carpet,
which were waxy with the sweet filth of the freeway filtering
in over the years. The pain was steady, a boulder. And then
at times there was the ecstasy, the orgasmic scoop. It made
him stagger up. The bathroom's white porcelain, cool as
heaven, loomed toward him. He never turned off the bedside
lamps. He had stopped sleeping and waking at the usual
hours. Day or night, he would doze for periods, kneeling or
cross-legged. What was sleeping, what waking? If the pain
let up for a while, he might walk out to the 7-Eleven on the
corner. When he thought of Beverly, he wished he could get

a message to her, that he loved her. Then the rough twine in his guts kept jerking, and he would stagger up toward porcelain. If he imagined this agony going on and on indefinitely, he pictured himself outside, in the shelter of the rear wall of the 7-Eleven—there was something almost cozy about the picture—hunkering down among the diamonds of shattered windshield glass and the concrete tire stops and the stacked plastic milk-carton crates by the Dumpster where the south sun would be warm even in winter. And then, when the pain came back, he couldn't think about anything for a while. The floor of the bathroom rose up, a raft he could cling to, cool on the forearm, the forehead. The pain kept pushing at his middle until, like bliss, it made him stop resisting it and go limp and let it stir him and fold him. Bracing himself, he was a stanchion in the earth. And then suddenly it was over. It was a translucent grain that held the light. As soon as he saw it, he fell asleep dreamlessly on the bathroom floor. When he woke up, he remembered he had passed the stone. It was all over. He sat up slowly, with a sensation of brokenness, and of mending.

He got up on his feet, testingly, and felt just fine. He pushed his shoulders back, away from the habitual curve of molding himself around the boulder. Which had now disappeared. Everything was before him. How *quiet* everything was! He put on some new clothes, which rustled.

It was a tiny dull jewel, not so sharp edged as he'd imagined. A soft dawn was trapped inside. Carrying it in his hand in his pocket, he walked out his door and into the parking lot. It felt like midmorning, judging by the sun angle and the activity in the neighborhood. But he didn't know which day of the week. He started walking in the direction of the freeway, carrying the stone in his hand. What should he do with it? He could save it in a jar and show it to people, ridiculously. Or just throw it away; just toss it on the construction site beside the freeway, where it would be churned under in the original surf of earth. He wanted to show it to Beverly, which was probably ridiculous. He just kept walking, diagonally out of the parking lot, north toward the freeway, epaulets of sun on his shoulders weighing him to relaxation. If he kept walking along the frontage road, he would eventually go past the Shakey's, now owned by somebody else. The smell of the earth of the construction site in the warm sun rose to him like fresh-baked bread, and he stopped at the curb of the frontage road and just stood there, at the edge of the freeway, holding out in the palm of his hand this new stone.

SO FAR YOU CAN'T IMAGINE

●

Susan Dodd

"IT JUST GOES ON AND ON." Schachter, elegizing the latest tumble of his daredevil heart, shoved his cuffed fur hat down lower on his perspiring brow. The skull-shaped pelt, souvenir of his diplomat-father's glory days in the Moscow embassy, was snow dampened and spiky. It wreathed Schachter's sorrowing face like a crown of thorns. In the roseate light he might have been sweating blood.

Boston was writhing in the grip of a record-breaking cold spell, shared misery become the local claim to fame and mender of fences. Out on Boylston Street, blue bloods succumbed to a contagion of empathy, scattering coins behind them as they ran to waiting cars. The vox populi was a wheeze.

The Japanese restaurant was overheated, but the chill of incompletion lodged in Schachter's dank and salty bones. "Does despair become me, do you think?" he asked.

Monica, his former therapist, who had been forced to refer him elsewhere when Schachter insisted she was his best friend, leaned forward, her small succulent bosom resting on the edge of the black-lacquered table. She wore a patterned sweater of gray and salmon. It matched the sushi on the plate between them.

"Schach, Schach." She shook her head. "May I ask an impertinent question?"

"Does the Mona Lisa ask leave to luminesce?" Schachter had recently made a brief but ambitious expedition through Europe's major museums, where beautiful women with time on their hands were said to loiter. He'd returned without acquisition, another illusion dashed on *fin de siècle* rocks. Cultured women were all in offices now, it seemed, even in Paris.

"Is that a word?" Monica asked. "Luminesce?"

"Allow me my superior vocabulary, at least," Schachter pleaded. "Your impertinence . . ."

"What is it exactly . . ." Monica chewed thoughtfully on a shred of tentacle for a moment. "I mean, do you know, really, what it is you're looking for?"

"Shouldn't that be obvious?"

"Who to?" Monica said.

Schachter winced at her laissez-faire grammar. She knew better. "You *are* impertinent," he said.

"I used to get paid for it." Her inquisitive bosom nosed closer to the sushi. Her green eyes glistened. "You used to give me less lip."

"Budgetary considerations," Schachter said.

"Are you going to answer me?"

"Though it pains me to state the obvious." He nodded. "I am looking for love."

"Don't be simplistic." Monica smacked her faux ivory chopsticks down on the table, creating turbulence in the pools of soy sauce. Schachter watched an island of wasabi sink.

"Why not?" he said. "Isn't the desire ... elemental?"

"I hate it when you whine."

"So do I," Schachter confessed. He poked the tip of a chopstick into a dab of green paste on his plate, then lifted it to his mouth. When his eyes welled up, he looked like a child on the verge of a tantrum. "My heart may be a little slovenly, but its longing is impeccable."

"Oh, please," Monica said.

"Love," said Schachter, still sucking on the chopstick. "Is it so much to ask?"

Monica drew back into her chair, her bosom departing from the table. Her small pale face looked icy. "Maybe it is," she said, "when you've got everything else."

Schachter, the youngest vice president of Boston's largest bank, had the grace to look abashed. He owned a three-bedroom condo overlooking the Charles, not to mention the house on the Vineyard his maternal grandparents had bequeathed him. Monica was still subletting a Somerville studio. He understood her bitterness.

But she really wasn't, Schachter thought, any great shakes as a therapist.

His friends Grayson and Boyd, being in love, were much more inclined to sympathy. Grayson, a balding man of fifty-two with the body of a high-school gymnast, was a CPA. He'd met Boyd English, now twenty-seven, two years ago, when the temp agency Boyd worked for had sent him over to help Grayson through the last few weeks of the tax rush. Grayson had been married at the time, a cordial union of twenty-five years that had produced two sons, a granddaughter, and a painstakingly restored farmhouse in Concord.

"When he turned twenty-six," Grayson had once told Schachter while massaging Boyd's neck, "the worst was over statistically. I'd never again be twice his age." His fine pale hands lowered to knead his lover's shoulders. "Quel relief! You can't imagine."

Boyd and Grayson had been living together for less than a month when Schachter had made their acquaintance in the courtyard of the Isabella Stewart Gardner Museum. It was March. The Fenway was gray and sodden. All the flowers in the atrium were white. Grayson could call each blossom and leaf by name, which was a good conversation starter. (Schachter, in concert with his expansive hopes, made it a point to be interested in everything then, even when heartbreak was fresh. You never knew when one thing might lead to another.) Boyd and Grayson had captured his attention because, though they offered no graphic illustration, they were so palpably in love.

"Grayson and Boyd?" Schachter had said without forethought when, after much botanical chitchat, they'd introduced themselves. "You sound more like a Beacon Hill law firm than a couple."

It was, as it turned out, the first time the two had been acknowledged as such by anyone besides themselves and the rather seedy divorce lawyer Grayson's wife had hired. Schachter's one-liner had seemed to the lovers a blessing upon their union, and they accorded him on its basis familial devotion. And sympathy. Boyd even introduced Schachter to a couple of the women he worked with. Love made people generous, Schachter observed, although neither of the women had panned out.

Boyd and Grayson invited Schachter to their Brookline apartment for dinner at least once a week. They served him a veritable Semitic buffet—knishes and borscht and kugel, tzimmes and half-sours. Their intent was to make him feel at home, of course. Schachter had been raised mostly on hamburgers and frozen french fries by a homebody mother who'd elected to sit out the end of the Cold War and the first blush of détente in Cleveland. His domestic pinings and a small streak of parochialism were his mother's doing, Schachter thought. Each week he acquired new tastes and bore to Brookline blood-streaked white parcels of bones and scraps for the blond Afghan hound, Farrah Fawcett, who had made Boyd and Grayson's conjugal bliss complete.

Sometimes, eating at the claw-footed library table Grayson had set with red bandanna napkins, hand-thrown pottery, and calla lilies in a bugle-shaped crystal vase, Schachter would want to weep for longing. The very walls of Boyd and Grayson's kitchen seeped love, he thought.

"So, boychik." Boyd's slender fingers were cool and tender for an instant on Schachter's steamy jowl. "You getting out? Meeting anybody?"

Schachter, abject, shook his head.

Grayson looked crushed.

"Been busy," Schachter said. "Mortgage activity's picking up."

"That's all right." Boyd slipped two pieces of rugalach onto Schachter's dessert plate, which was brown and speckled like a trout. "These things take time, sweetheart."

Grayson, his smile melancholy with memory, nodded.

Boyd touched his lover's wrist. "You've got to look in some pretty unlikely places," he said.

"Not to mention right under your nose." Grayson gave Boyd a deep loving look.

Schachter, pained, looked down at his lap. Farrah Fawcett, her narrow chin laced with drool, rested her head on Schachter's green wide-wale corduroy knee. Her eyes were liquid with yearning.

"Is it all right to give her one of these cookies?" Schachter said.

The Brookline men's group Schachter had joined in October suspended meetings in late May, just when he was on the brink of a breakthrough, he thought: at the last session he had almost brought himself to tears. Eight of the twelve members and the "facilitator" were tied up with a softball league. Schachter was lukewarm about sports. He wondered what he should do next, now that his Wednesday nights were about to go begging.

A woman he'd taken out to dinner—once, then never seen again—had told him about a class she'd taken the previous summer at the Harvard Extension School. She'd met a lot of bright, interesting people, she said. Schachter couldn't recall the woman's name—a flower, he thought. Daisy? Rose? No, something less common, like Dahlia or Larkspur. She had not, apart from her availability and a set of bracelets made from knotted elephant hair, been a memorable encounter. But Schachter remembered her when, sitting alone in a Cambridge café, he came upon a schedule of summer classes among the litter left on his table.

The course he chose (rather capriciously, he'd have to admit) was "Oral History: A Practicum." Schachter imagined balmy July nights in a dark, cool stone building with wide-open windows, reviewing videotapes of *Roots* as he sat surrounded by serious women in sandals and sundresses and light perfume.

The first class, however, swiftly divested Schachter of this propitious scenario. There were only seven in the class, which met in a stuffy cubicle in the basement of one of Harvard's more obscure libraries. Schachter and the professor, a rather plain, slight woman with a prow-shaped profile and odd ethnic clothes, were the only two in the room much under sixty.

The purpose of the class, Professor Geller explained in a voice Schachter sometimes had difficulty hearing, was to learn interviewing techniques. Although this was in no way what he'd had in mind, Schachter did not drop the class. He entertained some hope that it might, at the very least, make him a better conversationalist.

By the third week, Schachter was the only student in the class who had not begun interviews for the term project. His failure to so much as envision its scope made him feel as if he was in the hot seminar room under false pretenses.

Professor Geller spoke in a low, rapid voice that sometimes quivered with intensity. Schachter listened desperately to her lectures, hoping for a clue to her incomprehensible zeal, to his own opaque enthusiasms and possibilities. Personal stories were the true repository of human history, she said. "And sometimes"—her voice wobbled precariously—"it seems we have so little else to leave our children, their children . . ."

Several of Schachter's elderly classmates nodded sadly.

Looking down, Diane Geller fumbled with a small stack of note cards for a long, awkward moment. When she lifted her head, her dark eyes were skittish and moist.

"Maybe now's a good time for our break," she said.

During the fifteen-minute recess, the professor, who usually stayed to chat, disappeared. Schachter used the time to question his classmates about their plans. Jessica Katz knew an artist who had spent two years of her childhood in Terezin. Mrs. Yuan was writing a biography of her pastor, who had served as a missionary in Seoul. Mr. Grimes was interviewing residents of a local convalescent home about the Depression. Harriet Phillips had already made two trips to Alabama to record the scrambled memories of a hundred-year-old great-aunt, the daughter of slaves, and Martin Tilley had been interviewing homeless Vietnam vets for five years. He'd started out hoping to meet someone who'd known his son, still "missing in action" after twenty-four years. But the project "got bigger than both of us," Tilley said. He was taking the class, he told Schachter, because his narrative lacked shape.

"I know what you mean," Schachter said. "I hear you." He turned to Eileen O'Bannon, a plump and bashful woman of eighty or so. "And yourself, madam?"

Mrs. O'Bannon, her blue powder-puff eyes evading Schachter's gaze, blushed mightily. " 'Tis a somewhat rare circumstance, mine," she confessed at last.

"Oh?" he said. Schachter pictured Mrs. O'Bannon waddling through the Combat Zone in the wee hours, a mottle-covered composition book in hand, as she pursued fallen women with unrelenting curiosity and motherly chiding.

Mrs. O'Bannon shrugged, then looked down at the perforated uppers of her white orthopedic shoes. "I looked after the Kennedy youngsters a bit," she allowed.

"Ted and Joan's?" Schachter's smile felt arthritic.

The old woman shook her head.

Schachter waited.

"Caroline and John-John drop by now and then," she whispered. "On the way to Hyannis, you know." She sounded so penitent Schachter wanted to tell her to say ten Hail Marys and let up on herself.

"I'm not much help, I'm sure," Mrs. O'Bannon said.

"Au contraire, dear lady," Schachter said. "You are an inspiration."

Schachter began to view both himself and everyone he knew as woefully ... well, *limited.*

Monica was all over him, of course, when he owned up

to this. "Christ," she said, "you're such a defeatist. Not to mention supercilious. Limited?" She made a sound of disgust that seemed shockingly crude coming from a mouth that resembled a rosebud.

Schachter sighed. "Thirty-six years of hoping for the best." He shrugged. "So maybe I'm a little jaded."

Monica's laugh was heartless.

"It's too late now to drop the class," Schachter said.

"So what about your father?"

"What, he should write me an excuse?"

"He should give you an interview, meshuga. My God, that fabulous career, cooling down all those foreign hot spots . . ."

"Please." Schachter transformed the word into a groan. "I'd be listening for years."

"Would it kill you," Monica snapped, "to listen for a change?"

"I had a highly infectious childhood," Schachter reminded her. "My hearing is impaired."

"Well, your listening is, anyhow."

"What the hell kind of therapist are you, anyway?"

"Confrontational." She grinned.

"Great. Maybe *you* ought to talk to my father."

"I'd be delighted."

"Forget it," Schachter said. "Besides, he's down in Palm Beach, writing his memoirs."

"So fly down for a weekend."

"I'm not talking transportation," Schachter said. "I'm talking commerce. You think he's going to give me what Farrar and Straus are willing to pay for? He's already got an advance."

"My God, Schach, he's your *father*."

"He's in love," Schachter said. "Some goy divorcée. From the upper crust of Omaha yet."

"Don't tell me you're jealous?"

"My mother's remains are still tepid. Remember her? The wife who hung around Cleveland waiting for him for twenty years?"

"Your mother," Monica said, "died six years ago. I remember it was '89 because you were—"

"Are you planning a foray into privileged territory?" Schachter said. "My case records are sealed. Besides, my father—"

"The man's—what, seventy-five? How long is he supposed to hold out for the filial blessing?"

"You know, Monica," Schachter said, "you could seriously start to annoy me."

"Good thing I'm not your therapist, huh?" she said.

In sheer desperation, Schachter spent a day making plans to interview Grayson and Boyd. A love story for the nineties, he thought . . . the changing social fabric of New England . . . *yes!* And they would love to talk, would never make a mockery of his interest or misconstrue his motives.

But when Schachter started drawing up a list of the open-ended questions he'd ask them, he balked. It was just . . . too personal. And more than he really cared to know, when you got down to it. I need a stranger, he thought. I can't go into this with a vested interest.

Professor Geller, who had asked to be called Diane (with the result that no one in the class called her anything), arrived late that week, looking wan and flustered. Her apologies seemed a little panicky, Schachter thought. He empathized. He was feeling a little panicky himself. After tonight the course was half over. He was going to have to talk to her.

As always, Professor Geller spent the first half hour lecturing on technique—how to gain the subject's confidence, how to handle defensiveness, how to engender intimate conversation without breaching the proper distance, how to help the respondent regain focus after a digression. "You want to leave room for things to develop," she said. "But not let them get away from you."

"I have a question," Schachter said.

"Yes?" Professor Geller looked distracted.

"What if a person is..." Schachter's stubby fingers picked the air below his chin for the proper word. "I mean, what if they're boring?" he said.

The flush that rushed up Diane Geller's neck and engulfed her face filled Schachter with dismay. She thinks I mean her, he realized. His own face felt overheated and damp.

"Well." Professor Geller's wounded eyes fluttered around the edges of the seminar table. "Do any of you have suggestions for that?"

Mr. Grimes cleared his throat, opened his mouth, then shut it again.

No one would look at Schachter.

After a terrible moment, Mrs. O'Bannon raised a timid hand.

"Yes, Eileen?" Professor Geller smiled with relief.

" 'Tis my own feeling," Mrs. O'Bannon said, "that boredom's a thing in the ear of the beholder." She gave Schachter a sidewise but scathing glance.

One of the men stifled a laugh.

"Yeah," Schachter said humbly. "I guess that's right."

In the second half hour, when they practiced interviewing each other, Schachter was cast in the role of a philandering politician while Harriet Phillips fired questions at him like Geraldo. He wanted to ask if this was history, but he didn't have the nerve. By the time the break arrived, Schachter knew his madras shirt was bleeding, profusely blue, all over his undershirt.

He slumped in the corridor, bathed in accusatory

fluorescent light, as he waited for Professor Geller to emerge
from the ladies' room. Down the hall, in a would-be staff
lounge, the others were drinking the sweet iced tea the professor lugged in each week in a huge red plastic thermos.
Tonight Mrs. Yuan had brought almond cookies. Schachter,
alone in the corridor, felt quarantined by shame.

When Professor Geller finally came out of the rest room,
glancing anxiously at her watch, her face looked paler and
sharper than ever. She was wearing a black leotard and a
gauzy wraparound skirt of some dark Indian material shot
with gold threads. She was thinner than Schachter had noticed before, almost frail. A few droplets of water rested in
the shallow depressions of her collarbone, as if she had just
washed her face. He wondered if she were ill, or troubled
by something other than him, but it wasn't really his
business.

"Could I . . . detain you for a second?" Schachter said.

She hadn't noticed him leaning against the wall, and her
smile was startled.

"Of course, Howard."

"My question in there," Schachter said. "I didn't
mean—"

She made a small hushing sound, as if reassuring a
dreaming child. Schachter found its gentleness almost shock-
ing. Then she smiled again. "Let's face it," she said. "I *am*
boring. I get too wrapped up and—"

"My God," Schachter said. "*You* were the last thing on
my mind." Then his hapless words rebounded and struck
him dumb.

Professor Geller laughed softly. "Never mind, I know
what you meant."

"Thank you." He felt like crying.

"Was there something else . . ." She paused for a moment.
"Howard?"

"I'm kind of lost," Schachter said.

"Lost?"

"I don't have a subject," Schachter said. "I don't even know how to find one."

"I see." Her face was sympathetic and much softer full on, Schachter saw, than in profile.

"I wondered, could I come and talk to you sometime?" he said. "Like a conference or something?"

"See me after class?" she said, glancing again at her watch.

"I appreciate it," Schachter said.

The last hour of the class, they watched a videotape of Bill Moyers interviewing a famous poet. Diane Geller stopped the tape frequently, pointing out the subtleties of Moyers's skill. She paid a great deal of attention to his facial expressions and posture, leaning in and out of the dark to touch the small rectangular screen. Her hands flew like birds across the light, resting here and there on the journalist's grainy face, touching the corners of his mouth and eyes, hovering over the alert angle of his head, the easy slope of his shoulders.

"Couldn't you just fall in love with someone who *listens* like that?" Diane Geller sounded as if she were talking to herself.

In the darkness the other women murmured like pigeons under the eaves.

Late the next afternoon, after work, Schachter made his way, as agreed, to Diane Geller's apartment in Belmont. She lived on the first floor of a homely brown-shingled two-flat with a porch railing and shutters the color of Dijon mustard. A bright blue plastic recycling basket full of mineral-water bottles stood beside the door.

Diane Geller answered the buzzer only seconds after Schachter had pressed it. "It's me," he said. "I'm just disguised as a banker."

"Hello." She held the screen door open for him. "Right on time," she said.

"I wanted to do something right," said Schachter. "Change of pace."

"Relax." She smiled. "We'll get you straightened out."

"In four weeks?" Schachter said. "It's taken me thirty-six years to get like this."

She was dressed, as always, in dark clothes, a black cotton sundress with red-and-purple stitching around the neck and a purple vest that looked like fishnet. Her long brown hair was twisted into a knot at the back of her neck and anchored with two black things that looked like short chopsticks. They formed a dark X just above her nape, where her skin was the translucent white of dogwood petals. Schachter found her suddenly exotic.

The room into which she led him, however, was almost painfully plain: white walls, a bare oak floor, Crate & Barrel furniture the color of sand. An old fireplace was covered with a huge rice-paper fan. Plants in rattan planters hung at each of the three large windows. Schachter, playing for time, wandered to the nearest window and examined some tangled loops of vine with fuzzy purple leaves.

"Wandering Jew," Diane Geller said.

"That's me," Schachter said.

She smiled. "Me, too." She sat down in one corner of the shapeless sofa. Its linen cushions collapsed dejectedly as she leaned back against them. "Please," she said. "Sit down."

Schachter took the other corner of the sofa, leaving enough room for three people to sit between them.

"You want to tell me what's going on?" Diane Geller said.

"Not much," Schachter said. "That's pretty much the problem."

"Could you give me a little more to go on?"

"Well, like I said last night, I haven't got a subject."

She nodded.

"And I guess I don't really know . . ." Schachter was stumbling. Her eyes were patient and encouraging. He remembered her pale pliant fingers traveling gently over Bill Moyers's face. "I'm afraid to pick one maybe," Schachter said. "I don't know."

"Why would you be afraid?"

"Getting in over my head?" he said.

A phone rang, and Schachter's whole body flinched. The phone was at his elbow, but he hadn't noticed it before. An old-fashioned rotary model, it sat, black and malevolent looking, on a small blond kidney-shaped table beside the sofa. Its ring reminded him of the burglar alarm on the bank vault.

Diane Geller seemed paralyzed for a moment. Then she stood up stiffly. "I'm afraid I need to answer it," she said.

"Feel free," said Schachter. He wondered if he should offer to leave the room, she looked so tense, almost trapped. But she moved swiftly to the kitchen and picked up an extension there.

Her hello sounded breathless. She stood in the doorway, her back in full view. After a silence he watched her rigid spine soften. "Oh," she said. "Hi." She lowered her voice, but he could still hear her. "I don't really know anything yet."

Schachter got up and examined the plants again. He kept his posture nonchalant.

"I'm in the middle of a . . . student conference. Could I . . . yes, as soon as I know something, okay?"

When she returned to the living room, Schachter was as she had left him, on the sofa. She reclaimed her own place, seating herself with care, like someone with an injury. Her face was very pale. "You were telling me about being afraid," she said.

"Afraid I can't make ordinary people interesting enough, maybe." Schachter sighed. "I don't know anybody famous," he said. "Or . . . you know, remarkable."

"And what about you?" Diane Geller asked softly.

"Interview myself?" Schachter's laugh was rough and dry. "I'm not remarkable."

Diane Geller leaned forward, her elbows on her knees, slanting toward him. "I'm going to tell you a secret," she said. "The key to the whole thing. I was saving it for the last class, but I think you might need to hear it now."

"What?" Schachter sounded cautious.

"Everyone's remarkable, Howard."

He grimaced.

"You don't like my pet theory?"

"I don't like being called Howard."

"What would you like to be called?"

Schachter looked down. His blunt hands hung like dead things between his knees. He had always hated his hands, the square bluish nails on the stumpy fingers, the tufts of reddish gold hair between the knuckles. His father's were a musician's hands, graceful and competent. He kept them manicured and tanned.

"What would you like me to call you?" Diane Geller insisted quietly.

"Remarkable," Schachter said.

She did not smile.

"I guess I'm getting off the subject," Schachter said.

"Not really." A pale green bottle sat between two glasses on the teak coffee table. Her hands were unsteady as she filled both glasses, then stretched a thin arm down the length of the sofa toward him. Schachter leaned forward to meet her halfway, accepted the glass. The water was scented with lime.

"Thank you."

"You're welcome." She didn't touch her own glass, but

clasped her hands tightly in her lap as if to still them. "I'm not very good at this, am I?"

"What?"

"Interviews, conferences . . . teaching." She smiled sadly. "I haven't been doing it long, and right now I—maybe it's me in over my head."

"No," Schachter said. "You've just got a bad subject." He set his glass down on the table. "Me, I mean."

Diane Geller's hands flew out suddenly, as if reaching for him. "Ask me something," she said.

"I'm sorry?"

"Listen." She clapped her hands together, and Schachter jumped. "Okay, let's say you've got to get to know me. It's a matter of life and death, right?"

"Whose?" asked Schachter.

Diane Geller cringed, but then waved the question away like a mosquito. "You've got only moments," she said, "to cut to the heart of a lifetime that's making me tick."

"This sounds sort of like open-heart surgery," Schachter said.

"It is." She inched closer on the sofa, straining forward. He thought for a moment that she was getting ready to pounce. "Let's say you've got six questions. Just six strokes to sketch out the contours of my life, the shape of my . . . being." She held up her right hand, fingers spread, and her left thumb. Then she clapped again. "Six. What would they be?"

Schachter just stared at her.

"What is it?" she said. "What's the matter?"

"But who are you supposed to *be*?" Schachter said.

"Isn't that what you've got to find out?"

"You mean a guessing game?" Schachter asked. "Like you're Marie Antoinette or Madonna or something?"

Diane Geller's shoulders sagged just a little. "I thought I could just, you know, be. *me*," she said.

"Oh." Schachter frowned, then brightened. "Could I be Morley Safer?"

She shook her head and did not smile.

"You're my professor," Schachter said. "I can't just barge in here and start asking personal questions."

"*All* questions are personal," she said. "Besides, this is an assignment."

Schachter stood up abruptly. "This is all a big mistake," he said.

"Sit down." Her voice was firm. "Start asking."

Schachter, still on his feet, threw her a helpless look. "How old are you?" He felt blood rushing to his face.

"Thirty-two," she said. "That's a waste of one question."

"Where were you born?"

"Pennsylvania. Two down the drain."

Schachter began to pace. "I need to think."

"Yes," she said. "You do."

The soles of his wing-tips were loud on the floorboards. He loosened his tie as he crossed from the hall entryway to the far windows, from the fireplace to another door, covering the room with a large X. From where he stood he got a good glimpse of the kitchen, gleaming white appliances and pebbled beige linoleum, all out of date. A row of good copper-bottomed pots dangled from an overhead rack of wrought iron.

"You like to cook?" he said.

"I like to feed people," she corrected him. "You're doing better, but not great."

"I don't know where these questions are supposed to *come* from," Schachter said. "Can't you give me a hint?"

He stood in the doorway, his back to her, and continued to study the kitchen. He saw a neon-orange tricycle by the back door, a huge pair of filthy running shoes on the floor beside it. She would not answer him. An open box of cinnamon Pop-Tarts sidled up to a smudge-faced chrome toaster, surrounded by more than a dozen amber vials with prescription labels on them. A child's finger painting was clamped to the side of the refrigerator with two magnets that looked like Oreos. So she was married, had a husband and a kid and a life—why ask?

"Sit down for a minute." Behind him her voice sounded tired. Or maybe just tired of him.

Schachter turned around slowly. "I shouldn't be taking up your time like this."

"Sit down," she repeated, patting the sofa seat beside her. "Please."

Schachter, slumping somewhere in the middle of what had been the distance between them, imagined that his body didn't make a dent in the cushions. "Am I hopeless?"

"Just listen to me, all right?" Her face was damp and looked almost bleached. Her stare was irradiating.

Schachter closed his eyes. When Diane Geller started to speak, it sounded as if she were slowly moving away, though he could feel her there beside him still, a suggestion of heat and weight and molecular jostle.

"The questions," she said softly. "They come from your passion. Terror, torture, desire . . . the passion that's within you tapping into the passion in me. If you are full of fear, then that's what you have to work with. Let that guide you to what's in me." She hesitated, like someone about to reveal something painful. "It's that simple," she said.

"I am afraid." Schachter's voice was fractured.

"Of course you are. We're supposed to be."

Schachter thought he heard the ticking of a clock somewhere. His tongue was parched. He remembered the mineral water on the table, but he did not want to open his eyes. He pictured the drops of moisture trapped in the hollows below Diane Geller's throat, and he tasted salt.

"All you have to do is find the . . . the headwaters of that passion," Diane Geller whispered. "Not mine. Just your own.

Longing, sorrow...they will carry you...so far you can't imagine. And nothing will be kept from you. Nothing."

Somewhere above, a baby cried. Then light footsteps crossed a room, shut a door. Schachter waited for stillness.

"But how do you know?" he said. "When you're there?"

"Ssh," she said. "Listen."

He thought he felt a glance of breath on his cheek, like warm fingers.

"Take your time," she said. "We need to believe we have all the time in the world."

Schachter, his head bowed, heard the solitary beating of his own heart, frantic and brave. The husband and child would be home soon, and Diane Geller would feed them. The days were growing shorter now, it was nearly August. The air would soon cool, and by eight-thirty it would be fully dark. She would open the windows, drawing frail white curtains over them, against the night. Her fingers would brush the lids of a sleeping child, would caress the first lines at the corners of a man's mouth. The life Schachter craved was being lived, here in this house, without him.

Beside him, her breathing was quick and shallow, and he knew she was waiting, but he didn't know for what.

"Three questions?" Schachter said. "Three left?"

"I'm listening," she said.

Schachter took a deep breath, then let it go. "I want to ask you about love," he said. "How did you find it, or know when you did?"

His eyes were sealed, he was falling in the dark, he knew no fear at all.

A phone rang, and a small broken sound came from the throat of the woman beside him, but Schachter didn't hear.

"If you didn't already love someone," he said, "could you love somebody like me? Am I doing everything wrong?"

WOMEN LIKE THOSE

•

David Haynes

Bobby and julie are sitting by the window in Table of Contents eating sourdough bread and waiting for their salads. Fresh endive in a vinaigrette.

"You think you're so cute," Julie says. She runs her foot up and down his leg, tilts her head provocatively to one side. "See over there," she prompts.

Bobby turns his head and looks where she has indicated. "Bald guy with glasses?" he asks. "That's Professor Herbert Von Hymen. Religion, or at least that's what he teaches. His real field is transcendent ritual sex cults. Little number with him there, she's his sex zombie."

"Bobby!" Julie complains, rolling her eyes, but to no avail. He has her in his thrall tonight, and he knows it.

"You see she's wearing his ankle bracelet. Don't look now. Don't. Try not to be so obvious, would you?"

But Julie does look. At the bracelet and at the professor;

at the woman behind them eating alone, hiding the cover of the book she is reading; at the waiter with five piercings in his left ear; and at the well-tailored middle-aged woman with the young man whose ripped jeans and ponytail obviously make her uncomfortable. Bobby looks, too, and they make up stories about these people over pork medallions and salmon. And more stories while splitting the sautéed orange pound cake.

When it's her turn, Julie weaves a family history for the boy and the woman as complex as a daytime drama. She imagines characters who have long since died, remarried, or moved on to another city. The men are duplicitous, or rich and wise, and the women long-suffering but inevitably resilient, the ultimate survivors. Bobby says Julie's stories are generic, that they could be about anyone. And though he has never rebuked her for it, she often repeats herself. Tonight she says the woman with the book is a divorcée from the Coast beginning a new life in Saint Paul, just like the woman with the Monet scarf they saw in Palomino last week. Bobby is secretly disappointed at Julie's lack of creativity. He prides himself on inventing whole lives from the smallest of details—from a tattoo or a bangle or a scar. He likes his stories concise and simple, like the thirty-second news teasers inserted in the evening lineup on ABC. Julie encourages Bobby to add more detail to his stories. She accuses him of holding out on her, of going for the cheap laugh as a desperate stand-up comic would, but Bobby holds his ground. Like those news teasers, he wants her to stay tuned for more.

It is Bobby's month to do the laundry, and the washing machine in the apartment building has died. The landlord, Skjoreski, says he'll fix it, but they don't hold their breath. He's got them by the short hairs—cheap rent, long lease, and a prime Crocus Hill location he'd turn over in twenty minutes if they had any complaints.

"Think of it as an adventure," Julie says and encourages him to come back with lots of tales of Laundromat people.

He loads the car and drives over to Grand Avenue, but the machines there are full, and so are the ones on Dale. That's about it for the high-rent district. He heads out to the Midway.

Someone has propped open the door, but still the heavy, scented air assaults the lungs. He has washed at the Midway Coin-Op before and, if he can't get any closer to home, prefers it to the ones down on West Seventh Street, which are sometimes full of runaway teenagers and street people.

There are only two customers today, two women. Bobby loads his duffels and basket into three washers and sits back to read a biography of Frederick Douglass.

"I know one thing—black men sure are dogs," one of the women says. The other woman grunts her assent. Though he can't imagine she means him, she says it loud enough for him to hear. He sees her out of the corner of his eye, doesn't want to give her the satisfaction of looking directly at her. It is the heavyset white girl. She swooshes from the dryer a pale-colored sheet that Bobby thinks may have once been white but is now gray and threadbare and covered with stains shaped like mushroom clouds and giant amoebas. The black woman picks up a sock that dropped from the bundle and lays it in her basket.

"Lying dogs, every one of them," she says in Bobby's direction. He ignores them and goes back to his book.

When it is Bobby's month to wash, it is Julie's month to iron. He helps her fold and stack things in the basket to put away in the bedroom later. *The Cosby Show* plays in the background, but they are not watching. They have seen this episode before.

"So tell me, who was in the laundry today?" Julie asks. "Did you see Flo?" Flo is a bag lady who collects postcards. Julie claims that Flo used to be married to a world-famous jazz musician—whom Julie refuses to name—but that he dumped her for an equally famous actress—also nameless —and that now she is forced to live in the third dryer from the end in the Midway Coin-Op.

"What I saw was better than that old hag," Bobby replies.

"Was it that one Hmong girl—the one who has twenty-six kids?"

"It was Tammi and Tina," Bobby says.

"*Oh*, Tammi and Tina," Julie repeats, intrigued.

Bobby grabs a shirt to hang up and adopts his best storytelling voice. He says, "I go in, minding my own business, and this Tammi starts right in on me. She says to me, 'Them Maytags down on the end work best, hon.' "

Bobby gives Tammi a country accent. He can tell Julie likes all the details he is adding today.

"This gal's waddling all around the place like she owns it. She goes over to her friend, who's sitting there reading the *Weekly World News*. They huddle together and make some sort of snickering noise about me. They sound like pigs."

"Oh, so these wenches were flirting with you. Well, I just may have to go over there and cut me some Tammi and Tina."

"Tammi, she's this big white gal. She looks like she could take you easy. She's the kind that looks like all she eats is pork rinds and potato chips. You know, the kind my mother calls horsey."

Julie says she knows and then says, "Let me guess. She was wearing a halter with all this blubber sticking out so you could see her stretch marks. And shorts and thongs."

"You *have* seen this girl," Bobby says, though he remembers that what she was really wearing was a frilly pink blouse with long sleeves, even though it was summer and almost ninety degrees.

"Let's see, what else . . . I bet she had this real long stringy blond hair—no! Her hair was all wound up in those nasty sponge rollers."

"Listen to this," Bobby says. "She actually starts pulling those nasty curlers out of her hair right there on the table where people are sorting their clothes."

Julie makes gagging noises and says, "Tammi. And I bet she signs her name and puts a little heart right over the *i*."

He nods and says, "Now Tina, she was the black woman. Tall and thin."

Like you, he was going to say. She looked a little like Julie, too. But he doesn't have time to tell her that, because they are meeting Mike and Deanna for a late dinner down at Forpaugh's, and they are running way behind schedule.

Among Bobby's stories, Julie's favorite is the one he made up at her office Christmas banquet, where they had the misfortune of being seated at the same table with Naomi Shumacher, one of the company's executive secretaries. Everyone—including Julie—fears Naomi, who wears her tightness and authority as if it were a suit of armor. When Naomi excused herself that evening to go to the bathroom, Bobby told Julie that she was really Mistress Helga, a well-known Lake Minnetonka dominatrix who ran an all-night pleasure dungeon in the basement of her town house. For the rest of the night Julie had been unable to look anywhere in the direction of Naomi, and whenever the woman spoke Julie feigned a coughing fit to cover up her laughter.

Since then Julie often requests updates from Bobby, and he provides them, picking out Mistress Helga's clients in the most unlikely figures—local politicians, newscasters, even the principal of the school he teaches at. Bobby agrees this is his best story. It has all the right elements: pretentious characters, unlikely situations, even kinkiness. He knows that in whatever way it may offend Julie's virtuous side—the part of her that thinks it a sin to mock—a story like this one appeals strongly to her sense of justice, the notion they both have that there are an awful lot of people out there who need to be taken down a notch or two.

Tina has a little boy. Or the girl he calls Tina has a little boy with her when Bobby next goes to do the wash. Skjoreski hasn't fixed the washer and won't, at least not until after the beginning of the next month, after all the rent checks have cleared the bank. The little boy is about four years old and has tiny tortoiseshell glasses that make him look precocious and old for his age. Tammi also has a baby with her—a deep cream-colored baby with a head full of woolly, sandy hair, which indicates to Bobby that this is probably a mixed-race baby. Tammi has on sunglasses, too, and when she takes them off, Bobby sees she has an eye that is black and swollen shut.

"Are you sure it was a black eye?" Julie asks. "You know that type wears a lot of dark mascara and eyeliner."

"It was a black eye, all right. Looked pretty new, too."

Julie shudders. "Willie must have hit her," she sighs.

"Who's Willie?" Bobby asks.

"Troy's father, of course," she says, exasperated. "Dude with the Cadillac."

"Oh, *that* Willie. Nigger comes struttin' in there today, red silk shirt on, black tuxedo pants, some Stacy-Adams. Thinks he's something. He asks her for a twenty so he can get some gas. You should see all the dents on that car. Looks like it was rolled off a mountain."

Julie clicks her tongue. "Lazy bastard. Never had a job in his life. Lives off that poor girl's AFDC."

"What was the little boy's name?" Bobby asks.

"Todd," Julie answers, and they both laugh. This is funny because they know that women like those never name their boys Todd or Troy.

"Too bad about that girl's eye," Julie adds.

Bobby tells Julie that Tina told Tammi she had better take care of herself. "You know what she said?" he asks her. "She said that if a nigger ever hit her, she'd kill him."

"Good for her. And you know, I'd do the same thing myself." Julie says this and gives Bobby a look that tells him she means it.

Getting ready for bed that night, Julie brushes her hair up over the top of her head, away from the nape of her neck, where the hair is softer and not as knotted.

"Did that girl have any bruises?" she asks.

"What girl?"

"The one today. In the laundry."

"Oh, her." And he thinks and remembers and says, "A couple, I guess."

"What did they look like?"

He shrugs. "Like bruises."

"Well, you saw them. I mean, were they purple? Or what?"

Yes, he'd seen them today, and the other day as well, when they weren't quite hidden by the long-sleeved blouse. She was shameless about them, wore them almost as if they were medals. He bets she wears tank tops some days and things that barely cover her arms and her breasts.

Just then he isn't sure whether he and Julie are still playing the game, but he says, "They're gross. They're like crushed plums on vanilla pudding. That give you an idea?"

Julie turns out the light on her nightstand and rolls up in the covers. "That girl is crying out for help," she says.

Saturday they have dinner uptown in Minneapolis. Out the window are fashion plates and pseudopunks. A man—or a woman—with a tall purple Mohawk skates by. Rarely do Bobby and Julie have this much raw material, but she seems disinterested.

Bobby tries once. He says, "That woman there, the old one with the Red Cross shoes. She's Bill Clinton's secret lover. She's been hidden here in Minneapolis by the CIA." Julie laughs, but the laugh is halfhearted, so they give up and eat their plaza burgers.

The next week the white girl shows up after Bobby has begun his load. She is overburdened with clothes and the baby, and the black woman helps her to get situated. The girl sits at the next table down, opposite her friend, and picks her teeth with a fingernail covered in chipped pink nail polish. Bobby reads his book while the machines rumble and clank. In the cyclical silence he hears such things as "says he don't want no nigger babies in his house" and "ain't got hardly enough to wash these damn dirty clothes." Bobby looks up at the girl, and she catches his eye with a look as hard as iron and as cold and strong, too tough for tears.

"How do people get themselves into these things?" Julie asks at home that night. They are balling up socks quietly in front of *Seinfeld*. The game has shifted, and Bobby feels himself on unsteady ground. He wants to make Julie smile, to make things light again, but he doesn't know what she wants, whether he can, or if this is even a game anymore, for that matter.

"Who knows?" is his only answer. All he knows is that the city is full of girls like Tammi—tough little white girls, acting black, a baby or two, and no place to call their own.

He sees them all the time at school, and he's never given them much thought.

"Hey, maybe she likes it," he ventures.

"Don't ever say that!" Julie says. She snatches up all the clothes to be put away. "And don't tell me anything else about this. Ever. You hear?" She stalks away to the bedroom with the laundry basket.

"Why?" he asks, coming up behind her.

She tosses the basket on the bed. "Cause it makes me hate men, that's why."

He hands her some underwear that has fallen from the bed. "I'm a man," he says.

She doesn't say anything at all.

That is almost the last time they speak of those women. Skjoreski buys a new machine just when it is Julie's turn to wash; then it is Bobby's again, and life goes on with its usual routines. Yet he is curious about those women, and he knows Julie is, too, in the same way they are curious about former child stars and retired politicians. They want to know about them, though it isn't worth investing too much of their time to find out.

They are at Café Latte having cheesecake and cappuccino. It is about six months later, and Julie brings it up in a way he feels is probably a lot less casual than she intends.

"What do you imagine ever happened to that girl over at the laundry?" she asks.

Bobby knows immediately who she means and seizes the opportunity. He tells her he's glad she asked, because it seems the story has a happy ending after all. He tells her how, the last time he washed there, Tammi appeared and, even though she was still bruised, she acted stronger and more in control. She had brought the baby and had unloaded from a taxi what were probably all her worldly goods—two cardboard suitcases and three garbage bags, if Julie could imagine. He tells her that Tina got on the pay phone with Tammi and called around to some women's shelters until they found her a place, and he brags that he even chipped in some change for the phone calls without being asked.

He paints a picture of Tammi as Scarlet O'Hara, bravely swearing off Willie, black men, and all men for that matter. He raises a bread stick over his head to help Julie get the picture of Tammi, with baby Troy, riding off into the setting sun, west to Minneapolis. Julie can see this, he knows, because he can feel her relief, can feel the barrier that has stood between them crumbling, dissolving into the textured tile of the restaurant.

He is relieved, too, because at last the waters are still. It has been months since he has invented this story—months since they've enjoyed any other stories, either—and he is happy to have the chance to end it and be done with the whole episode forever.

The truth: the last time he went to the laundry, the black woman came in alone. They nodded at each other, and she put her wash in the Maytags. The little boy was with her, and she read to him from an abandoned *People* magazine.

Bobby helped her fold a sheet and asked her where her friend was. She looked at him as though she didn't understand.

"Girl that's always here with you," he said. "Big white girl."

The woman just shook her head and shrugged, in a way that told him she not only didn't know but didn't much care.

They both finished their laundry and left.

Sitting here, eating his caramel cashew cheesecake, Bobby does not feel the least bit guilty—feels satisfied, in fact, as if the story has had an ending just like the one he has told

Julie. Who knows what becomes of women like those in places like that? He only knows that he and Julie see all kinds of people all the time, and he knows that a lot of those people are looking right back at them and making up stories just like theirs, or worse. He knows it doesn't matter, the plots of those stories. He and Julie know who they are, separately and together.

They don't talk about those sorts of women or others like them. They don't have the opportunity to run into them much, and they have, anyway, learned their lesson. They save their eyes and their stories for the silly, the absurd, the fun: the man with celery in his briefcase, the nun with a masculine face carrying a kitten. Most of the time, it is as if the washer was never broken at all.

Sometimes, though, Bobby sees someone who is too hard to look at, someone broken by life, ragged or crippled, and he can feel Tammi's and Tina's presence, just as if they were ghosts of his own long-dead relatives. And he knows, when he sees such people, that Julie sees them, too, and that she remembers Tammi and tries to get them—and her—out of her head. He always hopes that she is able to do just that, and if she is not, he hopes that when she is remembering Tammi she isn't thinking of him at all.

LIBERTY

●

Julia Alvarez

Papi came home with a dog whose kind we had never seen before. A black-and-white-speckled electric current of energy. It was a special breed with papers, like a person with a birth certificate. Mami just kept staring at the puppy with a cross look on her face. "It looks like a mess!" she said. "Take it back."

"Mami, it is a gift!" Papi shook his head. It would be an insult to Mister Victor, who had given us the dog. The American consul wanted to thank us for all we'd done for him since he'd been assigned to our country.

"If he wanted to thank us, he'd give us our visas," Mami grumbled. For a while now, my parents had been talking about going to the United States so Papi could return to school. I couldn't understand why a grown-up who could do whatever he wanted would elect to go back to a place I so much wanted to get out of. On their faces when they talked of leaving there was a scared look I also couldn't understand.

"Those visas will come soon," Papi promised. But Mami just kept shaking her head about the dog. She had enough with four girls to take on puppies, too. Papi explained that the dog would stay at the end of the yard in a pen. He would not be allowed in the house. He would not be pooping in Mami's orchid garden. He would not be barking until late at night. "A well-behaved dog," Papi concluded. "An American dog."

The little black-and-white puppy yanked at Papi's trouser cuff with his mouth. "What shall we call you?" Papi asked him.

"Trouble," Mami suggested, kicking the puppy away. He had left Papi's trousers to come slobber on her leg.

"We will call him Liberty. Life, liberty, and the pursuit of happiness." Papi quoted the U.S.A. Constitution. "Eh, Liberty, you are a lucky sign!"

Liberty barked his little toy barks and all us kids laughed. "Trouble." Mami kept shaking her head as she walked away. Liberty trotted behind her as if he agreed that that was the better name for him.

Mami was right, too—Liberty turned out to be trouble. He ate all of Mami's orchids, and that little hyperactive baton of a tail knocked things off the low coffee table whenever Liberty climbed on the couch to leave his footprints in among the flower prints. He tore up Mami's garden looking for buried treasure. Mami screamed at Liberty and stamped her foot. "Perro sin vergüenza!" But Liberty just barked back at her.

"He doesn't understand Spanish," Papi said lamely. "Maybe if you correct him in English, he'll behave better?"

Mami turned on him, her slipper still in midair. Her face looked as if she'd light into him after she was done with

Liberty. "Let him go be a pet in his own country if he wants instructions in English!" In recent weeks, Mami had changed her tune about going to the United States. She wanted to stay in her own country. She didn't want Mister Victor coming around our house and going off into the study with Papi to talk over important things in low, worried voices.

"All liberty involves sacrifice," Papi said in a careful voice. Liberty gave a few perky barks as if he agreed with that.

Mami glared at Papi. "I told you I don't want trouble—" She was going to say more, but her eye fell on me and she stopped herself. "Why aren't you with the others?" she scolded. It was as if I had been the one who had dug up her lily bulbs.

The truth was that after Liberty arrived, I never played with the others. It was as if I had found my double in another species. I had always been the tomboy, the live wire, the troublemaker, the one who was going to drive Mami to drink, the one she was going to give away to the Haitians. While the sisters dressed pretty and stayed clean in the playroom, I was out roaming the world looking for trouble. And now I had found someone to share my adventures.

"I'll take Liberty back to his pen," I offered. There was something I had figured out that Liberty had yet to learn: when to get out of Mami's way.

She didn't say yes and she didn't say no. She seemed distracted, as if something else was on her mind. As I led Liberty away by his collar, I could see her talking to Papi. Suddenly she started to cry, and Papi held her.

"It's okay," I consoled Liberty. "Mami doesn't mean it. She really does love you. She's just nervous." It was what my father always said when Mami scolded me harshly.

At the back of the property stood Liberty's pen—a chain-link fence around a dirt square at the center of which stood a doghouse. Papi had built it when Liberty first came, a cute little house, but then he painted it a putrid green that reminded me of all the vegetables I didn't like. It was always a job to get Liberty to go into that pen.

Sure enough, as soon as he saw where we were headed, he took off, barking, toward the house, then swerved to the front yard to our favorite spot. It was a grassy knoll surrounded by a tall hibiscus hedge. At the center stood a tall, shady samán tree. From there, no one could see you up at the house. Whenever I did something wrong, this was where I hid out until the punishment winds blew over. That was where Liberty headed, and I was fast behind on his trail.

Inside the clearing I stopped short. Two strange men in dark glasses were crouched behind the hedge. The fat one had seized Liberty by the collar and was pulling so hard on it that poor Liberty was almost standing on his hind legs. When he saw me, Liberty began to bark, and the man holding him gave him a yank on the collar that made me sick to my stomach. I began to back away, but the other man grabbed my arm. "Not so fast," he said. Two little scared faces—my own—looked down at me from his glasses.

"I came for my dog," I said, on the verge of tears.

"Good thing you found him," the man said. "Give the young lady her dog," he ordered his friend, and then he turned to me. "You haven't seen us, you understand?"

I didn't understand. It was usually I who was the one lying and grown-ups telling me to tell the truth. But I nodded, relieved when the man released my arm and Liberty was back in my hands.

"It's okay, Liberty." I embraced him when I put him back in his pen. He was as sad as I was. We had both had a hard time with Mami, but this was the first time we'd come across mean and scary people. The fat man had almost broken Liberty's neck, and the other one had left his fingerprints on my arm. After I locked up the pen, I watched Liberty wander back slowly to his house and actually go inside, turn

around, and stick his little head out the door. He'd always
avoided that ugly doghouse before. I walked back to my own
house, head down, to find my parents and tell them what I
had seen.

Overnight, it seemed, Mister Victor moved in. He ate all his
meals with us, stayed 'til late, and when he had to leave,
someone from the embassy was left behind "to keep an eye
on things." Now, when Papi and Mister Victor talked or
when the *tíos* came over, they all went down to the back of
the property near Liberty's pen to talk. Mami had found
some wires in the study, behind the portrait of Papi's great-
grandmother fanning herself with a painted fan. The wires
ran behind a screen and then out a window, where there was
a little box with lots of other wires coming from different
parts of the house.

Mami explained that it was no longer safe to talk in the
house about certain things. But the only way you knew what
things those were was when Mami leveled her eyes on you
as if she were pressing the off button on your mouth. She
did this every time I asked her what was going on.

"Nothing," she said stiffly, and then she urged me to go
outside and play. Forgotten were the admonitions to go study
or I would flunk out of fifth grade. To go take a bath or the
microbios might kill me. To drink my milk or I would grow
up stunted and with no teeth. Mami seemed absent and tense
and always in tears. Papi was right—she was too nervous,
poor thing.

I myself was enjoying a heyday of liberty. Several times
I even got away with having one of Mister Victor's Coca-
Colas for breakfast instead of my boiled milk with a beaten
egg, which Liberty was able to enjoy instead.

"You love that dog, don't you?" Mister Victor asked me
one day. He was standing by the pen with Papi waiting for

the uncles. He had a funny accent that sounded like someone making fun of Spanish when he spoke it.

I ran Liberty through some of the little tricks I had taught him, and Mister Victor laughed. His face was full of freckles—so that it looked as if he and Liberty were kin. I had the impression that God had spilled a lot of his colors when he was making American things.

Soon the uncles arrived and the men set to talking. I wandered into the pen and sat beside Liberty with my back to the house and listened. The men were speaking in English, and I had picked up enough of it at school and in my parents' conversations to make out most of what was being said. They were planning some hunting expedition for a goat with guns to be delivered by Mister Charlie. Papi was going to have to leave the goat to the others because his tennis shoes were missing. Though I understood the words—or thought I did—none of it made sense. I knew my father did not own a pair of tennis shoes, we didn't know a Mister Charlie, and who ever heard of hunting a goat?

As Liberty and I sat there with the sun baking the tops of our heads, I had this sense that the world as I knew it was about to end. The image of the two men in mirror glasses flashed through my head. So as not to think about them, I put my arm around Liberty and buried my face in his neck.

Late one morning Mami gave my sisters and me the news. Our visas had come. Mister Victor had arranged everything, and that very night we were going to the United States of America! Wasn't that wonderful! She flashed us a bright smile, as if someone were taking her picture.

We stood together watching her, alarmed at this performance of happiness when really she looked like she wanted to cry. All morning aunts had been stopping by and planting big kisses on our foreheads and holding our faces in their hands and asking us to promise we would be very good. Until now, we hadn't a clue why they were so worked up.

Mami kept smiling her company smile. She had a little job for each of us to do. There would not be room in our bags for everything. We were to pick the one toy we wanted to take with us to the United States.

I didn't even have to think twice about my choice. It had suddenly dawned on me we were leaving, and that meant leaving *everything* behind. "I want to take Liberty."

Mami started shaking her head no. We could not take a dog into the United States of America. That was not allowed.

"Please," I begged with all my might. "Please, please, Mami, please." Repetition sometimes worked—each time you said the word, it was like giving a little push to the yes that was having a hard time rolling out of her mouth.

"I said no!" The bright smile on Mami's face had grown dimmer and dimmer. *"N–O."* She spelled it out for me in case I was confusing no with another word like yes. "I said a toy, and I mean a toy."

I burst into tears. I was not going to the United States unless I could take Liberty! Mami shook me by the shoulders and asked me between clenched teeth if I didn't understand we had to go to the United States or else. But all I could understand was that a world without Liberty would break my heart. I was inconsolable. Mami began to cry.

Tía Mimi took me aside. She had gone to school in the States and always had her nose in a book. In spite of her poor taste in how to spend her free time, I still loved her because she had smart things to say. Like telling Mami that punishment was not the way to make kids behave. "I'm going to tell you a little secret," she offered now. "You're going to find liberty when you get to the United States."

"Really?" I asked.

She hesitated a minute, and then she gave me a quick

nod. "You'll see what I mean," she said. And then, giving me a pat on the butt, she added, "Come on, let's go pack. How about taking that wonderful book I got you on the Arabian Nights?"

Late in the night someone comes in and shakes us awake. "It's time!"

Half asleep, we put on our clothes, hands helping our arms to go into the right sleeves, buttoning us up, running a comb through our hair.

We were put to sleep hours earlier because the plane had not come in.

But now it's time.

"Go sit by the door," we are ordered, as the hands, the many hands that now seem to be in control, finish with us. We file out of the bedroom, one by one, and go sit on the bench where packages are set down when Mami comes in from shopping. There is much rushing around. Mister Victor comes by and pats us on the head like dogs. "We'll have to wait a few more minutes," he says.

In that wait, one sister has to go to the bathroom. Another wants a drink of water. I am left sitting with my baby sister, who is dozing with her head on my shoulder. I lay her head down on the bench and slip out.

Through the dark patio down the path to the back of the yard I go. Every now and then a strange figure flashes by. I have said good-bye to Liberty a dozen times already, but there is something else I have left to do.

Sitting on the bench, I had an image again of those two men in mirror glasses. After we are gone, they come onto the property. They smash the picture of Papi's great-grandmother fanning herself. They knock over the things on the coffee table as if they don't know any better. They throw the flowered cushions on the floor. They smash the windows. And then they come to the back of the property and they find Liberty.

Quickly, because I hear calling from the big house, I slip open the door of the pen. Liberty is all over me, wagging his tail so it beats against my legs, jumping up and licking my face.

"Get away!" I order sharply, in a voice he is not used to hearing from me. I begin walking back to the house, not looking around so as not to encourage him. I want him to run away before the gangsters come.

He doesn't understand and keeps following me. Finally I have to resort to Mami's techniques. I kick him, softly at first, but then, when he keeps tagging behind me, I kick him hard. He whimpers and dashes away toward the front yard, disappearing in areas of darkness, then reappearing when he passes through lighted areas. At the front of the house, instead of turning toward our secret place, he keeps on going straight down the drive, through the big gates, to the world out there.

He will beat me to the United States is what I am thinking as I head back to the house. I will find Liberty there, like Tía Mimi says. But I already sense it is a different kind of liberty my aunt means. All I can do is hope that when we come back—as Mami has promised we will—my Liberty will be waiting for me here.

THIS TIME

•

Henry H. Roth

T H E L A S T T I M E he awoke in the sinister, glossy green recovery room, he was hugged by a pretty, flat-chested nurse, who nurtured him and whispered happily that he was all better. And she *was* proved correct. The last time there had been no pain afterward, and he was okay. In that dismal, hollow pit stop of long ago, the world suddenly was fresh and newly painted. Sunlight had streamed in. "Nothing to worry about," chirping birds reassured. "All gone," a nanny he never had gently soothed. The pretty nurse, slender, not frail, wonderfully resilient, swayed back and forth over and against him. The dapper and foolishly beaming surgeon had tap-danced in bearing a bouquet of dried and fresh flowers. Ten years ago there was a perfectly clean and clear happy ending.

———

This time, a fierce pain nailed him to the bed; the side slats barely contained his thrashing. Like an unwelcome jack-in-the-box, a stout, grim nurse appeared. For a while she perfunctorily patted his head each time he trembled and moaned. Later, when his cries and quivering continued, she groaned impatiently and politely insisted he try to be more still. Of course he ignored her. She didn't mind. She moved even closer. Exhausted, he looked away. Okay, okay, would he die soon, or would this fanciful cancer attack, retreat, hit and run, and mug him for a dozen more rotting years? A tough-looking, overmuscled Spanish punk orderly joined the implacable fat nurse. Neither foe was in any hurry to return him to his semiprivate cubicle. The orderly flexed many muscles while telling the devoted nurse a dirty joke. He cried out in pain and anger. The nurse laughed demurely. He napped, awoke, cried out again, and lay quietly in his sweat. They finally noticed him. Grudgingly, the punk lunged toward the bed; with dazzling grace the orderly spun the bed out of the recovery room and along the warped hallway floor into an openmouthed elevator. Next they exited the massive elevator, and he, now safe not sound, returned to a room that was even smaller than he remembered. Another luckless patient squirmed restlessly a few feet away. The nurse and the orderly waltzed outside the room. He felt lost. The other wounded patient, sucking a hairy thumb, slept desperately and loudly.

He stubbornly demanded attention. No dice. Sighs and grunts became his wailing chant. Still no dice. He yielded and fell asleep. When he awoke this time, the orderly had vanished; a weary nurse sat at the edge of the bed. Then a solemn surgeon in soiled three-piece pinstripe peeked in. The shy, frightened, bloodless medicine man could not approach his failed patient. Finally the surgeon fled. The nurse meekly followed. Neither had hinted at any optimistic final lab results. Quoting his favorite author, a former Nobel Prize winner and eventually a melodramatic suicide, he said loudly, "*Nada, nada,*" and added, "Nothing really to be said." Then he wept.

Each evening, a wife still thin, still pretty, always punitive, visited his shabby quarters. She dutifully arrived after work and joined him for a miserable supper. Everything she wore, planned to the last detail, quickly became frayed and drab. Fair, not fair, he thought. Both had erred terribly; their life, heavy and dark, was a constant reproach. He acted out infrequently, usually discreetly, with drinking and occasional affairs, delighted in the telling of splendid anecdotes, loved the hurly-burly party, and wanted a noisy, festive home. She could not deny or vanquish drink or sexual meandering, but, avenging ruthless dictator, she punched air and life from his public stances and desires. He was always ready to run to life; she, licking her colorless lips, blotted it out. Two sons sorted it out early, in time left for colleges in distant landscapes and never returned. They called every two weeks on Sundays, though, and their succinct letters and appropriate cards were not infrequent. He missed them greatly; she admitted nothing. They both hardened in an unfenced existence.

She said he looked better. He insisted it wasn't true. Then both were silent. They ate carefully—lonely people no longer astonished by their loneliness. She told him the chairman and the dean of humanities, among other colleagues, had called. He nodded, grinned, and pointed to droopy flowers and thick boxes of chocolate—visible tokens of how his pals worried about him and their own mortality. He knew they were all relieved that at the moment only immediate family could visit.

"You do look better," she insisted. He grudgingly agreed with her. "Sure, okay, maybe I am getting better." She crumbled an odd-shaped chocolate chip cookie. He wondered whether he was dying. What was she doing here, making crumbs in his room? Was she a bloodthirsty hyena? A vengeful wife prepared to knit, to prattle on, to make cookie messes? Fair, not fair, he chanted to himself, then felt sorry for the both of them. He breathed softly, sniffed loudly a few times, searching desperately for any odor of death or dying. Kindly, she offered him a box of Kleenex.

She left. Finally, she left. Depleted, he waited for his pleasing medicine. The newest nurse, a quicksilver erotic thing, offered superior drugs. Gratefully, he accepted—the pain was shunted away to a distant ledge, where it lurked for eight hours. Becoming drowsy, he determined to dream of his newest nurse; instead, there was another damn bus dream. He, a sole passenger in a ratty bus traveling to vague lands, was stopped at borders, where diligent guards refused to let him continue. Always he awoke to a dream image of being abandoned, sitting cross-legged under a leafless tree. However, this time he was not stopped as the bus sped past villages and cities with complete disdain for red lights, speed limits, and stop signs. When he awoke, he spotted several doctors bent over his fallen roommate a few feet away. "Sorry, sorry," blurred voices whispered. "Why, why?" he shouted back. "The man is dead." For the first time since the operation, his chest wound stopped itching. He cared only about himself. He spied the comrade he'd never spoken to being packed and zipped into a garment bag. And waved farewell.

Too soon, visitors were allowed, and like bad ideas they poured in: a careworn crowd of distracted male colleagues

—bearded, badly shaven, balding, smelling of the glory and rot of city life. The few awkward women who had backdoored into the unfriendly department were poorly dressed and categorically denied the existence of lovemaking bodies. They seemed even more restless than their male colleagues, uncomfortable this time in distress, but equally unhappy in better times.

Nurses impressed by so many professors of all ranks treated him like a ruined rock hero, a largesse he accepted humbly. Tired by all his duties as host to so many folk, he felt he might be able to sleep without a powerful pellet. So he slept lightly, sharp to any stray interruption. No solitary noise floated in from the outside, and nothing was happening in the silent ward. No one mopped to a shrill, fragmented tune; no soppy moans beckoned from the sleeping maimed; no static issued from the nurses' station. It was after three in the morning, and he was still celebrating a splendid day. At first he had shuddered resentfully when his colleagues had thronged in as if he were some hit film the *Times* had ordered its readers to see immediately. But soon the gathering had erupted into a noisy shebang. Though a party bereft of booze, food, and the most timid of love moves, it was a splendid occasion, and, ironies and cheap shots aside, he had been really glad to see and embrace every one of his dear colleagues. Tossing in bed, he reviewed the happy snapshots that so stirred him; it was impossible to sleep.

During the festive afternoon, he'd been accosted by Martin Cohen, a colleague of more than twenty-five years. The first of his peers to attain the fullest tenure, Cohen, despite his many years on earth, was still not used to all six feet four of himself. Still clumsy in his moving parts, but the wisest of observers of the human condition, Cohen elbowed his ailing comrade and asked loudly, "Who's the lady in the paisley bathrobe walking so damn fast to nowhere?" He, for the past few days gingerly tiptoeing around the premises, had seen her walking well past the speed limit for hours at a time and had wondered the same. No mumbler or hallucinator, an intelligent look to all her good features, the obsessive walker was extraordinary, but clearly she was not loony. Cohen, impatient for answers, shook his large head. "She's a find, you lucky scoundrel. I like them slightly used up like me, like us. Mark my words, look 'er up." Then Cohen rambled about his newest grant proposal and bored the both of them.

Afterward, she, still devoted wife of pain and anguish, had looked at him shrewdly, nervously, as if he'd been caught stumbling in from boisterous times, and he'd foolishly spilled out recent anecdotes that displeased and rankled her. Therefore she'd eaten her dinner sparingly and left early. Then both his sons, as if sensing her early exit and a lightening of the mood, called and reassured him, as he did them, how much they still cared.

It was almost four o'clock now. As he continued playing back the afternoon images, it was the woman in the paisley bathrobe's speedy hikes around the floor that flooded his landscape.

"Walk with you?" he asked a morning or two later. She nodded and bid him welcome. She didn't appear put off or surprised, but neither did she offer to shake hands when he introduced himself. He understood touching would come later.

They ambled along, conversing like old friends catching up on recent news. His was cancer of the left lung; she had lost two breasts. Her gray eyes narrowed but did not tear when she said brightly, "I'm not forgetful. They're not misplaced boobs, you understand. They're gone." Unable to reply, though still the concerned suitor, he scanned the lady, and her body remained not uninteresting, indeed looked promising. She, as if sensing a careful scrutiny, posed but for an instant and then went marching off again. "It's doctor's orders to walk and keep walking, acquire a new balance to compensate for my loss." He nodded sagely this time. "I was never full breasted at all, but the body fiercely mourns all losses, and punishes by making me stumble and forces my shoulders and back to sag."

"No," he argued. "You're fine. You walk better than a queen."

She bowed.

He insisted, "We're both fine," and vainly attempted to keep pace with her jaunts.

She turned to him. "My, you were popular two days ago."

"Proof of popularity," he defined, "is if the curious return."

She laughed. "No one's curious about me at all."

"Who've you told?" he wisely asked.

She smiled thinly. "I've no wish to boast about dying."

He looked away as if he might cry. She touched his shoulder. "Walk with me."

He desired only time alone with her. Gruff with any boorish visitors, he tolerated little small talk, insisting he required several naps in the afternoon, and his wife and he no longer ate together. Both were relieved. All the other times of day and night, he and the woman roamed the wards of the hospital. The eight floors held no secrets and became their countryside.

Already they were nostalgic. How did they become friends so quickly? They were both very shy, yet for once they lunged with boardinghouse reaches toward a center. Trust was immediate; confessions flowed like confetti and twirling banners. Nothing shocked or frightened them about each other. Both were obsessive, careful people, chewing over life happily and ruthlessly. So they walked, gossiping about the doctors, the nurses, their own concerns, their past and the present, not daring yet to peek into the future.

Once he said in delight, "We can have breakfast and lunch every day 'til Blue Cross interferes."

She clucked, walking off, not teasing now, "And you have a patient wife in the wings for supper if you wish."

Angry too, he let her walk away, knew she must retrace her steps. When she returned, he was at her side like a puppy.

"Be forgiving," she apologized. "I'm ill."

He said, "I want to have supper with you."

"And to walk with me?" she asked.

Now they held hands and shocked a half-blind diabetic man who'd recently lost a leg.

Later that night the woman singsonged to him, "Married twice, next I lived with a man who turned me out when I was diagnosed. But he sends flowers daily."

"Bastard!" he cried out. Doctors, nurses, maintenance staff, volunteers, patients, guests—everyone pushed forward to get a better view.

"He needed nurturing, even though he was past fifty, and I can't give him these." She pointed angrily.

The others moved in closer. He whispered, "You only need mending."

She, for the moment, looked too weary to walk. "We only need mending." Then she sped off. He followed slowly. The audience left quickly. He knew he'd catch up or she'd slow down for him.

Another day, he boasted, "My kids called again."

"They haven't visited?"

"I told you they live far away."

"So?"

"So I told them not to come unless I was dying."

She said simply, "But you are dying."
He said, "They listened and stayed away."
"Did they always listen to you?"
"What good to see me convulse?"
"Who then should be permitted to see you?"
"Only you," he said.

It was sunset. It was twilight. It was sunrise. There was a beach, a cove, and a cottage. It was an asylum, a battered home, a hospital. It didn't matter whether it was a dream or not. All he knew was that neither of them could sleep apart. Accidentally, they met in the barren hallway—lonely, trespassing people. It was such a quiet place now, a home, with the rest of the family safe and sleeping—an outstanding image that she confirmed, kissing him. They gently embraced. Both their aching empty chests were worse after the slight exchange. Then he asked her to his room. He gently yanked at her wrist; of course she followed.

Once inside the room, arching on the bed like hooked fish, they squirmed toward one another. Already his chest leaked, the set of her eyes revealed her discomfort, but, moving slowly, they searched for ways to fold together. Finally, at a sly angle, he fastened to her; both agreed to a sweet cantering and finally to the speedy gallop. Bruised, she spent the night with him; bruised, too, he held her as close as he could. It was all done, promised and decided on.

For hours she waited demurely for him in the visitors' lounge. When he finally arrived, wan and shaken, his bathrobe a heavy curtain ringing his narrow body, she did not chastise him.

He sat gingerly next to her. "I couldn't bend all day," he apologized.

"Were you searching for something?"

"No, why?"

"Why the need to bend?"

He held her carefully. "I want to be at my best with you."

She said, "Oh, it's too late for that, don't you see? And it doesn't matter at all."

Adjusting her trim paisley robe, she leaned to draw him up to her side, and, giggling like teenagers, they cruised noisily about the hospital.

This time, however, unlike rowdy, unformed children, they were eager and able to accept their power and grace. And they were never the same again.

I N   1 9 7 9

•

Mary Gaitskill

I T W A S 1 9 7 9 , and Chris was at his parents' house
in Saratoga, doing nothing. Usually, at this time of year, the
fall, he and his girlfriend–Frisbee partner would be storming
across the country in their truck doing Frisbee acts in high
schools, colleges, or anyplace else that would pay them. But
Jenny had throat cancer, and she was lying in a hospital in
Canada with tubes up her nose. She was only twenty-six,
and the cancer made her furious. It made her so angry that
she didn't even want to see him until she got better. Even
if it hadn't been for the cancer, he wasn't sure they'd be
driving around in their Frisbee truck. He'd been playing
Frisbee professionally for seven years, and he was beginning
to wonder if it was maybe a dumb thing for a thirty-one-
year-old to be doing.

His parents were in Florida, so he was in the house alone,
answering the phone, taking in the mail, and listening to

the heater click off and on. He hadn't come to house-sit; that was an excuse. He'd come for refuge, to lie around watching TV and eating the snack foods he knew his parents would leave behind. He had spent most of his time in the rec room watching TV and drinking beer, his arm in a bag of potato chips, thinking melancholy and disconnected thoughts.

In this suspended state he thought of Elin.

He had met her in Canada in '72, shortly after he'd deserted the army. He had been twenty-four years old. He had been living in Toronto for six months, in a broken-down filthy boardinghouse, with John, his best friend since high school, who was a draft evader. The landlord was a pimp who lived on the top floor with a group of other pimps and a twelve-year-old girl and her dog, until somebody threw the dog off the roof. Chris and John shared a dank apartment in the back half of the first floor. The rent was only a dollar a day, so they never had real jobs. They sold street newspapers or did factory work for temporary agencies and spent a lot of time sitting on the front porch of their house. Their hair was shoulder length. They always wore jeans and tennis shoes.

People became very reverent when he said he'd deserted, and told him what courage and conviction he had. He came to believe it eventually, and thus became pleased with himself, even though it discomfited him when his mother called and cried. He didn't know what else he was besides being a deserter. He hadn't ever done anything but factory work in New York. He'd never been able to think of anything he wanted to do. The thing he liked most was to play Frisbee with John. Even then, they were good enough to go downtown to the main drag at night and find a quiet side street to play on. They'd collect a little crowd, and people would throw them money. After, they'd walk around spending their money from bar to bar.

When he first saw Elin, she was standing on the street selling roses out of a small basket. She was taller than average, but so slender and small boned that she seemed little. Her wrists stuck out of her big sweater like a bird's ankles. Her thin blond hair was scattered down her back. She wore a skirt made of old blue jeans and various scraps of bright material that dragged the ground collecting public dirt. Her face was very young, with a full, wide mouth and large gray eyes that were distant but observant. She was pretty, but he didn't notice her until one night when she stopped to watch him play Frisbee. She stood there and stared at him with a look so direct and probing it seemed to split her quiet face, revealing something strange and fierce.

He looked for her when they'd finished collecting the money, but she'd gone. He didn't see her again until a month later. She was on the street selling flowers, in a long cotton skirt and a wrinkled pullover that came up to her chin. She was standing outside a bar and laughing with a middle-aged black man. When she saw Chris, she nestled in her wrinkled sweater and, still smiling from her laughter, stared at him with the same abrupt probe that was so startling in her child's face.

They went to Toronto Island with a brown bag of cheese sandwiches and three peaches. He was surprised at her quiet awkwardness. She didn't show him her odd stare; she glanced at him sideways when she spoke, like a bashful kid. Her voice wasn't the dizzy rush of sound he'd expected from a teenager with a cute face. It was soft and measured, almost flat, except for the odd inflections that stuck out from the rest of her speech and made her sound suddenly squeaky and vulnerable. At first he was disappointed. But when they talked, she began to surprise him, as she had the first time she stared at him. She spoke confidingly in her flat, babyish voice, as if she were reaching out to hold his hand. She was sixteen years old and, coincidentally, she was from New York State. She had run away from home when she was fourteen because her parents had wanted to put her in a mental hospital.

"Was it because you're a freak?" he asked admiringly.

"I don't think so," she said firmly. "Lots of kids were freaks and did drugs. I think it was because I'm really different, and they could tell. I wasn't being rebellious. Authorities never care if you're rebellious. I think they like it, in fact. But they hate it if you're really different."

"Everybody likes to think they're different," he said.

"No they don't."

A month later, she came to live with him in the boardinghouse. When John spent the night at his girlfriend's, they had the whole apartment to themselves until late the next afternoon. They could sit across the table from each other naked while they ate one of Chris's tuna-noodle casseroles. They could take acid or Quaaludes and listen to John's albums. They could go up to their bunk-bed lair hours before dark.

They were near the ceiling in the top bunk, and the apartment was close, so they were surrounded by lush smells, from kitchen and bathroom, body and bed. He didn't mind the warm smells; they were like a bower of leaves that kept them from the harsh cleanliness of the outside world. When he held Elin in his arms, he smelled her armpits, her crotch, even the sticky perfume of her belly button, the smell he could never decide was sweet or nasty but was always on her, because her navel was freakishly deep and couldn't be completely cleaned. Her smells reminded him of a newborn animal that didn't know about embarrassment yet.

They could talk for hours. She told him that she'd been an ugly kid who wore blue plastic glasses. No one wanted her on their team; she could never hit the ball. She never wanted to play their dumb games anyway. She told him how cruel her parents were, especially her father. How they'd sent her to school after school, how she'd gotten kicked out of all of them, until they put her in a detention center. "It's not that they don't love me," she explained. "They're just sort of crazy and helpless, and they didn't know what to do with me. My mother sends me long letters telling me how much she loves me." She told him about hitchhiking around the country, about how she'd been hurt by men who'd used her, how she'd learned to take care of herself the hard way.

He told her about being a skinny suburban kid with tight pants and cleats on his shoes. He and his friends dragged girls around the playground by their hair and beat up fat boys and queers. They roamed the deserted netherworld of model developments, spray-painting garages and shattering windows, sometimes breaking into the houses so they could screw girls on the beds. He told her about his first girlfriend, Maureen, a leggy thing with a runny nose and black eyeliner. He told her how all his friends grew up and got fat or alcoholic or successful in businesses like carpeting or refrigerators, how he didn't want to do anything but play Frisbee. He even told her the truth about deserting the army. "It wasn't because I was against the war, although it did seem pointless to me. I just didn't want to wear those ugly uniforms and cut my hair that ugly way and be with all those dumb guys. You know when I knew it? When we were out doing drills, and this chipmunk ran across the field, and the sergeant pointed at it, yelled, 'Kill!' and all these guys charged it, screaming and shit. I was, like, oh, man."

She looked at him and her eyes flickered, as if something inside them had darted in a particular direction. "You are like a cat or a wolf," she said slowly. "You're all impulse, and that is very pure."

He'd thought it was a strange thing to say, but he liked it. He wasn't so sure about some of the other things she said, especially when she went on about how different they were from other people. She brought that up often, sometimes out of nowhere.

"Why do you think we're so repulsed by the jobs and lives that other people have?" she said once. "Why is it that

I couldn't stand high school, and you had to leave the army? It's not because we're stupid or lazy, it's because everything about us is against normal society."

"Why do you always bring that up? We're not that weird."

"We are too weird, and it means we can't count on society for anything. We have to make our own place."

"What's wrong with that? Wouldn't you rather do that anyway? Look at me and Frisbee. I'm not going to be playing in the street forever, you know. I'm going to go professional. Like baseball players and shit. And this could be really big, because there's nobody else doing it. I'll have to create it practically."

She loved to talk about this with him. She didn't have such specific plans for herself. She was clear on only one point: she was going to be in a position one day to do what she wanted, be free to piss on ordinary society. And she loved the idea of struggle.

"We'll be fighting against everything," she'd say.

Eventually, John said he couldn't stand three people in the apartment. They moved upstairs to stay with Chris's other buddies, Ed, Joe, and Dan, carrying only a bag of clothes and Chris's radio, the cord trailing behind them on the stairs. It was a small room painted an ugly brown, and there were only three beds, so everyone took turns sleeping on the floor.

Elin hated Dan and called him Dan the Man behind his back. "He's mean," she said. "He's got a bad attitude toward women." It was true. Dan beat up winos, he robbed drunk teenagers, and some people said he was a rapist. He would disappear for weeks at a time into the apartment of some girl he'd met at a bar, finally emerging with a TV under his arm, sometimes a radio, too. Then he'd tell ugly stories about the girl for days. Chris didn't approve of these things. Still, there was something about Dan he admired. Besides, Dan was always generous with his loot.

Dan was funny about Elin, too. One night, when he and the others came into the room drunk, Elin sat up in bed naked, blinking like a seven-year-old at an Easter parade. Dan pulled off his shirt and stared at her sideways with flat, drunk eyes. She lay back down and curled herself up facing outward, with a curious, pleasant expression on her face, as if she wanted to make friends. Chris went to use the toilet down the hall, and when he came back, Dan was lying on top of Elin, holding the blankets up to her chin, pressing his face against hers, and telling her, "You keep yourself covered. Don't show your tit. I'm telling you this because I love Chris and he's my brother. Do you know what that makes you? My little sister. My little sister! And you don't want anybody to see your tit except Chris. Because you're his." Then he went over to his bed and passed out. Elin looked at Chris with an expression of puzzlement and affability that, in his memory, came to be a warning he should've heeded.

The first snow was wet and ugly. Elin walked around in tennis shoes the whole time. When she came home, her feet would be pink and damp and stiff with cold. She would open the stove, turn it on, and stick her shoes inside it, dangling her socks from a coat hanger strung from the main dial. Chris wore big brown boots, but they leaked.

"We should go to California," he said one day as they walked down the street, their feet swollen with melting ice. "It's warm there. We could live outside."

Chris bought a fake American ID that would enable him to travel in the States, and they got a ride to California off a bulletin board. The ride was a white van that gave the appearance of listing to one side when it stopped. They traveled with a young, shy Japanese man and a recent veteran of Vietnam who rarely removed his sunglasses and almost never spoke. Chris and Elin loafed voluptuously in the backseat, tossing fruit peels and cores out the window and on the floor. When they weren't talking or making out, Elin would pounce forward like a spaniel, dangling her arms over the front seat and straining to stare out the front windshield, her back straight with expectation.

They entered California in the early morning. There were orange groves along the highway, and the sky was fierce and cloudless. At the border checkpoint, a friendly uniformed man asked if they had any fruit to declare and took their last two bananas. "It's like saying good-bye to our old life," said Chris. "No more cold and wet! We'll eat oranges now."

It was late afternoon when they arrived in Berkeley. Backpacks strapped to their shoulders, they held hands and walked toward the campus. It was chilly enough for Elin to wear her blue parka and her red scarf. They saw people with colored patches sewn into their jeans and people in masks of paint miming on the street. Black men afloat with perfume wore turbans and earrings and little stylized fists ironed onto their jackets. Women wore long denim skirts embroidered with stars and mushrooms. There were doughnut stands everywhere.

They spent the next five nights at a youth hostel with peeling walls and mattresses that smelled like damp dogs. They emerged from the hostel at daylight as if from a secret semiconscious state and walked around the streets looking at people.

They ate in a church that gave out free meals in bright yellow trays divided up into sections for different servings. Once they went to a Hare Krishna feast in a park. It was only a pile of yellow rice and vegetables in sticky sauce on a paper plate, but they enjoyed the huge, bright papier-mâché float of Krishna as it drifted and reeled through the park on the shoulders of three bald men in butterfly-colored robes. They noticed quite a few of the church eaters, paper plates heaped with rice on their laps, leaning against trees or on their elbows with their ankles crossed, rested and replete, as though at a family barbecue.

They spent their last two dollars on a banana, a jar of peanut butter, and a loaf of bread. They made peanut-butter-and-banana sandwiches, using a white plastic spoon the disapproving grocer had given them. They sat on the curb and ate their sandwiches, and Chris said, "When we're in houses with families and normal jobs, we're going to look back on this time of eating bananas and peanut butter, and it'll be a good memory. It'll be the time when we did what we wanted and had fun."

"What makes you think we're going to have families and normal jobs?" said Elin. She paused. "All right," she said intensely. "I'm going to remember this very moment. I'm going to save it up for ten years, and I'm going to look at it and see if you were right."

He had been discomfited by this remark.

After their money ran out, they tried to think of something to do. Chris said that even with his false ID, it would be too dangerous for him to do anything legal, because of his being a deserter. Elin had never done anything to make money but sell flowers, panhandle, and baby-sit. She had always sold the flowers for florists or wholesalers, and she didn't know how to do it by herself. "I can't do anything," she said one night as they lay in the dark.

"You can do anything. What are you talking about?"

"No. There are certain things I can't do. I've been fired from every waitress job I ever had."

The next day they were asked to leave the hostel, which allowed only a one-week stay. They walked into the street with their packs strapped on and their arms full of dirty clothes, dripping socks, and underwear. They stopped at a tube-shaped restaurant. They stuffed the dirty clothes under the table and ordered pancakes. They talked desperately, the laundry climbing around their ankles like a squiggly animal.

Chris suggested wiring their parents for money.

"I don't want to ask parents for money," said Elin.

"Maybe you could buy flowers wholesale and sell them."

"I'll bet that's illegal here."

"Maybe you could work in one of those massage parlors."

"I thought of that."

"I was only kidding."

"I've never thought there was anything wrong, morally, with that kind of thing."

"Do you want to do it?"

"I don't know." She cut up her pancakes and pushed them around in the syrup until they were completely sticky.

"You haven't done it before, have you?" Chris asked.

"No. But not because I think there's anything wrong with it. I just never wanted to do it. Especially not with some ugly old businessman."

"Why don't you think there's anything wrong with it?"

"Do you?"

"No. But I don't know how I'd feel if you did it."

"If you thought badly of me because of it, it would mean you didn't really respect me."

He went with her to Executive Massage. She'd made an appointment to talk to Ralph, the manager. They'd decided that she'd only give massages, no matter what else went on in there. Not because there was anything wrong with it, but because she wouldn't want to do it with the kinds of middle-class creeps that would come in there.

The Executive Massage was on the fifth floor of an office building. It was like a dentist's lounge. Soft rock music coiled through the room. There were magazines on little tables, and women who didn't look like whores.

Ralph had a large, cunning body and eyes that skimmed

surfaces and sniffed corners. Chris worried when he took Elin to a back room to talk. Tom, Ralph's partner, stayed in the main room and tried to soothe Chris. He was a young, slender man with long black hair and a kind manner. "My main interest is film," he said. "I just do this to make money. You wouldn't believe how expensive film is."

"Why is it taking so long?"

"I don't know," said Tom. "But this is just a routine interview. We really like to know who's working for us."

One of the women glanced at Chris and smirked.

Elin and Ralph appeared. Ralph told her she should come back the next day.

"What went on back there?" he asked her on the street.

"Oh, nothing. He wanted me to take my clothes off. Then I put them back on, and we talked. He asked me about men a lot—to find out how I get along with them, I guess. He wanted to know my sign. We talked a lot about astrology. I think he's pretty dumb."

"He didn't try anything when you took your clothes off?"

"No. He told me I should try to put on weight. He probably just wanted to see what I looked like and to make sure I wasn't freaked out to be naked in front of people."

"What did he say about sex?"

"He said that's where the money is, and I could do whatever I felt like doing. I didn't tell him I wasn't going to do anything, so he probably assumed I would."

"I guess, in that kind of profession, it's not a big deal to see women naked. He's like a doctor in that way."

Elin made a lot of money at Executive Massage. They were able to find an apartment sublet that they shared with a philosophy student named Mitch. Their life became calm and easy. She would get up late in the morning and go to the massage parlor. He would get up a few hours later and make a lunch of cheese sandwiches, carrots, and fruit. He

would meet Elin for lunch outside, and they'd eat their sandwiches while she told him stories about the creepy people
she'd seen that day, how they'd tried to induce her to screw
them, and how she'd resisted. Sometimes there'd be somebody
she felt sorry for, maybe an old man with a hearing aid who
was too shy to take off his underwear.

When she went back to work, he'd go to the university
campus and play Frisbee on the sunny concrete plaza between buildings with healthy, steak-eating students. He'd
met a few of them before, at Frisbee tournaments in Toronto.
He would play all day and then go home and wait for Elin.
She usually came home with a bag of treats, like oysters and
egg bread, or cream cheese and peach pie, and they'd have
a big dinner.

Sometimes they'd go for walks at night and watch people
playing guitars or mimes doing skits in front of hats filled
with coins. They'd always see the church eaters. They felt
sorry for them and gave them quarters. Elin always gave a
dollar to a bum she called the Monster. The Monster was
over six feet tall and had a huge head. His skin was like a
red, bumpy cactus. His waist-length hair was a greasy skein.
His nose was so humped and gnarled that his fierce little
eyes seemed to look over it instead of around it. Elin thought
the Monster was always staring at them. It seemed to Chris
that Elin was always staring at the Monster.

Elin enjoyed telling people she worked in a massage parlor. "Most people can't stand to have their stereotypes chal-
lenged, especially when it comes to sex," she said.

But when the spring came and they went up to Vancouver,
she didn't want to do that kind of work anymore. She told
Chris he had to get a job or she'd move out. He tried to
convince her that they should bake cookies and sell them in
Stanley Park. They talked about it in the Peter Pan restau-

rant, a dive frequented by street whores and homeless people.

"We could even make our own baskets to sell them in," he said. "Instead of those ugly things they have in department stores."

"Do you know how to make a basket?" she asked.

"Anyone can learn how to make a basket. They have booklets on it."

"Basket weaving is more complicated than that. They actually have classes in basket weaving that last for years."

"Yeah, for retarded people and mental patients."

"We are retarded people. And we should be mental patients."

"Why are you being so negative?"

"I'm not being negative, I'm being realistic. Besides, do you really think they let anybody sell food in public places? What about assholes who'd put razor blades in their cookies?"

"We could get a nice apartment and open our kitchen to inspection. We could wrap our cookies in cellophane. Individually, so people would know they were clean."

"It won't work."

He got a job as a popcorn vendor in Stanley Park, and she sold flowers in little wire stands outside liquor stores. They met a couple named Ed and Debby and moved in with them to save money. Ed and Debby both had naturally platinum hair. Ed wore dark green glasses and an army jacket and smiled more often than not. He had come from a rich family in Washington, where he'd been supported by his parents. They'd stopped supporting him when he deserted the army. He had adjusted his life with no apparent pain. Debby was a tiny woman, recently divorced, with a broken nose and a beautiful mouth. They made money by passing out industrial flyers and spent most of it at the races. At night the four of them played cards together. Sometimes Ed would sing and play his guitar, which had "Uncle Ed" written across it in shimmering letters.

Chris played Frisbee with Ed every chance he got. Elin liked Debby, but they never really became friends. "All we ever talk about is you and Ed," she said bitterly, as if that were his fault. She spent a lot of time in her room alone, reading or writing in a journal she'd started. She lost so much weight you could see her ribs. Her hair fell out. She picked fights with Chris almost every day about how selfish he was or how he wasn't listening or what a terrible attitude he had toward women. Sometimes, after fighting with him all morning, she'd show up at his popcorn stand and keep fighting with him there, in front of people, where he couldn't get away.

Later in the spring John came to Vancouver. They spent every day in the park playing Frisbee or talking about how to make money from it. John was cautious. "We couldn't charge admission for people to watch us play for two hours. They'd be bored."

"People watch baseball and golf for longer than that. We could invent a game. We could make money playing for just ten minutes. You know how excited people get when they watch us. We just have to find the right way to package it. Can you imagine how rich the guy who invented baseball is, man?"

When they played in the park, they began to draw crowds, often made up of businessmen on their lunch breaks.

"When they watch us, it's not just the Frisbee going back and forth. It's the way we are," he said to Elin in bed one night. "It's us."

"That's because you're very good-looking," said Elin. "And you just happen to fit the media trend about ramblin' gamblin' men who do their own thing, who are too manly to compromise with the wifey and the business world. It's their fantasy."

"It's the way I am."

She laughed.

As the weather turned hot, Chris began spending late nights with John in bars, meeting girls who'd admired them in the park during the day. There was one girl he saw often, Kelly, a college freshman majoring in economics, a robust, sweatless, blue-eyed blond who laughed big and talked about everything. Sometimes, when he saw Kelly, he thought of leaving Elin.

But there were still the times when she'd come to his popcorn stand at lunchtime, smiling, a bag of cookies and fruit in her hand. He could be sitting next to her on a bus, and he'd see her in profile, her high, pale forehead with its purple vein at the temple, her sharp little nose, her long, pale lashes; she'd be staring at someone or something with that weird blend of kiddish curiosity and fanatical concentration that had so attracted him to her. Then she'd turn to him and blurt, as if it was the most exciting thing in the world, "Chris, did you see that thin middle-aged man sitting across from us, the one that just got off? He was eating his ice-cream cone with the strangest, nicest look . . ." And he'd feel full of pride and sweetness.

In midsummer, Chris and Elin went back to Toronto. They returned to their old boardinghouse, because they had no-place else to go. They found it deserted and full of garbage, but they crept in anyway. It was so hot they dragged a mattress up to the roof and slept there. They woke under blistering sunlight, in a field of antennas and chimneys, their noses full of rotting blacktop smell. A couple of Pakistani guys in shirt-sleeves were sitting in lawn chairs on the neighboring roof, drinking beer and grinning at them. As if to defy them, Elin stood up naked and walked across the hot blacktop, tar sticking to her feet, her face flat with anger.

Her expression was very different from what it had been that time she'd sat up and looked at Dan as though she were waiting for an Easter parade.

They dragged the mattress back inside, into a room that had a ghostly TV in it. They stayed for days, waiting for John to return from Vancouver so he and Chris could play Frisbee. Chris spent all day wandering the streets with his shirt off and his headband on, drinking juice and meeting teenage girls. Elin sat in the old house eating Hostess pies and writing in her journal.

One night when they were in bed, she began crying that she wanted to die and grabbing at him with her arms and legs. "I'm a nothing," she wept. "I'm seventeen years old and I haven't done anything."

"Nobody ever does anything when they're seventeen," he consoled. "When I was seventeen, I was in my parents' basement playing bass guitar and doing acid."

"At least you finished high school."

"Just because everybody else did. Besides, I thought you thought it was stupid."

"It is stupid, and I'm so stupid I can't even do it."

When John came back to Toronto, Chris told Elin he didn't want to live with her anymore. She said okay, and they moved into separate places. But he gave her a key to his flat, and every night when he came home she would be waiting for him, naked in his bed.

After she moved out, her health improved. A doctor told her she had malnutrition and gave her a food chart with bright pictures of carrots and broccoli on it. She became fascinated by healthy eating and gained weight. But her face remained still as a wall, and it was unusual to see her smile. He was aware that men no longer looked at her on the street. She was often more like a familiar atmosphere or an ever-present noise than a companion. She grew more vague as the summer went on. And, as he'd predicted in Vancouver, he and John were discovered playing Frisbee on the street.

That summer, the main street was blocked off from traffic by the city and was turned into a mall. Every kind of gawker came to walk back and forth in the mall, even people who said they hated it. It was jammed with expectant teenagers in tight jeans, hot, grinning Americans up for the weekend, men in cowboy hats and undershirts selling heaps of leather belts, women selling macramé or candles, sweating vendors pushing carts of nuts and ices, underage kids dispensing strip-joint coupons, and girls with baskets of roses. There was always a group of Jamaicans skillfully beating music out of steel drums and garbage cans. The rhythm of it battered through the streets for blocks. Late at night, drunk, mostly middle-aged people danced to it, their faces sated and determined.

Chris and John took off their shirts and put on their headbands and became known within a week. "It's the Frisbee players. Let's watch them!" They would play for over an hour straight sometimes. They never missed, even if they had to hit the ground to make a catch. People would come up to them full of admiration. "I just want to tell you, I really like what you're doing. I'm a businessman, and it's great to see somebody making money off something like this." Teenagers wanted to learn how to do it. And girls, long-haired, in jeans or cotton skirts, would just stand and look and smile.

Chris was not surprised when the public relations people from a beer company approached them. The next week, he and John went into a huge air-conditioned office building and met with them. The beer executives spoke to them as though they were foreigners. Sometimes they were condescending. Chris was sure they were jealous. By the end of the summer, he and John had become the beer company's Frisbee team, which meant that they had to do a weekly series of demonstrations at high schools and colleges all over

Ontario, wearing a beer logo on their shirts, for two hundred dollars a show.

One night a local television station came to film them. "What made you think of doing this?" asked a reporter with long frizzy hair.

"The same reasons I deserted the army," said Chris into the microphone. "There's so much compromise of values in the business world—if you want to keep your integrity, you've got to practically make your own world."

"Would you say you're a dropout?"

"No, we're just making our own rules."

"Do you think there's much future in this?"

"Today the mall, tomorrow the Olympics," said John.

When Elin saw it on TV, she said, "Oh, puke."

The next week, the *Toronto Star* interviewed them and did an article called "Outsider Entrepreneurs." A month later, *Toronto Life* ran a piece called "The Tao of Frisbee," complete with full-page photographs. The journalist who wrote the piece began paying Chris and John to give him Frisbee lessons. Even though he was paying them, he was still so grateful for the lessons that he invited them to a special Frisbee party at his house.

Everybody at the party knew about the Frisbee team, and many of them had seen Chris and John play in the mall. They stood by the snack table, eating sandwich after sandwich, answering questions about how they got the idea and why Chris deserted the army and what it was like to live outside society. Then everybody went downstairs to the rec room to watch a home movie of Chris, John, and the journalist playing Frisbee to the sound of rock music. When it was over, some of the men took off their jackets and leapt all over the furniture in a pretend Frisbee game. Chris thought it was embarrassing, so he went into the kitchen to get more alcohol. He was rooting around in the pantry when he heard some women talking about him.

"It's a pretty funny thing to do for a living," said one of them. "But he's ... he's like a beautiful Jack Nicholson. Like in *Five Easy Pieces.*"

"Yes! He's got ... romance and ..."

"You'd never guess he used to be a pimp, would you?"

Elin's voice. He heard her laugh. "Oh, I'm only joking."

The beer people doubled their fee and made them sign a contract promising not to play Frisbee with anybody else. There was talk of the Rose Bowl.

Elin began drinking almost every night. She became friends with an eighteen-year-old stripper named Angeline, a beautiful, tiny girl from Halifax. He'd see them walking through the mall together, wearing high heels, bracelets, and tight pants, taking small, fast steps, giggling behind their ringed hands, and talking urgently.

When he came home at night, he no longer found Elin in his bed waiting. She was out with Angeline. If she showed up at all, it would be after the bars closed. Once she came in at six in the morning, dull eyed and shivering with unhappiness, her skin covered with gooseflesh lace. She turned on the light and slumped onto the floor, mumbling too low for him to hear. She pulled off her dress, and he saw that the crotch of her pantyhose was completely torn out. He felt pity and contempt and something else, a strange, greedy feeling that rose through him quickly and dispersed before he could feel it all the way. She got into bed with him, still half dressed, hiccuping and cursing absurdly. He stroked her hair and murmured to her, pretending he hadn't noticed the bruise welling up on her cheek.

They were having toast and coffee one morning when she told him the truth about the massage parlor. "Did you really think I was making all that money giving straight massages?"

She swore she only jerked them off, that it wasn't really any different from "massaging" the other parts of their bodies, except for the blow jobs, which she hardly ever did.

"Did you swallow it?"

Solemnly, she shook her head no.

"Well, that's all right. I got off on the idea of your turning tricks anyway." It wasn't true, but he wanted to hurt her, and he knew that would work. "You looked so innocent, and all the time you were in there jerking guys off."

"Well, so what?"

"It's disgusting, that's what. Giving blow jobs to gross businessmen with those ugly black shoes. And I'll bet you did swallow it. Whores do whatever they're paid to do."

She stood up and planted her sneakers and put her hands on her hips. "If I'm a whore, then what does that make you? You lived off me while I was working there, and even if I wasn't jerking anybody off, it was the same thing rubbing oil over their gross asses."

"Sure. I don't care. I just think it's lame. You say you're going to piss on ordinary society, and meanwhile you're sucking dick."

She jerked her arm as if she was going to smack him, but she just stood there panting furiously, her jaw loose and stupid like a monkey's. Then she turned and ran away.

When he came back at night, the apartment was silent and dark. He walked through it turning on the lights and calling her. He was sorry he'd hurt her, and he wasn't sure the blow jobs were so bad after all, even if she did swallow it.

He found her crumpled up on a filthy orange sleeping bag in a corner of the kitchen. Her eyes were swollen, and the delicate places on her face were faintly purple. He led her to the bedroom and put her under a sheet and brought her a cup of tea. She drank it and cried. He sat on the edge of the mattress and stared at the dark room. He was still sweating from playing in the sun that day.

They fought about it for days, insulting each other viciously. She threw a cup of hot coffee at him, and he knocked her across the room. They stopped talking about it.

To his surprise, it was she who left him. It began with fitful moods. She'd be chatting with him about some movie or book, and then she'd burst out, "Why don't you ever say anything? You never have any ideas." And she'd watch him with a distant, probing look, as if he were a curious object she'd never seen before.

It wasn't a clean break. For months after, he got weird letters, hysterical phone calls, and smiling declarations of her desire to be his friend, one of which ended in a loud argument culminating in her getting thrown out of a restaurant. Then she left town without saying good-bye. Somebody told him she'd gone to Montreal with Angeline.

Six years later, in Saratoga, he turned off the TV. He still played Frisbee, but it was different now. He and John had found out that those beer company assholes had been robbing them and snickering about what dumb hippies they were. John, who was tired of the whole thing anyway, went home to live in his parents' basement. Chris met Jenny, a redhaired girl with eyes like broken glass, who could play Frisbee as well as any guy. When the president pardoned the deserters, they went to America and started playing Frisbee with Sunrise Yogurt on their shirts.

But people had gotten jaded and bored. Frisbee wasn't enough; they had to play on roller skates to disco music or punk rock. It was sort of humiliating to skate around throwing the Frisbee while some lousy PA system screamed, "Now I wanna sniff some glue! Now I wanna have something to do!" and a bunch of people gawked.

He hadn't thought of contacting Elin until now. It wasn't because he was indifferent. His memory of her was like a velvety bag with music in it and smells and bits of words, scraps of pornography, a film starring him and her, everything part of a sweet slice of time when he was a Frisbee star and she was his girlfriend, however bitter.

He knew that her parents lived in a nearby suburb, so it was easy to call them. The mother wouldn't give him Elin's number. "Why don't you give me your number?" she said. "I'll tell her you want to get in touch." He agreed, smiling. Six years later, he was still cause for alarm. He hung up and paced to the picture window with wide steps, smiling into the small, square front yard. He was surprised at the dance of happy feelings in him and at the solidity of those feelings, which were like the rush of gratitude you feel on waking from a dream to remember who you are.

Her voice had the same flat, childish sound, but it was rounder, calmer, without the lumpy disturbances he remembered. She was glad to hear from him. She was living in Syracuse, where she was studying commercial art at the university. They agreed that he would drive to Syracuse the next day. When he put down the phone, he said the words "commercial art" out loud. The words sounded pretty and spindly and serious to him. He thought they suited Elin.

He enjoyed the drive to Syracuse. He played the radio, and he sang pieces of songs he didn't even like. The sky was a bright, shouting blue. He imagined Elin sitting at a slanted drawing board, concentrating. He imagined her looking bitter and saying, "Oh, puke." The thought made him smile and faintly nod his head. They wanted to see each other again, and that made him glad. He wondered what she would look like. He wondered if she wore pointy boots and black spandex tights and what that looked like on her.

She lived in a dilapidated residential neighborhood. The houses had A-line roofs and porches, some of which had chairs on them. On Elin's porch there was a card table on which sat flowerpots full of old dead dirt and an ashtray with a cigarette butt perched on its lip. He went up the steps to her apartment feeling almost as if the encounter had already happened and he was on his way home, satisfied.

But he didn't know the girl who opened the door. He stared at her, suspecting a mistake, until she said, "Hi!" and put a plump arm around his hip—plump! She was plump and healthy, with round breasts and thighs. She wore corduroy pants and a striped blouse. Her hair was cut above her shoulders, and it looked as though it had been styled. He saw something in her expression that he remembered, but it was covered over by other things. The glasses were the worst blow, although he realized she couldn't help it if she needed them. They were large and beige and abysmally functional.

"How long have you had those?"

"Five years. It was a relief to be able to see. No wonder I could never play Frisbee."

They stared, standing in her small apartment. He saw a desk with books on it and scrawled papers and a greasy plate with a fork and granules of salt on it. She had a mug in the shape of a smiling rhinoceros, out of which sprouted dull, dense crayons. Soft gray dust slept on the surfaces of things, disturbed in places by a blurred shadow of her fingers.

"You've changed," she said.

"Yeah." He had forgotten. He looked different, too. His hair was short and his beard was gone. With a sinking feeling, he thought he saw her notice his weak chin. "You have, too."

She smiled as if it were a compliment. Most people probably would think she looked better than the girl she had been. But he didn't. She asked if Frisbee was an Olympic sport yet.

He told her, not bothering to conceal the failure. The beer men's double cross. John in the basement. The roller skates and the punk rock. How he and Jenny lived in a truck half the year and went south in the winter. How they couldn't afford to keep the dog Jenny wanted. He didn't tell her about Jenny's cancer. Who would've guessed it? Weak, pasty Elin, who was always feeling for the lump, never got cancer. Instead, Jenny, with her tough little calves and sunburned nose, was lying in a hospital. He looked at the wholesome stranger with resentment. "It's still all right, though. I'm getting ready to copyright an official player's manual."

"That's good."

"What about you? What did you do when you left Toronto?" He was suddenly so depressed he didn't know why he asked.

"I went to Montreal, then New York City. Made money stripping. It was okay."

He thought he heard an insecure bump in her voice, and his heart moved tenderly. But she didn't look insecure. She just looked friendly and curious. He thought he saw another expression, too, but he couldn't quite identify it. To his discomfort, he sensed she was trying to hide it from him.

"What made you come back here?" he asked.

"I wanted to go to school. It was easy. All I had to do was take an equivalency test. School was so easy, I couldn't believe it. After all that pain about not being good enough."

"But you said you were too good."

Something subtle moved in her eyes. "Well," she said softly, "I would say that, wouldn't I?"

A small orange cat leapt onto the desk and gracefully squatted to lick the dirty plate Elin had left there. He thought of Jenny, alone in the hospital, too angry to be afraid. "So you must be happy," he said. "You're going to be successful."

A hint of feeling slowly touched her face. She almost looked as if she wanted to tell him something true. "I'm happier than when you knew me. But I'm really lonely."

"But you've probably got boyfriends and shit."

She smiled. "Shit, mostly. People here are jerks. I'll be glad when I can leave."

When she said this, he saw the way she hadn't changed. She was smiling, but stillness cramped her face, and sadness came from the very bottom of her eyes. Then he saw the way she had changed. She was looking at him as though she felt sorry for him.

NEWS ABOUT
PEOPLE YOU KNOW

●

Robert Phillips

"MINERVA, DO YOU HAVE any news for my column?" Bryan Lee's mother asked into the telephone. It was perhaps her two dozenth call of the morning. His mother had decided they needed a second income. There were four children, and his father was a high-school teacher whose salary totaled fifty-four hundred dollars a year. Things were so tight his mother was contemplating dismissing their once-a-week cleaning lady, a black woman named Congoleum. Congoleum would clean all day for three dollars, but even three extra dollars were hard to come by some weeks.

Before she married Bryan Lee's father, his mother had been a secretary. But that was in Roanoke, a then prosperous Virginia city. He brought her back to Public Landing, Delaware, population two thousand. There were no secretarial jobs in such a small town. Oh, perhaps two or three: the superintendent had a secretary in the school office. And Mr.

Chevrolet Worthington had a secretary in his lumberyard office. There may have been one at the Daisy Flour Mill. But that was all.

So after Hortense Jones—Horty to her friends—died, Bryan Lee's mother applied for her job at the *Southeast Breeze.* At the time, his mother wondered why Horty had killed herself. It seemed most peculiar. On the morning of her weekly bridge-club afternoon, Horty had put on her best suit, gone to the beauty parlor, and had her hair permed. Then she had gone home, pulled a plastic dry cleaner's bag over her head, and lain on her bed until she was asphyxiated. When she didn't show up for bridge club and didn't answer the telephone, one of the ladies had gone to investigate. Horty'd left the back door open. At least she had made things easy for the funeral parlor, dressed in her best suit with her hair all done. Her doctor told whoever asked that she'd been depressed, but he went no further than that, professional ethics being what they were.

It wasn't really a "job" at all. Bryan Lee's mother didn't have to go into the office. There were no regular hours. What it amounted to was writing up all the social news for the *Southeast Breeze,* the town weekly. Horty's column had been called "Here 'n' There," but Bryan Lee's mother had changed that to "News about People You Know." She thought it was more friendly. Public Landing was a friendly town. Outside the town limits, at each end of the dual highway, the chamber of commerce had erected signs: IF YOU LIVED IN PUBLIC LANDING, YOU'D BE HOME NOW. There was also a diner with a sign EAT HERE OR WE'LL BOTH STARVE. It was those homey little touches that made a town friendly.

Every weekday his mother hunkered over the telephone receiver trying to extract tidbits from the town's citizenry. It was like pulling teeth, she said more than once.

"Didn't I hear your son just went off to college? He did? I thought so. My land, we have to write that up! What college

is it? Tusculum? I always thought that was a school for elephant trainers. Ha, ha. Just kidding. Did he get any kind
of a scholarship? He didn't? Too bad, too bad, maybe next
year . . ."

"I understand you and Floyd took a little trip. Down
the Skyline Drive? How exciting! What all did you see?
Was the autumn foliage out?" Then, abruptly, she would cry
out, "Congoleum, would you stop rattling those venetian
blinds with that feather duster? I can't hear myself think!"
It was important to let people know you had help.

"Peg, is it true your mother-in-law is visiting you? What's
her name, and what place does she hail from? Cincinnati?
I'm never sure how to spell that, but never mind. I can look
it up. How long will she be staying? A month? Oh, poor you!
Sorry, but I always say houseguests are like fish. After three
days they begin to stink. Ha, ha."

This went on five days a week. On Saturday the paper
came out. And Sundays she took to be the day of rest. But
Monday mornings she was back on the telephone. Occasionally someone—always a woman—would call and volunteer
an item. But this was rare. It took a lot of doing to fill the
column. Sometimes the "news" was as tame as "Mr. and Mrs.
Herbert Hastings had Mr. and Mrs. Elmer Workman for
Sunday dinner," to which Bryan Lee ad-libbed, "They were
delicious." His mother was not amused. Despite the fact that
she had a wonderful sense of humor—everyone said so—she
took her "job" seriously. She called her page the society page,
though there clearly was no society in Public Landing. In
Public Landing the residents of Tobacco Road would have
been the country club set, or at least that's how it seemed to
Bryan Lee. He was thirteen and cynical.

His mother wasn't the only family member to get a job
that year. Bryan Lee had been asked by their neighbor, Mr.
Winky Lowe, if he'd like to empty his garbage cans once a
week. The Lowes had their matching aluminum cans behind

their garage, and Bryan Lee would load them onto his red wagon and pull them to the public dump, which was only a quarter mile away. Sometimes it took him more than one trip because the wagon could hold only two cans at a time. Some days he felt ashamed to be lugging garbage down the Sharptown Highway for all the world to see. But it was his job. He tried to do it on days that Billy, the Lowes' son—two years Bryan Lee's senior and really his only friend—wasn't around. Billy had three bicycles, a collie, and a learner's permit to drive his mother's Studebaker, and he had been to Bermuda twice. It probably was beneath Billy's dignity to haul garbage. (Or perhaps Mr. Lowe wanted to help out his son's friend with a little spending money. Everybody knew how little schoolteachers made.)

Several afternoons a week they'd sit on the floor in Billy's bedroom and play games like Monopoly or Parcheesi or listen to the radio and talk about books. Billy had an entire bookcase filled with every Hardy Boys adventure ever published. Or they'd romp out back with Spooky, Billy's black-and-white collie, who loved to fetch a Frisbee for hours. Somehow life seemed nicer in Billy's house.

Billy was taller than Bryan Lee, of course, being older, and he wore glasses. He had straight black hair that fell across his right eye, and he was forever tossing his head back to remove the forelock. A spray of freckles ran across his nose, and Bryan Lee noted that hair sprouted in Billy's armpits, something his own pits—smooth and bare as a baby's behind—so far lacked. When Mrs. Lowe wasn't at home to hear them, they'd lie across Billy's bed and talk about girls. They'd talk about how Brenda Johnson's titties had blossomed into full-fledged boobs at age thirteen. They'd talk about how much they wanted to "make" Bambi Breslow, the drum majorette for the high-school band. Though Bryan Lee would never admit it, he wasn't quite sure what he'd do with Bambi Breslow if he ever got her alone and she said yes.

But it was good to have someone to talk over these important matters with. Bryan Lee's father was never around. He taught by day, and by night he manned a ham-radio station in the basement. Some days Bryan Lee and Billy would take drives in Mrs. Lowe's Studebaker. Billy would practice parallel parking or making U-turns, getting ready to take the test for his driver's license. Other days they would wrestle on the floor in Billy's room. They lunged, then subsided, lunged, then subsided. It was mindless and meaningless, but somehow the physical contact seemed important to Bryan Lee. It was as close as he had ever gotten to anybody. He even looked forward to the special smell of Billy, a combination of sweat and peanut butter and talcum powder.

Garbage days, Bryan Lee was fascinated to see what was in the Lowes' cans. There were always quite a few empty beer cans and liquor bottles, a phenomenon new to him, since his parents didn't drink. The bottles made quite a rumble when he dumped the cans, glass against tin. Four Roses, the labels said. Why would anybody want to drink something that tasted like roses? Mrs. Lowe discarded all her magazines the minute she read them—slick publications called *Harper's Bazaar, Glamour, Vogue,* and the like. Occasionally he would fish a couple out of the garbage and take them home to his mother. But usually they had gotten soiled, smeared with grease, or stuck with coffee grounds. Some of them cost as much as three dollars apiece, and Mrs. Lowe just threw them out.

Bryan Lee couldn't imagine such waste, just as he couldn't imagine it was worth five dollars a week to have him cart away their garbage, but that was what they paid him. Mr. Lowe obviously had a good income. He ran the local five-and-dime, and it was especially busy after he installed a doughnut machine up front. It was the only place in town where you could buy fresh doughnuts. Mr. Lowe also got something Bryan Lee's father called veteran's com-

pensation, because he had been shell-shocked during World
War II. That's why he was nicknamed Winky. (His real name
was Ernest, but no one called him that.) He constantly was
winking and blinking. He couldn't control it. His eyes were
always snapping open and shut. Bryan Lee tried not to stare,
but it was fascinating to watch. The winking was an oddity,
like the roof of the Lowes' house: it had been apple green
asphalt shingles, but Mrs. Lowe had it spray-painted red.
The spray paint didn't take, and the shingles had been shred-
ding red strips over green ever since. In Bryan Lee's opinion,
it looked like a deformed Christmas card.

One weekday Bryan Lee saw that Winky Lowe's Plym-
outh was in his driveway, so after he returned from his trips
to the dump he knocked on the Lowes' front door. There was
no regular day for him to get paid. He would simply catch
Mr. Lowe when he could, usually once a month, and Mr.
Lowe would peel off a fresh twenty-dollar bill from his wallet.
When no one came to the door, Bryan Lee knocked again,
this time harder. Mr. Lowe finally appeared, barefooted,
bare-chested, wearing only his slacks. His enormous pot belly
rolled over his belt.

"Oh, it's you, Bryan Lee," he said, blinking like an owl.

"It's only me."

"I suppose you want to get paid."

"If it's convenient." Bryan Lee had been taught to be
polite. On the wall behind Mr. Lowe he could see the tapestry
of Adam and Eve fleeing the Garden of Eden. He studied
it each time he came to visit Billy. It wasn't every day you
got to look at a bare-breasted woman, even if she was just a
tapestry. He knew it was Adam and Eve because there was
a big snake wrapped around the apple tree. He went to
Sunday school every Sunday and to vacation Bible school
in the summer. With her fashion magazines and her naked
Adam and Eve, there was no question that Mrs. Lowe was
modern.

"Who is it, Winky?" a woman called out.

"Just the boy next door."

"Well, don't stand there all day. You'll catch your death," she said. Behind Mr. Lowe, beneath the tapestry, Bryan Lee caught a glimpse of a woman in a chenille bathrobe. She was not Mrs. Lowe. He had never seen her before. Her black hair was long and hung down her back. It was so long, Bryan Lee realized, she could sit on it—though why anyone would want to sit on her hair was beyond him.

Mr. Lowe blinked at Bryan Lee. "That's my wife's sister, Thelma Smith, from Salisbury. She's come to visit us this week." He pulled out his wallet and produced a twenty. The wallet looked like crocodile, but it could have been plastic, something from Mr. Lowe's five-and-dime.

"That's nice," Bryan Lee said, accepting the bill. Mr. Lowe closed the door, and Bryan Lee pulled his empty red wagon back home. His mother was at the sink shelling peas.

"Mrs. Lowe's sister is visiting from Salisbury," he told her.

"Oh, really? However do you know that?"

"Mr. Lowe just told me. Besides, I saw her."

"You wouldn't by chance know her name?"

"Thelma Smith," Bryan Lee said knowingly. "She's staying a week."

His mother dried her hands and made her way to the pad by the telephone. She began to scribble. It wasn't as exciting as the twins Mary Jane Womach had just given birth to, but an item was an item. It had been a slow week, and she got paid by the inch. She had almost been ready to write up the chicken and dumpling dinner Congoleum had orchestrated out at the all-black True Vine Baptist Church.

The column was published the following Saturday. Late that afternoon, Bryan Lee saw Mrs. Lowe emerge from the house with Billy, a pile of matching suitcases, and Spooky on a leash. Billy carefully packed the luggage in the trunk of the Studebaker, and Spooky hopped into the backseat. Billy opened the passenger door for his mother and she got in. He solemnly slammed the door, walked around, and got behind the wheel while Mr. Lowe stood in the yard blinking and shaking his head, as if in disbelief.

It was obvious that Billy was moving away with his mother or Spooky would not have been along. Yet Billy hadn't even come over to say good-bye. Bryan Lee wanted to run the short distance between the houses and find out what was going on, but before he could move, Billy backed out of the driveway, and the car disappeared down the Sharptown Highway.

It was rumored that Mrs. Lowe and Billy moved to Salisbury, where they had recently gone to visit Mrs. Lowe's sister. It was also rumored that Mrs. Lowe got a big divorce settlement—so big that Mr. Lowe was reduced to living off his veteran's compensation and couldn't afford to repair the doughnut machine in the five-and-dime store when it broke down. The town has gone without fresh doughnuts ever since, while Mrs. Lowe, it is said, gave her Studebaker to Billy and drives around Salisbury in a new Cadillac. Someone told Bryan Lee's mother that, in addition to his license, Billy now has a girlfriend, crazy about him, who looks like a movie star. "Yeah, Lassie," Bryan Lee quipped. "Trigger! George Gabby Hayes! Marjorie Main!" he shouted. "They're all movie stars!"

Mr. Winky Lowe now lived alone. He stayed home, away from the five-and-dime, many days. The woman with the long black hair was never seen again. (Did she exist? Bryan Lee wondered. Or was she the naked Eve in the tapestry, come to life in his imagination?) Mr. Lowe never asked Bryan Lee if he was responsible for planting the newspaper item, but it must have been apparent that he was. Bryan Lee sensed things had gone terribly wrong. He had no one to talk to after school now. The afternoons were as empty as an old dried-up well. He tried to make amends to Mr. Lowe. Bryan Lee would tell him it had been a month since he'd been paid when it really had been six weeks. Or he'd say it had run up to six weeks when it actually had been two months. Mr. Lowe didn't know the difference. He never questioned Bryan Lee. He paid whatever he was asked. Bryan Lee felt better taking less money for his work than he deserved. Mostly he missed Billy.

Winky Lowe's blinking seemed to have worsened. On, off, on, off he went, like a traffic blinker. The number of liquor bottles in his trash increased alarmingly. Some weeks it seemed that was all there was—no remains of food, no newspapers, just empty Four Roses bottles and beer cans. Some afternoons Bryan Lee tossed a Frisbee around the backyard, pretending Spooky was there to catch it, pretending he and Billy were having a high old time. Bryan Lee's mother missed the occasional fashion magazines. But mostly she couldn't stand the look on Bryan Lee's face and his constant tossing of a Frisbee into the empty air. A short time after the incident, she gave up her society column. She said she understood perfectly why poor Horty did herself in. The job simply was too hazardous for anyone's health.

OFELIA RODRIGUEZ

●

Judith Freeman

I N T H E F I N A L D A Y S preceding my mother's death, an odd thing began happening to me. Our bodies seemed to merge and become one. After hours of sitting at her bedside, it seemed I had examined and memorized her until I began to absorb her in some way.

I became aware of this at odd moments. In the night, waiting in a chair near her bed in the hospital room, I would pull the blanket covering me up to my chin and suddenly have the feeling that I was covering her body instead of my own. Or later, lying on the bed in the motel where I was staying, I would put a hand on my stomach, and for a moment it was as though it was her stomach I was touching. My hands began to look no different to me than her hands. I saw myself everywhere in her—in her legs, bare and white, protruding from her hospital gown. I couldn't help noticing the same sheeny paleness to our flesh.

During this time—those last days of my mother's life—
the nurses were very kind to us. I think of that quite often
now. How kind the nurses were. How they wept when she
died.

"I just need to weigh you," one of the nurses said as she
came into my mother's room one morning pushing some sort
of portable scale.

My mother looked up with large, uncomprehending eyes.
I imagined she was thinking, "Why weigh a dying woman?"

I'm sure she didn't want to be weighed—not then, not
ever. Her heaviness had always been a source of great sorrow
to her. But she was weighed anyway. "You've lost a few more
pounds," the nurse said to her cheerily when she'd finished
the task. My mother smiled at that.

"You're down to two hundred and twelve," the nurse
added.

I wanted to say a prayer for her that night before she
died, but I found I didn't know any. There were no prayers
except those I could make up, and I wanted an old prayer
and there weren't any I could remember. I tried to recall
the one that goes, "The Lord is my shepherd; I shall not
want. He maketh me to lie down in green pastures." But I
couldn't remember anything more except these fragments:
"Yea, though I walk through the valley of the shadow of
death, I will fear no evil. . . . For thine is the kingdom, and
the power, and the glory, for ever. Amen."

This was the best I could do. Some half-forgotten prayers
that I struggled to remember from the Sunday school classes
of my youth.

The next morning I was alone in the hospital room with
her. Her legs and feet were bare. She had kicked the covers
off, and her pale legs were white against the sheets. They
appeared as firm and sheeny as alabaster. She was breathing
heavily. Her eyes were closed.

Every once in a while she moved her toes. Sometimes she opened her eyes.

Two days earlier, she had asked for a pen and a pad of paper and had written me a note: "No more surgery, let me die." The note was penned in a shaky, wavery script. Later she wrote another note saying she was willing to have more surgery if the doctors thought she could survive it. The doctors did not think she could survive it, and I had to tell her this.

Around noon that day, Mary Miller, an old friend of my mother's, came to visit her. She approached my mother very quietly and took her hand gently, waiting for my mother to open her eyes. Then Mary Miller leaned over and spoke softly into her ear. She said, "Oh, Alice, my dear Alice, I've loved you for so many years." My mother couldn't speak because of the tube down her throat, but she took Mary Miller's hand and clasped it, and their eyes met for a long time. A great deal seemed to pass between them in that look. Then Mary Miller said, "I'll be back, my dear," and left the hospital room.

Later, in bed back at the motel, I lay propped up on pillows and looked out the window at the setting sun. I could see out over the whole valley. The most incredible light was falling over the lake, not penetrating its opacity but shining on the surface and making it look as hard as a sheet of tin. On the ridges of the Oquirrh mountains there was fresh snow. I thought, "This is what it was, this is what it's become," apropos of nothing.

I arrived at the hospital early the next morning and sat with my mother, who dozed on and off, her eyes opening occasionally. The respirator was gone. The tube down her throat had been removed during the night, and now she appeared much more comfortable. She was mostly conscious and seemingly relaxed. She could talk now, and I was glad for that, but not nearly so glad as she was. She seemed to want to talk, not only to me but to the nurses who came and went. I was surprised how strong her voice sounded, how normal it was.

"What's my blood pressure?" my mother asked the nurse who arrived to take her vital signs.

"One twenty over sixty."

"Oh, that's good."

"Couldn't be better."

"Just like a kid."

"Well, you are a kid," the nurse said, and my mother laughed, a dry, harsh sound.

When the nurse left, my mother summoned me to her bedside. Her eyes were moist and the palest green.

"I want to ask you to do something for me," she said.

"Okay." I smoothed the hair back from her forehead. Such beautiful silver hair, I thought.

"I'd like you to find Marie. Find out where she is and how she's doing. Will you do that?" my mother asked.

I told her I would try.

"Promise me," she said.

I promised.

"I'm leaving all the grandkids a little money. Not that much, but a little for each one. If you can find Marie, I'd like her to have her share. Only I don't want Ofelia to get it. I want it to go to Marie. Promise me you'll find her for me." After she said this, she turned her head away and closed her eyes.

She died a few hours later, just after noon, while I was downstairs in the hospital cafeteria eating lunch. When I came upstairs, the nurse stopped me in the hallway and very gently gave me the news. Holding my hands, she said, "Your mother passed away a few moments ago. It was very fast." She asked if I would like to go into the room and see my mother, and I said yes.

For a long while I sat with her body, until it had turned from warm to cold. Her face looked quite beautiful in death. I kept thinking this, that there was such beauty in her face. All her strife was gone and all the appearance of suffering. Her skin had taken on a translucence; a light seemed to emanate from her skin, faintly pearly and blue. The nurses had placed a towel beneath her chin to keep her mouth closed. One eye was open slightly, and I could see the emptiness there. Her pale waxen hands were folded across her breast, hands that no longer seemed to resemble my own in the least. Whatever feeling connected our flesh had been broken. She was gone. And I was still there, in a body that felt very much like my own.

The nurses came in after a while and stood at the end of her bed and wept. "She was so sweet," one of them said.

"Yes," I said, "she was sweet," and then I lost it, all the composure I'd hoped to maintain.

Awhile after my mother's death, I began to think of the promise I had made her to try to find Marie, the grandchild she had lost track of many years ago. I remembered my niece only as a heavy, dark child, burdened with a slowness that had seemed to mark her from birth. It had been many years since anyone in my family had seen her. Over the years rumors persisted of terrible things that had happened to her. None of us knew the true story, however, though I felt I was perhaps on the verge of discovering it. That was, if I could find Ofelia, Marie's mother. It would be necessary to locate Ofelia in order to find Marie, and that might not be easy.

I had no idea what Marie might look like now, nor even her exact age, though I figured she'd be almost forty. Nine years younger than I was. Nine years seemed a rather inconsequential age difference now, compared to how it had felt in 1954. I had been nine years old the summer my brother died, in a hospital in a different state, and his wife and baby turned up in our small town for the funeral.

Marie was the daughter of my brother Sam and his Cuban-born wife, Ofelia. Two years before his death, Sam had dropped out of high school and joined the navy. I recalled him as being handsome in an unusual way, and old photographs confirm this memory. He had dark wavy hair and a face that bore a strong resemblance to James Dean. He had that sort of James Dean sultriness, too, a sense of vulnerability or woundedness leaking from him. How he met Ofelia Rodriguez I didn't know. Perhaps it was in a bar or a waterfront dance hall. All I knew was they met in Miami in the 1950s—my brother, an American sailor, an eighteen-year-old farm boy from the West, and Ofelia Rodriguez, a twenty-five-year-old Cuban beautician who had recently arrived in this country.

One thing you have to say, looking at photographs of them, is that they made a striking couple. He was so handsome, she was so beautiful. The other thing you might notice—in the wedding pictures, at least—is that when they married, Ofelia was already very pregnant with the child they eventually named Marie. And Sam, though you can't really tell it, was already very ill.

By the time Marie was born, my brother was dying of bone cancer in a naval hospital in Alameda, California. A few months later, at the age of nineteen, he was dead, and Ofelia was a widow with a tiny baby. No matter what my parents later said about Ofelia, I believe she loved my brother, just as I think he loved her. Anybody looking at old pictures of them could tell this much. But my father thought that his son had married a whore and that the baby she carried wasn't his. He announced this to anyone who would listen. Nothing ever made him change his mind.

My brother died on the seventh of December—Pearl Harbor Day—with Ofelia and baby Marie and my parents at his side. His body was brought home to Utah for burial. The funeral was difficult for my parents. Difficult for them to lose their son at such a young age. Hard to bury him on a cold winter day. Above all, it was difficult having Ofelia there among their neighbors and friends, with her broken English, her tight clothes, her uncensored grief. She was inconsolable, and she ended up making a scene at the open casket. She refused to let it be closed. I remembered her weeping as she tried to force a ring onto my dead brother's hand at the last minute. My father had tried to restrain her. What I recalled was the image of my father grasping Ofelia, pinning her arms against her body, while she continued pushing that ring against my brother's lifeless knuckles. As for Marie, even then she seemed silent and slow, a dull little baby who never made a sound.

In the years that followed, my parents kept in touch with Ofelia, writing to her occasionally out of a sense of duty, or perhaps guilt. But they lacked any genuine feeling for her or their grandchild, and so these efforts were few and far between.

A few years after Sam's death, however, we heard from Ofelia that she'd married again, choosing a Miami policeman for a husband. In very little time, they had two children. They took a trip across the country and stopped to visit us. Ofelia seemed happy. But Marie did not. Her half brother and half sister, John and Lisa, were attractive, lively children, but Marie was sullen and quiet. They stayed only a few hours and were gone. And then we heard, just a short while later, that Ofelia had become a widow again. Her policeman husband was killed in the line of duty, shot while attempting to stop a burglary.

Following the death of her second husband, Ofelia's life must have become hard. Once during this time, my aunt visited her in Florida and found a gaunt woman living in squalor, trying to raise three kids. She had converted her garage into a small beauty parlor and worked out of her home. She asked my aunt for a little money, which my aunt reluctantly gave her. I think now that this was the thing my parents feared most from Ofelia, that she would want something from them, too, that she would come asking for money one day.

Over the years, we heard from Ofelia mostly in the form of cards at Christmastime. Each year she sent a new picture of Marie, who had not grown into an attractive child. The pictures showed an overweight girl with a blank look on her face. Ofelia began referring to Marie's "problems," and then she began asking my parents for money, just as they had suspected she would one day. She needed the money, she said, because Marie needed special schooling. She was slow—"no dummy," as Ofelia said, but a child with special needs. To my parents, it was clear their granddaughter was retarded in some way, and this they found difficult to accept.

Then one day Ofelia wrote and asked if she might send Marie for a visit. My parents made excuses as to why this wouldn't be possible. But Ofelia asked again, pleading this time, saying Marie missed her grandparents and often talked of them. She pointed out how good it might be for Marie. Finally my parents relented, and Marie came for a visit. The visit did not go well, and it was the last time they agreed to see her.

A little while later, Ofelia sent a short note telling us that she'd married again. Her new husband was a much older man named Jim Simpson. In their wedding photograph, he looked like her father. Except he was white. White, and not attractive.

This was the point at which the story for me turned to tragedy. A few years after Ofelia's marriage to Jim Simpson, Ofelia wrote my mother that Marie had gone to live in a home. Ofelia said Jim had not been good for Marie, and that was why she had to leave. She must have said other things, too, because it was then that my mother began referring to the bad things—the *terrible* things—that had happened to Marie to make her the way she was. These were not things she could even bring herself to talk about, at least not to her children. The whole thing, she said, was too sordid and painful to contemplate. But I figured it out for myself, and later she confirmed what I suspected. Jim, Ofelia's third husband, had sexually abused Marie for years, even before their marriage. He had assaulted a retarded teenage girl, his own stepdaughter, and in an attempt to protect Marie, Ofelia had sent her away to a home. My mother was right. It *was* too painful and sordid to contemplate.

"How could she stay with a man who would do such a thing to a child?" my mother later asked me, when I finally got her to admit the truth. I think we all had wondered about this. How could Ofelia stay with such a man? The answer seemed beyond our grasp, but I do remember thinking that Ofelia must be desperate—desperate and damaged herself—to be able to stay married to Jim Simpson.

I also remember thinking, during those years when all this was coming out—because, after all, I was a young woman by then, in my twenties, a college student, and certainly more worldly than I'd been when I'd first tried to guess what was going on—I kept thinking that there was something I really ought to do about all this. Some way I should try to help Marie. But then it never seemed as if I knew what that thing was. The damage, it seemed to me, had already been done. Marie was in an institution, perhaps mentally retarded, perhaps not, but definitely an abused and unhappy girl. Ofelia had married a monster, and Marie had been the one to really suffer.

Once during this time I wrote to Ofelia and got a Christmas card in return, signed by both her and Jim Simpson.

She included a short message saying she was glad to hear from me, glad that I'd "bothered to find her," as she said, and asked me to keep in touch.

But I didn't keep in touch. In time, Ofelia and Marie disappeared from my life—from all of our lives. They were more or less forgotten. Every once in a while, at some family gathering, somebody would bring up their names, and my mother would shake her head and say unhappily, "I don't know where they are. I don't know what's become of them." And then they wouldn't be mentioned again for a very long time, because nobody seemed to care.

I knew that my mother suffered more over all this than she ever let on. To my father, it was pretty cut-and-dried: Ofelia was a stranger and always had been, and Marie wasn't really his flesh and blood. But to my mother it was a much more complicated matter. Once she told me she felt that she had let her son down. She had failed Sam because she hadn't taken better care of his child. But it was not an easy thing to do, she stressed. It had not been an easy thing at all. Occasionally, in her later years, my mother would speak of this. She would sigh and say, "I feel terrible, just terrible, about Marie," and then she would drop the subject, as if nothing more could ever be said.

I had meant to begin looking for Marie soon after my mother died, but I put it off. A terrible lethargy seemed to overtake my life. So many things were so easily ignored, including the promise to my mother. I guess a lot of people go through hard times after the death of a parent. It seemed particularly hard for me. I no longer wanted to leave my apartment or see friends. I found it difficult to make plans or to carry out the simplest tasks.

Finally, however, one day when I was going through a box of family photographs and letters, I came across one of the old Christmas cards from Ofelia, on which was written an address and phone number. Immediately I called the number. Ofelia didn't answer, but a relative of hers did. The relative didn't speak English, so I had to wait until a man came on the line who did.

I explained who I was and asked if he knew where I could find Ofelia.

"Why you lookin' for Ofelia?" he said.

"My mother died," I said. I knew I needed to say something more, that this really wasn't an explanation. "I just want to get in touch with Ofelia again," I added. "I haven't heard from her in a long time."

"She and Jim are living in a trailer park out in San Bernardino, California." I was surprised to hear she was living in California, not far from where I lived.

He wouldn't give me her telephone number. I didn't know why, and I didn't ask. But he said he would take mine and also my address, and the next time he talked to her, he'd give them to her. As soon as I'd given him these, he said, "Fine, then," and hung up.

Unexpectedly, I heard from Ofelia rather quickly. A card came the next week.

> What ever happened to you? How come you don't get in touch anymore? Why did you try to find me now? Did your parents tell you not to keep in touch with me because they might be afraid I would try to contact them because of Marie? I wonder if you know what they did to Marie. Anyway, it's okay, if you prefer not to contact me anymore just let me know, but here is my address. Love, your Sis always, Ofelia.

I didn't answer the card immediately. It took some time to formulate a reply. In the back of my mind, I kept thinking, "What does she mean, 'I wonder if you know what they did to Marie'?" As far as I knew, my parents had never done anything to Marie except try to forget she existed. Their relationship with her had been almost nonexistent.

In fact, Marie had only come to visit my parents that one time, when she was thirteen. She was already an overgrown, heavy child, slow and quiet, and yet also temperamental and unpredictable. I had not been there for the visit. But afterward I heard it hadn't gone well. I heard it hadn't gone well at all.

She had been "difficult to manage," as my mother put it, from the moment she arrived. She used foul language, talked crudely about sex—shouting out things in public places— and if she didn't get her way, she threw a tantrum, punching out and kicking like a small child. My parents were frightened of her. They concluded that she must be retarded or unbalanced in some way, not only because of these things but because she kept asking the same questions over and over again until my mother said she thought she'd go crazy.

But that wasn't the worst of it. The worst of it was the violence, they said. The worst of it was what had happened at the senior center.

My father made the mistake of taking Marie with him one afternoon to the senior center, where he often went to play cards. He left her alone, reading a magazine in the card room, while he went to use the rest room. While he was gone, Marie became restless, then agitated, and began wandering the hallways, looking in rooms, opening and slamming doors. She discovered some lightbulbs in a supply closet, and, without warning, she took the lightbulbs back into the card room and began throwing them one by one against a wall, where they exploded like little bombs. The old people who had been quietly playing cards were terrified. The staff stood by helplessly. It took several people, including my father, to finally subdue Marie. By then there was broken glass everywhere, and people were very upset. Throughout it all, Marie laughed. A crazy sort of laughter, my father said later—a *demented* kind of laughter. Embarrassed and angry, my father led his granddaughter away and took her home. The next day she was put on a plane and sent back to her mother.

So I did not understand what Ofelia meant when she said maybe I didn't know what my parents had done to her. What had my parents done to Marie except admit they couldn't deal with their estranged and damaged granddaughter? What was their crime except one of rejection and neglect?

I finally got around to answering Ofelia's note. I wrote a short and simple letter telling her about my mother's death and explaining her last request to me—to please find Marie. I asked if she could tell me where Marie was and how she was doing. I didn't mention anything about the money my mother had left Marie, only that I wished to know where my niece was and how she was doing.

Then I mailed the letter off and waited for a reply.

I lived on the third floor of an old stucco apartment building overlooking downtown Los Angeles. It had once been a nice neighborhood, but that was no longer true. Back in the thirties and forties, the area had been called Westlake and had attracted people who built nice houses near the park. But it had gone downhill over the years. Now the big houses were carved up into apartments, where immigrant families from El Salvador and Guatemala and Mexico crowded into a few roach-infested rooms. Drugs and crime were rampant. It used to be that it was only really dangerous to be out on the streets after dark. But recently the sense of danger in the neighborhood had extended even into the daylight hours. The woman who lived in the apartment next to me had been attacked on the front steps one morning at ten as she was returning from the corner store. A man with a knife had demanded her purse and then, not waiting for her to disentangle the strap from her shoulder, had grabbed the purse and dragged her halfway down the stairs before she managed to free herself. My neighbor was left bruised and dazed on the steps, calling out for help in the bright light of day, while her attacker walked calmly away.

I was aware of something going on all around me that I could only think of as a terrible degeneration—a gradual, slow process of erosion of all things familiar and beautiful. The decay around me was palpable. Yards once watered and groomed were left to dry up in the heat. Graffiti covered every imaginable surface—trees, walls, doorways—even the skinniest little lamppost had strange and undecipherable markings. I kept thinking it was a new language I ought to understand but didn't. The streets around me were filled with the homeless and mentally ill. Parks I had once walked in either were no longer safe or were being transformed into something other than parks. Construction of a new subway station had encroached on the oldest and loveliest of these parks, and the lake had recently been drained in order for a tunnel to be constructed nearby. In the bottom of the now dry lake lay heaps and layers of trash, items dumped into the water over the years—skeletons of shopping carts and garbage cans, the remains of sunken paddleboats, hundreds of bottles and rusted cans, baby carriages and bicycles and parts and pieces of objects now undistinguishable and un-nameable, just an accumulation of disregarded things lodged in the mud.

Sometimes I emerged from my apartment to make a trip to the store a block away and felt startled to find the world still intact. One morning when I went out, it had been raining for days and everything seemed clean and luridly green, as if unnaturally alive. The sun was shining and, since I had been in my apartment for days, the light hurt my eyes. I put on dark glasses and began walking toward the park.

I passed people I recognized. I had lived in this neighborhood for many years, long enough to recognize familiar faces, yet these were people I never spoke to and whose names I did not know. I passed the same faces, the same people, week after week, year after year, without ever changing my expression or uttering a word.

At the corner, near the market, I came across some Salvadoran boys selling dope. One with a pockmarked face came up to me and said, "Hey, where you been? What you want? A dime?" Even though I hadn't really planned on buying any smoke, I said, "Yeah, give me a dime." Then I added, "Make that two dimes," and gave him a twenty. He handed me the marijuana, wrapped up in little packets of newspaper—a Spanish-language newspaper that had been torn up and the pieces neatly folded around the dope with the ends tucked under to make a little envelope. I put the dope in my pocket and continued down the street.

Inside the store, I picked out a few things—two small cans of V8 juice, instant-soup packets, some oranges and cans of tuna—and paid for them at the counter. At the last minute, I added a packet of cigarette-rolling papers. I was aware of the dope in my pocket as the clerk handed me the cigarette papers. I looked into the broad flat face of the Korean boy waiting on me and noticed how he didn't once look at me but managed to complete the transaction without ever lifting his eyes to mine.

Ofelia's letter came just as I had begun to give up on ever hearing back from her. It arrived on a day when something had happened that had left me badly shaken.

I was in my bedroom, not really sleeping but only half awake. It was around noon. The windows to the alley were open. A pair of ravens had built a nest in a tree, and I could see the nest from where I lay. It was a lovely spring day. The eggs had hatched, and both parents could be seen frequently flying in and out of the tree where the nest was. I watched them ferrying meals to their young, first one, then the other parent feeding the chicks.

Then I saw both adults fly to the nest at the same moment, and I thought to myself, "Both mommy and daddy have arrived"—even though the moment I thought the words mommy and daddy, they seemed so silly I instantly felt foolish. But it was true those birds seemed incredibly attentive to their young, constantly checking on their babies and feeding them, flying in and out, never leaving the nest for long. I had never seen more concerned or watchful parents. I began thinking then about my own parents, both now dead, and about how little I had known them. In fact, it occurred to me how startlingly little we ever really know about each other. And I thought, "Is it possible birds know their parents better than humans do?"

As I was having these thoughts, I heard noises in the alley—loud voices, some sort of argument being carried on in Spanish. It went on for a while, and then I heard another noise. It was a thud—not a very loud thud, but a rather gentle thump—followed by a lengthy and disconcerting silence.

I couldn't say exactly what it was that made me get out of bed and go to the window—after all, arguments in my neighborhood were common, and this one hadn't even been particularly loud or alarming. But something prompted me to get up and go see what was happening.

When I reached the window and looked out, I saw a body lying motionless, facedown, on the pavement at the end of the alley, near a row of Dumpsters overflowing with garbage. My first thought was "Someone's been shot," even though I knew this wasn't likely, since I hadn't heard any gunfire. A small boy was standing directly below my window, straddling a bike and looking in the direction of the body.

"What happened?" I called down to him.

He looked up and said, "That guy, he just fell out of that window."

He pointed to a third-story window above where the body lay. It was true—the window was wide open and the screen had been ripped and the edges of the screen were now lifting gently in a breeze. Everything was very still. There was no noise now except the chattering of the ravens in the nest. I looked up and down the alley. It seemed that no one but me and the small boy below knew that anything had happened.

But I was wrong about this. By the time I got dressed, ran downstairs, unlocked the door to the alley, and reached the place where the body lay, a small group of people had gathered. The group included an old woman in an apron, several men, and a pregnant woman with a small child in her arms—all Mexican or perhaps Central American. They stood well away from the body, clustered together on the opposite side of the alley. They were just standing there staring across the alley at the body.

No one in the crowd said anything as I approached. I looked down at the man who lay crumpled on the asphalt. He was badly injured, that much was clear. He was bleeding from his head and mouth, and his limbs formed odd angles, as if he might have broken something in the fall. The sight of him was very upsetting to me. I turned away and spoke to the small group of onlookers. I said, "Has anyone called nine-one-one and asked for an ambulance?"

A small dark man in a white shirt and a baseball cap said yes, he had already called the *medicos,* and they were on their way.

Suddenly I heard the man on the ground moan, and I looked down and saw that he was trying to lift his head. Until that moment I had thought he might be unconscious, or perhaps even dead. I was surprised to see him turn his head and gaze up at me with one eye.

I went to him and knelt down near his head, which he

262 • JUDITH FREEMAN

again tried to lift off the asphalt, only to have it wobble and fall to the ground with a terrible, sickening thud.

"Don't do that," I said. "Don't move. Try to lie very still." I placed my hand lightly on his head. His hair was thick and black and sticky with blood.

Someone across the alley, the old woman in the apron, said, "You shouldn't touch him."

"Why not?" I asked, looking up at her.

"The woman on the phone at nine-one-one say, 'Don't touch him. Don't go near him. Just wait for ambulance.'"

Automatically, I took my hand away and stared at her, but then I began thinking, and again I was suffused with that feeling that had overcome me so often lately of some deep degeneration, some unraveling of the fabric holding things together. There again was the sense of confusion and decay all around that had made things unfamiliar and incomprehensible to me. A man lay bleeding and injured, and people did nothing but stand at a distance and stare at him. Was this right? Could this be the right thing to do?

What, I wondered, is happening here?

The man was bleeding badly, and his moans suddenly became louder. Like an animal struggling in fear, he kept trying to lift his head, which flopped back heavily to the pavement with those terrible sickening thuds. I bent closer and laid my hand gently on his head again and began talking to him softly, letting the words come in a continuous stream. I told him that he must lie still, that help was coming, that an ambulance was on its way, and in just a few minutes the paramedics would be there and would know what to do, but for now he must try to stay very quiet; it was very important that he not move his head. I talked to him this way for what seemed like a long time. Everything's going to be all right, I said—though I didn't know whether I really believed this.

He grew a little quieter after I spoke to him. His head was turned to the side, and occasionally he opened his eye, rolling the eyeball to the far outside corner, where it fluttered in an effort to look up at me. Twice he said, "Thank you, lady, thank you," the words formed and spoken through bubbles of blood caught between his lips.

The minutes passed very slowly, I don't know how many, maybe ten or fifteen. I didn't have a watch. It seemed to take a long time, a very long time, for help to arrive, and I felt helpless and rather sick with fear as I crouched there, compelled to stay by his side and yet useless. Blood now pooled thickly around his head and covered my hands and stained the knees of my jeans. His eye had grown glassy as he sank deeper into shock. The crowd across the alley had grown. More and more people had joined the throng of onlookers, who stood mute, looking over at me and the injured man as if we were part of a play unfolding before them.

Finally two policemen arrived in a squad car. They pulled up and got out of the car. Instead of coming over immediately to help me, they stood frozen for a moment, surveying the situation. Then one said to the other, "This is beautiful, this is really beautiful," and as he spoke a little smile spread over his face.

The policemen walked unhurriedly toward the place where I knelt, bent over the injured man. Then an ambulance pulled up, and the medics got out and came toward me, also moving at an unhurried pace. I stood up, stiff from kneeling there for so long, and backed away as they approached. Nobody even looked at me or spoke a word.

The paramedics cut away the injured man's clothes, leaving only his shorts. Everyone now stood staring at the mostly naked man and at the scars and tattoos on his back. I listened to the questions the paramedics asked him in order to determine the degree of his consciousness. They asked him things like "What day of the week is it?" and "Who is the president of the country?" The man got the day right, but he didn't reply to the question of who was president, and it occurred to me that he might not know or could possibly be thinking of another country, perhaps one far to the south where he'd been born.

The paramedics handled him roughly as they loaded him onto the stretcher and wheeled him toward the ambulance. I thought they should have been more gentle. They seemed astonishingly unconcerned about his condition. An attitude of boredom seemed to mark their expressions, but then I thought, "Maybe this is just the way they get through their job, maybe this is how they manage to do it, how they deal with all sorts of accidents. They just stay removed, and maybe what looks like boredom to me is really a professional, studied calm."

Still, I thought they were rough with him. I didn't think they needed to be so rough.

After the ambulance had taken the injured man away, the police began questioning some of the people standing around, including me, but when I couldn't tell them anything about what had happened, how the man came to be lying on the pavement, they quickly lost interest in me.

The man in the white shirt and baseball cap turned out to know the most about what had happened. He was the manager of the apartment building where the injured man lived. He said a plumber had been doing some work in the man's apartment, and the plumber and the man had begun arguing about something. The manager had heard the fight and gone upstairs to see what was going on. He said the man was acting violent and was trying to push the plumber out the window. Instead, the plumber managed to free himself and left the apartment, with his tools, saying to the manager on the way out that he thought his tenant was crazy and on drugs and he wouldn't do any work in that apartment unless he was gone. When the plumber left, the manager said his tenant had simply walked over to the window and thrown himself out.

"Drogas," said the woman in the apron when the manager had finished his story. She clucked her tongue and shook her head. "Muy mal, drogas," she repeated, as one of the policemen wrote something down on his little notepad.

I returned to my apartment. There wasn't anything left to do or see out in the alley. Yet I felt shaken, and I wished I could have hung around outside and talked to someone about what had just happened. I thought about calling up one of my friends and telling her about it. But I had been out of touch with my friends lately, and it seemed crazy to just call one of them up now and tell her this story. So instead, for the next few hours I sat in a chair and listened to music and looked out the window at the ravens' nest. I kept turning the same thoughts over in my head. Why had the man jumped out the window? Was he going to die? Was the manager's account of what had happened really true? Something about it didn't seem right. I could see the man arguing with the plumber. I could even see him trying to push the plumber out the window. Or falling out himself during a struggle. But to just walk over to the window and throw himself out *after* the plumber had gone, it just didn't make sense.

I felt very edgy, jarred and jangled by every little noise I heard outside. I smoked part of a joint and things got worse, just as I had known they probably would. I found I could not separate these two images—the sight of the man lying injured on the asphalt and the last image of my mother lying in her hospital bed.

I looked down at my hands, as if from a great distance, and saw traces of blood still there. Although I had washed carefully when I came upstairs, I saw now the little crescents of red caught under my nails and quickly closed my hand into a fist.

Around four in the afternoon, I heard the mailman, the rustle of his keys as he opened each box in the alcove beneath my window, and I went downstairs to see what he'd left for me. There was only one letter, and it was from Ofelia.

> Dear Sis, I am sorry to hear about your mother. Maybe you will come see me and we can talk about Marie. There's too much to put in a letter, and I'm not so good at writing anyway. We're living in San Bernardino. Not too far from you. Thursday is my day off. Why don't you come this Thursday? We don't have no phone, so you can't call. Just come Thursday if you can. Around two o'clock is okay. Your loving sister, Ofelia.

The following Thursday, I arose earlier than usual and was on the freeway, headed east, by eleven o'clock. The day was dreary and overcast. A warm dirtiness hung on the air, which was laden with humidity. I drove in a semisomnambulant state. In the glove compartment was the last of the marijuana I had bought. I was saving it for the return trip. I wanted to be clearheaded when I saw Ofelia, to be my unadulterated self at the moment of our reunion. That was the thought that came to my mind: "You need to be your unadulterated self."

As I drove, I thought of the woman I remembered from all those years ago. I remembered the first time my brother had brought her home to meet his family. I was eight at the time, a shy girl with thick glasses, and I remembered the visit very clearly. We lived in a little stone house overlooking the north end of the Great Salt Lake. The land between our house and the lake was taken up by acres of orchards. Sometimes the lake rose and encroached on the orchards, turning the land white between the trees, and sometimes the lake receded, leaving acres of green mud. They arrived in the depth of winter, when there was snow on the ground and the mud near the lake was frozen.

They came across country by bus, and my first sight of

them was in front of Ruby's Diner, a café that also served as the bus station. They were standing with their arms around each other, Sam and his new wife, with a single battered leather suitcase sitting at their feet. My brother wore his navy uniform. Ofelia was bundled up in a bright red coat. The color seemed lurid and startling against the grayness of the winter day, against the dead trees and the gray stone cliffs. And she herself was rather startling. Pregnant. Exotic. Different. She had large dark eyes, which were heavily made up, and bright red lips. Her hair was black and sleek and very shiny, and her skin was so dark she could easily have been mistaken for a black person. (That was what my father said later: "She looks like a Negro to me.") The moment I saw her, I thought she was the most exotic-looking person I had ever seen. She was also one of the most beautiful.

The visit wasn't much of a success. My parents didn't bother to hide their disapproval of Ofelia, and a stiffness, a certain tension, permeated the house during the time they were there. But if Ofelia felt my parents' coolness toward her, she didn't let it show. She was a happy, energetic person. She had a natural vitality and confidence, a high-spiritedness I found infectious, and she won me over completely. She was so different—with her singsongy voice and strange diction, her luminous hair and dark skin—and she doted on me. She seemed to single me out for attention. She took walks with me along the lakeshore. She gave me a haircut and told me I was pretty, and she began calling me sister.

When finally the time came for her and Sam to leave, she took me aside and said I must always remember that we were sisters now. Then she boarded the bus with my brother, who looked drained and tired. The two of them waved from the window as the bus pulled out, taking them back to Miami.

———

I arrived in San Bernardino forty-five minutes early, so I decided to kill some time in a few thrift stores that were lined up one next to another on a dreary street called Baseline Road. The stores were all dismal, offering an array of shabby goods. There were racks of clothes, shoes, cheap furniture, and broken children's toys. I didn't know what I was looking for, what I thought I'd find there among the remnants of other people's lives, but I believe I was seeking the thing I always sought in these places, some little overlooked treasure, a primitive painting, a piece of pretty china or festive pottery—*something*, whose value only I would recognize and appreciate and which I would buy for next to nothing.

Ofelia's trailer was painted pink and white. Flower boxes filled with faded plastic geraniums lined the windows. New grass-green indoor-outdoor carpeting had been laid along the walkway leading to the front door. The dirt driveway came right to the edge of the carpet, and you could see where someone had tracked big brown shoeprints against the green.

I knocked, and almost immediately the door was opened. It seemed to me that she'd been waiting for me, perhaps watching my approach from a window. I didn't believe I ever would have recognized her if I'd met her on the street by chance. But the moment I heard her voice, speaking my name, I knew it was Ofelia.

"Hello, Ofelia," I said.

"Come on in," she answered.

The woman who stood before me was stooped, her back curved into a prominent widow's hump. Beneath her eyes there were deep bags of dark flesh. Her hair was short and no longer black, but gray. Yet beneath all these signs of aging I could still make out the traces of the beautiful young woman she had been. Most of all, something fierce, some spark of that high-spirited woman, was still evident in her eyes.

I thought we might embrace—I mean I had prepared myself for this—but as I stepped toward her I realized her arms remained limp at her side. She did, however, turn her face aside, and I planted a kiss on her cheek. Her skin felt dry and cool against my lips, and she quickly stepped away.

"Come in, come in," she said again, pulling the door open as she did so. She was shoeless and wore a simple cotton dress, yellow with some sort of darker pattern covering it.

"Sit down," she said. She indicated I should take the sofa, and she crossed to a chair, one of those large chairs that tilt back. She sat down and raised the footrest on her chair. Then she leaned back and looked at me long and hard.

"How many years since we last saw each other?" she asked. "Was it at the funeral?"

"I think it was after the funeral," I said. "When you brought Marie and Lisa and John for a visit with your second husband."

"Ah, that time. That was a long time ago. You've changed."

I laughed, and then she laughed, too. I said, "I guess I would have changed. I was still a kid then."

I looked around the room, taking things in, particularly the row of photographs sitting on a shelf near the TV. I wondered if any of the people in the pictures might be Marie.

"Well, he died in '54," she was saying, and it took me a moment to realize she was talking about my brother, Sam. "Fifty-four to ninety-four—that's forty years, plus one. It's been forty-one years then since he died."

"Forty-one years," I repeated.

"A long time."

"A very long time," I said.

"Half a lifetime."

"At least."

She said, "I'm turning seventy this year."

"And I'm almost fifty."

"You're almost fifty!"

"Well, I'm really only forty-eight. I think I say 'almost fifty' because I'm trying to get used to the idea."

"You married?" Ofelia asked. I noticed how her head bobbed to the side as she asked this, as if in shyness.

"No."

"Not married?"

"No."

"How come?"

"I don't know. Too old, I guess." I laughed, but she didn't laugh with me. "I live alone."

"In a house or apartment?"

"Apartment."

"Oh. So you don't own, then?"

"No. I rent. It's not the best neighborhood either."

"So many are bad now."

I stood up and crossed the room, heading for the row of family photographs. Ofelia watched me as I did this. At the last moment I veered away from the photographs and looked briefly at the china cabinet and a ceramic cat sitting behind the glass. Then I casually strolled over to the row of photographs.

"Boy, lots of pictures here. All of your family?" There were snapshots of kids of all ages. Adults with babies. Pictures of babies and children without adults. Wedding pictures, school pictures. Even a picture of Sam in a sailor's uniform. She didn't answer my question, so I tried again.

"Is Marie in any of these photographs?"

"No. Marie isn't there. Those are mostly pictures of Jim's kids from his first marriage. Kids and grandkids. But that's Lisa and John there, the one you're looking at now. You remember Lisa and John?"

"Of course I do. I remember them from the time you all visited, and also from the photographs you sent us."

"I sent lots of photographs to your parents. Didn't mean a thing to them."

I cleared my throat. "So, where is Marie now?"

"Here."

"Right here?"

I thought she meant here in the trailer, perhaps napping in a back bedroom, or in the kitchen or out in the yard. But Ofelia corrected this impression. By "here" she meant that Marie, too, was living in San Bernardino.

"Does she have her own place?" I asked.

Instead of answering my question, she said, "Marie's at work today."

"Where does she work?"

"I'll take you if you want to see."

I smiled and said, "Yes, I *would* like to see her. I have something for her, a little something from my mother."

She gave me a completely strange look. It was a look, I thought, of either disbelief or distrust or perhaps distaste. In any case, it lasted for a few moments, and then she said, in what I thought was a rather flat voice, "I'll take you to see her in my car."

In the end, I wondered why we even bothered to drive from the trailer park to the place where Ofelia took me. We could as easily have walked the four or five blocks. Instead we drove, and I did all the talking. Ofelia, for some reason I didn't understand, seemed to have grown silent since we left the trailer, and she didn't speak again until we reached our destination.

We pulled up in front of a small factory building, a place on the corner of two busy streets. It had frosted windows and a locked security gate and a high fence surrounding it. The neighborhood was old, a mixture of small stucco houses and old shops and offices. Ofelia parked at the curb on one side of the factory, near a row of windows covered with a wire mesh. Through the window I could hear the rhythmic clatter of machinery.

Ofelia switched off the ignition and turned and looked at me. It was not a pleasant look—I realized this even before she began speaking and before I heard what she had to say.

"You can see Marie," she said. "I'll point her out to you. We can look through that window. But I don't think it would be a good idea to talk to her."

"You mean we shouldn't interrupt her at work?"

"No. I mean I don't want her to see you. I don't want her to have any contact with you. I think it would just upset her." She hesitated, in order, I thought, to let these words sink in.

"A long time ago I decided I was going to protect Marie," she finally went on. "She needs protecting. Marie's not like everybody else. I had to make the decision to protect her from anything that could hurt her."

"How will I hurt her?"

"The hurt's already been done. You'd just remind her of it."

"Remind her of what?"

"Your parents and what they did to her."

"And what did they do to her?"

I waited for her to answer. I was thinking, "What about that asshole you married and what he did to her?" This was running through my mind, so to speak, as I stared at her and waited for her to say something.

Finally she said, "What they did to her was very cruel. It was very bad, very bad and very mean. It hurt her a lot, and she didn't get over that. And I didn't either. I guess they thought it was nothing, though, what they did."

"What did they do?"

"You know that trip when Marie came to visit them in Utah? When she was thirteen?"

"Yes." I thought, "The trip where she threw light-bulbs..."

"When she came home she was pretty upset."

"My parents were upset, too. It was hard for them, that visit. But I don't think they actually harmed her, did they? They just found that they couldn't ... quite ... handle her." I tried to choose my words carefully.

"Okay. I know. They couldn't deal with her problems. But you know what else they did? And this was the part that hurt her. After she left, they packed up all the pictures we'd ever sent them—all the baby pictures of Marie, the pictures from school, Christmas cards, her letters to them, everything—and they sent it all back to us. She got the package in the mail. It was addressed to me. But she saw everything. And she knew that her grandmother and grandfather didn't even want one picture around to remind them of her anymore. Believe me, that hurt her. That hurt me."

I didn't know what to say, so I didn't say anything. It turned out I didn't have to, because Ofelia got out of the car then, and I did the same.

I followed her over to the row of windows that stretched along the side of the one-story brick building. The closer to the window we got, the louder the sound of machinery became, a sort of pleasant, rhythmical sound, like *tickety-tock, tickety-tock*. I could now smell a wonderful odor on the air. Like the smell of a cake baking.

Ofelia pressed her face against the mesh covering the window, and, using both hands, she shaded her eyes in order to peer into the darkened interior of the factory. Following her example, I did the same. As my eyes adjusted, I could make out various pieces of large machinery of differing heights but all somehow connected by pipes and tubes and all emptying something onto a conveyor belt—some small, conical item—which was being carried toward a row of waiting women, all of whom stood at the end of the conveyor belt, three to a side, wearing uniforms and translucent caps and gloves, and packing these objects into boxes.

It took me a moment to realize it was an ice-cream-cone factory, that all the machines were stamping out cones, which tumbled onto the belt and were carried along toward the workers. The women scooped them up, one after another, expertly stacking an exact number of cones, putting the stacks into the boxes next to them, and then scooping up more cones. The work required steady attention to the conveyor belt and to the boxes, which had to be filled rapidly, in order to keep up with the flow of cones, and then moved on when full. And yet the women were conversing while they worked. I could see them talking to each other, occasionally laughing, chatting while they gathered up and stacked the cones very rapidly.

"There. Look," Ofelia whispered, though she certainly didn't have to whisper. She couldn't possibly have been heard over the sound of the machinery, and, in any case, the screen hid us from view. "That's her facing us. On the end. The last girl."

I looked at the girl she pointed out. The girl was not a girl at all, but a small, round-faced, middle-aged woman. A woman who I thought looked nothing like Marie. A person in whom I could detect no trace of either my brother's features or Ofelia's. She seemed absorbed by her work and also rather clumsy, as if she had been placed at the end of the line in order to give her the least-demanding job. Still, it seemed as though she had to think carefully each time she picked up a cone. There was an odd, mechanical rhythm to her movements. She wasn't talking to the other women. Nor did she appear to be listening to them. She looked as if she was lost in her own world. She appeared tired to me. Or perhaps sad. We didn't stay long. After a few minutes, Ofelia led me away.

Ofelia didn't invite me to come inside the trailer again. When we got back to the trailer park, she pulled up next to my car and left her engine running. She hadn't said a word during the drive back. Now she turned to me and said, "I've got to go to work now. Normally it's my day off. But someone's sick today."

I was going to say, "Where do you work?" But something told me to drop it, that it was a good time to part and it would be stupid to try to start up another conversation with her at this point. Instead, I told her I had something for her and asked her to wait while I got it out of my car.

I gave her a little needlepoint pillow with a picture of a Dutch boy on the front, the only thing I'd found in the thrift store that seemed worth anything. I told her it was just something I had bought for her on the way and I hoped she liked it. She said she did, and I believed it was true. She looked at it for a long time, really taking in the fine needlework, the skating Dutchman, his rosy cheeks and china-blue eyes, and then she pressed it against her chest before setting it down on the passenger seat.

Then I handed her the envelope in which I had put ten hundred-dollar bills earlier that morning. "This," I said, "is for Marie. It's from my mother."

She didn't take the envelope, but rather just stared at it for a while. She looked at it in silence, a silence that to me seemed laden with contempt. I believed we both knew what the other was thinking during that silence. She knew there was money in that envelope, and she both did and didn't want to take it. I believed she felt she was being compromised. And I thought she knew I wanted to say something about Jim and what he'd done to Marie and how I didn't think that what my parents had done was so bad compared to that. I believed the thoughts in both our heads were so clear and so strong that they almost radiated from our heads as words coming out in bubbles. Finally I just dropped the envelope in her lap. She picked it up and set it down on the passenger seat.

"I shouldn't take it," she said.

"She wanted to make up for what happened." I was talking about my mother, of course, and I felt tears begin to come to my eyes. My voice grew wavery. "It's the best she could do. It's not much, but it's something."

"It don't make up for anything," Ofelia said.

"I don't think she thought it would." I blinked back the tears and smiled at her. She did not smile back.

"Maybe we'll see each other again sometime."

"Maybe we will," I said.

She shrugged and gave me one last long, sad look, and then she drove away.

Driving home, I smoked the joint, all of it, three times the amount I normally smoked at any one time, and of course things were becoming very unclear. I was back to my old adulterated self, though it was a self that appeared quite crystal clear to me at that instant.

On the other hand, you could say that things had never been very clear for me, especially when it came to Marie and Ofelia. I had the strangest feeling that Ofelia might have tricked me, that the woman she had pointed out to me, that middle-aged, sad, clumsy woman packing ice-cream cones into boxes, wasn't really my niece at all, but some stranger she had selected for just that purpose. Thinking of that, I began to laugh. What was I laughing at? Just the craziness of it all.

REMEMBER WHY
WE'RE HERE

•

George Singleton

My wife kept talking about convection ovens. I thought she said "conviction" at first—which brought up weird visions of capital punishment—and then I thought she said "confection," even though we don't eat that much candy outside of the holidays. Already we owned a microwave and a regular electric thing in the house she bought outright. On the porch was a hibachi I'd had since before meeting her and a larger gas grill I didn't trust, seeing as flames seemed to pour out of the bottom more often than not. I'd read an article one time about some poor insurance salesman or banker outside with a spatula in his hand when a stray bullet hit his tank. His family saw everything, too.

My wife said, "There's a new self-cleaning convection wall oven out that can cook a thirty-five-pound turkey. It can cook a dozen loaves of bread. It has a convection roast mode, and a convection bake, and a thermal bake."

I said, "*Thermal* bake? What does that mean, Jerilyn? What do you want to cook that needs a setting called thermal? Why don't you wait a couple years, and I bet they come up with something catering to people who need different circles of hell." It just came to me, like that.

She said, "For piping-hot casseroles," and from the way she said it I knew she'd been memorizing some advertisement. Jerilyn said, "Convection ovens use circulating heated air, which roasts meats faster while leaving them beautifully browned outside and juicy inside."

I kept a can of Sterno in my backpack, too. There were dry sticks out in the yard, and probably pieces of flint scattered around somewhere. I'd never been in the Boy Scouts, but a couple of my buddies growing up were, and they taught me how to build a fire, tie a knot, and skin a snake. I said, "I don't know how to say this. I know I said when I came into some money it was yours for what you wanted, Jerilyn. But I thought you'd have something more in mind like a swimming pool or a good minivan. We don't have a swimming pool or a minivan. But we do have ovens. We have stoves. We got us some appliances is what I'm saying."

Jerilyn did not stick her bottom lip out and pout. She stared me in the face and made it clear how circulating heated air was the best thing for us. She said, "I want the convection to go in the kitchen of our new mountain cabin up past Tryon." Then she unrolled one of those free real-estate guides she always picked up off racks outside of places we went that served all-you-can-eat buffets. She said, "Some guy just bought most of the whole top of White Oak Mountain where there used to be a Baptist church camp. I called the real-estate agent, and she said they tore down all the old stone structures and strategically placed the rocks in the lake so bass and bream would bed better." She said, "The developer started in on a dozen little cabins around the lake but ran out of money and wants to sell them off fast."

Jerilyn nodded and kept eye contact. For some reason, I said, "Why'd the Baptist church camp go under?" I thought Baptists still thrived hard here. I said, "I bet there are a bunch of rattlesnakes and copperheads up on that mountain, and I bet those Baptists were a little on the charismatic side." I didn't go into detail about probable snake handling and lack of antivenin.

"You said you're finally the man of the house, Spoon," Jerilyn said. She wouldn't take my last name when we got married, but she sure used it more than my first.

"Circulating heated air that roasts meats faster. Thirty-five-pound turkey," I said, walking toward the answering machine. "I better think of more and better things for the babies of America."

"Uh-huh," she said.

We'd just gotten back from visiting Jerilyn's cousins down in Charleston. They wanted to throw a little party for me, seeing as I'd finally made it in their eyes. In the past, I'd always tried to find a way out of these visits on account of I felt somewhat the oddball. I didn't have family money, and although I went to college and tried to do well, I didn't have two houses on the same island. I said, "Well, I guess that hot-air theme kind of runs in your family, doesn't it, Jerilyn?"

The week before, I'd gotten my first check from the lawyer who took care of whatever needed getting done. I'd come up with a line of baby diapers that had LOADING ZONE emblazoned on the back side. The people up in New York said that it was perfect timing—that kids now had a new fascination with heavy equipment and that a tiny picture of a dump truck releasing its load on the back of a kid's butt was just what America needed to remember its blue-collar roots. I even got an offer for a regular nine-to-five job with an ad agency up there, but I told them I'd rather stick to teaching at the technical college, where I had enough time to come up with new ideas. Jerilyn said something about how I must not have that much time or I'd've come up with more than one idea in a decade.

Anyway, we went down to Charleston and ended up with Cousin Dargan—who went by Dar, which always sounded kind of stupid and Cro-Magnon at best—and his sister, Ashley. Ashley's good-hearted doctor-husband, Sam, and their two kids were there, plus Dar's latest girlfriend, named— get this—Anise, who got some weird theology degree from a place I'm sure sent diplomas through the mail, but it gave her the right to preach at a church way left of the Unitarians. I'm no psychiatrist, but I'd take bets that Anise got called Anus a bunch in her life and joined the odd church in order to cast hexes on old high-school classmates.

We sat there at a table with however many seats we needed one block off the Market. The waiter came up and took our drink orders. This was not a typical tourist restaurant, either. There were no fishnets filled with starfish hanging from the ceiling. There were no fake sailfish on the walls.

There were no prices on the menu is what I'm saying.

Dar was last and said, "I'll have one of your house micro beers, but don't bring it with so much attitude, man." Dar'd sold real estate in the past but now talked about going to New Mexico in order to learn about pressure points, channeling, acupuncture, aromatherapy—you name it. Dar still had a broken-off needle in his arm, if that matters, from the old days when he went to college and didn't care about doing well 'cause he knew he had family money and would end up owning two houses on one island.

Sam leaned over the table and said, "Don't start up, Dar. Remember why we're here." We were there, of course, to celebrate my newfound success. "While I'm at it, could you please watch your language around the kids?"

Well, this didn't go over well at all. Even though Dar cherished the wayward-family-member archetype, he always bowed up when confronted with his behavior in public. Dar said, "Why we're here? I thought we came here to have a good time, man. The waiter acted like he had to go stomp hops and barley by himself. I don't need that."

Sam and Ashley's girl said, "Your name's Anise," pronouncing it the wrong way.

Dar said, "Goddamn, tell your own girl to watch her mouth. I didn't come to wish Spoon well and listen to people talking buttholes all night long."

I said, "Hey," all diminuendo. Dar sat back and stared at his knee.

Ashley said, " 'Loading Zone'! That's so cute. It almost makes me want to have another baby. How much money are you going to make off this deal, Spoon?"

The waiter brought our drinks and served Dar first. He didn't say anything. I squeezed Jerilyn's knee under the table twice to let her know I wasn't comfortable. I may not come from some kind of aristocratic family, but my parents knew enough about minding their own business. I said, "I get a lump sum up front and then a penny for each diaper sold. They're going to be marketed in twelve and twenty-four packs. I got a good lawyer." I squeezed the leg again, once and long, which I consider the international sign for "keep quiet." My parents taught me to mind my own business—and lie big.

"That's great," Sam said. He came from a working-class Chicago family, and out of everyone in Jerilyn's family I connected with him best. When he talked about my liver, he didn't preach.

I said, "Thanks." Anise looked at me and moved her lips. I said, "What?" but then realized that she was chanting or something.

Dar said, "When I was in college, I beat off into a sock so much I grew a toenail on my pecker." He held his right hand in a loose fist, poured beer into the cup he'd made with

282 • GEORGE SINGLETON

his fingers, and said, "Look at me—I'm getting my date for tonight drunk!"

Sam got his children up first, then Ashley ran after them. Anise said, "Your family doesn't understand that you offer them unconditional love, Dar. They don't yet know agape."

Dar held his eyebrows high, shook his head in disbelief, and said, "Did you see those entities coming out of my sister's chest? Man, no wonder her husband's projecting so much. I wish they could see what I can see. I can tell two things: when meat's gone bad and when a bad marriage is going on."

I caught myself nodding up and down until we finally left for that hotel room my wife said we'd checked into but hadn't really. We'd always stayed with Dar before. Jerilyn talked about how our suitcases were already inside the Holiday Inn, et cetera. I caught myself thinking about a more peaceful time, like when I got hit by a car at age twelve or like a couple years later when I cut off my thumb up at my dad's shop and had to get it sewn back on.

This, of course, happened before my knowledge of convection ovens. Had it happened after, I'd've caught myself thinking of perfect heat, too.

The man who'd yearned to transform most of White Oak Mountain from a defunct Baptist camp into a circle of modern tin-roofed A-frames with lofts had got caught poking a female contractor who'd come down from an experimental design school in Vermont to work on the project. That was the real-estate agent's story. That was why the cabins had unfinished interiors and low prices. She said that ours wasn't made by that developer, though, that ours was bought and unfinished by another man totally, like it'd matter. The big developer didn't get his hands on everything, was her story.

About two minutes after I gave in to the oven, Jerilyn and I drove the sixty miles north to our cabin. The real-estate agent's name was Penny. Although I normally don't trust people named after currency or people in the same line of work that Dar'd been in before getting all spiritual, she and I hit it off well. Penny offered my wife and me cigars.

"Is your real name Spoon, Spoon?" Penny said when we got out of her car. She drove a regular car, a Ford something.

I said, "My last name's Spoon. Everybody's always called me Spoon. My first name is normal. Call me Spoon."

Jerilyn walked alone to the edge of the lake and turned around. She said, "With all the trees, you can hardly even see this cabin here."

I said, "Trees have limbs that get heavy in winter. They crack and fall on the roof."

Penny said, "You could cut them down. Or you could learn how to lay tin. Your insurance will pay for it, Spoon."

Jerilyn yelled, "I've always wanted to grow a shade garden. We're not cutting down any of these trees. Our other house doesn't have trees, and I'm tired of growing only corn, tomatoes, and peppers."

There was no one on the lake. That made me think that maybe some dead Baptists were submerged and had spooked people away. Penny said, "This lot here is three-quarters of an acre, and you have the creek on your property." She held out a map. The land wedged right into the lake, almost halfway in.

I said, "I can roof. I can also nail down one-by-twelve planks on the particle board for the floor and insulate the walls and put up drywall. I know how to do those kinds of jobs. A lot of people think pine's too soft for flooring, but you get a good kiln-dried southern yellow pine and it's good. I don't want no tongue-and-groove."

Penny folded up the map. Jerilyn skipped toward us. "You'll have to get a licensed electrician and plumber. There's a permit for the septic tank. I think it'll go over there," Penny said, pointing to the side of the property farthest from the creek. She said, "You can get something called builder's risk insurance until the cabin's finished. It'll cover if the place burns or if someone gets hurt."

I said, "I only believe in car insurance. You see, if you start feeling puny and think you've come down with a major illness, all you got to do is get in a car wreck and yell out, 'Ow, I got whiplash! I got cirrhosis of the liver, too!' I'm pretty sure it's a scam you can get away with."

We walked inside, and within a minute Jerilyn figured out where the sink would go and the refrigerator. She told Penny how she'd seen a glass-doored china cabinet on sale at one of the junk stores in town already. My wife held her hands out three feet, pointed to the wall as if she were bringing in a 747 on a runway, and said, "This is where the convection oven will go."

I looked up at the hole in the ceiling. I would have to make a staircase or buy one of those prefab wrought-iron spiral things. I'd have to invest some of my "Loading Zone" diaper money in that series of do-it-yourself books sold on late-night television. "This might be too much for us, Jerilyn," I said. "We can afford something that costs a little more and takes less work."

Penny said, "People never plan to die, but they die to plan." I didn't know what that meant. It sounded like something taught at a pep rally for insurance agents. "You can do a lot with this place. If you want to cover the area underneath, you'd have basically a three-story house," Penny said. "I think that's a good idea about what you mentioned about making a patio under the front porch," she added. Then she put her hand to her mouth.

I said, "I've been here the whole time and haven't heard about any patio. Who said something about a patio? I didn't say anything about it. Jerilyn was down at the lake doing her thumb like some kind of old-master portrait artist. She didn't say anything about a patio."

Penny tried to cover herself. She turned her back to me, looked at the wall, and said, "What do you teach at the tech college, Spoon?"

I said, "Logic, speech, and rhetoric," which wasn't really true.

Penny turned around and looked at my wife. Jerilyn said, "I've been up here a couple times before, Spoon. As a matter of fact, I've already written a check for the earnest money for the place and agreed to what the man selling wants to get."

In the old days I'd've gotten mad. Well, in the old days Jerilyn could've pulled out a hundred grand from one of her trust funds, which were growing at the same rate my student loans were because of the default, and she could've bought anything. I'd've pouted then, feeling that I wasn't man enough to be a man. But now just catching her and Penny trying to act suave gave me enough satisfaction. I said, "Earnest money?"

Jerilyn said to Penny, "Spoon doesn't know what that means." To me she said, "I had to put down a deposit that said we wanted to hold the place until we checked everything out. Earnest money isn't cashed, and it goes against the bid."

I looked at that big hole in the ceiling where the stairwell would go. I said I knew what "earnest" meant. I said, "Did you check to see if there're termites, Jerilyn?"

Penny said, "Termites don't eat into cedar siding, Spoon."

I said, "I know. I'm just checking on you two again," and caught myself nodding just like in the priceless restaurant. I said, "I can probably afford to quit teaching for a year and finish this place off." I made a point of saying I wanted to close the deal as soon as possible.

My wife and my real-estate agent did some kind of double holding-of-hands thing I'd only heard about. It looked a little like this contra dancing I'd seen on the local news. On the way home I said to Jerilyn, "How long have you known Penny?"

She said, "About a month. Actually I met her outside of all this. Right before you got the good news is when we met. Right after, I happened to pick up the real-estate guide and see the cabin. It was some kind of synchronicity thing, Spoon."

We took all the switchbacks slowly and stopped completely for vistas and waterfalls. I said, "Some kind of karma thing, huh? Some kind of predestination, that's what you're saying?"

Jerilyn sat there. She looked out the window. In the distance a red-tail hovered, almost still. My wife said, "Don't compare me to Dar. I see what's coming."

"So how did y'all meet before? I want to know this story about y'all meeting before I sold the diapers." A work truck pulled over so we could get by. I waved, as neighbors-to-be should.

Jerilyn said, "The first day I came up to the cabin, there was this old man on the other side of the lake pulling fish out every time he threw in his hook. Is a pound a good-sized bluegill? He said he'd caught eight one-pound bluegill. I didn't know if that was good or not. I told him my husband once caught a four-pound brown trout fly-fishing. Remember that time you caught that big thing, Spoon?"

It was a gravel road, and every vista point had a house owned by the same people Zarathustra passed on the way down, I'm sure. It came to me, just like that. I said, "Hey. Hey, don't change what I asked you. Where'd you meet that real-estate woman before you met her again?"

When my wife told me she hadn't really joined a bowling league, that she'd actually joined a church of women that met on Thursday nights and that the congregation sat in a circle and talked about their bad childhoods, I wasn't surprised. Per usual, I didn't mention how my father had spent some time unemployed or how he'd had a physical disability or how he'd whipped my butt when I needed it.

I drove, and paid attention.

Jerilyn said, "We've been married ten years this Halloween, Spoon. You can't hold it against me for wondering if things could be better. I just wanted to hear other women tell their stories. I'm not in love with anyone else, if that's what you want to know."

Of course I didn't exactly hear her. I asked where she got the address for women meeting to complain. I asked if she'd been watching all those talk shows in the afternoon. I said, "What, have you seen some entities flying out of my chest or something?"

My wife put her hand on my leg. She laughed and patted and shook her head like a wet dog. She said, "Spoon, we're not on this land for very long, considering. It's okay to strive for more. What I learned when it comes to marriage, it's better to ditch a plan than plan a ditch."

I damn near missed a curve right then.

By accident I called the lawyer's dog the lawyer's first name. The lawyer kept her cocker spaniel in the office for some reason. I don't know if she did a bunch of work for the SPCA. The lawyer's name was Baiba Brousseau. Jerilyn couldn't come close to saying it, really. I'd taken enough French in my lifetime to say the last name, but I still wasn't sure about the first.

I practiced "Ba-ee-ba, Ba-ee-ba, Ba-ee-ba," forever. It seemed like a trick to me.

We went in to sign the papers, and the dog came up, and Baiba said, "That's Daisy Mae. Say, 'Hey, Daisy Mae,'" et cetera, et cetera.

I petted the dog and said, "Ba-ee-ba!" like that, stupid. I said, "What a nice dog you have. Hey, Daisy Mae," trying to cover myself in a way that only wives and real-estate agents can, evidently. I probably looked at the wall or ceiling, I don't know.

I doubt it mattered.

That's not the big thing. At the time it seemed like the hook to a good country song, but my self-revelation wasn't close.

Baiba couldn't afford air-conditioning, and it must've been two thousand degrees in there. I didn't like lawyers in the first place—none of them, not even public defenders who supposedly care about people like me—and one with a dog on her sofa seemed overly obvious. She said, "On my sixty-five-acre farm we have horses, goats, cows, cats, and dogs. Daisy Mae just got kicked, so I'm keeping her here. I've got her on herbs."

Jerilyn squeezed my leg once, knowing what I'd say, which was, "You ain't got no manatees or emus? We want to raise a litter of emus under the house and manatees in the lake." I didn't smile or anything.

Baiba said, "My husband and I have an order in for llamas. I'd like to raise some llamas, and some angora rabbits. You can make a bunch of money off them. Unfortunately, y'all have a zoning law up on that mountain that keeps you from raising anything. You'd need three acres before you could think about a farm. Now, there's a chance you could jigsaw a farm—there's a lot ten lots away from your cabin that you could buy, and in time you might be able to buy all the lots in between, one by one. But for now the home-owners' association will take care of making sure no one oversteps the rules."

We sat around a big table waiting for Penny and the guy who sold the land. Baiba had on an electric fan down on the floor that didn't help whatsoever. I felt in my coat pocket for the certified check. I said, "Uh-oh. There's a homeowners' association?"

"You don't want any trailers next to you, do you? That vacant lot right next to yours might come up for sale. You don't want someone plopping down a single-wide within your view, believe me."

Now, I know all about depreciating land values and what not, but I still don't like people telling me what I can or can't put on land I own. I'm no member of one of those militias or anything. Occasionally I catch myself thinking how I'd like to own and drive a tank, but that's about it. I said, "I was born in a trailer, Ms. Brousseau. I'm probably not the person to tell what I would or wouldn't want to see outside my window. As a matter of fact, I'd probably like to have a good neighbor in a mobile home next to me, as opposed to the smell of horses, goats, and cows."

My wife said, "You weren't born in a trailer, Spoon." She looked at the lawyer and said, "He's just kidding. I wouldn't be surprised if we got up there on the mountain and he decided to become a stand-up comedian."

Baiba Brousseau stared at me as if she'd just noticed horns sticking out of my scalp. Penny walked in with the owner of the cabin and said, "Sorry we're late. Hey, Spoon. Hey, Jerilyn. Spoon and Jerilyn, this is Reverend Jimmy Splawn." We shook hands all the way around. I thought about shaking my own wife's hand, but Marx Brothers routines probably don't go over well inside a lawyer's office during the signing period.

I said to Reverend Jimmy, "Hey, I know you. I get a letter from you once a month asking me for money. You run that Faith Ministries place, right?"

Understand, if I'd've known that a preacher once owned my unfinished cabin, I doubt I'd've gone ahead with Jerilyn's bid, et cetera. Call me a bigot.

Reverend Jimmy pulled out some fake tears and said, "We loved that cabin. It gave us so many memories. But my wife's mother got real sick, and my daddy died, and I just don't know if we can go up there anymore." He said, "We felt so lucky just getting a part of the old camp before the developer could yank it up."

I said, "I send y'all ten bucks a month to help run your food bank. I'll be damned. It's a tiny solar system, ain't it?" I said, "Did you use to run the Baptist camp up on the lake? Man, I bet they really had an assembly line up there doing baptisms."

Penny sat next to Reverend Jimmy. She was on the seller's side, of course. It was some kind of North Carolina law. We even had to sign a document, that day my wife and the agent did their odd dance, saying we understood how the lines were drawn.

Baiba went on and on about things I didn't understand concerning deeds, septic-tank placement, moving the driveway, permits, et cetera. I looked over at Reverend Jimmy and knew he wasn't selling the cabin because of sick relatives or sad memories. I knew, too, that I'd met destitute men outside bars down in Greenville, and when I offered them a ride to the shelter Faith Ministries operated, no one took me up because they didn't like having to feign guilt, humility, and obedience for a plate of mashed potatoes and green beans. More than once I'd given a man two dollars and said, "Don't lie to me about what you'll spend it on. I don't really care. Booze or BLT—it doesn't make any difference."

Now, I'm not saying this to prove some kind of martyr thing. I just don't care. If things don't go all that well for you here on the planet, it's probably best to forget. That's all I'm saying.

Reverend Jimmy said, "Miracles happen up on that mountain, Mr. Spoon. Miracles. It's not just the clouds flying by or the sunset. You will see things that will change you forever."

Baiba said, "Sign here," and handed me whatever she'd been talking about earlier. She said, "As they say, it's better to stake a claim than it is to claim a steak." She said, "First you got to plan your work and then you got to work your plan."

I withered in my humid chair. I cannot explain the lawyer's voice, but in that moment I realized that either the preacher'd gotten caught doing illegal things with a boys' youth group or a member of the choir, or he'd had an uncomfortable revelation about the Truth, and that's why we'd gotten the deal. At that point I knew I'd spend time scared and paranoid in the cabin, waiting for Reverend Jimmy's regretful and holy and rationalized return. I'd look down at the lake and wonder why our bodies seemed more water than dirt, more dirt than air or fire. I knew right there at the lawyer's miserable conference table that if Jerilyn and I lived to be two hundred years old, we'd never figure out those old metaphysical questions, and that I'd stoop to ask Dar or Anise if they'd picked up on anything at some kind of weird gathering in Asheville or Santa Fe.

I signed. My wife performed Morse code on my thigh. I didn't understand anything whatsoever. The only thing I would've bet on that day was that I'd bend my thumbs odd with a hammer soon and have to come up with another patent or copyright to help all of us against people afraid of mobile homes and strangers.

When Jerilyn and I left the lawyer's office, we drove straight up the mountain, like we planned, and unrolled our two sleeping bags over the particle board in what later would be our den. I went downstairs and built a fire from fallen trees, caught and cleaned four bluegill from the lake within an hour, and placed the fish on ice after I pulled a champagne bottle out. My wife and I sat there quiet until pure darkness set in, until we couldn't make out bats flitting overhead. We didn't mention money or morality, cause and effect, or luck. We didn't niggle each other to remember a time when our marriage wasn't so secure. I talked myself out of thinking about times when I insisted on eating nothing but sardines and Slim Jims just to prove how poor I'd grown up.

I said, "I don't want to sound holier than thou or pessimistic, but I didn't come out of Baiba's office feeling so good about buying a place without floors or walls from a preacher. Did you see that guy's hair? I don't believe a word he said."

Jerilyn put her arm through mine there at the fire and said, "I smell fish. You need to wash your hands."

I nodded. I thought about how there wasn't a place to wash my hands except a lake that smelled of fish already. We didn't have a sink yet, of course, much less a hot-air hand dryer. It wasn't the time to bring up disagreements we might have about major appliances and what we could or couldn't hook up in the cabin, conventional or not.

Instead, I pointed upward and didn't pretend to distinguish stars, planets, and satellites shining above or to explain why some are brighter than others.

PENNY DREADFULS

•

Heidi Julavits

STATEMENT OF PURPOSE,
GORDON T. ANGSTROM FELLOWSHIP,
AMERICAN ORNITHOLOGICAL ASSOCIATION
"...But it is the postgestation period of the Caspian tern
that is of greatest interest to the ornithological world. The
Caspian tern, at least that species particular to the subequatorial regions of Asia, abandons its nest to take up residence in the hollow of a tree during this postgestation period
referred to as 'cocooning' (so named by my colleague Charles
'Choppy' Laughton in his article 'From Butterfly to Caspian
Tern: Cocooning as Metaphor for Reincarnation'). The
mother and newborn chicks reside in this temporary abode,
while the father remains on the 'outside,' taking care of such
necessities as the gathering of food and the guarding of the
permanent nest. Once inside the 'cocooning' residence, the
mother works obsessively to secure herself and her offspring

by filling in the entryway with mud and small stones, leaving just enough space through which the father can pass insects. This wall remains intact until, in a beautiful act of symmetry, of passing the torch, so to speak, the now fully grown terns break through the mud wall, thereby freeing themselves and their mother from their temporary captivity.

"In order to best record this transition from birth to adulthood, I plan to cut a small, round incision in the trunk of a tree inhabited by a mother tern and her chicks, then cover it with Plexiglas so that I can observe and record the never-before-seen events that transpire between birth and adulthood. My wife, the artist Poppy Frankenweiler, will be on hand to function as the project illustrator. Ultimately, I envision a finished work that is accessible to all levels of bird lovers—from the trained scientist to the mere hobbyist."

MIRI, SARAWAK, MALAYSIA, 5/6 (REEL #1, *HOMO SAPIENS SAFARIS IN DESERTO,* DOCUMENTARY FILM FOR THE BLIND)

We first meet Poppy Frankenweiler just seven days before her death. She is seated upon a footstool of woven river reeds that crackle as she wriggles her wide khaki bottom, trying to interlock herself with the knubbly underlying pattern. She leans her meaty back against a tall tent stake and sends the concave canvas swooping this way and that. This causes her to jump back, in a nervous, wiry way that seems unsuited to her soft, expansive frame. It is evident that the presence of a film crew makes her anxious.

"Poppy," says Franz irritably, putting a hand on the curved roof to soothe its swaying. We see Franz. He is a willowy man dressed in similar drab dress, his stockings pricked at by brambles and sticking out from his calves in strange, woolly loops. According to the notches Poppy has cut in her walking stick with a mud-matted Swiss Army knife, it has been fifty-two days since Franz has made love to her. He is a salt-speckled blond, his hair a dulled metallic tangle of iron-wool curls, his goatee long, the part beneath his nose swirling to the left and right in graceful wings whose tips catch in the corners of his mouth as he speaks. This irritates him, but he channels the irritation to his ropy forearms that cut wood with the vigor of fingernails attending to an itch. Franz is not one for grooming, despite his Boston Brahmin upbringing. Yet Franz is a marvelous open-fire cook and, given a sack of lima beans, some curry powder, and a conch or two, can whip up a feast of unimaginable elegance. Poppy sometimes calls him a house husband as she sits reading in a low-slung canvas chair before the fire, stuffing her pear-shaped face full of Franz's fabulous gruel and reading to him from a coverless and rather war-torn paperback entitled *Pure Bliss*. Typically, Franz does not react to her taunts. Either he is confident in his own masculinity and feels no need to stoop to his wife's occasionally petty level, or he has a terrible problem with anger and must choke it back if he is not to reach out and instead throttle her petal-jowled throat. We cannot be sure.

As the sun has not yet set, Poppy is reading in the shadow of the tent in order to avoid excessive exposure. Like many *Homo sapiens safaris,* she is cursed with a pinkish white skin, poorly suited to the treeless plains and subtropical forests in which she usually finds herself.

Cut to Poppy on Archival Footage, Tape #10B, Dar es Salaam, 2/28. "I find I drink in sun and heat like a dry sponge." (Poppy concluded that the Tanzanian physician she consulted for heat exhaustion was a "witch doctor" and a "quack" and ignored his advice that she get a breast reduction as "more evidence that the myths of the first world have even succeeded in colonizing the minds of purported scientists." She, like many of her species, does not consider herself first world or third world. She is, in a word, otherworldly.)

Poppy is giggling to herself as she reads. "Listen to this, Franz," she calls.

We cannot find Franz. He has hidden himself behind a shrub to urinate. Even on a deserted beach on the coast of Borneo, Franz is a relentlessly modest man. As with all animals, logic does little to alter the patterns established by habit or instinct.

Poppy begins to read to the swaying brush.

"I beg you, Bliss, do not be swayed by the gravest of sins—the Sin of Omission," the king said to his kneeling daughter, his brow furrowed like the prosperous fields of his kingdom, knowing that she held something from him in her tightly bound bodice that seemed to burst forth with its untold secret. "Kindness is not immune to procrastination, my darling. Beware of slow compassion as you tend to your affairs." And with that the king placed what was to be the final kiss upon his daughter's dew-soft cheek, pushing a familiar curl of blue-black hair from her pearly forehead, wondering if perhaps he might find her secret scratched there. Although there was nothing—not a blemish, not a clue—he could smell her betrayal, the way a foxhound smells a fox. As he watched his daughter's form floating away from him over the stone floor, he was suddenly struck with a spear like an icicle in his heart. The words bloomed like a wound in his chest—Byron the Scoundrel. The man he had exiled from his kingdom. The man he knew his daughter loved—maybe even enough to betray her own father. His eyes filled with tears, tears of both despair and utter rage, at the thought of Byron's rooty peasant hands thumbing his daughter's soft hips.

Poppy looks at her husband's twig-dotted form emerging from the brush. "Quite a hoot, n'est-ce pas?"

Franz makes a face that causes the tips of his mustache to touch like the handle on a pair of pliers. "I don't know how you can abide those damned penny dreadfuls," he says.

Cut to Poppy rummaging through a pile of bloated, coverless paperbacks on a blanket in a marketplace in Bangkok (Archival Footage, Tape #12C, Bangkok, 4/20).

"Well, darling, it's not like Billy Shakespeare's available in abundance here in the bush." Poppy smiles sweetly and thumbs a thick page. "Not like you couldn't use a little romantic instruction yourself, Franz, honey," she adds with an evil smile.

Franz tosses her a glowering look. "Harlequin rubbish," he mutters.

Poppy laughs again and waves him off with her pink and sweat-sheened palm.

"You laugh." Franz bristles, eyebrows cocked. "Little do you know, my dear, the insidiousness of those poisonous little paperbacks. I've scientific proof—my Aunt Edie was an unfortunate victim of reading penny dreadfuls. Couldn't shake the notion from her spinsterish head that a prince was supposed to locate her on her porch in Council Bluffs, Iowa, swaddle her in silks and chinchilla blankets, and sweep her off to a castle on the moors. She was discovered by a member of the Council Bluffs Volunteer Fire Department—no Prince Charming, I assure you—on her birthday. Sad old thing."

"I know, I know," Poppy says, dismissive, impatient. "They found her on her sixtieth birthday in the middle of the lake dressed in a polyester bathrobe and wrapped in an afghan."

"An orange afghan, Poppy. Penny dreadful in her pocket. Being a scientist, I couldn't help but put two and two together. *Amber Moon,* if I remember the title correctly. The woman tries to kill herself by walking into the sea but is saved at the last minute by her Poseidon lover, who ravishes her on the beach. The end. Poor Aunt Edie." Franz shakes his head. "I'll never forget the look on her face, Poppy. It was, it was . . ."

"Pure bliss?" Poppy chuckles again, then presses her form through the meager tent opening and disappears from view.

MIRI, SARAWAK, 5/7—MORNING (REEL #2, HSSID)

The Frankenweilers spend a sleepless night plagued by squeaking torrents of bats flying over the ill-placed tent near the mouth of the Sarawak. (*Insectus volaris,* Poppy and Franz should know, follow the river from the interior to the sea each evening to catch insects. They travel up to three hundred miles round-trip every day.)

"Look," Franz says to Poppy, pointing to the black ribbon winding through the sky.

"The noise!" Poppy cries, as she spoons a meager breakfast of cold curried beef from a can into her petulant mouth. Franz is too exhausted to build a fire. The Frankenweilers could buy a doughnut and a half-decent cup of Nescafé at the concession stand near the ferry, but such "concessions" to modernity, we have noticed, are repellent notions to most *Homo sapiens safaris,* as is sleeping at the Howard Johnson's conveniently located near the boat landing.

"The noise!" Poppy cries again, holding her hands over her cinnamon-bun ears. They are doughy and scarred a permanent purple from years of intense African and sub-Asian ultraviolet exposure.

On the way to the boat, Franz points out the flora and fauna. "*Dora ignomus insipidus,*" he says. "Look."

The boat the Frankenweilers are to take to the interior of Borneo is named *The Mulu Voyager.* Franz wrinkles his nose at the name, points to it bobbing on the hull, looks directly into the camera to convey the depth of his discontent to the folks back home. Poppy, it appears, is unperturbed by this evidence of cultural contamination. She has already struck up a conversation with a small white man, dressed in neat hiking shorts and a wide-brimmed panama hat. He is conspicuously clean shaven. Franz approaches the man warily through the underbrush of bags and rope-tied cardboard boxes littering the dock and waiting to be tossed into the hold.

The camera follows just over Franz's shoulder. As we near the pair on the dock, snippets of conversation catch in the mike.

MAN: . . . runway photographer in Milan, but of course, as you can imagine, it was hardly fulfilling, at least from an artistic standpoint.

POPPY: So you're an artist?

MAN: An *artist,* ho, ho. Well, not in the traditional sense. I use the term loosely, you see. Art to me is synonymous with passion. Your passion may be banking or ditchdigging or train sets, for all I care. It is the depth of feeling behind any activity that elevates it to a higher level. I use the word only because our pitiful language has no other. Quite unlike the Zulus, I might add.

FRANZ *inserts himself in the conversation, and quite literally between* POPPY *and* MAN: Ah, yes, well, the Zulus. Heh, heh. It's unfair to compare ourselves to them. Now there's a top-notch linguistic system if ever there *was* one, at least in the post-continental-drift era.

MAN *turning to face* FRANZ, *missing but half a beat to size him up:* And so underrated, don't you agree? I mean, what with all that bunk about the Eskimos and how they have more than two hundred different words for snow—light fluffy low-water-density snow, wet heavy fell-on-a-Tuesday snow, and so forth and so forth. Totally untrue, of course. Just another desperate stab by some anthropologist to come

up with an original statement of purpose for a grant
proposal.

Franz and MAN stare at each other territorially from a
safe distance. Their nostrils twitch. The revving engines of
The Mulu Voyager prompt a timely conclusion to both the
awkward silence and the awkward conversation. This seems
a particularly poetic moment to fade out.

*Pan upward to the sky. Cut in sequence of bats, filmed
at dawn, returning to the interior, an ominous black ribbon
snaking its way across the sky. Cut to bat's-eye view of river,
winding in a similar fashion into the rain forest. Reinforce
ominous quality of images with a few bars of Hildegaard von
Bingen's Hilarity #6. Fade to black.*

MULU LODGE, MULU NATIONAL PARK, SARAWAK, 5/7
(REEL #3, HSSID)

Franz, Poppy, and MAN arrive safely at the Mulu Lodge
in a dugout canoe with a mosquito-pitched Evinrude driven
by a local guide. The lodge is a modest log cabin raised on
stilts, built on the marshy edge of the river. A long dock
extends into deeper water.

Later the three of them are sitting on the porch drinking
small cups of rice wine offered to them, with great flourish,
by the proprietor. We assume this is excruciatingly distasteful stuff, if their forced smiles and quick gulps are any in-
dication. MAN is cleaning his camera. Franz is chatting with
the proprietor about his research on Caspian terns in half-
intelligible Malay. The guide's English is far superior to
Franz's Malay, but this is a linguistic reality Franz is either
unaware of or choosing to ignore. Poppy has her face well
buried in the depths of *Pure Bliss*. Since she assumes no one
can understand her, she begins to read aloud. Her voice

carries over the flat water but is swallowed by the forest on the other bank. There is no echo.

After days of walking on rutted roads through hamlets inhabited by mute peasants who drooled at the hem of her linen robes, Bliss stumbled toward the shoddy gates of Rensselaer. Once a castle belonging to a viscount whose lecherous passions had infected half the valley with his poisoned progeny, Rensselaer was now an inn located at a muddy crossroads and patronized by the rogues who ran mead between Crotchton-on-Stratton and Harbinger. Bliss retrieved a piece of softened parchment from her robe and looked at the ink, now blurred by the dewy moistness of her palms, and checked it against the blackened brass plaque bolted to the stone gateway. This was the place. A shiver ran down her spine as she imagined Byron's strong hands rubbing their burrs against her soft skin.

"My lord, it's nearly pornographic," exclaims MAN, and gives a lewd chuckle. Poppy ignores the interruption and reads louder.

Once situated in her dank room—number seven, as specified by her lover—Bliss again unfolded the parchment, soft as a piece of chamois, and read aloud the poem Byron had bled into the surface with his quick-spilling ink, the poem he had asked her to read as she waited for him. She didn't even need to light the lamp, for the moon was full and shot a clear beam of moonlight through a hole in the shutter, illuminating the page. In a hushed voice, as if reading an incantation, Bliss began. "A jar of honey chanced to spill, its contents on the windowsill, in many a viscous pool and rill."

There is no echo.

"The flies, attracted by the sweet, began so greedily to eat, they smeared their fragile wings and feet."

No echo.

"Feet," says Poppy.

"FEET!" says Poppy.

"Poppy, do keep it down!" says Franz. "So, the Pinnacles, you say . . ."

Poppy stands and, with the book outstretched in one palm like a Bible, moves to the edge of the porch as if it were a stage.

"With many a switch and pull in vain they gasped to get away again AND DIED IN AROMATIC PAIN."

"PAIN, PAIN, PAIN," says MAN.

"And what do you think the final line is?" says Poppy, turning to MAN. She makes it clear: this is a test.

"Don't forget the forest for the trees?" suggests MAN.

"Oh no, no, you silly fool. It's all a matter of seeing with you photographers." Poppy returns to the edge of the porch and yells into the wet forest.

"O foolish creatures that destroy themselves for transitory joy."

Poppy, less pained by her drink now that she's grown accustomed to the taste, polishes off her paper cup in one swallow. She puts a hand on MAN's blue-white thigh. She leans forward and whispers in his ear. We cannot catch what she says.

The proprietor serves dinner—curried beef, this time warmed over a propane stove. Rice. The proprietor is low to the ground and has big feet that grip the warped porch boards as he walks. Mosquitoes pool in the yellow eddies of tinned candles lining the railing. The sound of insects is deafening beyond the slight overhang.

"Dinner music," says MAN.

"Voices of the still-to-be-slain," says Franz.

During dinner, MAN explains in covert tones that he has been sent to Borneo by a Toronto-based environmental magazine to locate a Swiss man named Bruno, who is living with the Penang (a nomadic rain-forest tribe native to the region) and inciting them to take violent measures against the logging companies. The result has been a backlash in government policy toward the Penang, and a dozen or so longhouse "projects" have recently been established along the river in an attempt to keep the tribal people in one place.

"Bruno sounds like a *very* interesting *man*," Poppy gushes drunkenly, shooting a less-than-veiled look at MAN and shouldering out Franz in a less-than-subtle fashion.

"You've never seen a sadder thing," says MAN, coolly ignoring Poppy's interruption while cultivating the flirtation. ("I used to be an actor, you know," he whispers aside to the camera, then, donning a John Wayne voice, "Y'all don't scare me a lick.") "These people don't even know how to inhabit a building, you see. They all just congregate on the steps. No one ever goes into the rooms. Saddest thing. Like seeing animals in a zoo. But Bruno"—dramatic shake of the head—"he's a real controversial character. Puts spikes in trees and pours mud into the gas tanks of some pretty pricey machinery. Four loggers have died on account of him, and now there's a twenty-five-thousand-dollar bounty on his head," whispers MAN. "Of course, it's my cynical opinion that he's started on this more violent, attention-getting tack as a result of the small amount of publicity he received. Amazing what having an audience will do to a person."

MAN explains that he is to wait at the lodge until

otherwise notified. Bruno will send Penang tribesmen to fetch him, once the coast is clear, and bring him to their secret coven deep in the labyrinth of the Mulu caves.

"Did you know," MAN continues, "that there is an underground river in the caves? Apparently cold as can be, and, given the abundance of calcite deposits, it glows green if you shine a light on it. Rumor has it, however, that no one can swim in it, though the cold tempts you. Apparently there is an underwater current that will immediately suck you under and drag you to a chamber deep in the middle of the caves. Sort of like the Styx, the river to the mysterious underworld."

Shot beneath the table. Poppy has her pudgy warm foot nestled beneath the blue-white leg of MAN.

After dinner MAN pulls out some photos he has pressed between the pages of his *Malay for Laymen* phrase book. He presses them to the wall with wax from the candle. They drift downward, then stutter to a crooked stop as the wax catches in the splintery grain.

Pan from left to right: spokes of a bicycle, with a partially cropped knot of figures involved in some unfocused violent act in the fuzzy background; brain coral, an extreme closeup; an empty room, with the bottom half of a windowpane and a hand pressed to the outside filling the top of the picture; the back side of a painting canvas.

"What an eye you have!" says Poppy.

Cut to Poppy later in rattan seat. "I was just trying to get him in the sack," Poppy admits. In reality, the borders and perspective disturb her. To her they are violent. She says she found herself craning her neck, as if there were something more to be seen by pressing her face close to the photo and trying to slide a sideward glance along the seam. This is nothing new to her. She is used to the world as a succession of images randomly cropped to suit someone's tastes. Not her own.

After dinner Franz goes to his room. Poppy follows, and the door shuts.

Close focus on the wood grain: bulbous rings, the grotesque spirals force-fed to obesity in the fecund environment of a rain forest. A roach of notable length, equally well nourished, its wings a shiny chestnut, gleams in the damp moonlight and crawls along the hinge, balancing delicately, feelers waving like the pole of a tightrope walker. We catch the vague scratches of snores inside the room as they scrape the lower octaves, the higher whistles muffled by the humid air.

The door opens. Poppy emerges wearing a gauzy cotton slip that barely curtains from view the soft rolling hills of her stomach and breasts. She looks about furtively, as if conscious of being watched, as if wanting to be fully seen. She walks into the good light cast by the moon through a triangle of rotted shingle overhead. We catch her perfectly, looking positively alabaster as she opens the neighboring door without knocking and, with one last look over her shoulder and a plump finger to her lips, disappears inside.

Close focus on the wood grain.

BASE CAMP, THE PINNACLES, MULU NATIONAL PARK, 5/8 (REEL #4, HSSID)

We join our subjects (now most enthusiastic about our presence—even, it appears, courting our lens in a rather competitive fashion) deep in the heart of Mulu National Park, after a two-hour trip through the shallow, mud-choked river in the Evinrude-powered dugout, then a grueling hike through ten miles of swampy rain forest. (The equipment fared less than well; two battery packs and a light meter were abducted by a monkey at lunchtime.) Our camp for the next week will be an old shelter, blessedly raised from the insect- and millipede-dotted ground on a wooden platform atop thin stilts. The lean-to was built as headquarters for the British Cartographic Survey Expedition of 1973. During that year, over three thousand kilometers of cave were mapped beneath the Pinnacles, extending northward toward the South China Sea. This included the discovery of one of the biggest caverns in the world, which could hold in excess of five hundred Boeing 747 airplanes.

Previously explored territory—no matter how subterraneous and labyrinthine—appears to be of little concern to our subjects.

Poppy shows us her bloodied sock.

"A leech," she says. She turns her ankle this way and that, to provide a full view. She pulls off her sock, and three bloated leeches the size of grapes tumble onto the ground. Franz immediately torches them by igniting the aerosol emitted from a can of insect repellent.

"It's not as if they are on the brink of extinction," Franz offers us by way of insincere apology. (See *Archival Footage, Tape #6C, 1/12,* Franz's participation in a panel discussion titled "Treading Lightly versus Leaving Your Mark," held at the Fourth Annual Third World Ornithological Explorers Convention at the University of Nairobi.)

Our subject group has diminished to two: MAN disappeared around five this morning in an engineless dugout. He and two men of smallish stature and long earlobes poled away silently to avoid detection by the proprietor, whose political loyalties are still questionable.

"I hope he's been abducted by the proper people," Franz comments.

"Oh, I am quite sure he's just fine," Poppy replies vaguely, then winks at the camera. (Poppy has slowly warmed to the camera over the past few days of filming. She has even taken to wearing lipstick and carefully brushing her honey-blond curls into a knotted polka-dot scarf each morning, using the steam from the coffeepot to mold her curls to her head.)

Soon Poppy has set up her watercolors. She rests her watercolor pad on her fleshy knees and is not looking at anything as she paints. Franz returns from a dip in the nearby river (we are certain he wore his boxer shorts) and watches her painting amorphous shapes of slate blue and gray. They are not even the colors of the sky just now, with the sun settling into its own pink juices.

"Poppy," he scolds, and pulls her up by the wrist. He leads her to the shelter and sets her up in front of a bird's nest a foot wide in diameter wedged in the eave of the shelter. A bird-sized predatory spider clings to the outside like a big burr to a sweater, its weight threatening to bring about its own demise. "There," Franz says. "Let's see if we can't get you sketching something a bit more relevant to the task at hand, dearest. I tell you what—think Audubon and we'll be doing just fine." He mumbles to the camera as he walks away: "We're going to get our Angstrom revoked if she keeps painting that sort of crap. I warned her that artistic distractions would not be tolerated on this trip."

Shot of the back of Poppy's head. She is humming Hildegaard von Bingen's Hilarity #6 to herself as she wipes the watercolor brush on the thick-weave paper. We cannot see her pad from this angle. We zoom to her head, but there is no telltale snoring to be discerned beneath the thick grain of her mouse-colored hair. There is no sound at all but the scratch of the brush on the paper, the sound of her humming, and the sound of bats' wings overhead as they stream steadily from the cave entrance at the base of the Pinnacles.

Cut to a searing red sunset filmed in Poppy's hometown of Duluth, Minnesota. Drown the sound of humming with the sound of Franz's voice delivering the eulogy at Poppy's funeral behind a bland, midwestern podium. "Life is essentially extravagant. We court various survival instincts, but in the end we resolutely desire precisely that which imperils our life. It was the sacrifice of character that seduced her, a succumbing to drama, a lethal infusion of life with art, a violent end to an otherwise passively tolerated existence."

JOURNAL ENTRY, FRANZ FRANKENWEILER,
THE PINNACLES, 5/9

"Today I found the perfect subjects for study—a mother Caspian tern and her two babies. They have chosen the hollow interior of a *Dilapidus rigna* in which to hibernate for the coming weeks, a fine tropical hardwood that breathes but is impervious to ants, termites, and other such abode-threatening pests. Using a very thin jigsaw, I managed to cut a hole precisely five inches in diameter in the trunk of the tree opposite the entry hole. I then covered this with a sheet of Plexiglas to ensure maximum viewing while eliminating any drafts or crosswinds that might prompt our subjects to change residences. (Like the government in this country, we must do our best to discourage nomadic forms of living!) Unfortunately, I suspect we have caught these birds at a fairly late stage in their development. One chick is already noticeably bigger than the other. It also appears that there has been some sort of trauma suffered by the wall—one large chunk knocked out of it, perhaps by a curious monkey or a harsh wind. Subsequently, the mother spent a good part of this first day (after recovering from the vibration of the drilling—this seemed to cause her quite a bit of distress, and she sat on both her offspring with her head firmly lodged beneath her right wing for the better part of an hour) rebuilding the wall with bits of dirt and excrement rolled into small balls. Subjects, fortunately, do not seem to be aware of my presence. It seems hopeful that I may actually collect reliable data from these creatures that have remained mysterious to the men of science for far too many millennia!"

BASE CAMP, THE PINNACLES, 5/10

A certain inexplicable pall has fallen over the campsite. We assume this is because Poppy attempted to seduce Franz last evening and failed. Or rather she failed due to a particular sort of failure on Franz's part. At any rate, the record now stands: sixty-five days. Poppy has taken to painting the number on her watercolor pad and holding it up to the camera each morning like a cue card. Franz pretends not to care, but he has taken to avoiding us except when he is talking about his study of the Caspian tern.

Poppy is also sulking because Franz refuses to accompany her to the caves. She is insistent on seeing the river mentioned by MAN.

"Why, why, why?" she whines.

"I can give you three immediate answers: bats, Poppy, innumerable bats; bat shit, bat shit—there's so much of it, I believe it should count twice. Then of course there are the cockroaches and the scorpions and the deadly poisonous *Milli morticus pedus*. Need I say more?"

Franz leaves for the tree with his leather ledger, a small tape recorder, and a can of curry beef for lunch.

"You're not coming today, I assume?" Franz tosses a look at her watercolor pad.

Poppy shakes her head. "Tomorrow," she says, picking at a pink blister bubble on her heel. "Maybe."

Poppy sulks on the rattan stool for a half hour or so, then pulls *Pure Bliss* from where it has been lodged beneath her meaty thigh. The spine of the book has cracked in the heat, and Poppy tosses away each page after she reads it.

After the fifth day, there came a knock on the door. Bliss raised her head, weak as a pussy willow after a rainstorm. She had not eaten a thing since she arrived, her body and heart, in fact, becoming the bitter-tasting meal of her all-consuming sorrow. Could this be he? She pulled herself to the rough-hewn wood door, heart pounding. With a breath she opened it—and found, on the other side, a pudgy chambermaid with blemished skin. Suddenly the world began to swim, the colors orbiting around each other like a shadowy kaleidoscope. When she awoke there was the sound of water, and when she cracked her eye she saw the same chambermaid, her unpretty features pulled into a look of concern as she sponged Bliss's forehead with a grimy cloth. "Yer fainted, miss," the young girl croaked, her prepubescent mouth already toothless.

Clutched in the chambermaid's callused paw, Bliss could see a shard of parchment. She fluttered a hand weakly at the woman's hand. "What . . . is . . . ?" she managed to ask before trailing off.

"Ah, 'tis for you, milady. Knocked on yer door to give it to yer, but yer fainted dead away afore I could."

Painfully Bliss unfolded the parchment, glued shut with that familiar blood-red wax seal stamped with the familiar crest. Tears of relief and confusion welled in her eyes as she read the mysterious poem scratched on the parchment's surface.

Suddenly Poppy is silent. She reads to herself for a moment longer, then stands with languorous, corpulent difficulty and heads for the river. She ignores us in such a way that it seems clear she expects us to follow her. We oblige.

Jumpy shots. The walkway (nothing more than a few randomly placed flattish stones even in its glory days) is thickly overgrown with coarse spiny grasses. Then the blades peel away with a long hiss to reveal a naked back and round, naked buttocks that plump outward at the side before descending to the crease of a knee. Poppy does a slow dance, her back to us, as her hips weave invisible patterns in the air. Slowly, slowly she slips into the water until her hair is just a mass of kelp spreading snakelike across the surface.

JOURNAL ENTRY, FRANZ FRANKENWEILER,
THE PINNACLES, 5/10

"Today subjects appeared calmer than yesterday, their short-term memory having already emptied of the drilling incident and the broken wall. It was not long, however, before I began to notice signs of irritation exhibited by the smaller offspring. It continued to squeak at perfectly timed intervals of seven seconds (a torture that, as with any infant's ceaseless crying, began to fray the mother's nerves until she became equally agitated) and continued to look in my direction. Eventually the mother noticed my handiwork. (Though the Plexiglas is perfect for eliminating winds and the odd disruptive human smell, it does, unfortunately, permit an inordinate amount of light to enter the nest—an unforeseen design flaw.) It was not long, thus, before I found myself being bricked in (or bricked out, as the case may be), the mother doing her best to plaster my viewing hole with deftly placed excrement. Fortunately she left me a tiny crack through which I could view her. When her back was turned, I quickly removed the Plexiglas, wiped it with my shirt sleeve (a hasty move I regretted immediately afterward), and replaced it. Within moments she was in the process of covering the hole yet again. Ah, the persistence of women! Though I know it is a scientifically insupportable (and vastly unpopular) claim, it occurs to me more than once how the behavior of the sexes seems to freely traverse the species barriers!"

BASE CAMP, THE PINNACLES, 5/10

"Positively idiotic, my dear. Might I point out that you are damned fortunate to have a film crew following you around, so that someone is always on hand to rescue you from the seething depths? Or were they the reason for this little stunt? Trying to cook up a dramatic suicide attempt for the camera, loved one?"

Franz is quite displeased with Poppy's morning display. We had quickly surmised that Poppy hadn't the faintest notion how to swim (at first her hysterical thrashings were read as the heightened climax to her dance begun onshore) and had jumped in to save her from the ferocious current that courses under the river's deceptively placid surface. Needless to say, haste makes waste, and a second light meter in a shirt pocket was drowned in the process. This incident did, however, raise a bit of an ethical dilemma: given our attempts to remain as detached as possible from our subject matter, we felt that saving Poppy from her death was perhaps against the interests of the film. The purity and integrity of the final work will undoubtedly suffer from this intervention. We have now altered the course of reality rather than just dutifully recording its existence apart from us.

In the end, however, her gasping face got the best of us, and in we went. (Might we add that we had a long discussion afterward and decided that if such an incident happens again, we must do our best to remain behind our cameras and resist the emotional involvement that might seduce us again to influence the lives and behavior of our subjects.)

More talk ensues between our subjects about going to visit the caves. Poppy has begun to give daily dusk readings from *Pure Bliss* directly into the camera.

Shot of Poppy reading, no audio.

Franz is no longer around at sundown to listen as he tries to use every moment of daylight to observe his subjects.

"One cannot work at night, of course," he explains. "Any unnatural light source would cause an evident interruption of their routine."

For this reason, we are not allowed to film Franz watching his birds. "Those damned spotlights," he says, shaking his head.

For this reason, Poppy refuses to accompany Franz to the nest.

"What are they going to film, Franz, the empty tent?" Poppy asks. "Poor guys. It seems we owe them that much, after dragging them all the way out here."

"A lot can be learned from an empty nest," Franz replies.

JOURNAL ENTRY, FRANZ FRANKENWEILER,
THE PINNACLES, 5/10

"Mother tern continues to be agitated. Has spent the last five days in relentless pursuit of covering my peephole with blasted bird dung. I have been forced to wipe the slate clean, as they say, as much as thrice daily. Fortunately, I have come prepared with a stack of fresh banana leaves with which to do the dirty work, thereby saving my shirt sleeves for cleaner acts of cleaning up, such as wiping the sweat from my brow. It is hellishly hot here, and no one can deliver any bunk about it being a dry heat, like those fool tourist brochures in Nairobi that attempt to reason you out of being miserable at 113°F. No, no, if one were to grab a chunk of this air with a fist, one could squeeze a cup or two of water from between the fingers. But back to my subjects. Though the mother tern has become somewhat of a repetitive bore (not to mention a nuisance), the two chicks have developed their own unique personalities. Of note is the discrepancy in their sizes: one is nearly twice the size of the other. Emotional and physical development appear to have some sort of proportional relationship in these birds: the bigger tern has become noticeably restless in the past day and has even begun to peck at the wall (the original wall) opposite my viewing hole. He walks by and takes random if halfhearted potshots—truly the adolescent offspring, making motions toward adulthood but unable to actually break from the nest!"

BASE CAMP, THE PINNACLES, 5/11 (REEL #6, *HSSID*)

Sundown. The usual arrangement. Franz is going over his notes, eating cold beef curry from a can with the blade of his Swiss Army knife. Poppy is wrapped in mosquito netting. (The particularly bloodthirsty variety of *Boirus sanguinous* found in subequatorial Malaysia seems overly fond of poor Poppy's juices, while finding Franz utterly distasteful.) The netting is draped around her head like a veil. She holds her book inside the gauzy tent it forms, careful to keep the ripe fruit of her hands as far inside her slight shelter as possible, to avoid the persistent reachings in. Mosquitoes circle her head in wispy throngs like vultures.

And with her poor breast heaving through the frail lace of her bodice, Bliss pulled herself through the wicked underbrush that tore at her cheeks and threatened to put out her eyes with its sharp talons. She recited in her head again the lines of Byron's poem as she contemplated the black entrance to the cave.

Just when you think you've gone too far,
you have barely yet begun, my star.
Wander through the Devil's Hair until you come across his
*   tears,*
a hot and roiling river which will tug upon your maiden's
*   fears.*
Throw yourself into this moat to prove your steadfast devotion;

I shall appear from behind the nearest tree,
and save you from this wicked ocean.
But your life is what I ask, my love,
your entire being and nothing less;
Put yourself upon the altar and put my insecurities to rest.

Poppy concludes and stares wistfully, tragically at the setting sun. Deep sighs send her bosom rising and then crashing like a tanker nosediving into the troughs between stormy swells. She picks a dead butterfly (*Laitus ailerus bellimo*) from the ground and pulls its legs off one by one, examining each spindly member as if it were a torn petal before casting it dramatically into the nearby bushes.

JOURNAL ENTRY, FRANZ FRANKENWEILER,
THE PINNACLES, 5/12

"After two days of wiping bird shit off a piece of Plexiglas with banana leaves, my dedicated observation has begun to pay off. Though the mother tern continued with her neurotic plastering, the more developed offspring began to peck at the wall in earnest—first hesitantly, as if testing the strength of its own beak, then gradually applying more and more force until, like a drill, it broke through to the daylight on the other side. This is all well and normal, completely conforming to our knowledge of the typical growth cycle and 'cocooning' phase of the Caspian tern. Suddenly, however, around noon, I began to notice some unusual activity in the smaller bird. It was busily moving along the wall carefully patching the holes created by the larger bird. No sooner had the larger bird made a successful plunge through the wall than the smaller one stopped it up quickly with a small bit of dung! This remarkable and highly comical routine ensued for the rest of the day, until the sun set and all three birds collapsed into their own tired corners of the nest without even eating the food the father had so diligently pushed through the peephole that morning. Tension is such inside the nest that I feel certain tomorrow will bring some sort of climax—in the form of a simultaneous victory and defeat. Ah, it rivals the impatience one feels during the final intermission of mystery theater. An unsurpassed desire to see things artfully clarified!"

BASE CAMP, THE PINNACLES, 5/13 (REEL #7 *HSSID*)

It has been three days now since Poppy has eaten anything.

"I don't feel a fever," Franz says, kneeling over her catatonic form and pushing his wrist against the clammy flatland of her wide forehead. Then, turning to the camera, he says, "There's really no need to be concerned. This sort of lethargy is quite common in such a hot, humid climate. Just a severe form of heat exhaustion that those of, shall we say, *denser* consistencies are far more prone to experiencing." He gives Poppy a loving, if distracted, pat on her plump wrist. "What do you say, love? How about a little splash in the shallows? A little—and I stress *little*—river water might help to cool you down."

Poppy moans and shakes her flushed, fleshy face. "Bliss, you know, Franz, was nothing more than a cornered animal. She was merely responding to the limitations, to the expectations, Franz, of her audience. I mean, my *God,* Franz, she had an artistic obligation to fulfill. Of *course* she had to pursue Byron, that elusive hunk of a man. What, was she going to just sit back and take it like a stoic druid? That's no way to become a classic. People want blood, Franz, blood, honey. She couldn't disappoint her viewers."

Franz gives an exhausted look to the camera. "You don't mind watching her, do you? I hate to ask such a thing of you, but, well, I've got to get back to my terns. I don't think she's in any shape to draw, and, well, this is the crucial day. After all, it's not like you're not going to be *watching* her anyway. Heh, heh, heh." Franz chuckles and flashes a weak smile. Then he administers a chummy pat on the back. *Frame shakes, then stabilizes.*

We hear the wet crunch of Franz's retreating footsteps over the knatty field of *Verdigris thornicus.*

Camera remains on Poppy. She appears to be sleeping fitfully, rolling around on the planked wood floor of the shelter. It is unusually hot today. The heat is like a drug, weighing down the body, the spirit, the eyelids until one can no longer help but relinquish oneself, blessedly, to a state of unconsciousness and immateriality.

Jumpy shots of the ground. We are running (no easy feat with a hand-held camera) in pursuit of our escaped subject. A quick rewind of the tape (before the battery died) showed Poppy rising from her tangled bedding, then, after a single look in our direction (as long as it took, no doubt, to discern that we were fast asleep), wrapping herself in mosquito netting and heading out of the frame to the left. We assume, given the subject's obsession with the Mulu caves, that only this can be her destination.

The entrance to the caves is itself an understated mockery of the endlessly knotted interior. From a slight distance, it looks like nothing more than a shadowed oblong dimple in the rock face, just below an overhanging tangle of flora that Franz most likely knows by name, genus, and species. Tensions are high, and we squabble over which light to bring into the cave. I say the five-hundred-watter for clarity; he wants something more diffuse for a gentler cinematic effect. Neither of us dares believe that all our observations have been for naught—to lose our subject at a heightened moment.

"It is," I say, "missing the murder in the foyer for filming the potted palms growing in the salon."

I am almost filmed by mistake by my cameraman as he turns to throw me a disgusted look, but fortunately I am quick and duck just in time.

"Watch it. Don't get *me* with that thing," I scold.

Once inside the cave, we know we are on the right track—fresh footprints newly padded into the guano. Given the cave's inhabitance by nearly thirty million bats, it was estimated by the British Cartographic Survey in 1973 that the fecal matter generated would cause the floor to rise an average of two inches every year. This same survey predicted that the cave would be "buried from within," so to speak, by the year 3334. We track Poppy through the bat shit. The smell is wet, fetid, fecund. Just as a precaution, we tie a bit of string to a stone outcropping by the entrance and unravel it as we go. The cave begins to open gradually, until the ceiling is curving nearly a hundred feet over our heads. A brief overhead shot shows the ceiling to be fluttering, stirring. Another shot shows a muddy Timex. It is nearly sundown.

A few paces from the opening, we spot something white, square, glowing against the powdery, dimpled mounds of bat shit. It is a page from *Pure Bliss* only a quarter filled with text, obviously the end of a chapter.

> was aware that someone was watching her, she could even feel their eyes (she thought they were loving) boring into her back, pushing her toward the eroding riverbank, beyond which the river frothed and roared, its ropy emerald currents cutting ever deeper into the bed that so barely contained it. Bliss turned around to look at the dark wall of trees but could see nothing. Still, she knew she was onstage, that this was her final and

most important performance. With a deep breath, she slowly pulled her ripped and muddied garments from her shoulder, let them slip to a heap around her bare ankles. Then, with her heart filled with love and trust and, yes, fear, Bliss walked toward the edge, the sense of those watching eyes driving her into the depths that rushed up hungrily, frothing at the shore, at the slightest scent of her.

The cave continues its gradual expansion until soon water can be heard. It sounds like a far-off waterfall. As we get nearer and nearer, the sound is as deafening as that of an automotive factory in Detroit. The water slides through the rock floor with the scream of metal upon metal. On the shore is a figure. At first look, there appears to be one, then two, as in two lovers pulling apart, then one again as we shine the light. Behind our subject, the river glows a brilliant emerald green shot through with bits of foamy white. We watch as our subject begins her slow movements, her hips moving back and forth. The sound of the water has become unbearably loud. Then we realize it is the combined din created by the flapping of thirty million pairs of wings as the bats begin their mass exodus through the cave's tiny opening. Poppy turns to face the camera, looking directly into it as she backs slowly down the embankment, her arms flapping softly. Our subject hesitates, it seems, as if waiting for some reaction. Upon getting none, she puts one foot in the water. Still no reaction. It is not until she is knee-deep that the current catches her. She appears to snap like a matchstick into the raging froth and is quickly lost from view. We approach the shore. Poppy is fighting the current, her arm reaching out toward the camera mere inches away from her. We film her fingers, which claw at the air, and her face, which is plaintive and confused and the furthest thing from blissful. Then her pinkish body sinks from view beneath the green surface.

Close focus on the water. The only thing to be seen is the reflection of a million bats, stirring the river depths to a blackened frenzy.

EULOGY, POPPY FRANKENWEILER'S FUNERAL,
DULUTH, MINNESOTA (REEL #10, HSSID)

". . . I am a scientist, a man hemmed in by logic, and so I can only draw factual parallels in an attempt to elucidate a grander meaning surrounding the death of my wife. As it happens, at the time of her death I was making the final notes on my study subject, the Caspian Tern. As some of you in this audience may know, the Caspian tern is distinguished in the ornithological world by its instinctive act of cocooning, in which the mother and her newly hatched chicks brick themselves into a hollow tree trunk. What transpires within the confines of this cocoon no one knew until my very recently completed study. This has long interested me because of my subscription to the little-favored theory that birds are profoundly obsessed with mortality and, conversely, immortality. Cocooning, it seems, is a way for the mother to reexperience a gestation period and rebirth—though this time on her own, cognizant terms, the act of repetition that seems to me to indicate a yearning for the immortal state. On that final day, however, I learned that no amount of scientific or artistic overlay can prepare one for the instinctual love of irrationality one finds in all of nature. On my last day of observation, I hurried to the site fearing that perhaps the birds had already left the cocoon and thus preempted my attempts to understand the events leading up to this final breaking out. To my utter shock, I returned to the nest to find all my birds dead, brutally bludgeoned, it appeared, by a small, sharp instrument—a beak, one would logically deduce. It appeared that the mother's wounds, all about the chest area, were self-inflicted, and her beak was covered with greenish yellow blood from tip to toe. On closer inspection, however, I saw that the mother was still alive. She was looking directly at me with a beady eye, addressing me through the Plexiglas, and emitting a plaintive, pathetic squeak. Of course I thought about taking the bird back to the laboratory and nursing her back to health, but what would have been the point? She could hardly have served as a case study once she had grown accustomed to being with humans, so completely divorced from her natural habitat. I can only ask myself—what did that bird want from me? And what did my wife want? These are questions that no amount of science will explain. And so where science fails, I believe art succeeds, if not in *explaining,* then in *celebrating* that aspect of things that we can never completely understand—the seduction, if you will, of ambiguity, of the enigma. For what is it that drives us forth, artists and scientists alike, if not that seduction of the unknown? Science tries to disarm it, art tries to preserve it, but it is, in the end, the same impulse. I insist that we all view Poppy's death as the ultimate artistic act a human being—or any other animal—is capable of. Life, after all, is essentially extravagant. We court various survival instincts, but in the end we resolutely desire precisely that which imperils our life."

Cut.

CONTRIBUTORS

JULIA ALVAREZ is the author of two novels, *How the García Girls Lost Their Accents* and *In the Time of the Butterflies*, as well as two collections of poetry, *Homecoming* and *The Other Side*. "Liberty" is a fictional story based on her childhood in the Dominican Republic. She is currently a professor of English at Middlebury College.

FREDERICK BARTHELME is the author of two collections of stories, *Moon Deluxe* and *Chroma*, and six novels, *Second Marriage, Two Against One, Tracer, Natural Selection, The Brothers,* and, most recently, *Painted Desert*. He teaches writing at the University of Southern Mississippi, where he also edits the *Mississippi Review*.

PO BRONSON is the author of two novels, *Bombardiers* and *The First Twenty Million Is Always the Hardest*. An archive of his humor writing is located at http://users.aol.com/pobronson/humor1.htm.

MICHAEL CHABON is the author of two novels, *Mysteries of Pittsburgh* and *Wonder Boys*, and a collection of short stories called *A Model World*. His articles have been published in the *New Yorker, GQ, Vogue,* and the *New York Times*. A Washington, D.C., native, he now lives in California with his wife and daughter.

SUSAN DODD is the author of two story collections, *Old Wives' Tales* and *Hell-Bent Men and Their Cities*, and the novels *No Earthly Notion* and *Mamaw*. She has taught at Vermont

College, the Iowa Writers Workshop, Harvard, and Bennington College. She lives in Ocracoke, North Carolina.

J U D I T H   F R E E M A N is the author of a collection of stories, *Family Attractions,* and three novels, *The Chinchilla Farm, Set for Life,* which won the Western Heritage Award for best novel of 1991, and *A Desert of Pure Feeling.* She reviews books regularly for the *Los Angeles Times* and lives in Los Angeles with her husband.

A L I C E   F U L T O N is the author of *Sensual Math, Powers of Congress, Palladium,* and *Dance Script with Electric Ballerina.* She has received fellowships from the MacArthur Foundation, the Ingram Merrill Foundation, and the Guggenheim Foundation.

M A R Y   G A I T S K I L L is the author of the novel *Two Girls, Fat and Thin* and a collection of short stories entitled *Bad Behavior.* Her stories and essays have appeared in numerous magazines, including the *New Yorker, Harper's, Esquire,* and *Mirabella.* She has been a visiting lecturer at the University of California at Berkeley and Hollins College.

J A Y   G U M M E R M A N is the author of a novel, *Chez Chance,* and an acclaimed book of short stories entitled *We Find Ourselves in Moontown.* A graduate of the University of California at Irvine, he lives in Southern California with his wife.

D A V I D   H A Y N E S is the author of *Live at Five, Heathens, Somebody Else's Mama,* and *Right by My Side,* which won the 1992 Minnesota Voices Project and was selected by the American Library Association as one of 1993's Best Books for Young Adults. He has also worked as a teacher and as a teacher-in-residence for the National Board for Professional Teaching Standards. He lives in Saint Paul and Washington, D.C.

L O U I S   B.   J O N E S is the author of two novels, *Particles and Luck* and *Ordinary Money.* He lives in California.

HEIDI JULAVITS is a native of Portland, Maine, and a recent graduate of the Creative Writing Program at Columbia University. She continues to reside in New York City, where she is in the process of completing her first novel. "Penny Dreadfuls" is her first published work.

GARY KRIST is the author of two short story collections, *The Garden State,* which won the Sue Kaufman Prize from the American Academy of Arts and Letters, and *Bone by Bone.* He lives near Washington, D.C., with his wife and daughter.

JILL MCCORKLE is the author of four novels and one short story collection. Her fifth novel, *Carolina Moon,* is being published in the fall of 1996. She currently teaches creative writing at Harvard University and in the Bennington MFA program.

ROBERT PHILLIPS is the director of the Creative Writing Program at the University of Houston. He has published two collections of short stories, *The Land of Lost Content* and *Public Landing Revisited,* as well as five collections of poetry. He is the recipient of an Award in Literature from the American Academy of Arts and Letters.

HENRY H. ROTH is the author of two collections of fiction, *Boundaries of Love and Other Stories* and *In Empty Rooms: Tales of Love.* He also wrote *The Cruz Chronicle: A Novel.* He currently lives outside New York City.

GEORGE SINGLETON has published over forty stories in such national and regional magazines as *Playboy, Georgia Review,* and *Fiction International,* one of which was selected for *New Stories from the South: The Year's Best, 1994.*

MELANIE RAE THON is the author of two novels, *Meteors in August* and *Iona Moon,* and a collection of short stories, *Girls in the Grass.* Her new collection, *First, Body,* will be published by Houghton Mifflin in January 1997.